The Silkie's Salvation

by

Laura Browning

The Silkie's Salvation

Contact Information: info@thewildrosepress.com

Cover Art by *Angela Anderson*

The Wild Rose Press
PO Box 708
Adams Basin, NY 14410-0708

Visit us at www.thewilderroses.com

Publishing History
First Scarlet Rose Edition, April 2011
Print ISBN 1-60154-940-7

Published in the United States of America

**The magic she works on him could restore the
heritage he destroyed but separate them forever...**

"I owe you an apology," she whispered. "For this
morning. You saved my life and I—I overreacted."

He smiled, his teeth white against the tan of his skin.
"Then dance with me, and you can tell me how sorry you
are."

His voice stroked along her eardrums like satin
sheets on bare skin. When he held out his hand, she
placed hers in it and he helped her up. The dance floor
was crowded; he pulled her against his broad chest. The
hand holding hers pressed it against his heart, while his
other hand splayed across her lower back.

"Relax," he told her, his mouth near her ear. "I won't
hurt you."

She nodded, but still found it hard not to be stiff
against him.

"Just listen to the music, Keeley, and let it go. Let it
go."

His cheek touched the top of her head. She closed her
eyes and inhaled the warm, familiar scent of him. She
hadn't realized how accustomed she had become to it, and
she wondered how he would taste. *Oh God! What was she
thinking?* She swallowed nervously. Her hand trembled in
his. The music, the wine, and the feel of him moving
gently, confidently around the floor were making her hot
and lethargic. The urge to lean into him so she could feel
the firmness of his body against her cheek, her breasts,
and her belly nearly overwhelmed her. When his thigh
brushed against her aching mound, Keeley gasped.

Dedication

To all of my fellow members in the
Heart of Carolina Romance Writers.
You are a constant source of inspiration.

Chapter One

"He's feeding her!" the maid whispered as she popped back into the kitchen with the salad plates and paused next to where Keeley was finishing dessert. "And she's already giving him *the look*."

"Too bad I didn't prepare peas, so he could retrieve them from her cleavage." Keeley scowled and turned back to spread a glaze of sweet, dark chocolate over the gateau. It hadn't turned out quite as she'd hoped, but it would have to do. She didn't have time to prepare another dessert. Besides, by the time lover boy got to the last course, he'd be more interested in screwing his dinner partner than tasting Keeley's cake. With the glaze done, she peeked through a crack in the hall door to see her employer leaning attentively toward a busty blonde. The bimbo giggled as he fed her a piece of meat. It was more than obvious from the heated looks she gave him it was an entirely different piece of meat sparking her interest.

Keeley frowned. That was no way to appreciate the veal she'd prepared. She huffed. Another excellent meal would go to waste while half the staff watched him work his magic on his latest date. Women seemed to fall over him like he held them in some sort of thrall. For his part, he usually looked like he could care less. The least he could do was eat the meal off his date's naked stomach, maybe lick the gateau off her...

Jeez! Keeley ignored the tingle in her breasts and between her legs watching Ciaran Clifton usually caused. Why the hell did he have to be so good-looking? Why the hell did she work for him?

Granddad. That was why. The job gave her enough money and freedom she could care for him at home. That was what mattered. He'd lived within sight of Long Island Sound his entire life. She couldn't ask him to change that. He was having a tough time with the chemotherapy this go round.

Keeley stalked back to the kitchen. All she wanted to do was get home. Granddad needed her. For once she wished Clifton would hurry with his dinner and his seduction so she could leave. She was tired of the long dinner table conversations that seemed to her at least like he was busy getting information instead of sex. It disturbed her enough thinking about him that way; she certainly didn't need the evening to drag on for hours.

She cleaned the kitchen, her movements automatic and efficient. While the dishwasher was quietly humming, she started a pot of coffee. On a tray she put sugar, cream, spoons, napkins and cups.

"They're ready for dessert." The maid updated her. It was like play by play at a soccer game. *He's already got one hand all the way up her thigh and the other's slipping the strap of her dress off her shoulder. He scores!*

Keeley snorted at her thoughts. "Well if they do it on the dining room table, all I can say is she'll never get that gateau out of her silk dress."

Mary laughed as she picked up the sweet and took it to the dining room. Keeley ran her fingers through her spiky hair and stared impatiently out the window over the sink. She loved summer when it stayed light so late, but watching sunsets the past two years was rare. She cooked for lover boy six nights a week, and saw him flattering and fucking well-heeled women nearly as often. At odd times, she caught his dark eyes watching her, and she faded quickly back into the kitchen. The last thing she needed was for him to notice her as anything other than a cook. She could never begin to satisfy somebody like him.

Right now, she just felt impatient. She needed to get home. Granddad would be sick and irritable. He needed her far more than Ciaran Clifton needed a gourmet meal.

"Where is she?" The kitchen door slammed back on its hinges at the same time the angry question burst from her employer's lips. In his left hand he held the plate with the gateau. "What is this?" he demanded furiously as he spotted her near the sink.

Keeley straightened to her full height, but still found herself looking at his chest. Tilting her head she met the fury in his black eyes head on. "It's a chocolate gateau."

He flipped the fragile china plate onto the counter top next to her. It skidded, crashed against the wall, and shattered. "Thanks to this crap, Francine is in the bathroom puking up her guts."

Keeley bristled. Nobody called her cooking names. "So you strike out with one seduction. There's always tomorrow."

If she thought his eyes snapped before, they positively blazed now.

****

Ciaran couldn't remember when he'd been so livid. He glared at his cook and considered the urge to put his hands around her skinny little neck. It would be easy enough to do since she wasn't much bigger than a kid. She stared at him with angry green eyes like some demon faerie. The warm, faintly spicy scent of her filled his nostrils and he growled low in his throat, a sudden surge of desire making him all the angrier because he already fantasized about her all too often. He took a step toward her and tripped over the garbage can.

What the hell? Where had that come from? He tried to catch himself as he fell, but then his foot

3

slipped on something gooey and he slammed down onto the tile floor, turning his head just in time so only his cheekbone cracked against the stone tiles.

"Damn it!"

Before he could scramble to his feet, Keeley backed away holding a meat cleaver in her right hand. "Don't you dare come near me!" she snapped, her green eyes narrowed and watchful.

A meat cleaver? Did she really think he would *hurt* her? Confusion warred with anger as he jumped up, brushing refuse from his silk shirt and low slung dress slacks. "Come near you? I have no intention of getting anywhere around you. In fact Miss— whatever your name is—you're fired!"

She advanced on him with eyes that burned with a green fire. Ciaran wondered whether he was the one who might really be in danger when she slapped the cleaver on the counter. "My name is Keeley Ann McNamara, you arrogant ass. I've worked for you for two years, and you can't fire me because I quit!"

He knew her name, just as he was conscious of every single time she set foot in his house, but damned if he'd let her know. For two years he'd been on the receiving end of her prim, disapproving looks. Ciaran stalked to the hall door and spun around to glare at her one more time. "Well I guess I'm just damned lucky you haven't poisoned anyone before now! When I get back from checking on Francine and changing out of this mess, I want you gone."

"Oh don't worry about that. Nothing is worth having to put up with an employer who acts like an alley cat and has the manners of a wallowing pig!"

Alley cat? Wallowing pig? Who was she to criticize him but a *human*, and an undersized one at that? He was a Silkie, a sea faerie, not some earthbound animal. *But you are just like a human. It's your punishment.* Fists clenched, he spun on his heel and left. Now was so not the time for his conscience to suddenly find a voice.

The door swung shut behind him. She was alone. Keeley realized she was trembling. Stupid man. Two years and he didn't even know her *name*? Idly she reached behind her, scooped a finger full of the gateau, and tasted it.

"Phht!" She spit it into the sink and closed her eyes in mortification. Oh Lord, she'd been so distracted over Granddad she used salt instead of sugar. She stared at the closed door. She should apologize. Keeley closed her eyes and dropped her head forward, and then a moment later jerked it back again. Damned if she would apologize to that pig! She could work as a sous chef at the Yacht Club or cook at one of the restaurants, someplace where they knew her name at least. Let him just try to replace her!

With a sigh, she looked at the mess on the floor and the counter. After righting the garbage pail, she found the broom and swept everything into the dustpan before dumping it back in the can. She cleaned up the broken plate and the remains of the fouled up gateau and disposed of them as well. When she was finished, the kitchen was once again spotless. She didn't do it for Mr. Clifton; she did it for Mary, the maid.

Keeley stared around the kitchen—her domain the past two years—for one last time. With its granite countertops, oak cabinets and stainless steel appliances, she knew she would never work in surroundings as pleasant and plush. She stripped her chef's jacket off with a small sigh and folded it over the back of a kitchen chair. It was time to go home.

****

"I want to go home right now, Ciaran! All you ever want is to talk about what Daddy is doing. I

5

wouldn't stay here if you paid me."

Ciaran scowled at Francine's petulant outburst. He had really hoped to seduce information out of her about her stepfather's latest investments. The man was reputedly sinking money into a new venture, and Ciaran wanted to know what it was so he could decide whether it was worth risking his own cash. But his means for ascertaining that looked pouty rather than passionate. He doubted he would get anywhere this night.

It hadn't taken long to figure out that flattery made most humans easy to read. Once he got them to lower their guards, it was usually easy to filter through their thoughts and find what he needed to know. Even with his severely reduced telepathy, he could still do that, especially with humans. Tonight though, he was screwed, all because of that green-eyed kitchen witch. Maybe Francine should go home. Her spoiled princess act could be irritating.

"Let me take you home, babe. And I just want you to know I fired my chef. I couldn't possibly keep someone who would harm a hair on your head."

She blushed and batted her eyelashes, instantly mollified. "Yes, take me home. Maybe if you're very good, I'll let you make it up to me once I'm feeling better." She stroked a bright red fingernail down his shirt-front and toyed with his belt buckle. It did nothing for him. He managed a slight smile and she giggled.

Ciaran sighed inwardly. Was there a woman anywhere who was not so easy, so transparent? Give them a few compliments and they'd reveal everything they knew. Yeah, he'd have the information he needed before the week was out. Francine would have her ego stroked and he would once again add to his growing fortune. So why did it all feel so empty? Four years ago, it was necessary to his survival. Was it now only habit?

For an instant, a vision of Keeley's irate expression came to him. She would never play the kind of games Francine did, but he had sent Keeley away. He looked in the rearview mirror as he headed down the drive. Would Keeley still be there when he got back?

After escorting Francine home, he pulled his Porsche into the garage and eased through the kitchen door. Part of him hoped his little cook was still in there. Ciaran was spoiling for a good fight, and he'd just bet she could give it to him. He grinned as he remembered the meat cleaver. What a fiery little thing! But when he went in the back door, the kitchen was dark and spotless. He frowned and absently rubbed his palm over the middle of his chest. She was gone. What had he really expected? He told her to go.

In the low light from the stovetop, he spied her white chef's jacket folded over a chair at the kitchen table, picked it up, and brought it to his nostrils. There were the usual scents of food, but in addition, he smelled the warm, clean smell of woman. Keeley. He inhaled, drawing her rich, spicy aroma into his head, not at all surprised when his cock got half-hard just from her fragrance.

In an instant his mind filled with her, eyes as deep and green as a sheltered cove, a complexion as rich as any pearl of the sea. He would lay her back on the warm sand, run his hands over that milky skin until he parted her thighs and...

He tossed the jacket down and stalked from the room. He was so not obsessing over her.

Not. At. All.

He grabbed the jacket and took it with him.

****

"Granddad? I'm home."

"In here." His hoarse croak came from the direction of his bedroom.

7

Keeley shut the heavy wood door and dropped her windbreaker on one of the pegs next to the door. Her grandfather's house wasn't large, but it was where he grew up and where he came back to after ill health forced him to retire from ship-building. She kept it spotless for him, making sure the wide pine floors were mopped and waxed, the windows washed, and everything dusted. Last summer she painted the Cape Cod style home a blue-gray trimmed with white. It took most of the summer, but Granddad's gruff hug when she finished made the effort worthwhile.

Keeley bypassed the steps leading to her loft room and stepped through the doorway just beyond to see him half-sitting in bed. Even in the dim light from the bedside lamp, she saw his pale skin and veined hands. He was once again losing his hair from the monthly chemo treatment. His fingers trembled on the worn double wedding ring quilt.

"Can I get you anything?"

"I can't keep it down. I've thrown up everything." Frustration made his voice harsh, but it wasn't directed at her.

"It will get better in a day or so, Granddad, but let me talk to your doctor. There must be something they can give you to relieve the sickness."

"You do too much already, girl. It's no worse than last time. You take care of you. Head out with your friends. Plenty of folk to enjoy now it's summer."

"I went out for a while last night."

It was true. She had gone out with her best friend to Stan's for clams and beer. She and Stephie played a little pool in the smoky back room, traded insults with some of the other locals, and then Keeley headed home, breathing deeply of the thick salt air. It was her usual Friday night of freedom from Ciaran Clifton, Mr. American Gigolo.

Andy McNamara just shook his head. "Young girl like you shouldn't be working so hard, cooking like a servant and then caring for an old man in your free time. Damn shame."

"Granddad! I work as hard as I like, and there is no shame in cooking. I enjoy it and I'm good at it." She wouldn't tell him yet that she was also out of work. He didn't need to know tonight. She patted his leg. "As for you…that's a labor of love. I have some things to do in my room. Call if you need me, I'm right above you. Tomorrow, I'm checking with your doctor to see if we can't get your stomach calm enough you can at least keep liquids down."

She shut the door quietly and climbed the steep, narrow stairs. Keeley ignored the simple décor of whitewashed walls and rag rugs over pine floors, already scanning her eclectic mixture of cookbooks, novels and accounting texts. No help there. What she needed was the Herbal.

She ran her hands along the top of the nearest bookshelf. Pawpaw built them for her when she first came to live with him, half a lifetime ago for her. Her mind skittered away from thinking of that long ago summer and the reason she lived with her father's father.

She crossed to another area where she kept the Herbal handed from one McNamara to another for generations. Keeley hadn't used it much. She was a cook, not a healer, but flipped through it anyway. There must be something to help his nausea. Ginger was mentioned, but Granddad wasn't fond of that. Peppermint and basil were also listed. Basil she had plenty of. It was one of her favorites for cooking; she used it both fresh and dried.

She had quit cooking school to return and care for her grandfather. They both danced around the issue, but Keeley knew deep down he didn't have much longer. This would be the last round of chemotherapy. He was already living on borrowed time. Though his doctors didn't say so, she saw it in their faces. Even more, she saw it in his. If the cancer didn't go into remission this time, he wouldn't submit to the chemo again. It was too much, and he was tired. She swallowed thickly.

Sounds of her grandfather back in the bathroom once more getting sick to his stomach made her hurry downstairs. Tea might work. Keeley slipped into the kitchen, set the pot on to boil and pulled the basil out of the cabinet. It took several minutes to hunt the infusion ball she was sure was around somewhere.

In a few minutes, tea steeped in a mug. This had to work. She couldn't stand seeing him go through the nausea and the weakness. Sometimes it was more than she could bear to know how sick and weak he was. In the early years at the shipyards, no one really understood the dangers posed by the asbestos they used. Now that they did, it was too late for him. Cancer was taking his life, sooner and far more painfully than it should happen.

She poured the tea and walked back through the living room to the bedroom. "Pawpaw," she said quietly. "I made a tea of basil leaves. According to your mother's Herbal, it should help. Will you try it?"

He grimaced but finally nodded. "I can sip it. At this point it can't hurt."

She padded barefoot across the floor and handed him the mug. With a small smile, she leaned down and kissed his balding head. "I love you, Granddad. You were there when I needed you, and I'll be here while you need me."

He sipped the tea, set it down and closed his eyes. "I wasn't there for you soon enough."

"You came. That's what mattered."

Early the following morning, Keeley threw on

her bathing suit, shorts, and running shoes and grabbed a towel. After checking to make sure Granddad was still sleeping, she jogged past the marina and down the street to the rocky public beach at the east end of town. No one was there so early in the morning, and that was fine with her. Granddad wanted her to get out, but this was her restorative, not an evening in a bar.

Keeley dropped the towel, kicked off her shoes and shorts and ran into the water. Several hundred yards out, she saw the gleaming white outline of a huge yacht. The *Skerry*. Ciaran Clifton's family home. Nothing like having the *QE2* to grow up on. Wasn't there some connection to the Barton family? Hardly mattered now. He wasn't her boss, so she needed to quit thinking about him. Keeley shook her head to clear it and flipped over onto her back. She did some of her best thinking in the cold salt water.

A new job was paramount, something where she could handle a dinner service. Granddad needed her help more during the early morning and day than in the evening. The Yacht Club was a possibility, but that might be a real overdose of stiff upper lips and Junior League pearls. She could hope for another private chef's job, but they would likely want a reference and she doubted Clifton would give her one, though Jonathan the butler might. She could always try Stan's. That should be easy enough. Steak and seafood. She could cook them blindfolded.

Keeley flipped onto her stomach, swam out to the navigational buoy and then headed back to shore. She shook her head like a dog when she stepped onto the beach and stretched. Seeing no one about so early, she flicked her fingers at her towel, grinning as it jumped from the sand into her hand.

Parlor tricks. Simple parlor tricks. She'd been doing them since she was a kid, usually to amuse herself. She'd done it last night when she moved the garbage pail just enough that Ciaran tripped over it. Too bad her gift couldn't save her grandfather, but then his own magic was powerless against his cancer. Why should hers be different?

****

Ciaran stood on the point near the end of town staring unblinkingly at the *Skerry*. His parents must be visiting Bell and Cayden. There was a grandchild now, or so he'd heard. A girl. He caught glimpses of his brother and his wife now and then, but mostly Ciaran avoided them, just as they avoided him. When the Silkie Council first banished him, he used every opportunity to rub their noses in his success, but he found no satisfaction in it anymore. Now it just made his ache for the sea and his family that much harder to bear.

Despite the fact that most modern Silkie mingled and lived among humans undetected, they knew the refuge and solace of the sea awaited them. They could transform whenever they needed to, blend seamlessly back into the wild freedom of the open ocean. But not him. The moment the Council forced him to surrender his pelt, he had lost that refuge and the magic that went with it. Still, like the other Silkie, Ciaran stayed as near the ocean as possible.

The sea and the land. As God promised the angels he sent to earth. The Silkie and the Faerie were to be the guardians of all that dwelt on land and in the sea, something Ciaran had forgotten in his jealousy of his brother.

At a movement on the beach his brows drew together. A black-haired waif ran into the water and disappeared beneath the waves. His dark eyes narrowed as she first floated, then swam strongly out to the buoy. He wondered if she had any idea how often he watched her swim there. He still wasn't sure what odd compulsion made him come to the shore nearly every morning. When she swam back again, he turned on his heel and left. Waif? No, only an annoying demon.

Envy warred with desire. If he could just feel the smooth glide of water over his sleek fur. It would take just seconds to reach her. Then what? Drag her under and drown her, or wrap that lissome body in his arms and hold onto her forever? He nearly took the path down to the water until he remembered there would be no change, no tingle of awareness as he reverted from man to seal.

Back at the house, Ciaran shouted for the butler. He was tempted to ask Jonathan how he could find Keeley McNamara so he could hire her back, but remembering her face from last night, he doubted she'd even consider it.

"Yes, Mr. Clifton," the man, not a hair on his iron gray head out of place, intoned from the sun porch door.

"Find me another cook. I fired that one. What was her name? Kelly?" *What a farce. Like he could ever forget her name.* But making people think he didn't give a shit was so much a part of his persona now it was hard to change.

"Keeley McNamara, sir."

"Yes, her. Get me another." *Someone just like her would be more than he could hope for.*

"Right away, sir."

A few minutes later, she still crowded his thoughts, and so did the temptation to call Jonathan to see if his butler could persuade her to come back. Ciaran tapped his fingers on the polished desktop. Right. That would be too much like begging. He opened the bottom drawer and stared at the cook's jacket neatly folded there. Against his will, he inhaled deeply and let the spicy hint of cinnamon flow through him. Something about her scent soothed him and made him forget his longing to be back beneath the waves.

He regretted the anger that made him fire her. The fact he now suffered regret didn't surprise him too much. He'd been obsessed with her ever since she began working for him, and she was a damn fine cook on top of it. But what did make him uneasy were the stirrings of—what—concern? In all the time she'd worked for him, she'd never made a misstep in the kitchen. Something had to be bothering her, but what?

Chapter Two

"This is hideous! God in heaven. Can't anyone find a cook who can cook?"

Ciaran slapped his silverware down on either side of his plate. What was supposed to be grilled salmon with parsleyed new potatoes and marinated asparagus on the plate in front of him instead looked like some sort of blackened cardboard, with mushy, cold potatoes and asparagus so overcooked it now looked like it came from a can. Keeley would never serve such trash.

"Jonathan!" Ciaran bellowed.

Less than a minute later, the butler opened the dining room door and walked to within a few feet of his employer.

"Tell me, Jonathan. What am I having for dinner?"

The butler peered at the plate distastefully. "Well, sir, it would appear you are having some sort of charred fish with peas and mashed potatoes."

"It's supposed to be grilled salmon, parsley potatoes and marinated asparagus, but how would you or I know that? It certainly doesn't look like it, and it very definitely does not taste like it."

"Shall I fire this one as well, sir?" Jonathan inquired with just a hint of relief coloring his clipped British accent.

Ciaran arched a brow as he shoved the food away. "Nearly poisoned you too? The sooner the better. How many chefs does that make?"

"Four, sir. Two the first week and two this week. This one was the last one the employment agency had to offer. Everyone else has been booked for the summer."

Ciaran drummed his fingers on the tabletop. One spoiled dessert and his temper cost him a fine cook. What was worse, he could not rid himself of either her memory or her aroma. They lingered in his mind and his senses. He had taken her jacket to his room, fisting his cock while he inhaled her scent like some gawky adolescent. Remembering made him shift uneasily. Until she was gone, he hadn't realized just how accustomed he'd become to her presence in his house, how much he missed it now.

"I'm going into the city tomorrow morning on business. See what you can do about a replacement." He stood and added over his shoulder, "I'll go into town to find something to eat. Toss this refuse in the garbage."

After stalking from the house, Ciaran revved the Porsche's engine and spun gravel on his way out of the drive. Even in the middle of the week, the streets were crowded. The summer season always brought the well-heeled from the city to the sound to play. The *Skerry* lay anchored in deeper water than the marina offered. His family might be in the same area, but his banishment made whatever distance impossible to bridge. The urge to anger them had disappeared, but he refused to examine the feelings that had him seeking a glimpse of the *Skerry* each summer. He turned away from the water.

Light and music spilled from Stan's Clam Shop, always a source for a decent meal. Ciaran nimbly avoided a tipsy couple stumbling from the doorway. The man's hands already made erotic forays under the woman's clothing.

Summer changed the whole mood of the town, not that he stayed much in the off-season. He preferred the city during the winter. Since the open sea was not an option, Ciaran chose to immerse himself in an ocean of humanity. Minds open for exploiting, and women eager to spill what they knew if he would just touch them, fuck them. He had taken advantage of that over the last four years and profited handsomely.

He stepped inside, his Silkie senses recoiling from the glaring lights and the mix of body odors and cigarette smoke. After weaving his way through tables and milling people, he reached the bar.

"What'll you have?" Stan demanded in his gravelly voice.

"Whisky on the rocks."

"Canadian Club all right?"

Ciaran stared at the bartender. "No. It gives me a headache. What else do you have?"

"I've got a nice, aged bourbon, Bulleit."

"I'll try it."

"Comin' right up."

A waitress scooted in next to Ciaran, flashed a smile at him even as her eyes did a quick check up and down. Her leg brushed against his as she turned to her boss. "Hey, Stan. I need another bucket of clams, and the couple who just came in wants two steaks, medium rare along with fries."

Stan nodded. The waitress grabbed the bottles of beer he placed on the counter and with another quick, flirtatious smile at Ciaran, she was on her way back into the crowd. Stan slid the bourbon in front of Ciaran and turned to the small window into the kitchen.

"Hey, Keeley, I need a bucket of clams, two steaks medium rare, fries on the side."

Ciaran glanced just in time to see a dark head flit past the window, one hand raised in acknowledgement. Even amid the smell of frying meat, her scent tickled his nostrils. When Stan returned to wiping the bar down, Ciaran looked from the window back to the bartender.

"Keeley?"

Stan grinned. "Yeah, Keeley McNamara. My regular cook went in for an appendectomy, so I called her. She'd stopped by just the day before looking for a job. I gave it to her, at least 'til George gets better. Business is solid enough, though, I'll probably keep her."

So she'd landed on her feet. He fought the urge to drag her from the kitchen and back to his house. Somehow, he didn't think that would go over well with her, or Stan. At least now he knew where to find her.

****

Back in the kitchen, Keeley, expertly flipped the steaks on the grill, checked the fries in the deep fryer, and then garnished two plates in readiness. While the meat sizzled, she pulled an iced bucket from the freezer and deftly dumped two-dozen clams on top. Hot sauce and lemon went into it along with a trio of seafood forks. Flitting back by the window, she set the bucket down and called. "Order up!" before continuing on her way to plate the steaks. The fries went into a holding area where the leftovers would stay warm. She scooped up what she needed, arranged them on the plates, and then carried them both back to the window.

"Order up!"

When Stan snatched the plates, he added another order of two burgers, all the way, with fries and onion rings. Keeley grabbed the orders and met Ciaran's dark stare. For an instant, the noise and the rush vanished as if they had never been, and their gazes locked. She watched his nostrils flare, felt the intensity of his gaze caress her cheek and brush her lips. Almost as if he actually touched her skin. Then she scowled at him. The noise bombarded her once more, and she moved on. The moment was broken.

Keeley worked on the fly all night long. She had expected it to be quieter in the middle of the week. When she finally got a minute, she slipped out the back door to cool off before going back in to clean up. Stan kept the customers comfortable, but the kitchen could get overwhelming. Keeley leaned against the wall next to the door and sucked in a deep breath of the cool night air.

She checked her watch. Customers could still get buckets of clams, those were always available, but the grill was closed. Once she cleaned her area, she was done. A college student handled the rest of it, so she would be free to go home to her granddad. She closed her eyes and put her hands to her face, rubbing tiredly.

Why did she have to see *him* tonight? As much as she hated to admit it, she missed her job at Ciaran's. If you could put up with the parade of women, she had plenty of license to create gourmet meals, not the steaks, burgers, and clams that were Stan's staples. Then there was that tingle of awareness. She'd never felt it with any other man.

Feminine laughter interrupted her thoughts and she opened her eyes to see a tall, stacked redhead stretching up to kiss Ciaran. For an instant, she wondered if she had conjured him, and on the heels of that, she wondered what it would feel like to kiss him the way the redhead was doing now. He leaned his hips against his sports car. The redhead's hands wandered down to grab his butt. Keeley's face flamed and she looked away uncomfortably. An instant later, she heard a low moan and glanced back to see the redhead wrapping herself around him like ivy. Keeley bit her lip to stifle the pulsing of her own body.

Heavens! Was he going to let the woman seduce him right there in the parking lot? She watched the redhead slip one arm between their bodies, watched as his head dropped back. When his eyes closed, heat pooled between Keeley's thighs. She really needed to get back in the kitchen before she humiliated herself.

A little interruption would do him good. Spreading her fingers, she let the energy flow through her hand toward the Porsche. A split second later the car alarm went off. She heard a muffled curse and saw Ciaran fumble for his keys to deactivate the alarm. Keeley didn't wait any longer; she quickly slipped back through the kitchen door.

An hour later, she was walking home. She sighed spotting the light on the porch. She really hoped Granddad would be sleeping, but he hadn't been lately. Keeley hated to admit it, but it seemed he was going downhill quickly. The doctor told her the latest round of chemo had not stopped the progress of the cancer. They would give him pain medication so she could keep him comfortable. So he could die.

He sat in his chair in the dark. He had withdrawn inside himself more and more of late. It didn't seem to be depression as much as separation.

"Pawpaw?" she reverted back to her childhood name for him.

"Keeley girl," his voice was not much more than a whisper. "I ate the food you left for me, even managed to get the dishes cleaned, but I'm wiped out now."

"I'll get your medication." She padded into his dimly lit room, found the correct medicines on his bedside table, and brought them to him along with a glass of water. "Here you go."

When he handed the glass back to her, he gripped her wrist. "I'd like you to call in Hospice, sweetheart."

The glass shook in her hand. "No Pawpaw," she whispered.

"It's time."

She looked into his eyes and saw not only the weariness, but the acceptance as well. Tears sprung to her eyes and rolled down her cheeks. He pulled her into his arms and stroked her shoulders and her short cap of black hair.

"I don't want you to go." Her voice shook. She couldn't help it.

"I'll stay as long as I can, but I can't fight it anymore. You and I both knew from the beginning it was a question of time." He touched her cheek. Hands now gnarled with age were the same hands that built her bookshelves, her bed, and her chest of drawers. They were the hands that bloodied her stepfather's face and pulled her from a household that was hell on earth. "You're a strong young woman now. You'll do fine."

She covered his hand with hers. "It's too much. First Daddy, now you. What good is our magic if we can't save ourselves?"

He frowned at her. "Shame, Keeley. The McNamara magic has never been selfish."

She sighed and bit her lip. "Doesn't mean I have to like it."

She called hospice the following morning. They would send a representative out to talk with her and her grandfather and make arrangements for his particular situation. Keeley straightened the house one more time while she waited. Andy McNamara insisted on coming into the living room and now sat in his favorite chair with his feet propped on the ottoman in front of him.

"Give it a rest," he sighed impatiently. "The house is neat as a pin."

"I'm nervous, Granddad."

"Then go cook something. That will get your mind off it. Always has."

She was working with a new twist on chowder

when she heard the door. She wiped her hands on the towel over her shoulder. "I'll get it, you sit."

She opened the door expecting to see the hospice nurse, but instead the spare, upright figure of Ciaran Clifton's butler stood there.

"Jonathan? What are you doing here?"

"I've come to offer you your job back, Miss McNamara." Keeley was shaking her head before he even finished. "Mr. Clifton has been through four chefs in the past two weeks. I can't find anyone else."

She stared at him. "I went after him with a meat cleaver. He won't want me back."

The butler pursed his lips and glanced at his feet before looking back at her. "Did he deserve it?"

Keeley's eyes twinkled. "I thought so at the time, until I realized after we'd parted ways I accidentally put salt instead of sugar in the gateau."

Jonathan's mouth twitched at the corners. "I can assure you, Mr. Clifton himself suggested I find you. Look, I'll give you a raise and an additional night off."

A raise and more time off? She closed her eyes. More money for food that might tempt Granddad to eat…

A car pulled up in front of the house. A middle-aged woman with a medical bag exited the passenger side. A tall, younger man stepped from the driver's side. She brought her gaze back to Jonathan.

"I'll have to get back to you later. My granddad's ill and the folks from Hospice are here so we can work out some help for him."

The normally staid butler took her small hand in his and squeezed gently. "I'm sorry, Miss."

Keeley soaked up the unexpected warmth. "I'll call you later and let you know."

He nodded and said a pleasant good morning to the two people coming up the walk.

Keeley stepped forward with a smile on her face. "Good morning. I'm Keeley McNamara."

The man, somewhere in his early thirties, shook her hand. Just over average height, he had dark blond hair and hazel eyes. Keeley supposed most women would find him attractive, but not her. She didn't find any men interesting in that way. For just an instant, a lean face with snapping black eyes and collar length dark hair flashed through her mind. She dismissed it immediately. If she thought of Ciaran Clifton at all, it was because he was such an arrogant ass, certainly not because his gaze could scramble her brain.

Keeley sat stiffly in the wooden rocker near the big stone fireplace as she listened to the hospice workers. While her grandfather might already accept the eventuality of his death, she couldn't. Not yet. But she wouldn't upset him. If this was what he wanted, she would do it.

Once they were gone, she stared at the closed door, trembling.

"Keeley?" Quietly, her grandfather shuffled across the room. He put his hands on her shoulders. "Ignoring it won't change it. I'm dying, girl. I'd like whatever time I have left to be as pleasant as possible. I don't want to die in a hospital with people sticking me with needles, poking, and prodding me with tubes and such." He paused for breath. "You've done a wonderful job caring for me, but I know, and you do too, very soon I'll need a lot more care. Enough you can't do it all. It's no sin to ask for help."

She rested her head on his sunken chest. "I don't want you to go. What will I do without you?"

He patted her hair. "You're a fine, strong woman. You'll make a life for yourself without an old man to step and fetch for. That's what you'll do."

Keeley shook her head. "I don't know. I just don't know. I-I need to go out for a bit. There are some errands I need to run."

He raised her chin and looked into her eyes. "I remember a girl who possessed so much fight she was ready to take on the whole world by herself. You've still got that."

She swallowed and nodded.

"Run your errands. I'll be fine."

She didn't immediately head to town when she left her grandfather's small house; instead she turned toward the point. She sat on the rocks and stared out over the bay for a long time. For fourteen years, this was the only home she'd known. She'd been so angry when Andrew McNamara arrived along the Maryland shore to get her. After plowing his fist into her stepfather's surprised face, he'd told her mother and Frank Wells to sign the papers he carried waiving their parental rights over her. If not, he'd have the police on them in no time and there'd be a nasty court battle to face, even if it took every cent he owned to fight it.

He never said a word about the note she'd left explaining what her stepfather was doing to her. And Keeley never mentioned it. She had spent summers with him since she was a girl, and it was shortly after one of those summers he showed up demanding custody. After telling her he would make sure it never happened again, all he ever said was it was not her fault and she was not to blame in any way. But they never really talked about it.

Still. He was her hero.

Keeley buried her face in her hands and struggled to regain her composure. Now was not the time to crumble. She would be strong for him. She would make sure his last days were as pleasant as she could make them. Swallowing back the lump in her throat, she squared her shoulders and stood. There were things she needed to take care of. Her first visit would be to Ciaran Clifton's house. Then, if everything worked out, she would walk back to town to give Stan her resignation.

By the time she reached the weathered mansion Clifton purchased two years ago, she had recovered her equilibrium. She walked down the drive and around to the back of the home. Jonathan opened the kitchen door to her ring.

"Miss! I didn't expect you to walk here. How is your grandfather?"

"I don't know how much time he has left. I might have to take time off," she swallowed, "but if you can deal with that I'll come back to work just so long as Mr. Clifton stays out of the kitchen while I'm here."

Jonathan pursed his lips and raised his brows. He hesitated, but finally said, "We can work with that. Your cooking is artistry compared to what has traipsed through this kitchen over the past two weeks. When can you start?"

Keeley stuck her hands in her pockets and stared out over the pool in the back yard. "I need to give Stan notice. What about Monday?"

"All right. Would you like to take a look at the kitchen before you go to see if there are any supplies you'd like me to have picked up?"

Keeley grinned. "Naturally."

****

Ciaran followed the older woman down the hallway of her upscale penthouse. He had taken her to an opening at an art gallery and then out for a late dinner. Now he hoped the evening would pay off. He liked the sway of her hips and the still-firm flare of her butt. Adrianne Shelton's husband was away on a business trip to Europe, so Ciaran was taking advantage of it to pump her for gossip. While her husband had no objection to the sexual side of their relationship, Ciaran doubted he'd be nearly as keen on his wife's penchant for gossip. With her husband's business connections and her position as one of the premier hostesses in the city, she always dropped profitable bits of information. The woman, with her expertly bleached blonde hair and her perfect makeup, turned in his arms as soon as they stepped in the bedroom.

"Ah Ciaran, you make me feel young again."

He smiled at her with practiced ease. "The years only enhance true beauty."

As he kissed and caressed her, he removed her clothing, praising each area he uncovered. While she reclined on the huge bed, Ciaran stripped, letting her absorb each part of his body as he bared it. The avid desire in her eyes and the way she stared so breathlessly at his crotch made him hard. Naked at last, he approached the bed. She sat up, cupping his testicles and took the glistening head of his cock into her mouth. He sighed.

If Keeley Ann McNamara thought he had the morals of an alley cat, what did that make Adrianne Shelton? Ciaran frowned and shut his eyes. He wanted to banish the evil little sprite from his thoughts, but she haunted him. And why was he thinking about her when a beautiful woman had his dick in her mouth? Maybe because it was her mouth he really wanted around him.

"That's it, babe," he murmured, but in his mind it was Keeley with her lips working their magic. He let Adrianne continue, reveling in the pure sensation even as he pictured someone else. Pushing her back on the bed, Ciaran climbed over her, stroking her with his hands and lips until she gasped out his name. He spread her open and buried himself inside her. His movements were expert, designed to get his lover off as quickly as possible and as often as possible until he, too, climaxed. That part was for her.

As impatient as he was to leave, Ciaran held her in his arms. This was where he picked up what he needed, and most of the time, all he had to do was listen.

He knew she wanted him permanently as a lover, and she was not unattractive. But if he learned nothing else from his exile into the world of humans these last four years, it was caution. All of his actions were determined according to what would best serve his interests in the long run. Not exactly the lesson he was sent among humanity to learn, but it was the lesson that enabled him to be successful.

"I saw your parents and your brother and his wife. They were in town for the opening of a new art exhibit. Carrick was talking to Jason Redman, the software guru."

"Really?" Ciaran feigned indifference as he did whenever mention of his family was made.

"They talked for quite some time along with Cayden and Taylor. You know, Annabel is pregnant again."

He didn't want to hear any more about Cayden and his wife. He didn't want to hear about a family that had so obviously moved on without him. It was just too painful. But the fact his father brought both Cayden and Annabel's brother into an extended conversation with Jason Redman did interest him.

Valuable information called for a reward. Ciaran kissed her, gliding his hands over her until he let her go with a regretful sigh. "I have to go. I have an early meeting with my attorney. As always, you have enriched what would have been a lonely evening."

As he rode the elevator down to the lobby of the building where the Sheltons occupied most of the top floor, Ciaran shut his eyes, his mouth twisting with disgust—at her or himself, he wasn't sure. Something had to change. He couldn't do this anymore. This wasn't about being Silkie. He felt like he was selling himself. And wasn't he?

He thought again of Keeley McNamara. He'd left instructions for Jonathan to find her and hire her back no matter what he had to pay her, what he had to promise her. It was only to himself he admitted the true reason. He missed her. Not just her cooking, he missed the feel and the scent of her in his house. He missed the way she always tried to avoid him, even when he caught that odd glimpse of sexual heat in her gaze. So many women threw themselves at him, but not her. What the hell was wrong with him? Introspection was not normally part of his nature.

Just before dawn, he stood on the terrace of his penthouse and stared at the city. The sea of humanity helped him the first two years to forget what was taken away from him, the feel of the sea, being able to dive and swim in the rich saltiness of the water. He dove naked into the pool that served as a pitiful substitute. Nothing could replace what he'd thrown away. The more success he achieved, the emptier his life became.

The Silkie Council sought to punish him four years ago. Ciaran could now admit the justice of it. In his anger and his jealousy he had gone way over the edge. He'd tried to murder Cayden and his human, and nearly killed his father as well. It wasn't something he was proud of. His punishment was to live like the humans he held in such contempt. Four years had done little though to change those feelings, not when he dealt with the Adrianne Sheltons and the Francines of this world. They demonstrated no loyalty for their kind and were so easy to manipulate he found it wearisome.

The Silkie Lords told him he must live as a human until he learned compassion, but Ciaran wasn't sure how he was supposed to do that. And he didn't know if he even wanted to try. What he did want was his home. Even if he couldn't transform to swim and hunt, he could be near what was more home to him than dry land. His whole body shuddered. He needed to hear the ocean, the cry of gulls, and smell the salt tang in the air.

****

It was Keeley's last night at Stan's. Tomorrow his old cook would be back and she would once again be ensconced in the Clifton kitchen. As she flipped a steak on the grill, the sizzle and hiss of burning fat rose into the air. The heat sapped her energy. If she never smelled another deep fat fryer in her life, it would be too soon. Stan's, she decided, was a lot pleasanter when you were the customer.

She felt more relaxed now about returning to Clifton's house. It would give her more freedom and more time with Granddad. The hospice nurse came by to set him up on a program of medication, and a hospice health care worker stopped by every day to give Keeley time to run errands. They stressed the need for her to be within reach, particularly as his condition deteriorated.

She brushed a hand across her forehead as she flipped burgers and threw another steak on the grill. They were busy tonight. A Sunday evening and no one felt like cooking. She deftly plated the burgers, added fries and garnish and carried the plates to the window.

"Order up, Stan!" she called.

A sixth sense made her glance through the window and her gaze met the dark eyes of her former employer. Scratch that. There was no longer any former about it. He smirked and lifted his bourbon to her. Keeley ignored the puckering of her nipples. Instead, she smiled and casually shifted her hand just out of his line of vision, feeling the rush of energy flow through her fingers. When he set his glass back down it was right in the middle of a bowl of peanuts. His eyes narrowed on her. Keeley nearly laughed out loud. She moved away and as soon as she was out of sight of the window, doubled over with laughter.

"You're losin' it Keeley," her helper mumbled.

"Private joke."

She was late leaving Stan's. Several orders came in right before cut-off so she had to finish those before she could begin cleanup. As she stripped off her apron and washed her face and hands, all she could think about was getting home and taking a shower. She knew she'd been a big help to Stan, but to be honest, it wasn't her kind of cooking. She much preferred Clifton's kitchen. And what she really preferred was not feeling like a giant grease ball by the end of each day. So as much as Ciaran Clifton might be a dickhead, she'd rather be in his kitchen than Stan's.

She said good night to Stan and slipped out the back. After having to fend off drunken advances on several occasions out front, Keeley switched the way she went home, now cutting down to the shore to walk along the edge of the dark water. At the outskirts of town, there was a small beach. She was relieved to see no one there. She slipped off her deck shoes, shimmied out of her baggy pants, and pulled her T-shirt over her head. The night air was cool, and she shivered slightly as she headed into the water clad only in her tiny excuse of a bra and the cotton boy shorts she favored.

The water still retained some of the heat of the day so it was warm compared to the night air. Keeley sighed and dove smoothly under the surface before bobbing up and shaking her head. She loved the water, loved swimming, and would spend nearly half her life doing just that if she only could. But tonight was just a quick dip, a way to get the kitchen grease off her skin. She floated quietly in the dark water, letting her body relax, and allowing herself to forget for a few minutes that the person she loved most in the world was slipping away. She didn't want to think about life without Granddad. He'd been more of a father to her than her real father. She immediately felt guilty for that thought. Her father could not be blamed for what happened to her.

With a regretful sigh, Keeley struck out strongly for shore. When her feet hit bottom, she stood and picked her way toward her clothing. The hair on her arms prickled and she jerked her gaze up to see the tall, dark silhouette of a man leaning against the post by the walkway. Sure he couldn't see anything in the dark, Keeley stuck her chin up and continued on to her clothing.

"Not a good idea to swim alone in the dark."

She'd recognize that gravelly voice anywhere. "As you can see," she responded coolly, "I'm fine. You can go."

With a deliberate casualness she was far from feeling, Keeley pulled her shirt over her head and yanked her pants up. Ciaran continued to simply stand there. His dark gaze made her nervous and uncomfortable. She didn't like men's eyes on her. She fumbled trying to get her shoes on.

"You really don't need to stay here, Mr. Clifton. I'm fine. I was just on my way home after work."

He straightened away from the post. "I'll walk you."

Great. Keeley eyed him suspiciously as she drew near. "Why?"

He shrugged. "There are lots of drunken temps around."

She laughed suddenly. "And I'm supposed to feel safer with you than the summer residents? The man who seduces a different woman every night?"

He looked her up and down. "Are you a woman?"

31

he drawled insultingly. "I hadn't noticed."

"Go to hell."

He laughed without much amusement. "Some days it's difficult to know if I'm not already there."

"I don't want you following me," Keeley hissed and stomped past him.

"Too bad." He followed her anyway. "I'm walking you home."

They reached the top of the stairs that led back to the sidewalk. A group of teens was a few yards farther, laughing and cursing, obviously drunk. She glanced from them to Ciaran's towering form next to her and wasn't sure for a moment who she feared most.

"Humor me," he murmured blandly, as if sensing her uncertainty. "I'm trying to redeem myself."

Keeley snorted. "That's a lost cause."

"A lot of people would agree with you there."

As she stalked along the sidewalk, he kept pace easily. A few of the teens called out ribald remarks. Clifton tried to put his arm around her shoulder, but she twisted away and waved her hand at the teens surreptitiously. She'd just give them something else to think about.

In the dark, they suddenly heard shouts. "Hey dude, what are you doing? Why'd you spray your beer at me?"

"I didn't spray my beer at you. You did it to me, jackass!"

Keeley and Clifton were forgotten.

"You don't have to walk me home," she said again, as the quiet of the night settled around them again. "I'll be fine. I'm sure you must have something else to do, someone to meet."

He ignored her. Instead he said, "Jonathan tells me he managed to hire you back."

Keeley stopped and faced him in the dim light

from homes nestled along the sidewalk across from the marina. "Did he tell you my conditions?"

"I have to stay out of the kitchen when you're there." She heard amusement in his tone.

"Yes."

"I have some conditions of my own." The amusement was still there, but trimmed with a hard edge.

"That's not part of the deal." Not losing her temper suddenly appeared an unreachable goal.

He laughed softly. "Perhaps I'm missing something here, but aren't you working for me?"

Keeley's nose went in the air. "I have decided to cook for you again, but I don't work for anyone."

When she stopped outside the gate to her grandfather's yard, he stared at her. "You have a very bad attitude Keeley Ann McNamara."

She glanced over her shoulder, ignoring him. "This is where I live." She put her hand on the gate and started to unlatch it.

"I could fire you again," he taunted.

She glared at him, refusing to let him see it mattered. "I don't have the time or the patience to play games. If you don't want me to work for you, tell Jonathan to call me before I walk over to your house tomorrow."

"You walk?" he asked incredulously.

She shrugged. "Sometimes I ride a bike."

"Don't you have a car?"

She shrugged again. No way would she tell him she sold it to help pay some of her grandfather's medical expenses not covered by his insurance. "I don't need one."

"Keeley—is that you?" Her head swiveled. Her grandfather stood grasping the doorframe, his voice querulous.

"I'll be right there, Granddad. I stopped for a swim on the way home."

The way Clifton's eyes assessed the house, her grandfather and finally her, made her bristle.

"Thanks for walking me home. You can go now."

The glow of the porch light highlighted his suddenly narrowed eyes. "Don't get in the habit of issuing orders to me, Keeley. I rarely take direction from other people."

When he reached out to touch her, she flinched away and hurried up the walk. Her hands trembled as she shoved them into the pockets of her jacket. Why did she have to feel such an attraction to him, especially when he half scared her to death?

Chapter Three

Ciaran watched her from the darkness. When she reached the doorway, she helped the old man back inside and closed the door. A moment later the porch light went out. *She lived with her grandfather.* That surprised him. As brash and aggressive as she was, he figured her for a party girl, someone with several roommates and a free flowing lifestyle. Something else surprised him as well. Two times that night she avoided his touch. She'd not made any kind of a production about it, just twisted out of reach.

Most women fell into his arms. That was his plan for her as well. He hoped he could seduce her, bed her, and get her out of his thoughts. More and more, he found himself holding that damn jacket with her scent on it and fisting his dick while he imagined fucking her. Hell, he hardly knew her. Other than their fight when he fired her, he'd barely spoken more than a handful of words to her. She wasn't even his type. He preferred his women sweet, blonde and statuesque, not waiflike, black-haired and vinegar-tongued, which was precisely why he didn't understand this strange fascination.

He walked a few feet down the road, then stood in the shadows of a large maple and stared back at the house. After a few minutes, a light came on upstairs. He'd been in a few small Cape Cod style homes and knew the upstairs was probably set up like a loft, with dormer ceilings and the two windows at either end. He shook his head. What he needed was a good lay, but somehow he just wasn't in the mood. If he were honest, he hadn't been for some time because every time he considered it, all he could think of was Keeley.

****

The nurse, Susan Levine, came by in the morning to see Andy McNamara. She asked him if he was having any pain, how he was feeling, eating, and sleeping. Keeley excused herself to go into the kitchen. She prepared a couple of meals and snacks for her granddad he could easily grab and eat without help. Since it was her first day back at Ciaran's, she wanted to get there early, see what was available before she set menus for the week. Jonathan could then run those past lover boy so she could get busy.

Keeley ducked her head back in the living room. "I have to go to work, Granddad. Remember I'm back at the Clifton house if you need anything."

"All right, Keeley girl." He turned to the nurse. "My granddaughter's a chef. She cooks like a dream, trained at one of those fancy schools in New York."

Keeley grinned. "I'll see you later, Granddad."

The sun was hot, but the walk wasn't bad. She didn't take the road, instead cutting across the point to where the house stood on the opposite side of the cove. She followed the path up through the gardens. Hearing splashing and laughter from the pool, she glanced over to see Ciaran perched lazily on the edge. Two nubile blondes played in the water; what she could see of them was bare. One girl swam over and stopped between his legs, lazily running a hand up his muscular thigh. Even from this distance she saw his cock straining his shorts.

God! The man simply could not keep his dick in his pants.

As if he'd heard her thoughts, his head snapped up and his black eyes met hers. When she glared at him, he arched one brow and deliberately reached out to caress the woman's breast. The other blonde surfaced next to his other side and he immediately leaned down and kissed her lingeringly on the lips. The girl leaned in to rub her custom breasts against the bulge in his shorts. His gaze challenged Keeley, and he smiled slowly.

She'd seen enough. After stomping into the house, she tossed her backpack into the closet and pulled out her chef's jacket.

"Ah, Miss McNamara," Jonathan greeted, no doubt hearing her slam the kitchen door. "May I be the first to say what a pleasure it is to see you once again in the kitchen?"

She smiled at him. "You may. And I will confess what a pleasure it is to once again be in this kitchen, though you would have to put bamboo shoots under my nails to get me to confess that to Mr. Clifton."

The butler sniffed. "There will be three for dinner this evening."

Keeley snorted. "Judging from what I saw, French cooking will be lost on the blonde bimbos. About the closest they've probably come to haute cuisine would be French kissing. I'll keep it simple and go with baked halibut, a salad of baby greens and twice baked potatoes. If you will run that by Mr. Clifton for his approval, I'll get started."

Jonathan glanced out the window toward the pool, a small smile hovered on his normally firm mouth. "I suspect I should wait a few minutes."

Keeley knew she shouldn't look, but she did. Though the hedge shielded some of it, it was pretty obvious the two blondes were nude, and Clifton stood watching whatever they were doing with an appreciative smile on his satyric face. She sighed in disgust and disappointment. For a while the night before he seemed like a different man. She should have known better.

She turned away. "I'll prepare the menus for the

week, Jonathan. You can present them all at once that way."

"Very good, Miss."

Once he left the kitchen, she looked through the refrigerator, freezer, and pantry to refresh her memory and then sat down to work. She had nearly finished when the back door opened and one of the bimbos appeared.

"Ciaran wants sandwiches and drinks brought to the pool." The blonde looked her over. "Are you the cook?"

Keeley felt every nuance of the woman's contempt. The posture clearly said, look at me, I look like a woman while you've got the figure of an adolescent. It was tempting to tell the bombshell what she could do with her silicone boobs and her bubble butt. It was even more tempting to give her something to trip over so she'd fall flat on her face, boobs, or whatever hit first.

"I'm Mr. Clifton's chef."

White teeth flashed at her. "Great. Just bring the sandwiches out when you get them done."

Peanut butter and jelly? It was tempting, but too unprofessional. She made roast beef sandwiches with pasta and fruit to accompany them. Placing that with a pitcher of tea on a cart, she rang for Jonathan.

"Lover boy has worked up an appetite. Barbie was in earlier to say they want sandwiches." She slapped the notepaper with her weekly menu on it in his hand. "While you're out there you can discuss this with him."

It was an indication of how the afternoon would go. While he kept his word and never entered the kitchen, the blondes were there often with requests for drinks, snacks or anything else they could think of. After dessert was served, Jonathan came to tell her Mr. Clifton requested her presence in the dining room.

She stepped down the short hall and entered the room, her hands folded in front of her. The blonde bathing beauties now wore silk sheaths, one red, one blue. They were all but falling out of the tops of them as they leaned forward, one at each of Ciaran's elbows.

"You wished to see me, sir?"

"I just wanted to welcome you back and tell you how fine tonight's meal was. Liz and Emily really enjoyed it."

Keeley looked somewhere over his right shoulder and responded stiffly. "Thank you, sir. If that will be all, I need to finish in the kitchen."

It set the tone for the next two weeks. He antagonized her every chance he got, trying to make her lose her temper. Keeley refused not only to take the bait, but even to look at him. It became easier to ignore him as her grandfather's situation went rapidly downhill.

By the end of the second week, he could no longer leave his bed. The hospice folks moved in a hospital bed, helping Keeley to move her grandfather's four-poster into the storage building behind the house. She stood for a long time staring at the heavy maple headboard and footboard. Granddad had slept in that bed as long as she could remember, but he needed the mobility of a hospital bed now. Sometimes late at night, she sneaked down to check on him, to make sure he hadn't left without saying goodbye.

On her day off on Friday, Keeley got up early and jogged down to the beach. She wouldn't stay long, she promised herself, just long enough for a swim before she returned home to make breakfast. Stripping off her shoes and shorts, she ran lightly into the cold water and struck out for the navigational buoy. She hadn't been able to get out in a while and the exertion felt good. At the buoy, she stopped only a moment to catch her breath.

She couldn't stay long. Grandad needed her, so she let go of the buoy and began the swim back to shore. Not quite halfway, daggers stabbed through her right calf. The cramp knotted the muscle and doubled her up with pain. She stopped swimming abruptly and grabbed for the leg, accidentally swallowing water. The agony gripping her calf vied with the violent need to cough, and she flailed, suddenly frightened of the water she normally regarded as relaxing, and comforting.

****

He stood on the point watching her. She infuriated him at the same time she fascinated him. He longed for her scent when she wasn't there and fantasized about what he wanted to do to her. He closed his eyes, picturing her slender figure pressed against him. Damn.

His inability to get her out of his head made him angry. Deliberately over the past two weeks since she returned to work, he had gone out of his way to annoy and antagonize her. Knowing how it angered her, he'd fondled and flirted with as many women as he could where she couldn't possibly avoid seeing it. He did everything except enter the kitchen, her one condition for working for him. In the back of his mind was the unspoken knowledge that while he might taunt and tease her, he would do nothing to truly drive her away. Just her presence in his house once more eased his mind. He closed his eyes and shook his head. How pathetic was that?

This morning he stood watching the boats heading in and out of the bay, remembering the feeling of zipping through the water next to them and then diving down, the muffled sounds from the sea floor vibrating over his body. Even below water he could hear the echo of human voices from up top.

His eyes searched her out again. She'd reached the navigational buoy, but this morning she didn't linger as she often did. Instead she immediately struck out for shore. She was graceful in or out of the water, but especially in. He enjoyed watching her slender, almost boyish body. At some point, he realized with surprise, he'd stopped finding the Francines and the Lizzes and Emilies attractive with their oversized breasts and hips that would run to fat in their later years. But Keeley Ann McNamara was a different matter.

He was positive her small breasts would barely fill his hand, and he could probably span her waist with no effort at all. She wasn't tan like other humans he'd known over the years. What little time she spent on the beach seemed to be at sunrise or sunset, so her legs and arms were long and creamy. He wondered what it would be like to make love to her. As tiny as she was, it opened all sorts of possibilities.

Abruptly his musings came to an end. His body stiffened and his brows snapped together. Something was wrong. She'd stopped swimming and was struggling in the water. Ciaran hesitated only an instant. Her panic struck him as clearly as if it were his own. Stripping off his shirt and shoes as he went, he scrambled down the path to the water and launched himself into the bay. God if he could only transform he could reach her faster! Fear made his heart race, but this time it was fear for someone else and it nearly suffocated him.

Her struggles had grown sluggish by the time he reached her, but when he grabbed for her, she had strength enough to cling to him and nearly take him under as well.

"Stop Keeley!" he ordered harshly. "I've got you."

He towed her toward shore. When the water was shallow enough, he picked her up in his arms and carried her. She weighed next to nothing. As feisty as she acted, it was easy to forget how delicately she was made. She coughed, but he sensed that wasn't the main problem. After laying her on the sand, he knelt next to her. Pain contorted her features.

"What's wrong?"

"Cramp," she gasped.

He felt along her legs and then found the hard knot of muscle in her calf. He massaged it, ignoring her cries of pain. Slowly, the muscle relaxed and so did she. Her face was averted. As the muscle returned to normal, his massage changed to a caress. She was beautiful, like fine china or a delicate piece of blown glass, and he realized he wanted her more fiercely than he thought it possible to want a woman. His cock stiffened and his breathing changed as he studied her. His hand slid along the silky-smooth skin of her inner thigh, and his nostrils flared as he picked up the scent of her sex. How would she taste? How would she feel gloved around him?

In the next instant a tiny foot planted itself in the middle of his chest and shoved with surprising force.

"Get your damn hands off me!" She jumped to her feet and stumbled up the beach to her belongings, snatching them up and running for the stairs to the sidewalk. He caught her at the base.

"I save your life and that's the thanks I get?" he snarled as he grabbed her arm.

She cried out in fear and shook him off. Eyes snapping, she shoved a hand at him, but not with the intention of hitting him he realized in confusion right before he took a half step back and fell over the garbage can behind him. As he floundered, trying to regain his balance, she shot up the stairs and disappeared.

He stared at the tall green can in confusion.

How had it gotten there? He would have sworn it was a couple of feet away next to the light pole. In fact, how did they pass by it to begin with?

Ungrateful witch. He seriously needed to have his head examined. He couldn't believe now he had ever mooned after her and actually missed her. She was a skinny, annoying shrew. Thank God it was her day off so he didn't have to look at her or listen to her.

Turning on his heel, he stalked back along the beach. His shorts dried as the sun rose and the heat grew. All he needed to do was collect his shirt and his shoes. What on earth made him jump in to save her?

A splash of water near the point drew his attention, but when he looked he saw nothing, just a ripple of water. Probably a fish.

***

"I tell you I am not imagining things!" Annabel Barton Clifton snapped a few minutes later as she stared at her husband and her father-in-law. "I saw Ciaran race into the water to save a girl who was floundering. He hauled her to shore, carried her when the water was too shallow, and then massaged her leg, I guess to get a cramp out."

Cayden, her husband and Ciaran's older brother by a year, snorted. "Let me guess, and then he fucked her right there in broad daylight."

Annabel glared at him. "No. She kicked him in the chest and took off running. That's when the really amazing thing happened. He caught her arm and yelled at her. She shook him off and then the garbage can behind him *moved* so when he stepped back he tripped over it and almost fell right on his butt!"

Cayden put his hand on his wife's forehead. "Are you sure you're feeling all right, Bell? It's not the pregnancy is it?"

She pushed his hand away. "I am telling you the truth. The damn garbage can *moved*!"

Carrick cleared his throat and rubbed his bristly jaw with one hand. "Well, if he did go in after this girl, it's the first unselfish thing he's done since the Council stripped him of his pelt four years ago. I wish I could be more optimistic it's a sign he's trying to change."

"Hello?" She stared at both of them. "A garbage can *moved* by itself!"

When neither reacted, she shook her head and stalked off in search of her mother-in-law. Maybe Catriona would have some explanation for what she had seen. Annabel knew one thing for sure. She wanted a closer look at the girl. She seemed vaguely familiar. Maybe she should ask her brother, Taylor. He might know something too. He'd spent more time with the locals.

****

Keeley stopped a little farther down the sidewalk and slipped her sneakers and shorts back on before jogging the rest of the way home. In her mind she hurled every insult she could think of at Ciaran Clifton. How dare he touch her like that? It was one thing to massage the cramp, but then the feel of his hand changed.

What made her even angrier was it turned her on. As soon as his fingers skimmed her thigh, she felt as if a thousand butterflies danced across her stomach. It was wrong. She shouldn't feel that way about her boss, and especially not him. He had a different girl every night, and sometimes more than one.

She realized with a sense of deep mortification she was crying. Why should she care what he did? Why should it even matter? He was a pig, an arrogant, self-absorbed ass—and he had just saved her life. That thought made her flush with embarrassment. He saved her life and she kicked him in the chest and moved the garbage can behind him.

Keeley stopped on the front porch and wiped her face with her hand. Sand covered her, so she dusted that off as well. It was doubtful Granddad would notice at this point. It made her sad to think how quickly he was fading. The thought of losing him made her heart pound with panic. He had always been there, and haughtily she thought he always would be.

Now a definite end was in sight, she struggled to accept it as reality.

Quietly, Keeley opened the door. She exhaled softly as she saw he still slept. After a quick shower and a change of clothes, she slipped into the kitchen and prepared breakfast. He had reached the point where he could only tolerate soft foods and liquids, so she worked hard to make sure everything was as nutritious as possible.

When she poked her head back in the living room, he was awake and smiled at her weakly.

"Good morning, Granddad."

"Same to you, girl."

"Would you like something to drink? I have juice and I've fixed a pureed omelet."

He shook his grizzled head in disgust. "Never thought I'd see the day I had to have my food ground like a babe again. Bring me a straw and I'll see what I can slurp down."

She sat next to him, helping him eat and drink. He was weak enough now she had to steady his hand. He watched her between bites and sips. When he'd eaten all he could, he put his hand over her forearm to stop her from getting up.

"What's bothering you, Keeley?" When she started to shake her head, he squeezed her arm. "Don't lie, and don't try to avoid it. Something's got you rattled. Now talk. I can't do much else, but I still have a mind and can listen."

She blinked rapidly. "Sorry. You're right." She sighed. "It's a couple of things."

She told him about going to the beach, what happened and how her boss fished her out then massaged the cramp away. She felt his hand tighten on her arm as she described her fear she might drown.

"Then after he did all that, I panicked. I felt him touching me and I panicked. I kicked him and swore at him. Then when he tried to stop me, I moved a trash can behind him so he nearly fell over it." Keeley stared out the window. "Oh Granddad! I was horrible to him."

"Well girl, you know what I've always told you. If you wrong someone, it's best to own up and make up before too much time passes. That way no hard feelings set in."

Keeley squirmed. Apologizing was never easy, but to Ciaran Clifton? Impossible. Still, Grandad was right, like always. "I'll see him tomorrow. Is that soon enough?"

"I expect so. With the kind of girls young Clifton normally has hanging on him, it will likely surprise him you say anything at all."

Keeley made a face. Maybe he'd fall over from the shock of it.

As if he sensed where her thoughts took her, and he might have, he continued. "Now don't go judging everyone in light of your stepdad. Some men who go wild when they're young make the best husbands, considerate and faithful. You judge him for how he is with other things. Now, what's the second thing?"

She lowered her eyes and plucked at the sheet covering him. When she finally looked up, tears rolled unheeded down her cheeks. "I've tried to be cheerful and brave, but Pawpaw, I don't want you to go. It's too soon! Why would God take someone like you when he lets other awful people like my stepfather live? I want more time with you."

She scrubbed her eyes just like she had as a girl. Andy McNamara's face softened as he touched her cheek. "There's a reason for everything that happens. We might not always see the whys behind the plan, but they're there. As to wanting more time with me...why it's up to each of us to make the most of what we have each and every day. None of us knows when our time to move on will come. I could go tomorrow or I could go in a month, but counting the time won't make it any better. You've got to live it."

She sniffed and wiped her fingers under her eyes. "I know I'm being selfish, and then I feel even worse. Tell me what you want me to do Pawpaw. I want whatever time you have left to be the best it can be."

He smiled at her, then lay back and shut his eyes. "It is. I am home where I want to be. I have you here with me, the only family I need. I've asked the hospice folks to send someone over to sit with me this evening. And I called your friend Stephie. She's taking you out for a night on the town. You spend too much time locked up with a sick old man."

Keeley's mouth fell open. "You're kicking me out?"

He smiled tiredly. "No, not kicking you out. It will give me pleasure for you to go out and have fun. You're not even twenty-seven yet. Have your night on the town and then tell me all about it tomorrow. That will make me happy."

Stephie picked her up at seven, but as soon as she saw the shorts and T-shirt Keeley wore, she dragged her friend upstairs and started riffling through her closet.

"Your granddad wants you to have fun, and it's my job to make sure that happens." As she talked she pulled a short form-fitting black dress from the closet. "Put this on, then I'll do something with your hair and makeup. Do you have any heels?" Stephie continued to dig in the closet. "Oh wait, here's a pair."

"I can't walk around in those!"

Stephie laughed. "Walk hell! We're going dancing."

As Keeley protested, Stephie pushed her down on the stool in front of her mirror and slipped the high-heeled sandals on her small feet. Keeley saw Stephie's eyes widen at her bright pink toenails.

"Well at least you have some vanity, Keeley. Now hold still while I fix your hair and add some makeup."

Twenty minutes later, she came downstairs. When she stepped in to say goodbye to her grandfather, he smiled. "You look beautiful, just beautiful. It's a picture I'll never forget. You have a good time."

Stephie had her car parked out front. There was a supper club near the Yacht Club both the locals and the summer crowd enjoyed. Stephie squeezed her Volkswagen into a parking spot Keeley wasn't sure really was one and they headed inside.

"Do you have a reservation?" The haughty looking hostess inquired.

Before Keeley could open her mouth, Stephie stuck her head around and said, "Andy McNamara for two."

The hostess sniffed as she looked down her list. "Right this way."

"Shoulders back, Keeley!" her friend ordered.

All Keeley really wanted to do was run back to the kitchen, throw on a chef's jacket, and help cook. She felt half naked with her shoulders bare, and half her thighs on display. In fact, she was awfully afraid if she sneezed she might show something from one end or the other that would land her in jail.

"You look great. And you're already attracting attention."

"I don't want to attract attention."

The waiter seated them both and smiled widely at Keeley who ignored him. Stephie ordered two glasses of wine and then leaned over and tapped her finger on the table in front of Keeley. "You are supposed to have a good time, your grandfather's orders."

She started to reply, and then she smelled Ciaran's unique cologne. It always drew her attention no matter how unwillingly. She glanced up just in time to see him weave past their table, his hand resting casually just above the rounded butt cheek of the tall blonde with him. She watched in horror as the waiter seated them just two tables away, with Ciaran facing her.

Chapter Four

Ciaran scowled as he took his seat at the table. He still had Keeley Ann McNamara on the brain. In fact, he'd swear he smelled her tantalizingly spicy scent. As the blonde with him rambled on about her latest shopping trip to the city, Ciaran let his eyes droop and his mind wander back to that morning. Keeley. For just a moment, she'd been his. Her skin was as smooth and silky as mother of pearl. She was a feather, delicate, fragile, and soft, and just as quickly she had flown away.

So why could he smell her? He looked and his eyes narrowed as he saw the two women seated a couple of tables away. The blonde was just like the type he normally hooked up with, generous breasts and a nicely rounded ass, but it was her partner his eyes riveted on.

Short, black hair, stylishly mussed, a swanlike neck that blended into fragile, creamy shoulders, small, firm breasts, luscious lips and when she at last looked, he saw her wary, defensive green eyes. Desire shot through him like a bullet from a gun as he took in the curve of her jaw and the slight tremble to her lower lip. Keeley. But this was a Keeley he'd never seen before, never even imagined. It was all he could do not to get up and go over to the table.

"Ciaran! Have you heard one word I've said?"

He looked back at the blonde. Betsy? Bambi?

"Sure babe. You got a great deal on a Prada bag."

She smiled, took a sip of her drink and went on

again about a party the next day at the Yacht Club. He tuned her back out, his narrowed eyes focusing on Keeley. She and her friend talked easily, like people who've known each other for years usually do. Were they friends or lovers? As violently as she reacted that morning, he wondered. Were women what attracted her? He tried to envision her touching and caressing the blonde with her, but the image just didn't fit.

She picked up her wine with a movement as graceful as any ballerina. As she brought the glass to her lips, he watched them part, close on the edge, then release it. When the tip of her tongue appeared to catch a stray drop, Ciaran swallowed thickly.

"Do you want to dance?" Bambi, Betsy, Barbara asked.

He felt the wood he was sporting and shook his head. "Not right now." Not in this millennium if he couldn't get his mind off Keeley Ann McNamara long enough for his hard-on to subside. Resolutely, he turned away from her faerie form and tried to concentrate on his date.

****

Keeley snuck peeks at him all through dinner, but he seemed completely absorbed by his buxom blonde date. As she watched, he touched the woman's arm, put his arm around her shoulders and leaned close to hear something she said.

"So exactly what is it you find so fascinating?" Stephie asked with a laugh. "I've never seen you this distracted unless it was by a poorly executed puff pastry or a dressing with a drop too much vinegar."

When Stephie started to turn and look, Keeley put her hand on her friend's arm in panic. "No! Don't look at him."

Stephie's eyes narrowed. "Him?"

"My boss," Keeley huffed. "He's sitting two tables over with another blonde bimbo on his arm."

Stephie did laugh then, and Keeley caught Ciaran's smoldering gaze for just an instant, just long enough to ignite the heavy ache of desire in the pit of her stomach.

"How would that be different than any other night from what you tell me? It sounds like the guy is a sex machine with a 'blonde only' gear."

Keeley abruptly set down her knife and fork. "Yeah."

"Let's go into the bar. I'll get you an after dinner drink and maybe we can dance. No turning down guys," Stephie warned her. "Remember, your granddad said to have fun and you've got to be able to tell him more than 'I sat at the table and watched Stephie dance all evening.'" Stephie stood and Keeley followed suit. "Besides, you look smokin' hot. Make sure you wiggle that tush a little when you walk by lover boy."

Wiggling her tush was the last thing Keeley wanted to do. Nevertheless, she felt his stare as she glided past.

The bar was crowded. On a Friday night during the summer season it appeared everyone decided to dance. They found a small table not far from the dance floor. Almost immediately, a waitress appeared and set down two glasses of wine for them. "Compliments of a gentleman in the dining room," she told them and then bustled off again, back to the bar. Ciaran. Had to be. Keeley forced herself not to look that way, afraid he might somehow still be watching her.

The music was loud, but not so overpowering she couldn't hear herself think. She sipped her wine, watching humorously as a man dressed in a casually crumpled linen suit came to ask Stephie out on to the dance floor. Keeley tapped her foot to the music. She enjoyed dancing. It was just people touching her that made her uncomfortable. Instantly her imagination brought up Ciaran's fingers running over her calf, brushing the silky skin along her thigh as his dark eyes stared at her intently. Almost as if she conjured him, he took the floor with the statuesque blonde. It was a fast song, and his hips pumped with the beat. He was an uninhibited dancer, but then she would have expected nothing less. She lifted her gaze to his face and found him watching her. Heat flooded her face, and she was glad she sat in dim lighting that wouldn't reveal her blush. With a hand that trembled slightly, she snatched her wine glass and swallowed a gulp.

"Would you like to dance?"

The questioner was hardly more than a boy, and she wanted to say no, but she remembered what Stephie said. She owed it to Granddad to try to have a good time. He obviously had gone to some effort to set this up tonight. With a small smile, she nodded. She cringed away slightly from her partner's hand on the small of her back, and then forced herself to relax. It was a dance, nothing else.

After that, it seemed to Keeley she rarely sat. She made as many excuses as she could to avoid slow dances and contact. Between dances she sipped from a wine glass that never emptied and realized she was beginning to get just a little bit of a buzz. That was okay. At least she would be able to tell Granddad she enjoyed herself. Her skin glowed from the heat and the exertion. She glanced over at one point and saw Stephie snuggled up to a man wearing dress slacks with suspenders. Probably some Ivy League attorney type. Stephie was a magnet for the ones with money.

When the latest song ended, Keeley smiled absently at her partner, thanked him and headed back to the table. She was about to sit when she felt a hand at her back.

"Surely as your boss, I can get at least one

dance, Keeley Ann McNamara."

His smooth, deep voice sent a shiver down her spine, and his breath near her ear gave her goose bumps. A slow, jazzy piece began. Keeley found herself staring into those dark, mesmerizing eyes.

"I owe you an apology," she whispered. "For this morning. You saved my life and I-I overreacted."

He smiled, his teeth white against the tan of his skin. "Then dance with me, and you can tell me how sorry you are."

His voice stroked along her eardrums like satin sheets on bare skin. When he held out his hand, she placed hers in it and he helped her up. The dance floor was crowded; he pulled her against his broad chest. The hand holding hers pressed it against his heart, while his other hand splayed across her lower back.

"Relax," he told her, his mouth near her ear. "I won't hurt you."

She nodded, but still found it hard not to be stiff against him.

"Just listen to the music, Keeley, and let it go. Let it go."

His cheek touched the top of her head. She closed her eyes and inhaled the warm, familiar scent of him. She hadn't realized how accustomed she had become to it, and she wondered how he would taste. *Oh God! What was she thinking?* She swallowed nervously. Her hand trembled in his. The music, the wine, and the feel of him moving gently, confidently around the floor were making her hot and lethargic. The urge to lean into him so she could feel the firmness of his body against her cheek, her breasts, and her belly nearly overwhelmed her. When his thigh brushed against her aching mound, Keeley gasped.

She tilted her head back and found him staring. His dark gaze wasn't taunting, angry, or wickedly amused as she so often saw it. Instead, his hot, intense look nearly made her stumble. His hand on her back pressed her closer. Keeley inhaled shakily as his muscular thigh slipped once more between her legs. It was too much.

"Please," she whispered. "Please take me back to the table."

For a moment, she wasn't sure he would. She saw the raw desire in his eyes, the driving need to have her. Keeley's alarm increased. Denying himself was something Ciaran Clifton rarely did. Women fell into his arms, begged him to make love to them.

But not this one. She wouldn't be another notch on his belt.

He touched her cheek. "Do you hate me that much?" It would be so easy to give in to the liquid appeal of his velvety eyes. She averted her face and heard him sigh. "Come. I'll take you back to your girlfriend. I won't bother you again, Keeley. Enjoy your evening."

He melted into the crowd.

She stared at the table and swallowed. She felt suddenly smothered and wanted out. Stephie returned a moment later and Keeley looked at her.

"I want to go home, Stephie. I need to."

One of the things that made Stephie such a wonderful friend was her unquestioning sensitivity to Keeley's mercurial moods. She was the only person besides her grandfather who knew even a fraction of what made Keeley so wary of men. Stephie cast a look around for Ciaran. She took Keeley's arm gently.

"Come on, baby. Let me get you home then before you turn into a pumpkin."

When Keeley let herself into the house, her grandfather woke from a light doze. The volunteer who'd sat with him stood.

"Did you have a good time?" her grandfather

asked.

She plastered a smile on her face and came over to kiss him lightly on the cheek. "Yes, Granddad. I had a wonderful time. Thanks for arranging it. I'll tell you about it in the morning, okay?"

He smiled at her. "Okay."

****

Ciaran couldn't wait to drop Blabby, as he'd privately dubbed her, back at her parents' home. Nothing was worth taking her out again. After a practiced kiss that left him cold, he mouthed some platitude and slipped behind the wheel of the Porsche. He wanted to get home, but there was one place he had to check first. In a matter of minutes, he cruised past the tiny Cape Cod house where Keeley and her grandfather lived. After turning around, he stopped a few feet away, parked in the shadows and cut the engine.

God, now he was *stalking* her. What was wrong with him? He didn't allow anyone to get to him, to touch his emotions. He used them, got what he wanted, and moved on. What made her different?

An older woman came out the front door and got into a small sedan parked on the curb. Once she pulled away, the porch light went out. Only the dim light in the living room remained until, once again, light filled the upstairs window. He stared at it, imagining Keeley taking off the silky black dress. Heat instantly flooded his groin, stiffening his cock. Ciaran snorted in disgust. He was like some lovesick teenager, as bad as Cayden had been mooning all over Annabel Barton.

But this was different. Annabel returned Cayden's feelings. That was part of what spurred his jealousy toward his older brother. Annabel and Cayden's love for each other began when they were just children and stood the test of time.

The only thing Keeley seemed to do was fight or

flee from him. He paused and looked at the lighted window again. Her entire response to him was the classic way in which all animals reacted to threats. Was that the problem? Did she see him that way? A threat to what? Her job? Her? Was it his sex that made her so frightened?

He thought back over the two years she had worked for him. As his chef, she was around six days a week. Other than Jonathan, who got a kick out of watching Ciaran seduce women, she knew the most about his lifestyle. She saw firsthand the constant round of women, and had no doubt seen more than she wanted. Unlike Jonathan, Keeley avoided seeing the women Ciaran brought to the house whenever possible. His mind went back to the two blondes out by the pool. He'd done that deliberately, to antagonize her. He flaunted women in front of her a lot, he realized.

If she was frightened of men, frightened of sex, then it made sense. Her responses made sense. Maybe he needed to take a different approach. Obviously seduction, like he'd tried tonight, didn't get him anywhere. The most interaction he managed was when he pissed her off. She would stand and fight then. At least it was some reaction to build on.

He couldn't read her the way he could so many other humans. The only times he had were the day she nearly drowned and the day she came back to work. He'd heard her thought then as she'd walked up to see Liz and Emily all over him. Was that what he needed to get a reaction from her? He closed his eyes. He was desperate enough to try anything.

****

She dreamt of him that night, dreamt he whispered softly into her ear. His lean hands stroked down her body making her clothing magically disappear. He stood behind her and she watched him in a mirror, his dark, long-fingered hands cupping her breasts, touching her waist and stroking across her stomach down to the dark curls of her sex.

"Let me touch you, Keeley. Let me stroke you. Feel me inside you."

His words and the feel of him made her wet. She pulsed heavily with wanting him, her heart and her breath quickening.

Then the dream changed.

"Come on Keeley, touch it. That's it girl, put your hand around it."

Ciaran was gone. In his place was her stepfather.

Keeley woke with a gasp that turned into a sob. She curled onto her side, clutching her pillow against her stomach as she rocked. It was half a lifetime ago. Why did it still haunt her?

Dawn was just lighting the sky, but she wasn't ready to try swimming again this morning. Yesterday's close call was just that...too close. Instead, she headed downstairs and stood under the stinging jets of the shower trying to scrub away the dirty feeling that haunted her. It would never do to let Granddad see her this way. He would know at once something was wrong and would think it concerned last night. That it did, she had no intention of letting him know.

She checked on him on her way to the kitchen and found him sleeping. His breathing was shallow and labored. After starting coffee, she fixed a mixture of yogurt and fruit for him. She smiled sadly to herself. He would never have eaten this when he was healthy. Back then he'd said yogurt was for sissies, but the illness changed his tastes and he now professed to love it. She wondered sometimes if it was just a way to make her happy. And it did because it was one way she could get enough nutrition in him.

As she fed him, she told him about last evening,

only leaving out her dance with Ciaran. She described the other men she danced with, the Ivy League suspenders type Stephie danced with several times, and finally some of the music they listened to.

"There was no one special?" he asked.

Keeley started to say no, but then realized part of what the night had been about. He was worried she would have no one when he was gone. Swallowing the lump in her throat, she finally said, "There was one person."

He smiled as he laid his head back. "Tell me."

"My boss was there."

His eyes opened in confusion. "Mr. Clifton? The man you always talk about as having a different girl every night."

"The man who saved my life, Pawpaw," she reminded him. "He had a date, but he watched me through most of dinner, and he asked me to dance. A slow dance."

"Keeley," he said cautiously.

"I apologized to him, like you said I should. He was very nice, a gentleman."

"I should hope so. Did you have a nice time?"

"The best." She kissed the papery skin of his cheek. Each time she saw him, it seemed he grew frailer and frailer. She took his hand and stroked the veins on the back of it. "Do you think, when the time comes, you will see Grandma and Daddy again?"

He turned his hand over so he could hold hers. "Yes. I believe so. Why do you ask?"

"Because I want you to have people you love who'll show you what to do. I don't want you to be alone." Her chin wobbled.

"You mean like I'll be leaving you?"

Realizing too late the door she opened, she brushed away her tears. "Oh, but I won't be alone. I have Stephie, and Ciaran...I mean Mr. Clifton."

She hoped the lie was convincing. To make it

more so, she smiled brightly. "He's asked me out. We're...going sailing tomorrow afternoon, and then I'm cooking dinner for us. I know it's kind of a busman's holiday, but you know how I love to cook."

"Well you must have him come in when he comes by to get you. I'd like to meet this young man. I remember his reputation from a few years ago, and it wasn't good." Andy McNamara frowned. "Not because of the women. There were other things involving a feud between him and his family."

"Umm. Okay."

Oh lord, how could she get out of this? Could she have him cancel at the last minute? No, that would defeat her whole purpose. There was nothing else to do. She'd have to talk to Ciaran.

****

Liz and Emily. Those were the two who really pissed her off. Ciaran called them on his cell phone as he sat around the pool. They were more than happy to come over for a little private party. As he recalled, they really enjoyed a threesome, even if with those two, more often than not, he was the odd man out. He could still watch. Honestly, he'd rather do that than take a more active role, especially when they usually made him feel like not much more than a dildo. He laughed at himself. Deep down inside, he admitted if he couldn't have Keeley, he'd just as soon not have anyone. And how pathetic was that?

He told them to arrive after he was sure Keeley would already be working in the kitchen. He watched her walk through the dunes and through the gardens at the back of the house. She looked pale and drawn. For a second, he thought about tossing out the whole plan to make her angry, but he wanted a reaction, and it seemed anger was the only way to get it. As soon as he was sure she was in the kitchen, he pulled on his swimming trunks and padded downstairs barefooted. He stood in the doorway for a moment watching her study a cookbook. She was bent over the kitchen table while she read, her sweet little ass pointed right at him. He closed his eyes as he briefly imagined slipping between those round cheeks.

"May I come in?"

She spun, looking almost guilty and then blushed to the roots of her black hair. Her gaze darted away from his. "Of...of course. I needed to talk to you about something anyway."

He smiled as he stepped in and said casually, "There'll be three for dinner tonight. Liz and Emily are coming over in a bit. We'll want some snacks and drinks out by the pool, too."

Her hand clenched on the counter next to the cookbook she had open and her mouth thinned. "I'll see to it."

"Jonathan won't be back until later. Would you mind bringing it out?"

"Not at all, sir."

There was a bite in her tone. He smiled. "Good. Now what was it you wished to talk about?"

Her mouth opened and then snapped shut. "Just the menus for next week."

"Just bring them out with the snacks. I'll take a look at them then." He said it absently and then left her fuming as he strolled out to the pool. Liz and Emily drove up five minutes later. Even though he wasn't really interested, he had to admit, they were extraordinarily stacked. Oh sure, the boobs weren't real, but few these days were.

"Hi girls."

They kissed him lingeringly. From their already aroused nipples, he knew they had engaged in a little foreplay of their own. Great, he could just let them continue their own pleasure except for a few well-timed caresses that would suit his purposes.

****

Keeley fumed as she looked out the window. It seemed to her their hands were everywhere, but then she didn't want them touching him at all. How the hell could she talk to him about helping her out while the bimbos felt him up in front of everyone? Moreover, why did she even want to?

Granddad.

Why oh why had she opened her big mouth?

She worked furiously, creating club sandwiches, with homemade potato chips and cucumbers marinated with fresh basil and olive oil. After loading everything onto a cart along with glasses, fresh lemonade and a small cooler of beer, she pushed it out to the pool. As she backed through the gate, she nearly tripped when she saw one of the blondes with her hand resting high along Ciaran's thigh. Even more shocking, both women were kissing each other like lovers.

Keeley closed her eyes and averted her face. Quietly, she moved the tray to beneath the awning near the gate and cleared her throat. Ciaran looked over with a lazy smile. "Thanks, Keeley. Did you bring the menus?"

She nodded dumbly and pulled them from her jacket pocket. "Here," she squeaked, walking just close enough to hand them to him.

"Wanna join us?" he invited with a wicked gleam in his dark eyes.

Her eyes narrowed. "Fuck you!"

He smirked. "All right. As you can see, Liz and Emily are a little busy with each other. I'm sure they won't mind if you and I hook up."

Keeley was so angry she was afraid she would hit him. Without another word, she stomped out of the pool area, slammed the gate and then ran inside the house. What the hell had she been thinking? Why had she ever led her grandfather to think that...that lothario meant something to her? What made her even angrier was last night, for a few minutes, he made her feel special. Well, she didn't feel special now. She felt used, dirty. She felt like she had when her grandfather found her and brought her back home with him all those years ago. Right now, all she really wanted to do was run and hide.

She slammed her way through the kitchen, getting started on the preparations for dinner. When Jonathan came back from town, he got only snarled monosyllabic responses from her. She knew she was being childish, but couldn't stop herself. As soon as she plated all of the courses, Keeley cleaned her work area. Jonathan could serve.

Somehow, she would have to find a way to explain things to her grandfather. She wanted to make him feel better about leaving, wanted what little time he had left to be happy, but she was failing miserably. As she rinsed her utensils, her hands shook. When tears blinded her, she finally put her apron over her face and sobbed. The dishwasher hummed quietly in the background as she sank down on her haunches behind the center island and cried.

****

Ciaran entered the kitchen quietly with the intention of making Keeley blow a gasket. He'd request a tray with whipped cream, honey, and chocolate syrup for the bedroom. That should be enough to really send her over the edge. Where was she? Had she already gone? Then he heard, barely audible over the hum of the dishwasher, the sound of her crying.

Keeley crying? He'd seen her feisty and furious, even fearful, but never crying. Without a sound, he made his way back to the den where Liz and Emily were already topless and kissing passionately.

"Get dressed," he ordered. "I'm not in the mood

tonight. Take it home or over to one of your other friends."

"But Ciaran..."

"No buts. Go. I have things to do."

He walked them to the front door, waved them off and then headed back to the kitchen. She had taken off her apron and her chef's jacket and was getting ready to go.

"Is everything all right?" he asked quietly from the doorway.

She averted her head and nodded.

"Keeley?"

"I said it was," she snapped without turning to look at him. "What more do you want?"

"I want you to tell me why you were sitting on my kitchen floor a few minutes ago, sobbing like your heart was breaking. That's what I want."

She glared at him. "Don't you need to go back to the double D duo? Or have you become an unwelcome third?"

He took a few steps toward her. "I sent them home."

"How tragic for you. A night without getting laid."

Her dark lashes were spiky from her tears. Close up, he saw the purplish circles under her eyes and the way her irises practically glowed green.

"Don't," he ordered.

"What? Don't offend your delicate sensibilities? That doesn't seem to matter to you, does it?" As he continued to approach, she backed away. "I can walk out and see all manner of things, but you tell me 'don't'? God, and to think I..."

She headed for the door, but he caught her gently by the arm. "To think you what?" For just an instant, he pictured holding her, caressing her.

She shook her head warily, and continued as if she were talking to herself. "No. Even for him, I can't. I'll just have to tell him I lied."

As she said the last sentence, her chin wobbled and new tears welled in her eyes. Ignoring the stiff set of her shoulders, Ciaran pulled her into his arms. "What? What is it? Let me help."

She was stiff and resistant, making him worry she would pull away. Just as he began to say something to reassure her, he felt her give in.

"I just wanted to make him happy."

He stroked her hair and her back. "Who, sweetheart?"

"Granddad. He wanted to know if I had a good time last night, and I told him yes. Then he wanted to know if I'd met anyone. He's so afraid about leaving me alone. I told him you were there, you asked me to dance, and you were nice." She hiccupped against his chest. "He worries I'll be lonely, so I told him you'd asked me to go sailing with you tomorrow, and I was cooking dinner for us both tomorrow night."

She looked at him. "It was just supposed to be a white lie, you know, to make him happy. But he wants to meet you when you pick me up."

The last came out on another sob. Ciaran didn't see a problem. In fact, he couldn't have planned it any better. She managed to create the very opportunity he wanted. "Is that really what you wanted to talk to me about when you first got here today?"

She nodded. He closed his eyes and stroked her back with gentle hands. His timing where she was concerned was abysmal. He was such an idiot. "This sounds easy enough to resolve...Keeley Ann McNamara, will you go sailing with me tomorrow and then cook dinner for us? I can pick you up at your grandfather's home at noon."

She looked at him. "You would do that?"

He nodded. "If you'll come with me."

"You can't let my granddad know it's just an act," she pleaded.

"I won't," he promised. He would promise anything to see the sheen of tears disappear. Inside his mind reeled. She'd told her grandfather they had a relationship? He hardly dared to hope. Already he pondered the possibilities of how to turn fiction into fact. Once he slept with her, he was sure it would be just as it was with every other woman; he could move on and forget her.

Chapter Five

Ciaran wasn't sure what he expected when he arrived at Keeley's home the following afternoon, but it wasn't what he found. She answered the door with a nervous smile. He took in her shorts, tank top, and deck shoes. Well that still looked promising.

"Are you going to invite me in so I can meet him?" He arched a brow.

Keeley blinked. "Oh, yes. Right. Come in."

Ciaran kept his expression carefully neutral. Andrew McNamara lay in a hospital bed in the middle of the living room. He was just a shell of the man Ciaran remembered puttering around the marina just a couple of years ago. That man had been short, but wiry and vital. This man was dying.

"Granddad? Mr. Clifton, I mean, Ciaran's here to see you before we go."

The old man smiled, his papery skin stretching skeletally over the bones of his face. "Bring him over then, girl, where I can see him."

She looked at him a little uncertainly. Ciaran blinked as he saw how much she loved her grandfather. *Enough that she's willing to tolerate me for a day. She's even willing to risk going sailing with me alone.* Something hard inside him loosened, and it hurt. He had never inspired that kind of feeling in anyone.

He stepped up next to her, took the old man's hand carefully in his own and shook it. He draped his other arm casually around Keeley's tense shoulders. Her tension he could see, but he also felt the old man's. Ciaran was being measured and weighed; he wondered if he was also being found wanting.

"Good afternoon, sir. Don't worry about a thing. I'll take good care of your granddaughter."

Andy McNamara fixed him with piercing green eyes, and for an instant he sensed something more than human brush his thoughts. "You'd better. She deserves better out of life than what she's had."

"Pawpaw!" she hissed. "Please!"

She glanced over at the hospice volunteer. "We'll be sailing here in the bay. Isn't that right, Ciaran?"

He smiled and nodded. "I'll have my cell phone on in case of emergency, and there's also the ship radio."

"I'll be back after I finish supper, Granddad."

The old man smiled at them, his gaze once again dimmed with age and illness. "You two have a good time. I'm glad to know she's got a friend like you, Clifton."

Ciaran's anger simmered as he held the door for her and walked her down the sidewalk to the Porsche. Keeley hadn't exactly told him everything, and he didn't like surprises. Once he'd stalked around the driver's side and slipped behind the wheel, he frowned.

"What's wrong with him?"

She smoothed her palms down her legs to cup her knees. "He has cancer, from asbestos exposure."

Ciaran pressed his lips together as he turned the key and the car roared to life. "How long does he have?"

Her only answer was a shrug, but he caught the way she bit her lip to stop it from trembling. He reached out and pulled her chin around so she had to look him in the eye.

"How long does he have, Keeley? Days? Weeks?"

"I don't know," she whispered. "Not long."

"And you want him to think we have a

relationship, is that it?"

"Yes. He worries he's going to leave me alone."

Ciaran pulled out into traffic and headed for the marina. He kept a sloop there he could take out by himself thanks to all its bells and whistles. After parking the car, he faced her, his anger still lurking just below the surface.

"You didn't think you could let me know? That I wouldn't have given you the time you need to spend with him?"

She searched his face. "He doesn't want that," she whispered, and he felt the hurt inside her. He understood that pain, understood what it felt like to feel like your own family was pushing you away. It was all he could do not to gather her in his arms to soothe her.

Comfort. He could never remember giving it to anyone, even wanting to give it to anyone. "He wants to know I can go on without him."

"Can you?" he probed.

She closed her eyes, but he still saw the pain there. "I don't know, but I need to make him think so."

He did touch her then, just lightly on the cheek. "Let me take you sailing. You can have something to tell him tonight."

He helped her out and then fetched a picnic basket he'd placed in the trunk. "Sorry, you'll have to put up with my sandwiches this time."

"Peanut butter and jelly?" At his offended look, she laughed. "I almost served that to you the first time you sent one of the bimbos in."

He chuckled, casually taking her hand as they walked along the dock. *The Prankster* was a black-hulled sloop tied at the end of the dock, her mast gently swaying with the movement of the water.

"Oh! She's beautiful!" Keeley exclaimed. She walked around examining the sloop's clean, classic lines. She was slender, almost boyish, but he wanted her. He acknowledged it, but also realized he wanted her for more than one night, more than just casual sex. He'd never wanted another woman that way. It was more than just the way she looked. She intrigued him.

"I'm glad you like her."

He stepped on board, set the picnic basket down and then held out his arms to her. For just an instant, wariness flashed across her face and then it was gone. As she put her hands on his shoulders, he clasped her around the waist and set her on deck. He could span her waist with his hands. It was a graphic reminder of how delicate she was beneath her feisty exterior.

"Hang on while I untie, then we'll be on our way."

He used *The Prankster's* small motor to maneuver through the marina. After stowing the picnic basket in the cabin below, she came back up and went forward to perch on the bow. She sat with her knees drawn up and her face lifted to the sun.

"Need sunscreen?"

She laughed and looked at him over her shoulder with her tip-tilted cat eyes. "Oh, I don't burn. In fact, the sun seems to have little effect on me whatsoever."

"Famous last words."

Her look challenged him. "I don't see you putting any on."

"Oh I had Francine do that before she left this morning. She particularly enjoyed applying it to all the places I couldn't reach."

He hoped for a reaction and got it, just not what he expected. She threw back her head and laughed. His breath caught. He had seen her angry, sad, and even somewhat aroused, but he had never seen her laugh as uninhibitedly as she did now. There was something wild and free in it. A glimpse at a soul strong enough to stand up to the darkness in him? He didn't feel that side of himself when he was with her.

As if she sensed the intense interest in his gaze, she turned back around. "Isn't that your parents' yacht?"

Ciaran's brows drew together. The *Skerry* lay at her moorings off to their left. "Yes."

She watched him curiously. "You don't speak to each other."

It was a statement rather than a question, so he didn't respond. What was between himself and his family was his, not up to be examined or discussed. She lifted her face to stare at the gleaming white ship. "I don't talk to my mother. She's the only other family I have besides Granddad."

He saw the way her eyes stayed on the *Skerry*. Sensing he was being watched, he turned his head and saw his mother standing at the rail. Homesickness shot through him, but he pushed it away, turning the wheel slightly so *The Prankster* heeled a bit more and picked up speed. He didn't want to think about his family today. He wanted to concentrate on Keeley.

"Did you bring your swim suit?" he asked as he set course for the cove Cayden called Bell's Cove after his wife, Annabel. He hoped it would be deserted. Keeley would enjoy the quiet.

"Yes. Where are we going?"

"A cove. Very quiet. A wonderful place to swim with beautiful, clear water and all kinds of things to see beneath the surface."

She tilted her head. "Do you dive?"

"Not any more. Not for about four years." *Not since I tried to kill my family*. He wondered what she would do if she knew. This woman who was so devoted to her grandfather would never be able to

71

understand.

As the wind picked up, their conversation ceased. After a few minutes, Keeley stretched out on her stomach, her arms supporting her head. When they headed into the cove, Ciaran was relieved to see it was deserted. There were sheltering bluffs along two-thirds of it, a small section opened up into a narrow strip of beach. The rest was sheltered by tall pine trees. He lowered sail and started the motor, bringing *The Prankster* as close to shore as he dared before cutting the engine and lowering anchor.

Keeley still stretched out at the bow so he vaulted up and moved forward. Her face was resting on her arms; she was sound asleep. Shadows were still evident on her pale skin. It worried him. Now that he knew what was going on, he could imagine just how exhausted she probably was trying to help with her grandfather's care and also continue her normal routine. Eyes somber, he sat beside her.

"Keeley," he said her name quietly, reluctant to disturb her. "We're here, sweetheart."

She didn't jerk awake like so many people. Watching her wake was like watching the opening of a flower; it was a gradual becoming of awareness. At last she inhaled deeply and rolled over.

"You smell like pine and citrus. It's such a unique smell. I noticed it when I first started to work for you."

Just like I've noticed the way you smell, almost every night when I've got my cock wrapped in my fist. "I've dropped anchor. Did you want to swim?"

She stretched like a sleepy kitten. "I guess. This is really wonderful. It's been so long since I've been sailing. Granddad took me when I was a little girl, but he sold the boat the summer before he took me away from Momma."

He rested he arms on his bent knees. "Why did he take you from your mother? That's a pretty drastic step."

She rolled away as she sat up and shrugged casually. "My mother remarried. I didn't get along with my stepfather."

A flash of pain and fear jolted him, and he knew he'd read it from Keeley's subconscious mind. Obviously she wasn't nearly as unconcerned as she sounded, but no way would he press it. He stood and offered her a hand. "Come on, change clothes and let's swim."

When she went below, he kicked off his shoes and stripped off his shirt before diving over the side. He looked a few minutes later to see her perched on the side of the boat. The conservative racing suit fit her style, but still managed to show off a figure he found increasingly sexy. She surprised him by executing a perfect flip in the air and ending with a dive. He ducked below the surface. She swam lazily along the bottom. When he came near her, she pushed off with her legs and shot to the surface. He came up a moment later only to be splashed unmercifully.

Ducking beneath the water again, he grabbed her leg and jerked. They continued to swim and play in the smooth, quiet water of the cove. After a few minutes, she stretched out on her back, floating with her eyes closed and a faint smile on her face. Ciaran trod water, watching her. Following instincts buried deep inside, he moved closer and gently blew bubbles around her. She opened her eyes in surprise.

"What did you do that for?"

He shrugged, unwilling to tell her it was a mating ritual among the Silkie, afraid it would scare her off. It made him nervous enough, unsure as he was about the instinctive response. He had never felt anything like it. He smiled at her. "Come lie on the beach and I'll tell you the legend of the Silkie...the seal people."

Her eyes sparkled with amusement. "Race you."

It was no contest. Ciaran won easily, but she was a stronger swimmer than he'd expected. When she flopped breathlessly onto her stomach on the warm sand, he lay on his side next to her, propped on an elbow.

"So tell me about the Silkie." She smiled lazily with her eyes closed and her head resting once again on her arms. "I've always thought seals were cute with their big, soulful eyes and their long, silky whiskers."

"Then there's hope for me yet," he muttered and she laughed.

She rolled onto her back and put her hands behind her head. "Come on, tell me your tale like you promised."

He smiled slightly. "Some say the Silkie began as angels, who must now live their lives as seals. The angels who fell on earth became the Faerie folk, but those that fell into the sea became the Silkie. Others say they are mortals who were condemned to live out their lives as seals for some wrong they committed."

She opened one eye. "I like the angels that became Silkies or Faeries."

He grinned. "So do I. Legend says the Silkie love to take off their seal skins so they may dance as humans under the moon at midnight. And the males are known for their sexual prowess, charming women and then pleasuring them in bed." He watched for her reaction.

"Your cousins?" her tone had a bite to it.

Ciaran's mouth twisted ironically. "Why yes. How clever of you to guess."

She laughed. "Go on."

"It's said a human woman may actually call a Silkie to her by shedding her tears in the water at high tide. The Silkie will come and make love to her until she's happy again."

"And then he leaves her?" Keeley opened her eyes. "Can't a human and a Silkie stay together?"

"No. She can't follow him into the sea, and he can never truly be happy on land as a human."

"Does that happen?"

"Well if the Silkie loses his pelt, or someone takes it, then he can't turn back into a seal. He's doomed to live out his life as a human."

"That's sad, Ciaran." Her eyes were shadowed.

He laughed. "It's just a story. You don't really believe it, do you?"

She threw her arm across her forehead, just above her eyes. The green of her gaze held him spellbound. "I'm Irish. It might surprise you what things I believe. Faeries and Silkies and witches and warlocks. Why I might be a witch or a Faerie myself, and you could be my captive Silkie."

Silence stretched between them.

"May I kiss you?" Ciaran breathed. What was the matter with him? He never asked, just took. "I find myself thinking about it more and more. Like now."

She swallowed. Desire and wariness warred in her expression like sunshine and shadows scudding across the sea. Her gaze searched his face. Finally she nodded, and he felt as if he'd won a victory. When he put his fingers under her chin, she trembled. Easy, he told himself. The fear coming off of her was palpable. He lowered his mouth and gently touched his lips to hers.

"Relax. Open your lips to me."

He teased her mouth with the tip of his tongue, relaxing ever so slightly when she opened to him. They traded kisses back and forth. He felt her body responding just as his was. With a soft growl, he slid one hand down along her rib cage and around to cup her bottom. When his other hand moved to her

75

breast, she suddenly stiffened.

"I can't do this."

Oh but he could, and she tasted sublime and he wanted her breast in his mouth. He leaned over her for a deeper taste.

"No!" she rolled away from him and leaped to her feet. "I'm sorry. I can't do this."

She ran back into the water and raced toward the sloop. He watched in frustration as he slowly rose to his feet to follow. In any other woman he would have simply thought she was being a tease, but there were something else going on here.

****

Keeley climbed the ladder on the stern and scurried below to grab a towel. She had noticed earlier the interior of the cabin was spartan, built for function and safety, not seduction. It helped calm her. Ciaran had two very different sides. It seemed the side that sailed *The Prankster* wasn't the man she worked for every day, the man who had few compunctions about seducing anyone. The man like her stepfather? No. Never like that.

She heard a splash and the boat shifted. A moment later, Ciaran's form filled the doorway. She huddled in the towel, embarrassed and awkward with him now. She didn't dare look at his bare chest or the long, muscular legs. The curl of desire she felt once again turned to queasiness. She felt suffocated and trapped.

"What did he do to you?" His gaze was somber, but not judgmental. With one arm braced in the doorway, he waited for her answer.

"Who?" She stalled for time. She had never talked about it, not even with Granddad, not really.

Ciaran came forward, and even standing several feet away, his presence overpowered. It wasn't anything he did. He simply had a presence that made her constantly aware of him in a way she wasn't with other men. It frightened her.

"Don't, Keeley. You know who I'm talking about. Your stepfather. What did he do to you? Did he beat you? Did he *touch* you?"

She laughed bitterly and huddled deeper in her towel. He was far too close to a truth she kept buried deep inside. So Keeley went on the attack, hoping to distract him. "I'm sorry the big seduction didn't work out. I'm sure if you take me back now, there's enough of the day left you can find someone else to screw."

Anger flared in his eyes and the tightness of his face. "I didn't bring you out here to fuck. Remember, this was your suggestion. You're hardly my type now, are you Keeley Ann? As you always point out I like them blonde, busty, and with butts a man can sink his hands into. You hardly fit that description." His voice dripped with cool sarcasm. "What did he do to you?" He persisted and she resisted.

Her chin went up, and her eyes narrowed. "You arrogant ass! Maybe I just don't want to kiss or do anything else with someone who's slept with almost every female around the bay."

His expression cooled. "Lie to yourself, if you must, but don't turn it on me. I'll take you home."

In two strides he was back on deck. She heard the anchor motor, then the soft chug of the engine. She rocked forward with her arms wrapped around her waist.

****

A reddish brown seal watched as *The Prankster's* sails unfurled. The man at the wheel scowled; the woman was nowhere in sight. But it was not temper that radiated from him so much as concern. As the boat slipped silently back into the waters of the bay, the seal suddenly transformed into a beautiful auburn-haired woman.

Catriona Clifton stepped onto the deserted

beach, her nude, creamy-skinned body as attractive as it had been nearly thirty years earlier when she met her own Silkie Lord. She had hardly believed what Bell told her, but since then she had tried very hard to tune into her younger son, despite the Council's orders to look upon Ciaran as a human.

It had come as something of a shock to see him sail by the *Skerry* a couple of hours ago. Even more of a shock when she felt the wave of homesickness flow from him. She also saw the girl, the same one Bell described, and she made an excuse to follow them.

She watched the way her son was so careful with this woman. When he blew bubbles around her, Catriona's eyes widened. Why, he was in love with her! In love and not at all sure what to do. She wondered if he even realized. She concentrated on both of them. Ciaran was a blur. He had become a master at blocking her; he had spent so long as a human, her link to him was slipping. What surprised her was how clearly she could read the girl. She saw the attraction and the fear, felt how she was at once drawn and repelled.

Such a conflict must mean some sort of trauma in her past. Catriona probed deeper, seeing memories of loneliness and isolation, and then she hit a wall. There were certain areas of this girl's life she kept tightly locked from anyone's view.

When *The Prankster* disappeared back out into the waters of the bay, Catriona smiled slowly. It was time to contact the Council and call in observers. Ciaran was changing in ways that might open the door to regaining his pelt, and she wanted to make sure Silkie other than his family saw those changes. It was also time to talk to Carrick. He must find a way to forgive his son.

****

Keeley felt vaguely sick to her stomach. She was

ashamed of her reaction, but couldn't help it. It was cowardly, but she stayed below until the ship's motor cut on and knew he was getting ready to tie up soon. She couldn't look at him as she came up on deck, didn't want to see the contempt he must feel for someone her age who went into a panic over what was really nothing more than a few kisses.

"You can take me home," she said quietly.

He glared. "Like hell. You have a job to do. You're my chef, remember? And since I haven't even had lunch, I'd like a decent meal for dinner. You can join me."

"You can't be serious! You want me to cook and eat with you after this...this fiasco?"

He looked her up and down, and now the contempt was evident. "You're a lot of things Keeley Ann, but I never would have taken you for spineless. Wasn't the whole point of this day for you to give your grandfather the impression you had someone to watch over you once he's gone? Are you going to back out now over a few meaningless kisses? You disappoint me."

She squared her shoulders and glared right back. "You asked to kiss me! Can I help it if it was so bad it made me run away?"

"Oh don't feed me that bullshit. You ran because you're a scared little girl. Well stay that way. When I kiss someone, I want a woman in my arms."

He jumped up on the dock and tied *The Prankster*. When he offered her a hand, she batted it away. "I can get off myself."

He crossed his arms over his broad chest. "Well that certainly explains why you don't need me or any other man."

She gaped at him. "You are unbelievably crude."

He stalked along the dock with her hurrying now in his wake. A number of interested faces turned at the sound of their raised voices.

"Get in the car," he ordered.

Keeley took vicious pleasure in slamming the passenger door of the Porsche as hard as she could. Silence simmered between them as he weaved through town and out to his mansion near the point. Another car sat in the drive when they pulled up. As Ciaran opened his door, a tall, older woman came from the pool area.

"Ciaran, darling," the woman pouted. "I got bored in the city and decided to visit you here, but you've been gone." Her eyes flitted to Keeley and then dismissed her. "Now that you're here, I could use some lotion on my back."

"Adrianne, what a pleasant surprise." He turned to Keeley. "Bring us something to eat out here at the pool. Then you can start dinner."

Keeley was speechless with anger and hurt. When he followed Adrianne to the pool, she waved her hand at the ground in front of him. He stepped on a sharp rock, winced, hopped in pain and nearly fell over a coiled hose that suddenly blocked part of the path.

"Shit!"

"Did you say something, Ciaran darling?" Adrianne inquired.

"No."

"I've been so lonely since your last visit…"

The sound of their voices faded as they walked through the gate into the pool area. Keeley stood there for a moment fuming. He'd made it clear in both words and actions how little she meant, how little any of what happened today meant. It only reinforced the idea he was after nothing more than a quick lay.

She went into the kitchen. It was her haven, a place where she could hide. But this evening there would be no hiding from the fact the dinner she planned for the two of them would now be eaten by

Ciaran and another woman.

Keeley did her best to stay as far from her employer as she could. Jonathan took the food to the pool and Jonathan served the meal. She stayed in the kitchen, immersing herself in preparing a meal and then cleaning up afterward. As if Ciaran were somehow aware of how long it took her to accomplish things, he appeared just as she removed her apron.

"I'll run you home."

She looked carefully somewhere over his right shoulder. "There's no need. I can walk."

"This isn't about you, Keeley. It's about your grandfather. He would expect me to bring you home."

She swallowed and nodded slightly. "All right." Then because she couldn't help it, she added. "Won't your friend wonder where you are?"

"Adrianne left a few minutes ago. Her husband will be home early tomorrow morning."

"Too bad."

"Don't press your luck. After all, won't your grandfather expect me to kiss you when I get you home? Think about that."

She didn't want to, but she couldn't help it and he knew it. By the time they pulled up in front of her house, she was shaking from head to toe. He came around the car and helped her out. When she would have hurried up the walk, he touched her arm to stop her.

"Out here, Keeley, where he can see."

She stopped, still not looking at him. When he took a step forward, he cornered her, so her back was against the sports car.

"Put your hands on my shoulders," he said quietly. "Let's make this at least look good."

Her trembling fingers fluttered to his broad shoulders, and his hands spanned her waist. "Tilt your face, Keeley."

As he lowered his face toward hers, a soft whimper escaped her. She was instantly ashamed.

"Easy, sweetheart." His words and tone were suddenly gentler and more soothing than she had ever heard him. Instead of kissing her mouth, he touched his lips to her cheek and laid his face alongside hers. "He can't see you. Can't see exactly what we're doing. Just relax. All he can see is the embrace. Are you okay?"

"Yes." And she was, she realized. As all he did was hold her, she did relax. When he straightened, he touched her cheek with two fingers, and his eyes searched hers in the darkness. "I'm sorry," she whispered.

His hand drifted in a quick caress along her neck before he gently squeezed her shoulder. "Run along, Keeley. Take tomorrow off. Spend the day with your granddad. I don't have noble impulses often. Enjoy it while you can."

She looked at him, but his expression was shuttered and enigmatic. "Thanks."

He waited until she reached the door and waved. Then, he got back in the Porsche and drove away.

Chapter Six

She told her grandfather a marvelous tale the following morning, intermingling the truth with her own wishful thinking. She wasn't naïve enough to turn her day with Ciaran into a great romance. Even dying, Andy McNamara would never believe that. Instead, she made it into what it felt like out in the darkness in front of the house. Ciaran Clifton had made her feel safe there, as if he were a friend, someone she could lean on, someone who would not betray her trust. As she told the tale to her grandfather, she realized a part of her truly believed it. The other part of her simply wished with a weary cynicism it were true.

But distrust had been ingrained in her from an early age. From the moment her mother married Frank Wells when Keeley was nine years old, her world twisted into a waking nightmare. It wasn't until she was thirteen that Grandfather finally rescued her. He was her hero.

Sitting next to him now, Keeley touched the heavy Celtic knot that hung on the chain around her neck. It was a double trinity design. Her father told her that at the same time he told her what he was—what she was, what all the McNamaras were to a greater or lesser degree. Fey. Faerie folk. But to most people nowadays, they were simply witches, people who could do things other humans couldn't.

"I've seen you move things, Keeley Ann," her father whispered softly as he put her to bed one night. "You have a different gift than me. I see the future sometimes, the possibilities. Because of what

I see there, I want you to have this now." He slipped the necklace over her neck. "Use your gift carefully. Some will mock you, some will hate you, but one will love you just the way you are."

Two days later, her father died in an explosion at the plant where he worked. He went back in to rescue a woman trapped in the rubble and a large section of the roof collapsed on top of him. Keeley wore the necklace under her dress at his funeral.

Granddad looked at her now with his weary eyes. "You're the last of our line, Keeley. You must listen closely to me now and then you must call the hospice nurse."

"No, Granddad!"

"Hush!" his voice was harsh. "My time is almost up. I want you to cremate me. You must give my ashes and the box with your father's to one of the sea people. They can return us to the land of our birth. They'll know where. It must be done."

She shook her head. He gripped her hand with his own, surprising her with the strength in it. "You must do this! There is a key. Do not touch it with your bare skin. Give it to one of the folk from the sea. You will know when. You are the last of our line. If you follow your heart, you'll restore us and our honor."

He wasn't making sense, she thought sadly. She listened to the change in his breathing and realized he was fading. She made the call to the nurse and then returned to his side. She wanted to beg him to stay. All at once she felt like the wounded, traumatized teenager he'd rescued, and she wasn't sure she could even go on without him. He was her hero. He'd stayed by her side, asked no questions and gave her space to heal and grow. As an adult, he gave her a sounding board, the support and the confidence she needed to find her own path.

"Pawpaw," she whispered brokenly. "Please

don't go. There's so much I don't know."

He stroked her hair with a hand he could only barely lift. "I'm in such pain, Keeley girl. It's time to let me go home. Take our ashes to the sea folk." He was silent for a long time, only the sound of his labored, slowing breathing filled the room. It seemed the pauses between breaths grew longer and longer. She held his hand cradled against her cheek, pressed her face to it and let her tears wet the paper thin skin.

"I love you PawPaw. I'll stay right here. I won't leave you."

So quietly she could scarcely hear him, he murmured, "My time on earth is nearly done, a faerie child, a faerie son. Release me from this weight of clay; take me home to endless day. Release my soul and let it go, oh sweet goddess make it so."

The final words were released on a long sigh. Keeley felt the change almost immediately. As she reached to touch his cheek, pictures, vases, dishes all began to rattle. She threw back her head and released a long, low keening cry. The pictures fell off the walls, glass shattered and in the middle of the room, she lay sobbing next to her grandfather's body. Wind swirled around them, but disturbed nothing in the room.

****

Out on the *Skerry*, Catriona Clifton cried out, clutching her chest. Her elder son and her husband rushed to her side.

"What's wrong?" Carrick demanded seeing his wife's paper white face and the burning brightness in her deep green eyes. "Cat! What is it?"

"One of mine has passed." She looked at her husband. "I never knew. Andy McNamara. I never knew. He's one of the people."

Cayden frowned. "One of us?"

She shook her head. "A Faerie." She looked at

her husband. "Carrick. I know the ruling of the Council, but I must call Ciaran."

Her husband scowled. "Why?"

"Andy McNamara leaves an even more powerful Faerie behind him. Keeley is his granddaughter, and she's overwhelmed. She's also the woman Annabel saw Ciaran save; the woman I have seen that he loves. If anyone other than Ciaran walks in on her now, there will be hell to pay. Open your mind."

When he did, she let him see the picture of what was happening inside McNamara's house. Books flew off shelves, light bulbs burst.

He looked at his wife. "Shit! Do you think Ciaran can stop this?"

"Maybe…maybe not, but he's the best choice we have."

Cayden frowned. "Why does this matter to us?"

His mother sighed. "If one of us is discovered, it becomes the ruin of us all—Faerie or Silkie."

****

Ciaran was already throwing on clothes when the phone rang. He was out by the pool when he heard Keeley's cry in his head. He nearly didn't answer the insistent ringing of the phone, but at the last moment, snatched it up.

"Since you will not hear me any other way, I must use the phone to call you."

"Mother? I'm a little busy right now." He zipped his fly as he cradled the receiver between his ear and his shoulder. His tone was cutting. "Have the Silkie Lords gone soft? I thought no one was allowed to speak to the bad seed."

"Stop it, Ciaran! You must go to Keeley McNamara. You will have to break into the house…"

Cold dread went through him. "Why? What do you know about her?"

"Her grandfather just passed. She's wild with grief and has no control over what's happening right now."

"Happening? What do you mean? I heard her call."

"She phoned you?"

"No!" he snapped impatiently. "I-I hear her thoughts and feelings sometimes, usually when she's very upset, like now."

"You must ignore whatever she says, ignore what you see happening. You must hold her and let her vent on you. She may hurt you, but if you don't calm her, then everyone will know what she is."

Something cold grabbed Ciaran's heart. "What she is?" he repeated stupidly.

"She comes from a long line of Faerie folk. I can see it now her barriers are down. Even she doesn't understand the full extent of it. She only knows she's always possessed an ability to move things."

Ciaran thought of the times objects suddenly, inexplicably laid in his way. He had tripped, stubbed, stumbled, and fallen and it was usually when Keeley Ann McNamara was flaming mad at him.

"She can do more?"

"Some. You'll get a taste of it, but you must hurry. There's a hospice nurse on the way to the house. And Ciaran? I love you, son."

He stared at the phone for an instant, breathing heavily and blinking rapidly. Still yanking a shirt over his head, he raced down the stairs and out to the garage. The Porsche roared to life. By some miracle, none of the town's police force was about. Perhaps it was still too early in the morning, and on a Monday, many businesses in the tourist town were closed. It was a slow day when many folks slept in.

Tires squealed as he pulled up along the curb, then Ciaran raced up the walk and pounded on the door. From inside, came the buzz of what sounded like electrical gadgets shorting out, followed by thuds and crashes. Rather than shout, he took a quick look around. Seeing no one, he put his shoulder to the door and shoved. It fell back on its hinges. His eyes widened in amazed horror.

She stood next to her grandfather's bed, her head thrown back and her eyes wide and staring. She shook so much it almost looked like she vibrated.

"Keeley!" His tone was clear and commanding, but she didn't hear. She was locked in her own world. Remembering what his mother said, he rushed toward her. As he neared her, something or someone pushed him back. The sound of thundering surf roared in his ears. He stepped into a hurricane to reach her. It took every ounce of strength to finally grab her and wrap her tightly in his arms. Her body was ice cold, her teeth chattering and her breath coming in short pants, almost as if she were hyperventilating. She was board stiff in his embrace, her eyes still staring unseeingly.

"Keeley Ann McNamara!" he hissed into her ear. "Come back to me."

Glass shattered behind him, and then a barrage of books slammed into his back and his head. The sharp corner of one cut his cheek; another sliced his forehead. Still, he held tightly to Keeley, protecting her. There was more at work here than he thought he could handle. He needed help. It was an admission even a month ago, he would never have made. He cradled her head with his hand, nestling her face against his chest. As he held onto her, he reached out in his mind for his family. Whatever his own feelings, they were the only ones who would do. *Help me!* As he said the words, something inside him loosened just a little more.

Keeley stared at him, her green eyes blazing. "Let me go! I hate you! I hate all of you!"

More things flew as she raged. She worked her

hands loose, pummeling his chest and his face. He twisted and ducked as best he could, but he still refused to let go. She mumbled, speaking in a language he couldn't understand. Wind buffeted them, swirling around their locked forms until his feet lifted off the floor. *Jesus!*

"Keeley!" he ground out against the noise and the force of the wind whipping around them. "I will not leave you. I will not let you go. Hold onto me. Believe me."

As if from a long distance away, he heard others enter the house and could only pray it was his family and not the hospice nurse. With one hand, he forced her head back so she stared into his eyes. "I will not betray you. I will not leave you. I will protect you. I will help you. Believe."

Even as the words came out of his mouth, he realized he meant them.

His feet returned to the ground and he sighed gratefully. She still stared at him, but now the beginning of awareness appeared in her expression. The wind died as if it had never been. He stroked her hair, touched her cheek, but kept her firmly and securely against him.

"He's gone." She whispered so quietly he had to strain to hear her.

"I know."

She looked around her in confusion. "What happened?"

Catriona Clifton came forward and touched her cheek. "There will be time for questions later. We must act quickly before the nurse arrives. There are only a few minutes. If I work with you, can you get all of this back in place?"

Keeley's expression was wary and shuttered. "I don't know what you mean..."

Catriona waved her hand impatiently, and an overturned lamp suddenly returned to the table from which it had fallen. "This is no time for pretense. For any of us. Can you do it?"

Keeley moved out of Ciaran's arms and raised her chin defiantly. "Of course."

She closed her eyes, grabbed hold of her father's necklace, and inhaled deeply. She trembled again, but when Ciaran shifted toward her, his mother waved him away. Suddenly books, pictures, dishes and knickknacks flew back to where they belonged. Keeley opened her eyes and stared at Catriona.

"There."

The older woman smiled and then addressed her sons and her husband. "Ciaran, find a broom and dustpan and clean this glass up. Cayden, keep an eye out for the hospice nurse, and Carrick, find the light bulbs and replace them in all of these lamps and fixtures." She paused and looked at Keeley. "You, come with me."

Obediently, Keeley followed Catriona down the hall to the bathroom. The older woman ran water over a washrag and gently bathed her face and hands. "The nurse will be here in just a few minutes. All of us except Ciaran must be gone. He will help you deal with everything. You must trust him, but I need to know you can control your power."

"Yes."

Catriona looked deeply into her eyes. Green met green. "You cannot lose control again. You will expose yourself to humans. Have you been told enough to know you should not do that?"

Keeley's chin lifted. "I know what I am."

They returned to the living room to find everything in order. Someone had even straightened the covers over Andy McNamara's body, but the room was empty. From the kitchen came a curse.

"Damn it! That hurts. Ow!"

"No more than you deserve."

They looked in to see Carrick carefully cleaning

Ciaran's cuts with salt water. Keeley sucked in a breath. "Did I do that?"

Ciaran grinned at her. "You pack a wallop for such a little thing."

She sniffed. "I'm sure you deserved it."

Cayden poked his head in the back door. "They're here."

Carrick handed the rag to Keeley. "Just keep dabbing salt water on it; it will help it heal faster."

Then they were gone.

Keeley stared at the rag in her hand and back at Ciaran. He leaned against the kitchen counter, not sure what to say and half afraid he would set her off again. When she swallowed and looked everywhere but at him, he held his arms out.

"Come here."

With a lower lip that wobbled, she walked into his arms. "I'm sorry I hurt you," she whispered.

"It's nothing. It will be healed and gone by tomorrow." Something fundamental changed in those moments when he held her clasped tightly against him. "You let me know what you need me to do, Keeley Ann. I'll get you through this."

He did. Andy McNamara had already handled most of the arrangements with Hospice. They knew he wished to be cremated. The nurse looked at Keeley and said, "He did have one unusual request. He wants you to place a plate on his chest with dirt and salt on it."

Keeley bit her lip. "Why?"

Ciaran cleared his throat. "It's a Celtic ritual in some parts of Scotland and Ireland. The dirt represents the body's return to earth, and the salt represents the soul which does not decay."

The nurse smiled. "That's a lovely thought. Did you wish to take care of it, or shall I?"

"Keeley and I will do it."

While she found a small wooden plate her

granddad used to hold his trinkets, Ciaran gathered the dirt and found the salt in the kitchen. He watched her enter the room, concerned by how pale and quiet she was. Nevertheless, she held together while she signed the paperwork, dealt with the funeral home and watched them remove her grandfather from the house. The nurse began packing the medications, and then explained someone would be over in the afternoon to pick up the hospital bed.

It wasn't until the door shut behind her with a curiously final sound that Keeley began to tremble. Without waiting, he picked her up in his arms and carried her to the rocking chair near the fireplace. He sat, holding and rocking her. Her fist grasped part of his shirt, while the other crept slowly, hesitantly around his chest to rest along his ribcage.

They stayed that way until he realized she had fallen into a fitful doze. Cautiously he stood, careful not to awaken her, and carried her up the stairs. Her room surprised him. It was as neat as a nun's chamber. One corner contained photos, jars of herbs and a very large, very old looking book. It was an Herbal, he realized, probably handed down from one generation to another for centuries.

He laid her on the bed and then unfolded a throw to cover her. It was hard to believe this tiny woman was the same one who had wrought such havoc when he arrived. He had seen a small taste of what she could do, and realized she made his own powers fade into oblivion. He was never as telepathic as his mother or Cayden. In many ways, he was much more like his father, a warrior rather than a sorcerer. His were the traditional powers of the Silkie: strength, stamina, and an abundance of sexual prowess.

Except where she was concerned. He looked at Keeley's boyishly slender frame. He had barely done more than kissed her, though God knew he wanted to. He thought of her nearly constantly, to the point where even when Adrianne Shelton had done her best to seduce him at his house, he hadn't reacted. Now the woman he wanted until he was consumed by need of her lay asleep, and he wasn't at all sure how to reach her.

Chapter Seven

The next few days passed in a blur for Keeley. The only constant was Ciaran's presence. Without giving her a chance to say no, he slept on the couch in the living room, his black Porsche a sign to any Sounder in town that Ciaran was with her around the clock. While folks might look at it with a raised brow, no one said a word. Andy McNamara had been too well liked, and there had always been something just a little odd about that whole Clifton family that discouraged public gossip but not private wonder.

Only one person had the temerity to say anything. Stephie arrived the morning following Andy McNamara's death. She wore a militant look on her face when she walked in the door, her eyes narrowing suspiciously on Ciaran. He only stared back at her blandly.

"Stephie!" Keeley raced in from the kitchen and hugged her friend tightly. "I'm so glad you came. Do you know Ciaran?"

She nodded faintly. "We've met before."

He smiled faintly at her. "You'll want to be alone. I have some business to complete at the house, so I'll leave you to it. A pleasure to see you again, Stephie."

As soon as he stepped out the door, she turned back to Keeley with a worried frown. "Keeley, what are you thinking? The man is the biggest womanizer in the whole town and you have him *staying* here?"

"He's my boss, Stephie. He's been a good friend the past couple of days. I couldn't have handled all this without him."

Stephie looked around her nervously. "Maybe, but you could have called me, too. I would have helped. I could have stayed with you."

Keeley shrugged uncomfortably. She couldn't really explain without telling Stephie about her legacy from her father and grandfather. She shuddered to think what would have happened had Stephie been the one to walk in on everything flying through the air. Ciaran, though, accepted it as if it were no big deal. So had his family. And honestly, the more she thought about it the stranger it was, even if Catriona had righted a lamp. Why had they all acted as if it was perfectly normal to see her mentally destroying the house? Were they the same?

"Keeley? Are you listening to me? I said maybe we should get together and do something. I'll take you out to dinner, or we can go shopping. You need to get out of the house."

She shook her head. "I can't deal with that right now, Stephie. I have to take care of Granddad's arrangements. There's just so much. I found his will and I've contacted his attorney. He's in the city. Ciaran says he'll take me there."

Stephie put her arm on Keeley's. "I know he's being a big help, but listen to yourself. You've gone from being antagonists to best buddies? Less than a month ago he fired you!"

She shrugged, unable and unwilling to give Stephie an explanation for her about face. She saw the hurt in her friend's expression, and knew she was putting distance between them that hadn't been there before.

"I'm sorry, Stephie. I don't mean to hurt you, but he's been here for me..."

Her friend's face flushed. "And I *haven't?*"

"No. No, it's not that at all. Oh Stephie, you've been my friend for years and I love you, but he got here when I was falling apart and gave me something to hang onto. I never would have guessed. No matter what he might be like in some parts of his life, he does have influence and he knows his way around some of the legal issues I'm facing."

Keeley trailed off helplessly. "Please don't be mad. Please. I can't lose anyone else right now. I can't."

Stephie hugged her fiercely. "I'm sorry. It's just that I still remember what you were like when you first got here. You never talked about what happened with your mom and your stepdad, and I never asked, but I felt like we bonded. I guess I'm just a little jealous, a little hurt you didn't call me."

Keeley snorted. "I didn't call him. He just showed up. It was like he knew."

She discovered over the next few days Ciaran knew a lot of things. He dealt with the memorial service, the visitation at the house and even picking up her grandfather's ashes. She was so overwhelmed with grief she found it difficult to do anything. From somewhere in her grandfather's belongings, he produced a beautiful handmade double box. The inner box was made of elm, and the outer, carved with the same Celtic knot symbol she wore around her neck, was made from oak. He showed it to her, explaining gently the elm was considered to be the living place for the Faerie folk, while the oak was a powerful symbol of life and magic. She blinked as she held the box in her hands and stared at him in amazement.

"How do you know this?"

He shrugged.

"Where did Granddad have it?"

"In a trunk in his closet. Your father's ashes are in there already. There's room to add your grandfather's ashes."

"Then do it. It's what they both would want." It was a beautiful tribute to them both. Keeley worried her lower lip. She must still do what her grandfather asked. But where was she supposed to find sea people? Had her grandfather meant Silkies, like Ciaran told her about? It preyed on her, disrupting sleep that was already disturbed.

The day after the memorial service, a card arrived in the mail with no return address. Keeley tore open the envelope. When she saw her mother and stepfather's signatures, she dropped the card as if burned. Without a word, she went into the kitchen and got out ingredients to prepare dinner.

Ciaran, who'd been working on his laptop looked up, his eyes narrowing as he glanced curiously from the card lying on the floor of the doorway into the kitchen. Setting the computer aside, he stood, crossed the room and bent to retrieve the card. He turned it over and then checked the signatures. Alyssa and Frank Wells. It looked like an ordinary card, but her reaction was anything but normal.

He stepped into the kitchen doorway and leaned his shoulder against the doorjamb, his fingers tucked into the pockets of his jeans.

"Who are Alyssa and Frank Wells?"

"Shit! Ow!" She spun on him, holding the index finger of her left hand tightly. She went to the sink and ran cold water over the bleeding digit. She'd cut herself? Keeley never made a false move in the kitchen; she sliced any kind of food so professionally and fast he sometimes enjoyed just watching her. "There are bandages under the sink in the bathroom," she said. "Would you get me one?"

After locating the adhesive bandage, he returned to the kitchen and put it on for her. When she would have pulled her hand away, he held onto it with gentle, but insistent pressure.

"Who are Alyssa and Frank Wells? And why would their names be enough to make you cut your finger?" His tone became cooler, more insistent.

Her gaze skittered away and her expression closed tighter than a clam. She tried to slip her hand from his grasp, but he held firm. When she still would not look at him, he pulled her into his arms and tilted her chin, forcing her to look at him.

"Your mother? Your stepfather?"

"Yes!" She spat it at him. "Is that what you want to hear?"

He stroked her cheek with his fingertips, but she cringed away from his touch. "I simply want to know who it is that can turn the feistiest woman I've ever met into a nervous wreck. Why is that? And why is it the mere mention of them now has you once more cringing from me as if you fear I might attack you?"

She twisted away, and this time he let her go.

"Leave it alone, Ciaran," she muttered and continued chopping vegetables.

He closed the distance between them, his body tense and his manner wary. "Every time I bring up why you left your mother's home to live with your grandfather, you've twisted the conversation away, avoided answering. Now a simple card arrives and you're once again a bundle of neurotic energy. Yet you expect me to leave it alone?"

She shoved past him to add the vegetables to the salad.

"Yes, I want you to leave it alone." She spun on him. "I want you to leave *me* alone. Go home, Ciaran! Go back to your mansion and your women and leave me alone."

In two strides he towered over her, his hands wrapped around her upper arms, but not with so much power as to hurt her in any way. He leaned down enough so he could put his face just inches from hers. "I can't leave it alone. I can't leave you alone. And if I have to keep asking you for eternity, you will tell me why your grandfather took you out of your mother's house!"

Both of them were breathing heavily as they glared at each other. Keeley blinked first and twisted away. She stood in the corner between the stove and the sink and crossed her arms across her chest, hugging herself as she stared sightlessly at the countertop. When at last she finally spoke, he strained to hear. He took a step closer, but stopped with a couple of feet still between them when she withdrew into herself.

"Momma married Frank the summer I turned nine. She couldn't get time off from work to bring me here for the summer, so Frank said he would. We had a flat tire part way here and we had to spend the night at a hotel."

"Keeley..." He shook his head.

She spun on him with eyes that blazed. Through gritted teeth she hissed, "No! You wanted to hear it, so now you can listen to all of it.

"He ran a bath for me and said he'd help me clean up before bed. I told him even my own daddy didn't help me with a bath, but he said he was my new daddy and things were going to be different. He made me uncomfortable and when I got out, he told me what a pretty little thing I was and wrapped me in a towel to dry me off. Then he put me to bed. Even though he made me uneasy, I thought everything was okay."

She was rocking ever so slightly on her feet, and she'd begun to bite her nails, something Ciaran had never seen her do.

"But he didn't leave you alone, did he?"

She shook her head. "No."

Ciaran swallowed, hearing her pain and trying to control the murderous rage that flowed through him for Frank Wells. "Keeley..."

She glared at him. "I was nine years old. He told me afterward that it was our secret. That if I told my mother she would be angry. She wouldn't believe me and she'd hate me. I'd lose not only my dad, but her too. So I kept quiet.

"I hid out on the streets at night when I could get away with it. But it seemed like he always found me. Momma worked the night shift at the plant where Frank worked, so he had plenty of opportunity for his sick little games. He always waited until I was asleep, because he'd already seen some of the power I possessed. I wasn't nearly as good at moving things as I am now; I needed my hands. He knew so he'd sneak in on me and tie me up.

"I begged granddad to let me come live with him, but I wouldn't tell him why. Not until that last summer, when I turned thirteen. Things changed. I was growing up, and it was as if all holds on Frank's behavior evaporated."

She stopped and stared at Ciaran. He stepped close and pulled her into his arms. She was stiff and averted her face. Keeping his touch as gentle as he could, he rubbed her back up and down, over and over until she finally unbent enough to lean her forehead against his chest.

"That wasn't the worst part," she whispered. "I told Momma what he did, how long it was going on. Do you know what she said?"

He stroked her back. "What?" he murmured from above her head.

"'I don't believe you. Frank told me he caught you running away again. You're just trying to make trouble. He's right. You're a liar and God knows what else.'" She inhaled a long breath and let it out with the next words. "My own mother didn't believe me."

Her fingers dug into the shirt covering his chest. They were silent for a while. He held her wrapped in his arms and rocked her gently back and forth, his hands soothing her, comforting her.

"She put me on the bus the next day to visit Granddad."

"Is that when you finally told him?"

She shook her head. "I was so ashamed. I couldn't tell him even then. I finally got up enough nerve to write him a letter. I put some of what happened in it and left it where he could find it after I went back home. Two days later he showed up at our house in Maryland and beat Frank Wells until the man couldn't stand up. Then he pulled papers from his back pocket and made Momma and Frank sign them. It gave him custody. We came back here and that was it."

That was it. Ciaran suspected they'd never talked about it again. So she locked it all inside. He had heard about her during the summers when his family often brought the *Skerry* to anchor. Kids talk, and he heard she was stuck up. She wouldn't date anyone, didn't go to any of the school dances or even hang out at some of the places the rest of the Sounders did. She was a loner.

He closed his eyes as he continued to rock her. She didn't have to tell him there had been no one else. It was obvious.

Over her protests, he picked her up and carried her into the living room. After sitting with her in his lap, he pressed her head against his chest and stroked her short, black hair. "I can't undo what he did to you," Ciaran said at last. "All I can do is repeat what I've said before. I will not betray you. I will not leave you. I will protect you. I will help you. Believe me. Trust me."

"I want to." She breathed in on a sob. "You've been a really good friend."

He pressed his lips to her forehead, and where the knot of hardness in his chest once lurked, there was now only warmth. "If that's what you need, that's what I'll be."

She cried against his chest then, and he let her until her sobs stopped and her breathing deepened into an exhausted sleep. He shifted slightly so he could look at her. His eyes moved restlessly over her pale face, taking in the delicate bone structure, the thick sooty lashes now veiling those deep, emerald green eyes. Her small, deceptively fragile hand lay limply across her stomach.

He squeezed his eyes shut. His nostrils flared as he battled the murderous urge to hunt down Frank Wells and kill him. How could anyone harm a child? He knew he would feel outrage for anyone, but Wells had touched the woman he loved. He took a pure, trusting soul and damaged it.

Ciaran thought back over his own life, the lifestyle Keeley observed the past two years, and he marveled she still worked for him. How abhorrent she must have found his constant round of female companions. He thought back to some of the things she witnessed, some of the ways in which he taunted her, and felt shame.

His fingers gently stroked her cheek. He wanted her desperately, totally and completely, but he also wanted her whole. As much as he ached to suckle her breasts, to stroke her, and taste the sweet nectar of her, he would deny himself until she was ready. She would come first. If it was a friend she needed right now, then he would be that to her. They could continue much as they had, even if it was the last thing he wanted. Left up to him, he would introduce her to exactly how much pleasure a man and woman could experience together.

Chapter Eight

The house was quiet when Keeley awoke. Morning sunlight streamed through the white lace curtains at her open bedroom window. Outside songbirds chorused and the faint salt tang of the sea tickled her nostrils. In the distance, she heard the wavering cry of gulls and envisioned them wheeling and diving over the docks where the fishing boats tied up. It must be early. Maybe Ciaran was still asleep. She had caught him many times already, stretched out on Granddad's couch, too long for its length. Most times he had one foot on the floor and the other propped on the armrest at the other end.

He had done exactly as he said he would the morning of her grandfather's death. He stayed with her. The edginess that characterized him for the past two years was curiously absent these last few days. She saw new purpose in his lean face, and concern in his dark eyes instead of the contemptuous gleam that had so often colored his expressions. It would be easy to care for this Ciaran. And he said he would be her friend. But would he really? Could a man as sexual as him be just a friend?

She would make him breakfast. She was in the nightgown in which she normally slept, but she didn't remember putting it on. In fact, she remembered nothing after spilling her guts to Ciaran about Frank Wells. Her face flamed. She had never told anyone all that. Quickly pulling off her nightgown, she threw on gym shorts and a T-shirt. That would do until she could take a proper shower.

Afraid he would still be sleeping, she padded

quietly downstairs, but the couch was empty. His laptop and briefcase were missing too. There was a note on the coffee table. With trembling fingers, she picked it up.

Went into the city on business. Have a guest coming for dinner tonight. Can you cook?

She blinked and her mouth tightened. It seemed things were back to normal. Would it be one of the blonde bimbos? They seemed to be a favorite of his, but he usually escorted them together, like they were one entity. With a bitter twist to her mouth, Keeley stalked to the kitchen. She would grab a piece of toast and go for a swim.

By the time she finished and was lying on the beach to let the sun dry her off, she had calmed down. She had told him she needed a friend. What had she expected? He was a man who needed the adoration of the opposite sex.

"What, no tall, dark and looming protector this morning?"

She opened her eyes with one hand flung across her brow to shade them. "Hi to you, too, Stephie."

"It's the first time in days that I've seen you without Hulk."

Keeley closed her eyes. "He's not green, though he might be once I'm done with him tonight."

Stephie plopped onto the sand next to her. "Uh-oh. Trouble in paradise already?"

"Not trouble exactly. I'd guess you'd have to say things are just back to the way they were. When I woke this morning, he'd gone but there's a note letting me know he has a guest coming to dinner and could I cook."

"Why the dirty scoundrel! Imagine the audacity of wanting his private chef to prepare dinner."

Keeley rolled over onto her stomach and glared at Stephie. "Some friend you are. I'm in need of outraged sympathy and instead I get biting sarcasm...directed at me!"

Stephie leaned back on her elbows. "Oh get off it, Keeley. Did you really expect the new and improved Ciaran Clifton to last? I'd say he's simply reverted to form. And a good thing too before you let your emotions get out of hand over a guy who's just not real. So, are you going to poison him?"

Stephie's look contained more malice than mischief.

Keeley sighed. "No. Call it an overabundance of professionalism, but I just can't bring myself to screw up a meal on purpose. I think I'll divert my anger into overachievement and really knock his socks off."

Stephie grinned. "You go, girl. Personally, I'd opt for some laxative in the after dinner coffee. That would certainly put a different spin on an evening of romance."

"Eww. That's just gross, Stephie." When her friend merely shrugged and lay back on the sand, Keeley rolled onto her side. "Maybe I'll make a cake for dessert, shaped like a penis because he's such a prick."

Stephie snickered. "That is sooo wrong, Keeley."

"You wanted to feed him a laxative and you're saying I'm wrong?" She laid back and smiled. "You know, the cake idea is growing on me."

****

Early that evening, Ciaran paced back and forth in his room. Ever since his return from the city, he had forced himself to stay away from Keeley. He felt her anger the moment he walked back in the house. Though his telepathic powers were diminished locked in human form as he was, he was still perceptive enough her animosity slapped him in the face much as it had the entire time she worked for him. Then he'd taken wicked pleasure in tormenting her every chance he got, flaunting his sexual conquests in front of her and reveling in the waves of disapproval that flowed from her and over him. Now that was not his aim at all, and he realized what had seemed like an inspired idea that morning backfired.

His pacing stopped. He stood near the French doors leading out onto a rooftop terrace from his bedroom and stared out into the bay. The *Skerry* floated there quietly. Cayden would know what to do. His brother had always been wiser when it came to wooing women. Ciaran smiled, but there was no humor in it. Cayden would be surprised Ciaran thought that. There had only ever been one woman who touched his brother's heart, yet Cayden always knew how to reach her.

Ciaran had never tried to touch a woman's heart. Until now. He was far too interested in touching other places, which he had done so many times in the past he could scarcely keep track of it. They were nameless to him, simply ways to sate his own sexual hunger while he plied them for the information they were often privy to from husbands, lovers or parents. Lately all he wanted was the information without the need for anything else.

Because all his thoughts were centered on one woman? He sighed.

He stared around his room. His room. Not the room to which he brought all those nameless, faceless women. They were always in a guest bedroom, and he always went to them. No one was allowed here. Just as he had never taken a woman aboard *The Prankster* until Keeley set foot there. His room was his sanctuary, the place where he could acknowledge his heritage. He picked up the small crystal seal figurine he purchased in New York. It was a gift for her, but he was afraid if he gave it to her now, she would smash it. He wanted to offer her everything he was, but he couldn't give her his pelt, it had been taken away from him four years ago.

How could he reach her? How could he move her beyond her fear?

****

Keeley smiled wickedly as she plated the meal she had prepared. All afternoon she held her temper in check, concentrating on keeping things professional. She stepped back as she eyed the appetizer, the salad, and the entrée. Everything looked perfect.

"Ah, Miss McNamara," Jonathan smiled as he wheeled a cart into the kitchen. "Why don't you put everything on this. That way there'll be no interruptions to dinner."

Keeley smiled. Perfect. She moved the plates to the cart, covering them to keep them ready. When it was time to get the dessert, Keeley snapped her fingers. "Oh Jonathan, I forgot to get a bottle of wine. Could you pick out a nice white from the cellar to go with dinner? I'll finish loading the cart."

The older man smiled. "Of course."

As soon as he disappeared down the steps, Keeley hurried to the stainless steel commercial grade fridge and extracted the cake she'd prepared. While she topped it with a dollop of whipped cream, she waved her free hand at the refrigerator. A bowl of fresh cherries appeared at her elbow. After adding them around the base of the cake, she covered it and placed it on the bottom of the cart. Take that, Ciaran. If only she could see his face when he and the bimbo du jour reached the dessert course.

"Here you go. I thought perhaps a nice Riesling. You like that particular wine, don't you?"

Jonathan's voice startled her. Keeley swung around. "Yes, not that what I like matters. That will do nicely. Thank you."

He smiled. "I shall just take the cart out to the terrace then."

At last. She was alone in her kitchen. Keeley

rinsed dishes and loaded the dishwasher as quickly as she could. She wanted to be well away before Ciaran and his guest reached dessert. Just wait until she told Stephie. She would get such a kick out of her plan, Keeley almost wished she owned a camera so she could take a picture. She wiped down the counters, loaded the dishwasher and was already taking off her jacket when her sensitive nostrils picked up his distinctive scent.

His hand appeared from behind her and he set a flawless whelk shell on the counter in front of her. "A gift from the sea, Keeley Ann, and an invitation to join me on the terrace for dinner."

She refused to turn and look at him. "What's the matter, Mr. Clifton? Did today's menu selection stand you up?"

Big hands cupped her shoulders and turned her to him. An edge of impatience sparkled in his dark eyes. "You're my dinner guest, Keeley."

She wanted to disbelieve him, but there was no deceit in his gaze. Several emotions flickered through her before anger won. She planted a hand against his chest and shoved.

"You asked me to cook for *myself*?"

He nodded, seeming to be truly confused by her fury. "I wanted it to be a surprise."

She put her other hand against his chest and shoved again, this time with both hands. He took a step backward. "Cooking for *myself* is a surprise? And now you want me to just go out there and sit and eat dinner with you?"

Ciaran nodded, a little more cautiously. "Yes. Is that a problem? I put in a day of work. You put in a day of work and now we actually get to sit and enjoy the fruits of your labor. I don't see the issue."

Keeley's eyes narrowed and then suddenly she laughed, but there was a wicked edge to it. "You're absolutely right. Let's go enjoy the meal."

Relief lightened his lean features. He picked up the whelk and handed it to her. When she stole a glance at him, his expression was absurdly pleased that this time she accepted his gift. He guided her to the terrace with a hand resting lightly at the small of her back. Keeley couldn't remember him dining on the terrace before. It was usually the dining room or poolside. The scents of summer flowers hung heavy in the air. Jonathan had set the table, complete with cloth, crystal and candles, and the wine was cooling on a bucket of ice.

It was the perfect romantic dinner.

Except for dessert.

Keeley refused to think about that now. She would simply enjoy the meal. They started with a baked shrimp appetizer followed by a salad made of fresh greens topped by goat cheese croutons. The entrée was pan-seared tuna steaks served with spiced white beans. Ciaran complimented her throughout the meal, refilling her wine without her being aware of it as they munched through one of the best meals she had prepared in some time. Keeley was still savoring the last of her tuna when Ciaran sat back with a sigh.

"You really outdid yourself tonight. I can hardly wait for dessert. Jonathan said you were making some sort of cake but wouldn't let him anywhere near the kitchen while you worked on it."

The last bite of tuna nearly went down the wrong way. Keeley coughed slightly, grabbed her wine glass and swallowed the rest of the liquid. She was beginning to feel an ever so slight buzz from the alcohol, and the lack of food earlier in the day only made it worse. She smiled a little weakly.

"It will be a surprise, all right. Why don't we have some coffee first and let our food settle?"

While Keeley poured two cups of coffee, Ciaran stepped inside the house, coming back out with two small glasses containing a rich, golden liqueur. When she raised her brows inquiringly, he grinned.

"Irish Mist. A blend of whisky, honey and spices. Try it."

She sipped. It was quite good, and she was certainly feeling fine.

"How about this mystery cake," Ciaran suggested. "I have a wicked sweet tooth and I am curious you kept it such a secret."

Keeley coughed. "How about a walk? That way we could really build an appetite."

His eyes narrowed suspiciously. "The cake, Keeley."

She huffed air out, blowing her bangs off her forehead. "Oh all right."

She cleared the other dishes from the table, set out dessert plates and then bent to remove the cake from the bottom of the cart. After setting the covered dish on the table, she lifted the lid and kept her gaze locked somewhere over Ciaran's left shoulder. There was a moment of stunned silence. Keeley glanced at him nervously and then plopped in her chair when he threw back his dark head and laughed. It was a deep, full-bodied laugh that finally made her first smile and then giggle. He wiped his eyes.

"Is this a commentary on my character or my anatomy?"

When she blushed, he laughed once again. Keeley finally looked him in the eye and said with as straight a face as she could, "Will you cut or shall I? The base is chocolate cake."

He arched one thick brow. "It's the outside that's a bit intimidating. How on earth did you achieve such a lifelike look?"

"Well it did take a while to get the fondant just the right shade."

Ciaran poured her some more Irish Mist and held up his glass. "A toast then to the perfect cake for the perfect prick. Now which end did you want?"

She laughed as she swallowed more liqueur. "I really think you should choose."

"And leave you sloppy leftovers? What kind of a gentleman would I be? We'll compromise though. I'll choose for you."

His voice had lowered to a seductive murmur. He sliced off part of the cake, but then instead of putting it on her plate, he picked it up in his fingers, leaned over the narrow table and murmured, "Allow me."

Their eyes met as she bit into the piece he held in his hand. Heat seared through her, pebbling her nipples and settling into a hot throbbing between her thighs. What she hadn't eaten, he slipped into his own mouth. Her gaze was suddenly riveted to his firm, full lips. Keeley swallowed nervously.

"I should clean this up," she whispered.

He put his hand over her trembling fingers. "You should let Jonathan do it, so he can laugh at the cake while we walk out to the point."

She met his eyes and saw heat there. It roused conflicting emotions so she wanted to both pull away and lean toward him. It must have shown in her face.

He squeezed her fingers with gentle firmness. "Come with me, Keeley Ann. It's just a walk."

At her nod, he rose from the table and held out his hand, but released her as soon as she stood. They walked side by side. He seemed to sense her reluctance to have him too close, to have him touching her. Keeley had no idea how to bridge that distance, or if she even wanted to bridge it.

The moon lighted the way, showing the path through the sea grasses as a glowing streak as white as bone. It glimmered off the water, competing with the twinkling lights of the houses and boats surrounding the bay. She stared off into the distance when they reached the end. Still feeling a little loose from the wine and the liqueur, Keeley sat on a large rock at the end of the point. Ciaran sat next to her, still not touching her. She glanced over at his profile, just barely discernible in the darkness.

"When I was a little girl," she began softly, "I used to dream I was a mermaid. I was into that whole thing with the Little Mermaid. I wanted to be Ariel, and I dreamed I would find my own prince. Those dreams ended when Daddy died."

Ciaran appeared puzzled. "Who is this mermaid Ariel? I have always found the Mer folk to be spiteful and unfriendly."

Keeley looked at him, her mouth open. "You've never heard of *The Little Mermaid*? And you're serious, aren't you, about Mer people?"

She'd caught him off guard. He tried to laugh it off, but he'd caught her attention and aroused her curiosity. Afraid he might shut her down completely, she proceeded cautiously.

"Ciaran? Why do your eyes seem so luminous?"

He looked down and away from her. "A trick of the moonlight, that's all."

She twisted toward him and touched his shoulder. "I have to ask you something that's been bothering me."

He scowled. "I might not have an answer."

She studied the remoteness of his profile. She could back off and leave things the way they were or take a chance on pressing him. She would press. "The day you came to my house, the day Granddad died. How did you know I needed help?"

He shrugged. "Coincidence. I was on my way over anyway."

"Why didn't you freak out at what was happening? Not just you, but your entire family. Your mother knew exactly what I could do. Why is that?"

His mouth thinned.

"I deserve an answer, Ciaran. I at least deserve that. I saw what your mother did."

He glanced at her, and she still saw the luminosity in his eyes, like a buck or any other animal seen in faint light at night. His eyes seemed to soak up whatever small amount of light there was and reflect it back to her.

He smiled charmingly. "I love you, Keeley. Can't that be enough?"

Keeley's mouth tightened. "No. Don't break out the L word to distract me. Not fair. You know more about me than anyone, including my grandfather and my best friend, but I know almost nothing about you other than you're estranged from your family. You want me to take everything about you on trust, even when you know how nearly impossible that is for me. Are you Faerie folk like Dad and Granddad?"

He reached out then and took her small hand in his own. With his other hand, he traced the fragile bones of her hand from wrist to fingertips. She felt the hesitation in him, something not at all characteristic of him. "My mother was."

Keeley stiffened. "What do you mean was? You speak of her like she is no longer."

His eyes returned to the waters of the bay, and he swallowed. "She is something else now, like my father and my brother."

"And you? I notice you don't include yourself. What about you?" Keeley leaned back and stared at him.

Ciaran stood and walked a few feet away. His gaze was riveted on the sleek lines of the *Skerry*, its snow-white hull and decks visible in the moonlight. "What I was ceased to exist four years ago. Do you remember when I told you about the seal people, the Silkie?"

"Fallen angels. Those who fell to earth became

the Faerie folk, like my family. Those who fell to the sea became the Silkie. Like your family? Like you?" Her last words were a mere whisper of sound, but he heard. He spun around his whole posture stiff with anger.

"Like my family, but no longer like me. My jealousy and arrogance cost me dearly." His fists clenched and he thrust them into the pockets of his dark jeans. "I was always jealous of my brother. Only a year separates us, but because Cayden's older, he's the one who'll take his rightful place as a Silkie Lord." Ciaran paused and raked a hand through his long hair. "Oh, I would have a title, but not the power, and that was what I really wanted. The power. When Cayden was banished because he broke Silkie tradition, I foolishly allowed myself to believe I would become my father's heir. Then Cayden returned. All was forgiven, and my parents made it more than clear I would never replace him."

He closed his eyes. Pain etched his features. Keeley stood and went to stand next to him. She understood the rejection of a parent. She twined her fingers through his, but he didn't seem to notice.

"I went a little crazy. Hell, more than a little. I tried to kill my brother. I tried to kill Bell and my father. I nearly succeeded. I was captured. Put on trial." He stopped and swallowed several times. "The Silkie Council could have killed me outright. I suspect it was only my family's position and power that prevented such an occurrence. Instead, they did the next best thing. They took my pelt and condemned me to live as a human."

Keeley's fingers tightened on his and he finally looked at her. "You can never go back?" she asked in horror.

He watched her wonderingly. "You worry about me?"

He touched her cheek then brought their

114

entwined hands up so he could kiss the back of her hand. "They gave me a way back, if I could prove I had changed, had learned to put others before myself." He laughed cynically. "Instead I set out to prove how little I needed any of them. I survived on my own, figured out how to build my own empire and my own wealth. I was a success all right, but one that flew directly in their faces. I scorned everything they stood for, everything that was good and took only the bad. I seduced countless women. I used them. I used everyone I could to make money." He stroked the back of her hand with his thumb. "It's only recently I've realized I need to change—for myself and those I love."

Keeley shook her head, puzzled. "But your family. They didn't ignore you. They came to Granddad's house."

"They weren't supposed to. It was my mother's doing. She came to make sure what you are remained secret."

He touched her cheek. For just a moment, she wanted to lean into that touch, to beg him to touch her more. Instead, Keeley pulled back, stared out at the waters of the bay and changed the subject.

"Do you miss it? The sea?"

He followed her gaze. "Every minute of every day. I spent much more time in seal form than Cayden or my father ever did. At first it was an ache so powerful it curled me into a knot of pain at night when there was nothing else to distract me. I tried to erase it by sleeping with more women, partying, drinking. None of it worked. Gradually, though, something did make a difference."

She turned her eyes back to him in the darkness. "What was that?"

He laughed suddenly. "I had the most exasperating mosquito of a cook working for me..."

Keeley punched him in the arm. "I should have

poisoned you long ago."

He touched his finger to her nose. "But as much as I tried to ignore her, she haunted me. So I delighted in annoying her. I even fired her, but that didn't work. The only thing I had left was the jacket with her scent on it." He gave an odd, embarrassed laugh. "It's in my bedroom. I had to get her back. Then one day, while I stood right on this very point, I looked down to watch her swim, as I often did. This time, something went wrong. I didn't stop to think, could do nothing except what my heart told me to. I swam out and saved her. And she rewarded me with a kick in the chest."

Keeley swallowed, more affected by his words than she wanted to admit, so she kept her tone light as she said, "You were lucky. My aim was poor."

He laughed and pulled her against him. "You make me laugh. Even as you pester me and torment me, you make me laugh. I have never felt so light or free as I do when I'm with you, Keeley Ann McNamara. You make me feel like anything is possible. Good things are possible."

Something lifted inside her. The tightness that surrounded her heart eased and the shadow of fear that lingered in her brain dissipated. Her movements were uncertain, untutored, but no longer hesitant and no longer afraid. She stepped closer to him and stretched her hand up until she caressed the hard line of his cheek. Beneath her fingers, she felt him quiver.

"Keeley." It was a breath, a whisper on the evening breeze.

"Kiss me."

The glow in his eyes increased until she felt all the light of the moon and the sparkling lights of the ships and houses were reflected only in his luminous gaze. Gentle fingers tilted her face to his as he bent his head to her. Lips touched, brushed. His hand at her back pressed her closer. "More, Keeley," he breathed against her mouth.

She opened to him, her breath reduced to ragged, shaking gasps. He nibbled, tasted, giving her time to accept and respond. He was infinitely careful, knowing exactly how wary her past made her.

Tension ebbed like the tide and her hands crept up into his hair. It glided like silk against her fingers. This was his pelt now, the silk of a Silkie. Ciaran's hands drifted down, cupped her bottom, and lifted her against him. When she touched her tongue to his lips, an answering jolt shivered through him. He deepened the kiss, sliding his tongue between her lips, but still he kept it gentle, easy. She felt the tightly reined passion inside of him and realized with surprise she no longer feared it or him.

He broke the kiss, pressing her head against his chest. Beneath her cheek, his heart beat heavily, steadily, reassuring her. His hands stroked her back.

"Are you all right?"

She closed her eyes and sighed in relief. "Yes. Yes I am."

His arms tightened around her. "Come back to the house with me. I'll take you home."

She laid her hand against his cheek. "What if I said I didn't want you to take me home, that I didn't want to go home?"

He went completely still against her, even his breathing seemed to stop. She heard him swallow. "What do you want?"

Her lips trembled. "I don't know. Can you understand that? I don't know what it's supposed to be like. I've never…"

He pressed her against him, his arms circling her as much for protection as passion. He eased her back until they both sat on the rock, there on the point overlooking the bay. With one arm around her shoulders, he leaned his head against the top of hers.

"There's no rush, Keeley. My feelings won't change, and I won't do anything to hurt you."

She relaxed against him, leaning her head against his shoulder as she let the peace of the evening fill her. "I liked your kiss," she whispered, her hand resting on the firm muscle of his leg. "Your touch. Can we do that again?"

He chuckled quietly. "As long as you like, sweetheart."

Keeley got on her knees next to him so she could hold his face in the palms of her hands. He smiled at her encouragingly as she leaned closer. This time the kiss was not quite so gentle, deepening quickly into passion. Their tongues met, clashed. Lips stroked and tasted. When his teeth nipped at her lower lip, Keeley whimpered, feeling the heat coil deep in her belly. When he would have pulled back, she arched against him, rubbing her sex against his thigh without even knowing what she did, only that it made her feel hot and feverish. His hands spanned her back taking her with him as he eased them both backwards until she half lay across his broad chest. When she moaned again, he caught her hand against his chest.

"What Keeley? What do you want?" His voice was a deep rumble in the darkness.

"To touch you."

****

This time it was Ciaran who groaned. A vision of her naked body writhing and wrapped around him flitted through his fevered brain, but she wasn't ready for that. Instead, he held her hand, guided it inside the open collar of his shirt until her slender fingers stroked his broad chest. When her touch brushed the hardened point of his nipple, he

118

shuddered. He wanted to let her explore, knew she needed to, but God only knew how he would bear it. He felt nearly as uncertain as he knew she must feel. Everything was new again.

She leaned away from him, slipping open the buttons of his shirt until she could push it aside and bare his chest to her eyes. Her eyes widened. His vision allowed him to see her more perfectly in the darkness than she could possibly know. Her lips parted and her lids fluttered so sensuously he nearly groaned.

Her fingers caressed him, and this time he did groan. She kissed him again, but then left his mouth to trail her lips down his throat and across his chest. When her tongue touched his breast, he pushed into her. Her lips suckled him and she teased his flat nipple with her teeth. His balls tightened, and his cock pressed against the front of his slacks.

"Yes." His hands stroked her shoulders and her back. "I want to see you, Keeley, to feel you against me. As much as you can take, but no more than you can freely give."

She sat and stared into his dark eyes. With fingers that trembled, she grasped the hem of her scoop necked T-shirt and pulled it over her head. Only the thin white lace of her bra covered her breasts. They were small, high and all hers.

"You're beautiful," he breathed reverently, "so beautiful."

His hand stroked down from her shoulder and brushed the lace covering her already hardened nipples. Keeley panted. His fingers found the front clasp of her bra and then he was gently parting the material, baring the pale pink of her nipples to his hungry gaze. With a murmur he rolled to his side and pressed his lips against the swell of her breast. She threaded her fingers in his thick hair, and he suckled her gently, rolling his tongue across her

Laura Browning

nipple and drawing her deeply into his mouth.

When her breath came out on a sob, Ciaran stopped. "Is it too much? Am I pushing?"

She lowered her face to his again, kissing him hungrily. "No. It's perfect. Perfect."

He tugged her back on top of him and their bodies rubbed against each other as they continued to kiss deeply, passionately. It was a new experience for Keeley. He felt it in the ever so slight hesitation, as if she needed him to take just a faint lead so she could follow.

"All you have to do is say stop," he whispered against her lips. "Whenever it's too much, you tell me."

As much as he wished it would continue, as much as his cock ached with the need to be inside her, Ciaran knew she had nearly reached her limit. He unfastened her pants and slipped his fingers along her belly. When she arched toward him, he stroked her wet folds, teased the nub of her clitoris and continued to kiss her deeply until she arched against him in climax.

Her forehead dropped to his shoulder, her breath coming in surprised pants. When she laid her head against his chest, rubbing her cheek on him, Ciaran sat, cradling her in his lap.

"I think that's enough for tonight, Keeley." When she opened her mouth to protest, he put his fingers against her lips. "This isn't going away. I'm here to stay. Let's go back to the house. Let me take you home."

"You made it beautiful, Ciaran. What we did tonight, you made it beautiful. I'm sorry I couldn't…"

"Shh." The glow of trust lighting her expression touched him as much as her words. He stroked her cheek with fingertips as light as a feather. "It is beautiful. You're beautiful, Keeley, and anything we do together is beautiful because it comes from here."

120

He touched his fingers to her heart then his.

Keeley smiled at him and he thought it was like bursting from the dark depths of the ocean into the sunlight and air. They helped each other dress. Then as they walked back to the house, he kept his fingers twined through hers. As they neared the terrace, Ciaran asked, "Do you think Jonathan worked up enough nerve to try your cake?"

She giggled. "I'll bet he had a real ball eating it."

Ciaran laughed. "Remind me not to make you mad again. The next time you might really give me the shaft."

They both burst into laughter. They found the cake in the refrigerator, minus its other end and a note from Jonathan. *Absolutely the most delicious mountain oysters I have tasted. J.* They were still chuckling over it when they reached the Cape Cod style house that now belonged to Keeley.

Ciaran parked the Porsche along the curb and walked her to the door.

"Would you like to come in?" she asked as she unlocked it, glancing over her shoulder at him.

He touched her cheek and smiled at her. "No. It would be too tempting to stay. A kiss good night, Keeley Ann McNamara. That will have to do."

He turned her into his arms and lowered his head, brushing his lips across hers teasingly. "Good night, love."

He waited until she'd shut the door behind her then jogged lightly down the walk. He smiled as he drove home at the realization he'd never been so pleased about an evening that did not culminate in his own orgasm.

Chapter Nine

Ciaran stood naked on the terrace outside his bedroom as dawn broke over the bay and laughed at himself and the absurdity of how happy he felt. He was happier than he could ever remember being. Not just in the last four years. Ever. The bitterness of the past four years had been washed away with a kiss. It sounded like some children's fairy tale and made him laugh even harder.

What had happened no longer mattered. What he had once been no longer mattered. Keeley Ann McNamara wanted him just the way he was. She didn't judge him or condemn him for his past deeds. She didn't throw the women from his past in his face. He laughed again as he thought of the cake she'd served. She might not have thrown those women in his face, but she let him know what she thought of it. Tiny as she was, she could still stand with him toe to toe.

She hadn't said she loved him, but he saw it in her eyes and felt it in her touch. He knew as certainly as he knew she gave him her complete trust last night while they sat on the point. He thought again of kissing her, touching her and the way she looked as he brought her to orgasm. The feel of her exquisite breasts, her narrow back. The smooth play of the muscle beneath her fragile appearance. She was a lot stronger than she appeared, a lot stronger than he suspected even she knew.

She was perfect. She was his mate. If that meant he must live his life as a human, then he would do that.

He raked a hand back through his thick, dark hair and stared out at the bay to where the *Skerry* floated, glowing pinkly in the first rays of morning. Ciaran closed his eyes. For just a moment he heard the song of the Silkies, felt the splash of water and the smooth coolness of it flowing over sleek fur. The lure of the ocean floor pulled him in another direction. His hands clenched at his sides before he strode across his room to the shower.

Less than an hour later, he took a cup of coffee from the tray Jonathan held. "I must ask you a favor, Jonathan."

"What would that be, sir?"

He smiled and handed his butler a small envelope. "Take this to Miss McNamara, but stop at the florist on the way. I want a bouquet of yellow tulips; a planted pot would be even better...something living. Deliver them both to Miss McNamara's doorstep, but don't ring the bell. Simply leave them there."

"Let me see if I have this right," Jonathan said with just enough edge to his clipped accent Ciaran eyed him narrowly. "You wish me to have the florist open three hours early so you can purchase not only a flower not in season, but a specific color as well. Then you want me to deliver them to Miss McNamara, but not really. I'm supposed to simply leave them. Shall I ring and run as well, sir?"

"Only if you wish to be unemployed before lunch."

"Quite so." Jonathan smiled smugly and left the room. Ciaran had no doubt his butler would accomplish exactly what he'd asked him to do. He always did.

Ciaran sipped his coffee, his thoughts returning once again to Keeley. It was far too soon to ask her to marry him, but he wondered if she might consider moving in. They could have separate rooms. He was unsure just how ready she really was for an intimate relationship, but when he recalled once more how she'd let him touch her, pleasure her, he knew she was close. If she saw him at all hours of the day, and they could touch and kiss, perhaps it would speed things along. It would also show her she was the only woman in his life.

He leaned back. The only woman in his life. What would have seemed an impossibility just weeks ago was now the only thing he could envision. Was he more like his brother Cayden than he'd thought? Cay's single-minded love for Annabel Barton had baffled and angered Ciaran since they were just boys. Cay had loved his bride since they were children. When other Silkie were being called to a variety of humans, it was only ever Annabel who Cayden heard. Ciaran hadn't understood it before, but he did now. It was simply a matter of finding his true soul mate. For Cay it was Bell, and for him it was Keeley. The moment he'd seen her tears in his kitchen was his undoing. He felt as if he held the most delicate sea coral in his hand. A treasure, but a fragile one he would protect at all cost.

It would be easy enough now to pursue his investments without the help he'd gathered by flirting with the wives and daughters of the city's and the island's wealthiest inhabitants. Over the past four years, Ciaran learned and taught himself a lot. His investment base was now sound enough he could afford to relax.

He could afford to spend time with Keeley. He would show her she need not fear intimacy, that between the two of them, sex would be pleasurable and beautiful. He recalled the scent of her and the feel of her silken skin beneath his lips and fingers. His mind filled with images of Keeley from the previous night until he was hard with anticipation of burying himself inside all that tight wetness he had only touched with his fingers.

****

The knocking was loud enough to wake the dead.

"Just a minute! Just a minute!" Keeley finished stirring her muffin batter, let the spoon rest in the bowl and hurried to the front door. She yanked it open to see Stephie on her front step holding a big pot of yellow tulips. "You brought me flowers? Stephie! That is so sweet. What's the occasion?"

Her friend thrust an envelope in her hand, pushed past her and plunked the pot on the coffee table in front of the couch. "Not me, idiot. They were sitting on your front stoop when I arrived. So, open the card! Who are they from?"

Keeley slipped her finger beneath the lip of the heavy cream envelope. She pulled out the folded paper, opened it and scanned the note written in Ciaran's bold handwriting.

My dearest Keeley Ann,

Take the day off and let me take you out to dinner this evening. Nothing fancy and followed by a moonlit sail. In the meantime, enjoy the flowers. A little sunshine for you in return for what you've brought me. I'll pick you up at seven.

C

He hadn't given her just words last night. She could believe, could trust. For just an instant she closed her eyes and took a deep, healing breath.

"So? Who's it from? What's it say?" Stephie was trying to sneak a peek around Keeley's hand.

"It's from Ciaran. He's giving me the day off and wants to take me out to dinner tonight."

"Even after you humiliated him last night?" Stephie's eyes widened.

Keeley blushed. Stephie scowled.

"Okay, Keeley McNamara, spill it."

"There was no other woman. I was the guest."

Stephie's eyes widened and she hissed, "Please tell me you didn't make the cake in the shape of a dick."

Keeley nodded and then laughed. "I even decorated it in skin-toned fondant and garnished it with whipped cream and cherries."

Stephie doubled over with laughter. "Oh my God. And you served it? What did he do? What did he say? Oh why am I even asking—he must have loved it if he wants to take you out tonight."

Keeley's face flushed even more. "After he finished laughing, he cut the head of it off and fed it to me. Then he proposed a toast of 'the perfect cake for the perfect prick.'"

Stephie's lips twitched again and then she laughed until she had to wipe the tears from her face. Keeley grinned at her friend. It felt good to be able to talk about normal things like a guy. It was always one-sided before, Keeley listening to the recitation of Stephie's romantic woes.

"Come on back, Steph. I was just getting ready to put some muffins in the oven. You want a cup of coffee?"

"Sure. I never say no to your cooking or your coffee."

She perched on a stool at the small counter and watched as Keeley finished what she was doing. Keeley told her about the meal, about walking out to the point. She left out their discussion of Faeries and Silkies.

"Did he kiss you?"

"Yes."

Stephie sipped her coffee and set it down. "I'm sorry, but I have to ask. Don't you worry about all the other women?"

Keeley took off her apron and smoothed her

hands over the shorts she wore. "No. He's with me now, and that's all I want to think about."

Stephie bit her lower lip. "Keeley, you've never even really dated, honey. He's a very experienced man who's sure to have certain expectations. Certain desires. Are you prepared to handle that?"

Keeley looked her friend straight in the eye. "He won't rush me. He was the one who stopped last night. Stephie, he's so different with me than I've seen him with other women. It's hard to explain, but he is. I trust him."

"Trust? Him?" Stephie's coffee mug landed with a little thunk back on the tabletop. "Keeley, the man has had his hands and no doubt other parts of him, on almost every female from Montauk to Newark. Date him, enjoy him, even bed him if you choose, but trust him? You'd be a fool."

Keeley's chin hardened and Stephie held up her hands, palm out. "Okay, okay. I'll back off. I can see it in your face. Ciaran Clifton is no longer a topic of conversation."

"That's what I've always liked about you, Stephie." Keeley smiled at her friend. "I was thinking about going shopping. You want to come along?"

"Sure. I have to go to work at one, but we can hit some of the shops this morning. Anything specific?"

"I think I might get a bikini." Keeley darted a glance sideways to gauge her friend's reaction.

Stephie did a double take. "Miss *practical suits only*? You're finally going to take the plunge and bare your belly?"

"Yes. But nothing too risqué."

"Uh huh. You just put yourself in my capable hands. I'll get you set up right. You need to learn how to display your assets correctly."

Less than an hour later they stood inside one of the boutiques lining the main drag. It catered to well-heeled tourists, but Keeley and Stephie often found great deals when the sales started. As Keeley riffled through the rack of colorful suits, Stephie held up a tiny red thong and waggled her brows at her.

"I will not have something in the crack of my ass. Forget it," Keeley hissed. Snatching an emerald green tankini off the display, she held it for Stephie's inspection, but her friend put the nix on that.

"If you're going to look at those, you might as well stick with the racing suit you already have."

Keeley huffed. "What about this?" She held up a tiny triangle bikini in a cotton plaid. The miniscule bottoms tied at each hip. Stephie raised her brows.

"Try it on. Let me see."

Keeley looked around the shop. "I'm not going to step out here in it."

With an exasperated sigh, Stephie rolled her eyes. "If you can't let *me* see you in it, how on earth will you ever wear it in front of anyone else?"

In the end, Stephie poked her head inside the dressing room cubicle. "Oh wow! You really look great in that Keeley. As buff as you are? Wow."

Keeley frowned at her reflection. "I wish I had a little more to fill out the top."

Stephie laughed. "I think there's an old French saying that the perfect breast is just large enough to fill a champagne glass. I've always heard more than a mouthful's too much. I'd say you're just about perfect, honey."

Keeley's green eyes met Stephie's in the mirror and they both laughed. "Maybe I should put that to the test."

Stephie's mouth dropped open. "Keeley Ann McNamara! You have already been corrupted."

Keeley felt heat stain her cheeks as she pictured Ciaran's lips on her breasts.

****

After talking to his broker and his banker by phone, Ciaran changed into shorts and deck shoes, stopped by a couple of shops in town, and then headed for the marina at the Yacht Club. He wanted *The Prankster* ready for tonight. He'd always kept her furnishings sparse, but that was when he was the only person on board. Tonight, he wanted the cabin a little more comfortable. It had to be perfect for Keeley.

If she was willing, he hoped to take the next step forward with her. In addition to softer blankets and some throw pillows for the cabin, Ciaran added a thickly padded throw that could be used on deck, so if Keeley wished to stretch out like she had the last time, she wouldn't have to do it on hard, bare wood.

He put a couple of bottles of the wine he knew she preferred inside the fridge to chill, added some towels and almond scented massage oil. He wanted to show her touching between a man and a woman didn't always end in sex. That it could simply be a pleasure to touch.

Yeah. That was it, but since he got hard just thinking about his hands on her sweet little bottom he was concerned just how successful that experiment might be.

Ciaran came back topside with his mind still on Keeley. It took him a moment to see the two figures standing on the dock. When he did notice them, the smile faded. The hard knot in his chest returned in a heartbeat.

"Hello, Ciaran," his father greeted him without any apparent warmth.

With his dark eyes narrowed, Ciaran bowed his head. "My Lord. Brother." He met their eyes defiantly. "To what do I owe this honor?"

"Riordan has called the Council," Carrick informed him. "They are to meet at the end of this month to reconsider your case."

Ciaran's eyes flashed. "By whose request? I didn't ask for this."

"You can be damn sure I did not," Cayden snapped.

Carrick held up his hand in a staying motion to both of them. "Your mother requested it. She did so without my knowledge and apparently presented enough evidence Riordan feels it merits a meeting of the Council. We are here solely to convey that information to you."

Ciaran's nostrils flared as he looked from his father to his elder brother. "If I choose not to obey?"

Carrick's eyes sharpened. "Everything in life is not always yours to decide, Ciaran. It would be extremely unwise to defy the Council. They have already been more than lenient with you."

His jaw stiffening in fury, Ciaran ground out, "Lenient? Setting me adrift with nothing and no pelt was lenient?"

"It was more than you deserved!" Cayden snarled.

Ciaran closed his eyes, forced himself to calm down. This would get them nowhere. When he met their gazes again, his anger was gone. "I will await their summons. Now, if you will excuse me, I have plans for this evening and things I need to see to before then."

He vaulted from *The Prankster* onto the dock and walked away from them. Inside he still seethed. In the old days, he would have sought the water, reverted to his seal form and simply swum off his frustration, but he could no longer do that. Instead, he'd been forced to learn how to cope with his emotions. One way he did was by keeping his goals in sight, and right now the most important goal in his life was Keeley.

Just thinking about her helped the anger

dissipate. He rubbed his chest absently. Her slim figure and creamy skin. How sweetly she pressed herself against him last night, how passionate her kisses became. He swung open the door of the Porsche and slipped behind the wheel. For just a few minutes he allowed her to fill his mind and found it eased the rawness of seeing his father and his brother once more.

****

Keeley and Stephie ate lunch at a small café along the waterfront under the dappled shade of the trees that lined the sidewalk. As soon as she finished, Stephie stood and kissed her friend on the cheek. "I've got to run or I'll be late for work. Let me know how your evening with Mr. Clifton goes."

Keeley smiled. "I will. Bye Stephie." She settled back after her friend left and sipped the iced tea she ordered with her lunch. Two tables further down she saw a man and a woman seated at a table, a dark-haired toddler at their feet playing with a ball. Both the man and woman had honey colored hair with paler, golden highlights. Keeley's eyes narrowed as she studied them. For some reason, it triggered a memory, and she tried to place who they were. As she watched, a waiter hurrying to a table with a tray kicked the ball just as the toddler bounced it. The ball flew toward the street and the path of an oncoming car. Keeley saw the panic on the child's face. She concentrated on the ball and felt her energy touch the toy. The ball suddenly rotated, shivered and rolled back toward her. She picked it up and hurried over to the little girl.

Crouching, she handed it to her. "Here, sweetie. Your ball is just fine." She laughed. "The wind must have blown it back to you safe and sound."

Keeley looked into identical pairs of deep blue eyes. She swallowed as she suddenly realized why they both looked so familiar. Annabel Clifton and

Taylor Stokes—no Barton—he'd changed his name, as she recalled. She blushed at the way his eyes studied her with pure, male appreciation in them. She stood slowly, awkwardly, not sure how to treat these members of Ciaran's estranged family.

Annabel smiled. "You're Keeley McNamara, aren't you? Catriona's mentioned you."

"She has?" Keeley couldn't help the surprise that rocked through her. Ciaran's mother remembered her?

"Nice trick with the ball." Taylor's tone held a hint of teasing laughter.

Keeley stared at him with careful blankness. She must be more cautious. "Trick? All I did was give it back to the baby."

The golden-haired man arched one thick, sun-tinted brow at her. "If you insist."

"Will you join us?" Annabel asked softly.

Keeley looked around to see Cayden and Carrick Clifton strolling their way. For a moment, the similarity between Cayden and Ciaran took her breath away. They could almost be twins, but there was no doubt in her mind. Ciaran was by far the handsomer. Her gaze skittered nervously back to Annabel and Taylor.

"No. Thank you anyway. I-I should go." She didn't wait to hear anything else, escaping quickly back to her table. After leaving a couple of dollars for a tip, she picked up her bags. The sensation of someone watching her, though, made her turn as she left the patio and she saw Carrick staring after her with narrowed, dark eyes. But he wasn't the only one watching her. Taylor did too. He smiled, an easy, relaxed grin that brightened his already handsome face. Keeley blinked. Before she met Ciaran, someone like Taylor Barton paying attention to her might have meant something.

Keeley hurried home, grateful to get back inside

her granddad's house. Yawning tiredly, she laid on the couch, pulling an afghan over her that had been one of Granddad's favorites. She could still smell his spicy scent and it reassured her, comforted her as she drifted off to sleep.

She awoke in time to get ready. As she stood in the hot spray of the shower, letting the water sluice down her body, she recalled Ciaran's mouth suckling her breasts; desire uncurled deep in her belly. She had never felt that before, that heavy throbbing between her thighs, the wetness...Keeley leaned back against the wall of the shower, realizing she was panting almost as if Ciaran were with her now touching her as he had last night. Her fingers eased between her legs, but then she snatched them away. Would he do that again? She wanted him to.

****

Everything was ready. He pulled up in front of the house promptly at seven. He decided to keep the first part of the evening lighthearted and casual. He was taking her out for clams and beer. They could eat corn on the cob, buckets of clams and oysters and drink a couple of beers. His step was light as he came up the walk and knocked on the door.

She looked almost breathless when she opened the door, her green eyes glowing and her skin faintly flushed. She'd never looked better. Giving in to temptation, he leaned forward and gently pressed his lips to her mouth, tearing away as the kiss threatened to heat up. It was too soon. He had promised himself to take it slowly. She needed that and he did too. He wouldn't screw things up by trying to rush her into anything she wasn't ready to do.

He smiled slowly at her and tucked his hair behind one ear. "Ready, sweetheart?"

"Yes. Just let me get my bag." She grabbed the small backpack she used for a purse. He glanced past her and saw the tulips sitting on the coffee table. Catching the direction of his gaze, Keeley smiled. "Thank you so much for the flowers. It was exactly what I needed to brighten my morning."

He put his arm across her shoulders. "Then let me brighten your evening too. I know this great little dive where the clams are plentiful and the beer is cold."

"Mmm it sounds heavenly. I guess it's a good thing my boss gave me the night off, huh?"

He tucked her closer to his side and chuckled. "I hear he's a really great guy."

The clam bar was packed. Like most places during the summer, it didn't matter much what night of the week it was, restaurants were likely to be busy. Ciaran spotted a table in the back and guided Keeley toward it. In almost no time at all, a bucket of steamed clams sat in front of them along with corn on the cob and coleslaw. Frosty mugs of beer fought for space with the basket of crab cakes Ciaran had also ordered.

He picked up one of the crab cakes and held it out to her. Keeley leaned forward and bit into it delicately, closing her eyes as she savored the flavor of the crab and the subtle mixture of spices. Ciaran had always loved the crab cakes here because they actually had plenty of crab in them, not just bread crumb filler. He watched the concentration on Keeley's face.

"Do you find yourself critiquing when you go out to eat?"

Keeley laughed. "Not when I'm downing buckets of clams and corn on the cob." She took a sip of her beer. "I don't know that I really critique as much as I analyze. I don't know exactly how to explain it. I guess it would be similar to being a world-class musician. Just because I'm Sarah McLachlan doesn't mean I don't also appreciate Beyonce or Bonnie

Raitt. I enjoy and respect their different styles. It's the same way with eating another chef's food. We all use different seasonings and ways of preparing a dish. It doesn't make one good and one bad; it just makes them different."

Ciaran looked thoughtful for a minute. "You used the word analyze. I analyze financial information to come up with investment decisions. How do you analyze cooking? I mean to me it either tastes good or it tastes bad. Yours is superb."

"Except when I put salt instead of sugar into the dessert?"

He stroked a finger down her cheek. "You know at the time I was pretty furious, but looking back it is kind of funny."

Keeley fiddled with her silverware. "I hope you know I didn't do it on purpose. I was so distracted over Granddad's illness."

Ciaran took her hand in his, brought it to his lips and lightly kissed her palm. "I know you didn't. You would never deliberately make such a basic mistake. I know that about you now, and I realized it even then. I'm glad now it happened."

Her gaze was startled. "Why?"

He put her palm to his cheek. "There's no telling how long I might have drifted along in my own anger without ever really seeing the faerie witch making magic in my kitchen."

Her hand trembled against his cheek, and he smiled at her. "Now tell me, kitchen witch, just how do you analyze food?"

"It's a matter of using your senses. You've seen the way wine connoisseurs swirl the wine, sniff it, taste it, and swirl it in their mouths. Then even after they swallow, they look for the aftertaste. Food is the same way." She swirled her hand in the air over the pot in front of them. "Tell me what you smell?"

"Corn."

Keeley laughed, a merry, twinkling sound that made his gut clench. God! She was so beautiful.

"Let me tell you what I smell." She closed her eyes and inhaled deeply. "I smell garlic, pepper, allspice, and bay leaves along with the corn."

His fingers stroked her wrist. "Of course." He raised her wrist to his nostrils. "I see what you mean. It's just like your skin. I smell jasmine. There's the sweet, clean smell of an ocean breeze, and just a hint of spice. Mmm. Cinnamon."

She trembled and slipped her arm away from him. Her huge eyes fell, sheltered by thick, dark lashes as her fair skin flushed.

"Don't," she whispered. "Don't tease me like I'm one of your bimbos."

"I didn't mean it that way, Keeley Ann. I do smell all of those things on your skin. It's your scent, your fragrance. I can't help how it haunts me." He stopped, shook his head. "I'm sorry. Tell me what you taste."

She struggled for a moment to regain her composure and the lightness they had enjoyed so far that evening. At last she grinned at him. "What I want to taste is that pure, sweet burst of nectar and the creamy saltiness of the butter coating it. When I taste it, I don't want the spices I smell to overwhelm the flavor of the corn itself. And of course, there's the texture. That's important with corn on the cob. It's so easy, especially when you're cooking such a volume of it as they do here, to overcook it until the corn becomes mushy. You can also tell corn picked once it was too ripe by its texture as well."

Ciaran smiled at her. "A simple food that's not so simple after all. What started you cooking?"

"It was therapy as much as anything." Keeley bit her lip as she glanced around the crowded restaurant. "Oh, I don't mean the kind with a psychologist sitting back wanting to know 'and how did that make you feel?' I'm talking about my Granddad giving me a job to do, making me responsible. There was so much anger inside me and it wasn't going away. I started cooking at home for him, and managed not to poison either one of us. Then in high school, the guidance counselor steered me toward cooking in vocational education."

"Not college?"

Keeley blushed again and looked at the table. "I wasn't a very good student. It all seemed so meaningless to me, and math? I didn't get that at all."

Ciaran laughed. "But you use it every day, Keeley. You use it whenever you cook. You use it when you shop for ingredients."

"I understand that. It was just all those equations and the higher math you have to have for college. No. I decided on cooking school, and that was tough enough. Granddad helped as much as he could, but I had to work really hard. I lived in the city, shared a studio apartment with two other girls, and worked as an under chef in a small restaurant. I learned almost as much there as I did in cooking school. I had several offers, including one to work for Food Network."

"Then why come back."

"Granddad needed me, and I guess I needed him, too. I wasn't happy in the city. I missed the quiet of the island in the winter, the smells and the sounds of everything in the summer. This is home."

Ciaran understood that. He understood missing family and home, but he was also realizing the concept of family could change. His was changing. While he would give almost anything to be back on good terms with his parents and his brother, he didn't think he could give up Keeley to make that happen. She was quickly becoming the very core of his existence. He welcomed it as much as he feared it.

"Let's go for a sail. We can get away from the noise and enjoy the quiet of the night. I thought we might go back to the cove we went to before. Would you like that?"

When she nodded and smiled at him, his heart turned over. As he guided her from the restaurant, he glanced at a table near the door and saw Cayden and Annabel there. He nodded curtly to them, drawing Keeley closer to him. He wasn't sure if it was to protect her from Cayden's dark look or to draw comfort for himself from her presence. Even after they left the clam bar, he felt Cayden's gaze follow them. The marina was only a short walk away, so Ciaran guided Keeley in that direction.

The sun was just setting. From the boats around them floated the sounds of laughter, music that ranged from classical to salsa, and finally as they reached the end where most of the sailboats were moored, just the gentle lap of water against hulls. It relaxed him and helped him put aside the brush with Cayden. He wanted no memories of the past to intrude this evening.

He slipped *The Prankster's* lines, jumped on board and held his arms out to Keeley. With his large hands spanning her narrow waist, he lifted her down next to him. Just before her feet would have touched the deck, he dipped his head sideways and brushed his lips over hers.

"Welcome aboard. It's still warm. Did you want to go below to change into your bathing suit while I get us under way?"

She nodded at his suggestion. He watched her for just an instant, a smile curving his lips before he turned his attention to the cockpit.

****

Keeley noticed the changes as soon as she entered the cabin. The spartan interior was gone, tastefully softened with a plush comforter and some throw pillows. She swallowed nervously as she glanced around and saw candles scattered around. Nerves gave way to anger. She entered the small galley and opened the fridge. Two bottles of her favorite wine. Did he think he could so easily seduce her? What happened to all his fine talk about taking it slowly, not doing anything to betray her trust? *Being her friend?* Keeley's fists clenched impotently at her sides.

The engine rumbled to life and galvanized her to action. She raced up the stairs to where Ciaran stood at the wheel, his face lifted to the breeze as he began maneuvering *The Prankster* out into the channel.

"Turn her around you son of a bitch!" Keeley snarled letting the wave of energy slice down her hands, knocking him back a couple of steps. Ignoring his confused expression, she hurled herself at him and punched him in the chest. "Take me back! You're no different than *he* was!"

Ciaran grabbed her by the shoulders and held her far enough away so he could avoid her fists, so she launched into him with her feet instead, catching him in the shin. When her next kick looked like it was headed for a higher target, he jerked her sideways and scissored his legs around hers.

"Keeley! Stop it. What's wrong?"

She jerked her head back to glare at him. "Don't give me that confused look. You promised you would be my f-friend, that I wasn't another one of your bimbos."

"You're not, damn it. What's the problem?"

"The cabin! What's with all the pillows and the comforter and the candles?"

He stared at her agape and then closed his eyes and shook his head in chagrin. "Keeley...it's not...I never..." He stopped, sighed and looked at her. "I just wanted to make you feel more comfortable, and yes I guess I did want it a little more romantic. I've never brought anyone else on board *The Prankster*." He cut the engine and let them drift. "Come here," he said as he dragged her forward by the hand. "Look, I added a pad up here. You seemed to like lying there the last time, so I put the pad here to give you cushioning from the bare wood."

Between his abashed expression and his apparent thoughtfulness, Keeley felt herself waver. "What about the candles and the wine?"

He touched her cheek and stroked down to her chin. "I hoped you would let me touch you like I did last night," he murmured. "I enjoyed that. I thought you did too. Was I wrong?"

Keeley leaned into his caressing hand. "No."

Ciaran framed her face with his hands and kissed her. "I thought if you would let me, I would give you a massage."

Her heart fluttered and she instinctively started to pull away.

"No, sweetheart. Listen. I want to show you not all touching leads to sex, that it doesn't have to. Not if you don't want it to."

She shook her head. "I don't know."

"Think about it, but if you still want me to take you back, I will. I've never lied to you. I won't betray you."

She shook her head, shame and embarrassment making her bite her lip. "I'm sorry," she whispered at last. "I overreacted."

Ciaran touched her shoulder. "No. You were right to question, and I should have explained. Just next time, do you think you could ask before you wallop me with those powers of yours?"

Keeley laughed softly and smiled at him. "Yes."

"Good. Then let me get the motor started so we can get out of the way and on our way to the cove."

When they reached the sheltered waters, Ciaran

dropped sail and then anchored in the middle. The moon was just beginning to rise even though it wasn't full dark yet. Keeley swallowed. "Did you want to swim?"

He grinned. "Of course."

He was watching her and she wasn't sure she could make herself pull off the T-shirt to reveal the bikini. Her body trembled slightly as she lifted the hem. He watched her with those dark eyes, and she knew the moment he realized just how little she wore. His eyes narrowed slightly and his nostrils flared as if he were drinking in her scent. Deciding she couldn't back up now, she pulled the shirt off over her head and let it drop to the deck.

"My God! Keeley, you're exquisite." The heat in his eyes made her weak.

She resisted the urge to cover herself with her arms. "It's okay?"

"If it were any more okay, you would have to pick my tongue up off the ocean floor. I thought you were attractive in your racing suit, but this?" He smiled slowly at her. "Are you by chance on the dessert menu? Because if you are, I'd like to order one of you with whipped cream all over."

Keeley blinked, her mouth falling open and then she giggled. The giggle became a laugh. Spinning on her heel, she dove over the side of *The Prankster*, cutting into the black water with barely a splash. Ciaran was right behind her. She swam just beneath the surface, not daring to go deeper in the dark, and felt more than saw Ciaran at her side. When she stopped to tread water, he slowly swam around her blowing bubbles at her as he surfaced. It teased her sensitive skin, setting off the nerve endings all along the tender flesh now bared by her new bikini.

When he stopped in front of her and grinned she started to splash him and flip fluidly away, but he caught her against him and growled softly.

"God Keeley. I need to kiss you in the worst way. The beach or the boat?"

"Boat," she whispered, and she knew she was making a decision on where they would go from here.

Chapter Ten

He climbed in first then reached down with one arm and pulled her out of the water. Keeley stared at him, hardly daring to blink. Every once in a while he did something to remind her how physically strong he truly was. She shivered.

"Cold? We can go below deck."

"No not yet. I want to enjoy the moonlight." She tried to keep her body from trembling.

He tugged her forward then and they stretched out on the cushion there. He'd grabbed a couple of towels and now proceeded to dry her off. As his hands moved with the towel along her thigh, Keeley stopped him. "I can do it."

He handed her the towel a little quizzically, then took the other to swiftly dry himself. His eyes never left hers as he pulled her down to the cushion. Fingers like feathers, he traced the outline of her face, the shell of her ear and the soft parted opening of her lips. She took a deep, shaky breath.

"I love you Keeley," he whispered. "Whatever we do, you must remember that. If anything we do makes you uncomfortable, say so. I'll stop."

A tremor shifted through her.

"Are you cold?"

"No. Nervous."

His caressing hand slid from her cheek to the slender column of her neck, cupping it to draw her closer. Keeley's lips parted in anticipation, and now she already knew what was coming, she felt heat throb through her. She moaned softly. The sensations were so powerful they made her feel slightly out of control.

"That's it, love, let it go." He breathed the last words against her mouth and then began to kiss her. Again, he tasted, nibbled and caressed until she relaxed enough to open her mouth to him. When she did, his tongue teased her into touching him with her own. He turned them both on their sides, one strong arm cradling her back to press her against him. Their bare legs rubbed together and she felt the hard ridge of his erection press against her stomach. She refused to let memories intrude. This was Ciaran and he loved her.

When his hand slipped to the small of her back and then lower to cup her bottom, Keeley not only didn't protest his touch, she moaned in aching need. Her hands crept over the smooth muscles of his chest.

"Touch me, Keeley." His voice was rough with need and he guided her hand to the nub of his taut nipple. His groan matched hers. "Kiss me there."

She obeyed him instinctively, drawing his flesh into her mouth, flicking him with her tongue.

"Your teeth, Keeley. Use your teeth," he rasped, his breathing uneven.

She bit him, teasingly, but when he pressed her even closer, she bit down on the curve of his pec.

"Yeah." He groaned. "That feels so good. You feel so wonderful."

His cock twitched against her belly. Hot, wet heat exploded at her core. She was getting in too deeply, too quickly. Needing some way to lighten the sexual tension spinning out of control, she murmured. "Could we get a glass of wine?"

He touched her cheek and tilted her face to his. In his luminous eyes she saw the knowledge of what she felt. It wasn't fear, thank God, but it was an overload of sensation. Too much too soon and she did fear if he pressed her she would forget it was him.

Ciaran. Not the ghosts of her past, but the man who showed her more and more just how much he loved her.

"Wine would be nice." She heard the tenderness in his tone.

She shivered when he rolled away from her. Ciaran held out his hand to her. "Come below. It will be warmer there."

He led her down the steps. She sat on the bench at the table in the galley and watched him while he uncorked the wine and poured two glasses. After handing her one of the goblets, Ciaran opened the fridge again. "I have some cheese and apples. Would you like some?"

"Mmm."

Keeley sipped the wine, its coolness slipped down her tight throat, relaxing her and helping her restore some of her equilibrium. She couldn't believe she bit him. Her eyes skittered to his chest and she saw the mark her mouth left there. Heat suffused her cheeks, but embarrassment faded as she watched him slice an apple.

"Jesus, Ciaran! Give me that knife before you cut your fingers off." She jumped up and shooed him out of the galley. "Sit down and let the expert handle this."

He grinned at her like a little boy and she gave him an answering smile. All at once, the nervousness that had been eating at her evaporated. She felt his eyes on her as she quickly cored and sliced two apples and arranged them on a small plate along with the cheese. "Do you have any bread or crackers?"

He sipped his wine and nodded. "In the cabinet behind you."

After adding those to the plate, she brought them over, conscious of his dark eyes roving over her nearly naked body. She ignored the temptation to cover up, forcing herself to take a step forward. He obviously enjoyed looking at her and it bolstered her confidence. When she would have sat across from him, he slid over and patted the space on the bench next to him.

"Here, Keeley, next to me." His smile softened his words. "I might want to touch you, kiss you. A table between us would make that too difficult."

She looked at him and her mouth parted. He was a study in male perfection, tanned, toned, with muscles that bunched and rippled every time he moved. Her fingers itched with desire to slide over that smooth skin. Did she dare? She took another deep breath.

"We could take it into the cabin. It would be a shame to waste the pillows and the candles, don't you think."

Ciaran raked his hand back through his long hair, pushing it off his broad forehead. "You sure about that?"

"No." Keeley smiled nervously as she admitted the truth.

"Then..."

Resting one knee on the bench, she leaned over and picked the plate back up. "Help me out here, Ciaran. I'm trying..."

He let his hand rest at the curve of her waist, his thumb lightly caressing her stomach. "I don't want to scare you."

"I'll let you know when it becomes a problem. I promise."

He lit the candles and they stretched out on the double berth, the wine and food resting on a recessed shelf at the head of the bed. Keeley lay on her stomach while Ciaran rested on his side, his head propped on one elbow. With his free hand he picked up a slice of apple and held it out to her.

"Open up."

Obediently she did, but when she would have closed her mouth on the apple, he slipped it across her lips and popped it into his own mouth. His eyes laughed at her as she stared at him agape. He grinned and held out another slice. This time when he tried to tease her, she grabbed his wrist, struggling to hold onto it as he pulled the fruit inexorably toward his own mouth. At some point, both of them quit looking at the apple, staring at each other's mouths instead. He slipped the slice between her lips and then covered her mouth with his, taking a bite of the part of the slice still protruding.

"More?" His deep voice was little more than a growl.

She nodded, knowing it wasn't only food they were talking about. He continued to tease her and taste her as he fed her bits of food. When she fed him the last slice of apple, he sucked her fingertips into his mouth and touched his tongue to them. Heat shot through her, her eyes widening and her nipples hardening. She felt wetness between her thighs. Ciaran's nostrils flared as if he smelled the change in her scent and enjoyed the fragrance of her sex.

"I promised you a massage," he murmured throatily. "Are you up for it?" He followed the direction of her gaze. "Yes, I'm up for it, in every way possible, Keeley, but I won't do anything you don't ask me to do. So, again, are you up for it?"

"I don't know..."

He smiled. "Try it. There is absolutely nothing that will relax you more than a full body massage. If you get to a point where you're uncomfortable, tell me. I'll stop. Deal?"

He kept reassuring her of that. She wanted him, and wanted to believe him. If this would help her get to the point where she could tell him, show him, she was willing to do almost anything.

"Okay. What do we do?"

He smiled. "Roll over on your back. I'll start with your feet."

She let her eyes half close, watching as he put her feet on his lap. He picked up one and began to gently rub the sole of her foot, working from her heel to her toes.

He looked sidelong at her. "How does that feel?" At her nod, he continued, working first one foot and ankle before picking up the other. "Your feet are so tiny, like the rest of you, Keeley. Beautiful, delicate but only deceptively fragile. Now the other end. Sit up."

She smiled. "I don't know if I can."

"I'll help." He positioned himself behind her, bracketing her with his long legs and then he began the most divine massage of her scalp it melted her bones. Her hands rested weakly on his knees. "Oh. Mmm. That's incredible."

Even as he continued to massage, his lips touched the back of her neck as softly as a whisper. His fingers worked down through her scalp, stroking and kneading over her neck and shoulders. As her muscles relaxed, the heat in her belly intensified. His hands rolled and kneaded the flesh of her shoulders, and his face rested near her ear. When his tongue traced the silky shell, she shivered, her nipples immediately going to hard points she knew he must see through the thin top of her bikini. Her breathing accelerated.

"Lie down so I can massage your back." As she did, he reached past her for the bottle of almond oil. "May I untie your top?"

His voice rumbled, a deep vibration that sent waves of sensation straight to her core.

"Ciaran…"

"I need to be able to stroke from your neck down to your hips, love. That's all."

"All right." Her voice sounded thready, but she couldn't help it.

His fingers plucked the strings of her top and it fell away. Keeley forced herself to relax, her face turned sideways, resting on her hands. Out of the corner of her eye she saw him pour oil onto his palms and then rub them together. In the flickering candlelight of the cabin, his features took on an intense concentration. The only sound in the small room was the slick rubbing of his oiled palms and the erratic rhythm of her breathing.

She expected his touch to be heavy and forceful, but he stroked her skin lightly, running his fingertips from the base of her neck to just below the small of her back. Over and over, without her even realizing it, his touch grew firmer and deeper until she groaned with the intensity of the relaxation she felt all through her back. He shifted his weight to straddle her hips and for just an instant she felt the intimate bump of his erection as it brushed across her butt cheeks.

Keeley could do nothing to stifle the moan that escaped her. She wasn't sure where this was leading, but she had never experienced the heat and the wetness his touch ignited. A heavy, aching lethargy flowed out from her core until her entire body was one giant nerve ending. Her fingers itched to stroke over his body.

"That's it, love," he breathed near her ear as he continued to stroke and knead her back. His hands shifted more and more to her lower back and hips. "I want to massage your legs and your butt, baby. May I untie your bottoms?"

"Yes," she choked out. Anything to relieve the aching need! She felt swollen and wet between her legs, her nipples ached and she couldn't imagine anything she wanted more than to feel his hands on her butt and her thighs, or slipping between them.

"That's my girl," Ciaran murmured. "It feels good, doesn't it?"

"Oh yes." *Was that smoky whisper her?* What had happened to her not being ready for a lover? Right now all she could think about was having his fingers slide between the wet folds of her sex.

Was there just a faint tremor in his fingers as he untied the knots at each hip? She wasn't sure. And then she lost all track of thought as his big hands kneaded her bottom and the backs of her thighs. If she shifted just a little, she wondered, would his hands touch her? Touch the crease of her butt and slide farther down to her aching wetness?

"Keeley?" Ciaran's voice rumbled. "You okay with this?"

"Yes." Her voice was the barest whisper of sound. She almost cried out in frustration as his hands slipped farther down her legs to massage her calves, and then back again.

This time when his hands reached her bottom, they kneaded her butt cheeks and then stopped. She heard the harsh rasp of his breathing.

"God, Keeley," he ground out. "I have to stop. I promised I wouldn't...I have to stop!"

His hands squeezed her bottom once more. The berth shifted, and then there was silence. After a moment, Keeley rolled over, unconcerned with her nudity. He was gone.

"Ciaran?" She swung her feet to the floor, amazed she could stand at all as boneless as she felt. With a quick glance around she spied one of his shirts hanging on a peg on the wall. After lifting it off, she slipped the shirt over her head. It fell nearly to her knees, the short polo sleeves covering her arms to well below her elbows.

When she climbed the steps to the deck, she found him standing at the stern with his back toward her. She heard his ragged breathing and a deep groan.

"Ciaran?" she whispered.

He stilled, his posture stiff and his back still toward her. "Go away for a few minutes, Keeley," he ordered tautly.

She tried to see through the darkness, see what he was doing. "Did...I do something wrong?"

He groaned again. "No, sweetheart. Just seeing your gorgeous little ass and feeling how plump and soft it was under my hands...God! Just go below for a few minutes. I promised it wouldn't be about sex. I can't though. I can't be near you without wanting you. Let me take care of this. I just ache so badly."

Keeley blinked, then blinked again. "Oh."

"Yes, *oh*. Now go below for a few minutes."

She fled. She had felt his arousal earlier and hadn't really thought. Now all she could do was think, and her mind supplied a vivid picture of exactly what he was doing. But instead of revolting her, it sharpened the ache between her legs. Without thinking about it, without letting herself think about it, Keeley's lips parted and her fingers slid down until she touched herself. She whimpered as she made contact with her wet, swollen flesh.

She could see him, in her mind, standing on deck with his hand wrapped around his shaft, the oil from massaging her making his palm slick as he stroked the length of his erection from his balls to the tip. This was her imagination? It had to be, but it didn't feel like it. It felt like she was right there on deck with him, seeing the intense, almost pained expression on his handsome face, and then hearing his thoughts as well.

So hot. So soft and perfect. And I can smell her sex, smell the aroma of her juices. All I want to do is bury myself between her sweet thighs and hear her cry out in pleasure.

His hand moved faster, and Keeley's fingers

took up a rhythm of their own to match. Her thighs parted to allow her fingers better access, but then her breath caught on a sob.

****

On deck, Ciaran turned slowly, his cock still fisted in his hand. Slowly he pushed his shorts off until they dropped to the deck unheeded and forgotten and he walked back to the entrance to the cabin and down the steps, pulled as if bewitched. He stopped in the doorway, his gaze resting on Keeley's restless, frustrated expression. Her hand still partially covered her sex, but left enough uncovered he could see the glistening wetness he had created. He had done this to her, and now she didn't know how to finish it.

"Oh love," he crooned softly.

A tear slid from the corner of her eye. "I can't...I don't know..." she sobbed softly.

He crossed the cabin and knelt next to her. "I do, Keeley Ann. I do. Will you trust me? Will you let me?"

Her green eyes blazed at him through a veil of tears. "Please."

He picked her up, settled her across his lap and tilted her chin up. "You smell so good. Let me touch you and taste you and I'll make it better, I promise. I'll help you climax, just like before."

She shook her head. "I've never felt like this, never wanted to." Her eyes drifted down and his cock twitched in response, a drop of moisture glistening on the end. "What about..."

"Don't worry about me. This night's for you Keeley, just like it's always been."

He kissed her, deeply and passionately. It was a rougher kiss than any they shared so far, but when she met him without fear, he growled deep in his throat.

Easy, he reminded himself. He had never

attempted to make love to someone as inexperienced as Keeley. Never attempted to bring a woman pleasure based solely on emotional and physical need. The women he'd bedded in the past always understood the game and how it was played. But this was no game, and he found himself in the unexpected position of being nervous he would make a mistake with her.

He stripped her borrowed shirt over her head so she sat on his lap, naked flesh against naked flesh. For just an instant he closed his eyes and savored the feel of her round bottom nestled against him, the way her thigh rubbed his testicles and the base of his erection. With one arm supporting her back, he used his free hand to slide gently up and down her leg as he continued to kiss her deeply.

He laid her back again on the berth and returned to kissing her. His fingers tangled in her short hair as he plundered her mouth.

"Sweet, sweet Keeley. Touch me, love," he whispered against her lips. "Touch my chest where you bit me. Hell, touch me anywhere you want. I'm so close to coming right now, it doesn't matter."

Her eyes widened and then she smiled shyly against his cheek. She bit her lower lip and softly ran her fingers through his long hair. He watched her through slumberous eyes, the way her nipples tightened with desire for him and the soft flush to her pale skin. When his hands touched her breasts, she arched against him. There was no fear in her eyes. Their green depths darkened with desire and passion for him.

His. His Keeley. He had never experienced such emotion for a human, for anyone. His nerves stretched. He wanted to make this wonderful for her.

He eased his hand over her stomach until it slipped gently between her thighs. She stiffened, but only for a moment and then he felt the wonder of her surrender to him. Along with his lust, another emotion overwhelmed him. His chest tightened and he blinked away the sudden moisture in his eyes. His love. His mate.

She relaxed and let her thighs fall apart. His fingers stroked along the moist center of her before he slowly slipped his middle finger inside of her. When his thumb rubbed the bud of flesh nestled in the curls just above his slowly pumping finger, she jerked against him.

His breathing grew ragged and uneven. "All right?" he purred against her ear.

"Yes," she panted. "More Ciaran. I want more."

A soft chuckle rumbled through his chest. "Far be it from me to deny your request." He slipped an additional finger inside of her, continuing to stroke in and out of her tight passage as he kissed his way over her breasts and down across her stomach.

The smell of her! It was like the headiest of gardens, intoxicating and rich. He paused, his mouth just inches from her tender flesh and he stared in wonder at the dewy drops glistening among the dark curls.

"So pretty," he whispered and she arched up toward him. "That's right, love. I'm going to taste you and touch you, make you come for me. Only for me." He laved her with the flat of his tongue and his lips found the hard nub of flesh. Slowly, he began to suck and stroke her there, his rhythm matching what his fingers were doing inside of her until she writhed against him. Her low, keening cry built, filling the cabin.

The boat began to rock and pitch, the candles flickering and flaring. Ciaran raised his head and looked around in amazement, his dark eyes going back to Keeley, still in the throes of a magnificent orgasm. He laughed, the sound one of pure joy.

His.

"Do it," she urged him. "I want to feel you inside of me. Now Ciaran."

Her need was almost savage. Gone was the damaged woman in need of slow, careful attention. He lifted her hips, cupping her bottom in his hands and pushed his throbbing cock deeply inside of her. For a moment, he was afraid he was too big for her, but she stretched, accepting him and gloving him so he gasped and nearly climaxed.

It had never been like this before.

"Is this what you wanted, Keeley? Did watching me earlier make you want this?"

"Yes! Yes!" Behind them in the galley, he heard the wine bottle tip over. The candles blew out and then there was only the two of them thrusting hungrily against each other until their cries mingled, hers high and keening, his a hoarse shout of fulfillment before he fell away from her, nearly fainting from the intensity of his orgasm. Almost immediately, he gathered her against him, his hands stroking her, soothing her.

"Oh, Keeley, my love. Sweet, sweet. Are you all right?"

She snuggled against him and nodded. Her arms crept up around his neck and she pressed her cheek against his chest. For a moment, his breath caught. As he stroked from her back down to her slender hips, a tear rolled out of the corner of his eye. It was followed by another, then another. His breathing hitched, and he instantly stilled.

"Ciaran, what is it?" She looked up and touched the wetness on his cheeks wonderingly.

He buried his face in her hair. "Every time I touch you, I wonder why you're here. You make me feel things I've never felt. You make me believe I can do things I've never done. You make me want to be better than I am." He stopped and the hitch was back in his breathing. "I love you so damn much,

Keeley Ann McNamara. I don't know what I'd do if you left me."

"Shh." She stroked away the wetness on his cheeks. "I won't. I-I love you too."

He stilled and pulled back from her just a bit. In the glow of the moonlight, he searched her face, seeing the truth of her words from the soft, glowing look in her eyes and the tremble of her lips. Unable to stop himself, unwilling to deny himself, he lowered his mouth to hers, touching and tasting until his need made him press down harder against her lips. His tongue slid smoothly into her mouth, the tip touching her teeth and then tangling with her own tongue. For several minutes the only sounds inside the cabin were their soft moans against each other's mouths and the rustle of the comforter as their bodies moved and shifted, seeking to get even closer than before.

Ciaran's cock stiffened once more. He tried to ignore it. It was too soon. It would scare her off. He shifted away from her, more nervous than he'd ever been with a woman.

"Would you like something to drink?" he asked desperate for some excuse to step away for a few minutes so he could calm down. God, he couldn't want her again so soon. He'd never been this way with any other woman. Sure, with them he'd been able to last for hours, if necessary, but once he was done, he was done. He stared down at his rampant erection with something akin to horror. Far from calming down, he'd only grown stiffer.

"It's okay."

Keeley's quiet voice was just behind him, and he knew she'd slipped out of the berth too. Her hands slipped around his waist, her fingers twining just above the head of his penis, and she pressed her body against his back.

"It's too soon," he choked, staring down at her

156

hands so near his erection. She pressed a kiss to his back and her right hand slid down over his belly between his cock and his stomach. "Oh God." He groaned and closed his eyes for an instant. "Touch me, please Keeley, just touch me."

Somehow, she became the aggressor and all Ciaran could do was brace his legs slightly apart as he watched. Her delicate fingers encircled him, not quite meeting around his thickness. She flattened her palm against the sensitive underside and pressed him against his own stomach before she began massaging up and down his shaft. When her fingers rubbed across the head, he threw his head back and groaned.

"You like that?"

"Yes."

Her body pressed against his back, he felt the soft swell of her breasts, the hard nubs of her nipples.

"Tell me what else you like. Tell me what you want."

"Anything. Anything you do." His voice sounded weak and shaky even to his own ears, and he blushed in embarrassment. He was the aggressor. He was the one always in control, but he had lost control of this situation so now all he knew was the sensation of being a mindless, mass of nerves and heat. She continued to stroke him with one hand while her other slid from his belly, around his hip and over the firm flesh of his butt. When she squeezed and kneaded the muscles there, he jerked in her hand. Ciaran's head dropped forward. He stared at her hand working up and down and he groaned. Her fingers traced lightly down the crease of his butt and he was suddenly breathing as if he'd run a mile.

Keeley giggled and he laughed shakily. "Oh sweetheart, you are truly a witch. If you keep this up, I won't last much longer."

She giggled again. "Oh I definitely want to keep it up."

Now he glanced over his shoulder at her face and laughed. She was a constant surprise. "Then you had best get your hand out from between my butt cheeks and remove your other one from my dick. Otherwise, I'm going to lose it in just a minute."

She stuck her tongue out at him. "Spoilsport."

He lifted her to kiss her hard and fast on the mouth. "Light the candles, love, while I get us some more wine."

He went into the galley and grabbed a new bottle from the fridge. When he turned, he saw Keeley touch her finger to the wick of a candle. Flame glowed. She glided around the cabin, doing the same thing to each one and he watched her, fascinated once again. She caught him staring at her and flushed.

"How do you do that?"

She shrugged. "I don't know. I just do. I think about the heat and the flame, imagine my finger making the spark against the wick, and then it's there."

He poured wine and handed her glass to her. "Have you always been able to do that?"

"Yes, but Momma didn't like it. She wasn't comfortable with what Daddy and I could do. When she would go out, he would let me practice. Then after...after he died I didn't do it anymore. Only with Granddad. He made me practice."

She curled up in the corner of the berth, leaning back against the pillows. He set his glass on the shelf and sank down onto his side, his eyes traveling over her bare breasts, her flat stomach and on to the nest of curls between her legs. His still erect cock jumped, but Ciaran forced himself to ignore it.

"Made you practice?"

"I didn't want to," she said softly staring down into her wine. "They told me it wasn't normal; people would take me away and lock me up if they found out, so I just didn't do it."

Her face lost its laughter. Ciaran touched her thigh and stroked along its length. "If you touch me, I burst into flame, and you don't even need magic for that."

Her eyes met his and she laughed again. "I can see. It works for me too."

He leaned forward and sucked her breast into his mouth, teasing it, laving the pebbled nipple with his tongue and then releasing it to blow softly on it. "Like that?" He looked up to see such an intensely aroused look on her face he felt his testicles tighten in anticipation.

"Just like that."

Ciaran took her glass from her, set it aside and shifted into a half-kneeling, half-sitting position, his legs bent under him. He pulled her forward, his hands grasping her bottom. "Straddle me," he directed her softly. "I want to play."

****

She saw the hot, intense look in his eyes, the passionate fullness of his mouth and felt an answering tension in herself. "Yes. Play. That sounds good."

Putting her hands on either side of his face she leaned forward and kissed him quickly on the lips.

"What was that for?"

"For being you. For understanding, for making me feel normal."

His long fingers wrapped around the back of her neck, massaging almost roughly. "You are normal. Normal, beautiful and I love you." He kissed her hard. And then they simply stared at one another. Her hand slipped down, her fingers brushing over the mark on his chest.

"Does this mean you're mine now I've marked you?"

His hands stroked along her shoulders. "Everything I have—including me—is yours, Keeley Ann, for as long as you want them."

She slid her palms down his chest, over the ripple of muscle on his stomach and once again wrapped her hand around his engorged cock. "This too?" she teased.

He smiled. "Especially that."

As she stroked him he glided his hands slowly up and down her thighs. Her stroking intensified. He groaned and circled his hands around to begin kneading her bottom. She arched into his palms and he chuckled.

"You like that?"

She nodded, wordlessly and leaned her chest against him before dropping her forehead onto his shoulder. He stroked a finger down the silky crevice of her bottom until his fingers encountered the moist folds of her sex. She shivered, and he laughed. "You do like that, don't you?"

"Yes," she whispered. "It feels different when you touch me from behind."

Ciaran stopped and took a deep breath. "Lie down, Keeley. Let me touch you. If you don't like anything I do, tell me."

Her mouth felt swollen and soft and he kissed her quickly before easing her onto her stomach. Reaching up next to her, he grabbed a couple of pillows and tucked them under her hips, lifting her bottom. The position opened her, made her vulnerable to him in a way she hadn't been before. Keeley couldn't stifle the whimper that rose to her lips, but it was far from fear. Now there was only arousal.

"You are so damn alluring." He grabbed the massage oil and poured some over his hands, rubbing them together to warm them before he began to slowly massage her again, but this time his fingers slipped between her cheeks, a little deeper with each pass. When she groaned her approval he slowly slipped his index finger down until he touched the dewy flesh of her sex. I'm going to massage you again, a little differently than before. Okay?"

When she nodded, he reached forward again to grab the massage oil. Moments later he began to slowly stroke her again, his hands molding and rubbing the flesh of her thighs before he skimmed back and forth with the tips of his fingers, teasing her sensitive flesh. His lips touched her once more on her belly before his fingers slid down to stroke her aching sex. Keeley groaned her approval and he slowly slipped his index finger inside.

"Oh, Ciaran, it feels so good."

****

His chest heaved as he knelt between her spread thighs and guided the swollen head of his penis along her slit until it slipped slickly into her tight passage. As soon as he was fully seated inside her, he grasped her butt in his broad hands and stroked powerfully in and out of her.

Sweat glistened on both their bodies in the warm light of the candles. As her muscles contracted against him, he cried out, nearly coming right then. He had to stop for a minute and force himself to breathe slowly and regularly. He stroked his fingers down the slender line of her breasts and belly and realized his hands trembled.

He leaned over her, kissing along her neck to the sensitive flesh near her ear. "Everything okay still?" he asked shakily.

"Yes. It feels so incredible."

She clenched around him. This time he gasped as both of them lifted off the bed. His balls tightened and every thought left his head as sensation rocked through him. With a groan, he pumped his hips into her. As his body ceased shuddering, he grabbed her hips and rolled onto his back, still buried deep inside her. Easing her fingers out of the way, he stroked her swollen flesh, keeping his touch as light as a feather. When he felt her once again tighten down on him, he growled deep in his throat.

It had never ever been like this. He built to another climax and realized they were both lying several inches off the bed, suspended there by her thoughts alone.

"Come for me, Keeley," he panted. "You're so pretty when you come for me. Your whole body shakes with it. God, baby, I'm going to come again."

This time it was him who shouted out his pleasure. He shook with the force of his climax before he slipped from inside her and pulled her close, wrapping her in his arms as he rolled them both to their sides. He continued to whisper words of love to her until her eyelids drooped tiredly.

When she relaxed, he pulled a folded cover over them both. He never imagined when he picked her up they would make so much progress. He had hoped the massage would get her used to his touch, but he never imagined she would let him make love to her so completely, so intimately. He held her tenderly.

He wanted to marry her. He paused for a moment in amazement as he realized he would do anything to make her happy, to protect her. She was his mate, and there would be no others now, not anymore. He couldn't even imagine wanting to touch any other woman. Now all he had to do was convince her.

Chapter Eleven

Keeley stretched languorously, feeling the gentle tilt to the deck and the roll of the hull. With a soft sigh, she opened her eyes to find sunlight streaming through the porthole. She smiled. She had spent the night with him. Her heart swelled with love and desire as she remembered just how they spent a good part of that night. She slipped from underneath the comforter and made her way to the head. There was a small shower cubicle there, so she stepped inside and adjusted the spray before sticking her face beneath it. After washing her hair and her body, Keeley dried off and returned to the cabin to look for her clothes.

Ciaran had left them neatly folded on top of a trunk next to the berth. She tilted her head and smiled as she stared at the stack of clothing. Her experience of men was limited, but neatness was not something she immediately associated with them.

She slipped her bikini on, smiling softly as she remembered how Ciaran's fingers trembled when he untied her bottoms. Never would she have imagined him to be such a tender, considerate lover, but he was. With a quick shake of her head, she fluffed her fingers through her spiky hair and climbed up on deck. She spotted him at the wheel. He must have sensed her presence because he turned as soon as she reached the deck and smiled slowly and seductively. When Keeley blushed, he grinned and laughed, throwing back his head and letting the wind lift his long hair off his shoulders to blow in tendrils around his face.

He looked happy and carefree, two words she would never have used to describe the man he'd been just a month ago.

"Come, love." He held out one arm to her, then wrapped her tightly against his side and leaned down to kiss her. Other than the whistle of the wind and the sound of the water flowing past the hull, it was amazingly quiet. Keeley stretched against him, running her hands over his bare chest.

"Are you real?" she murmured softly. "Can you possibly be real or have I just imagined what I want to be?"

"I'm real, love." He placed her hand over the bruise on his chest. "Haven't you already marked me with your witch's brand? I'm your slave for as long as you want me."

She touched his cheek. "Forever, Ciaran."

His eyes darkened with passion and possession. "Move in with me, Keeley." When she hesitated, he continued, "I know it's fast, but I want to marry you. If you need that first before you will, then we'll do that, but I want you with me. I want you sleeping at my side. I want to roll over in the middle of the night and feel you next to me where I can touch you and love you. I want to find you in the middle of the day, sneak you into the pantry and bury my face between your thighs..."

"I get it," she laughed.

His finger slid along the thin barrier of her bikini bottoms. "So? What do you say?"

When she turned toward him, his hand slipped lower until he stroked her intimately. "I say stop by the house so I can pack a bag," she murmured in a husky, faintly breathless voice. "I'll sort everything else out later."

He smiled as he caressed her then dipped his head to kiss her softly.

"Ciaran! You can't play with me and sail *The*

Prankster, too."

He sighed and straightened. "Too right. However, once we tie up in the marina, we can certainly go below and play for a while."

Keeley blushed. He smiled at her. "Go. Away from me before I drop sail right here in the middle of the bay and make love to you right here on deck."

She moved nimbly forward and stretched out on her back on the padded mat near the bow. With her arms behind her head and one leg slightly bent, she watched the wind fill the sails. Higher up fluffy white clouds dotted the sky. Keeley couldn't remember when she had felt so happy and so complete.

Ciaran. She pictured him with his long silky dark hair, his eyes so dark a brown they were nearly black, fringed by thick lashes. A straight nose, broad cheekbones and a mouth that was at once soft and firm with its thin upper lip and a full lower lip. His neck was as muscular as his broad shoulders. She could almost feel the hard heat of his golden skin as her hands slipped from his shoulders to his firm, full chest, his flat stomach. She remembered the feel of his hard, muscular ass filling her hands. And his legs. Long strong thighs blended smoothly into powerful calves and large, arched feet. Everything about him screamed raw, masculine power. She saw again the way his aroused body gleamed in the candlelight.

With a groan she rolled over onto her stomach. As she shifted her arms to cradle her head, her sensitized nipples rubbed against the pad on which she lay. Lord! How long did it take to get back to the marina? When she thought she could wait no longer, she heard the whine of the motor that controlled lowering and stowing *The Prankster's* mainsail. The deck flattened out as the ship slowed and Ciaran started the engine.

Keeley sat and slipped her feet back into her sneakers. If she helped him tie up, then they could go below much sooner. She made her way aft, smiling at Ciaran as he stood at the wheel, guiding *The Prankster* toward the dock and cutting the engine to allow them to float in. With the first bump on the dock, Keeley hopped onto the wooden planks and caught the line Ciaran threw her. Once *The Prankster* was secured at both bow and stern, she jumped back into the arms he held out to her. He laughed as he let her slender body slide along the length of his.

"Come with me love," he murmured in her ear. She felt his cock already pressing against his shorts. "There are a few other things I'd like to show you."

She wrapped her arms around his neck and pressed her face against his throat. "All I could think about on the way back was touching you. I can still feel your fingers inside me from last night."

"I can give you much more than that." His voice was already rough with desire. Ciaran stroked her cheek. "Damn, Keeley. I never thought I would feel this way about someone. Do you know how special you are?"

"Show me," she whispered. She shivered in anticipation. As soon as they stepped inside the cabin, Ciaran kicked off his shoes and pushed his shorts down to reveal his rampant arousal. Thick with a nearly purple head, Keeley loved the way it bounced against his stomach as he stepped over to the berth and stripped back the covers. She swallowed as she stared at it. He laid back on the berth, one leg bent and one arm resting on his knee. With his other hand, he gently rubbed the length of his shaft.

"Is this what you were thinking about?" he asked on a soft chuckle. She nodded, swallowing at the sight of him touching himself. "Take your top off

Keeley. I want to see those pretty little breasts of yours. Touch them for me."

She licked her lips again, her gaze still focused on Ciaran's slowly stroking hard. Her bikini top fell unheeded to the floor. She rubbed her hands over her breasts, and then lowered her lashes as she rolled her nipples between her thumbs and index fingers.

"That's it, love," Ciaran praised her. "Now slide one of your hands down and touch yourself. Are you wet yet?"

"Yes. Oh, this is so hot."

He smiled tenderly as he met her eyes. "For me too. Slide the bottoms off, Keeley so I can play with that sweet derriere of yours."

She moaned, doing what he asked without question. When the bottoms dropped to the cabin floor, the movement of his hand increased.

"Lean over the chair, baby. Put your arms along the back of it and spread your legs."

She did what he asked, feeling vulnerable when he moved behind her. "Damn, sweetheart. You glisten like dew in the morning."

As he continued to describe how she affected his senses, he slid a finger along her folds and slipped it inside. He pumped it in and out, his other hand rubbing over her bottom. When he added a second finger, he bent over her to place a kiss on each round cheek.

"Ciaran!"

"Don't you like that?"

"I don't know," she admitted breathlessly as his fingers continued to tease her. He moved closer and rubbed against her. "Mmm."

"Is that a good mmm or a bad mmm?"

"Oh, good. Yes."

He bent over her, kissing and nibbling the back of her neck before his lips and teeth traced a path along her spine to the small dimples at the top of her buttocks. While his fingers continued to thrust and stroke he knelt behind her.

"Turn around and let me taste you."

He seated her in the chair and pulled her hips forward until her thighs rested over his broad shoulders. His dark eyes met hers and he smiled. Keeley's lips parted and her breath panted between them as he lowered his face to her. He kissed her intimately, sensation piling on sensation until Keeley thought she could take no more.

****

Ciaran watched her, emotion making his voice husky. "Why don't we take this to the bed, Keeley Ann, where we can both be more comfortable."

She nodded, her body still quivering with a surfeit of desire. He smiled slowly at her and rose to his feet in front of her. When her eyes lowered to where his erection throbbed, she licked her lips.

"You have no idea what that does to me," he growled.

"Show me," she whispered.

He laughed with pure enjoyment as he picked her up and set her on the berth. "Get on your hands and knees. I'm going to love you the way the Silkie take their mates."

She quivered as she did what he wanted. He tugged several pillows under her hips to support her, all the time softly kissing her neck, her shoulders. He ran the tip of his tongue down the delicate line of her spine.

"I've dreamed of this so often, Keeley Ann. I love how soft and white your skin is, the firmness of the muscles underneath. My feisty Faerie. But sometimes, like now, when I hold you and realize how small you are, I worry. I don't want to hurt you. I would never do anything to hurt you."

Once more he slipped his hand between her

thighs, stroking and rubbing her, spreading her juices. Her fragrance was spicy and just faintly musky and he wanted nothing more than to bury his nose between her legs in the soft curls there and inhale. It seemed he still had some of his Silkie instincts. His hands parted her cheeks and she gasped in surprise as his tongue slid along her swollen vulva.

"Please, Ciaran. Please."

"You want me in there, baby? You want me to take you from behind? To mate with you?"

"Yes. Oh yes!"

He leaned over and kissed her bottom as he slid his fingers in and out. With his free hand, he stroked himself, reveling in the sensation of his fingers easing in and out of her and the friction of his fist on his rock hard dick.

"Oh God, Ciaran, it feels so good. All I can think about is having you sliding in and out of me, filling me."

Her words made his cock jump and his balls tighten. God, if he didn't get inside her soon, he would come all over her beautiful little bottom. He began leaking and realized he wasn't helping himself calm down at all. He crooned to her breathlessly, kissing her back, running his free hand around her hip and over her stomach until he rubbed the spot he knew would send her over the edge. She jumped and moaned, her bottom thrusting toward his stroking fingers.

"That's it," he purred and arched over her. The Silkie half of his nature wanted to latch onto her with his teeth, to dominate her as he would if they were both in seal form. He fought back the urge, afraid he might frighten her.

"Now, Ciaran. I want you to take me now!"

He growled and pushed her legs farther apart before he stepped in close. He realized he was shaking as he guided himself between her cheeks and rubbed his tip back and forth along her slick opening. He was so close to losing it, losing the control at the core of who and what he was.

With his breath coming nearly in sobs, he positioned the swollen head of his cock at her opening. She gasped, and then it was his turn to suck in his breath as she pushed back against him, forcing him to penetrate.

They both cried out with pleasure.

"Easy," he commanded breathlessly. "I'm so close."

His voice trembled, an audible sign of the iron control he desperately tried to hold onto as he bracketed her hips in his hands and eased his cock in and out of her.

He heard her sobbing, but not with pain, with the incredible sensations this position brought to both of them. When she slipped her hand underneath her, touching them both, he moaned and grunted, shoving his hips forward forcefully. She arched and roared into another orgasm, her neck open and vulnerable. No longer able to stop himself he bent over her and closed his teeth on the nape of her neck.

Ciaran felt the force of her climax as she clamped down on him. He stopped thrusting for a moment while she rode out the sensations. His eyes were glazed with passion as he watched her writhe beneath him, his shaft still buried inside her while his teeth held her.

He released her and stroked his fingers lightly from the bruise at her hairline down to her bottom, chuckling as that light touch on her super-sensitized skin sent her rocketing into yet another orgasm.

He couldn't believe how perfectly matched and attuned to each other they were. His hands brushed along her thighs, and this time as her body gathered to come yet again, he felt a warm wind whip around them, like a thousand hands touched and caressed him exactly as he did her.

It was the magic inside her, he realized. She was sharing with him what she felt. All he could do was bend over her, his hands braced on the berth. Even as he stroked in and out of her, he felt the fullness she experienced inside himself. He groaned. He sobbed as he thrust back in and out again, feeling the glide and the pressure she felt along with his own sensations.

"Keeley, love! I don't know how you're doing this to me, but please, please don't stop. It's so damn incredible."

"Roll me over, Ciaran. Roll me over. I want to see your face while you make love to me."

He turned her slowly, his cock never leaving her. When she was at last lying on her back, he hooked her knees over his forearms and continued his smooth rhythm. Because of the sensation she created, he shoved her farther up the bunk so he could crawl onto it with her, afraid his legs wouldn't support him.

She watched him intently. "Come on, love," she crooned to him. He could do nothing to hide the tears rolling down his face. "Love me and let me love you. Do you like it?"

He could only nod, completely beyond speech as he felt her emotions and feelings along with his own. His slow thrusts speeded up until his control shattered. With a broken cry, he arched against her, spilling himself deep inside her.

He slipped from her and collapsed at her side, pulling her into his arms. Tremors shook him from head to toe. "Oh sweetheart," he gasped hoarsely. "Oh my sweet, sweet Keeley. I love you so much."

She stroked the hair back from his face and cradled his cheek against her breast. Tears rolled down his lean cheeks and he realized again just how greatly she'd affected him—changed him.

"I love you too, Ciaran. When I thought I never would or could love anyone, you came into my life and woke me up."

His arms circled her. "Sleep for a while. Sleep with me. Then we'll go home."

Home. The thought whispered inside his head. That sounded so good. It sounded so normal.

Chapter Twelve

He put her with him, the only option from his perspective. The house had been designed with a master suite that occupied nearly one full wing. As he led her through it, he realized a little uncomfortably just how huge it was compared to what she was used to.

Made up of two bedrooms, it also boasted a sitting room and a huge bathroom complete with walk-in closets between the two rooms. Separate doors led from the bedrooms into the sitting room and into the bathing and dressing areas. Keeley looked at it in amazement and then at Ciaran.

"This suite is bigger than the whole house where Granddad and I lived. Why would you buy something so huge when it was just you?"

His gaze slid over to the window where the *Skerry* was visible at anchor. "It was to prove a point, Keeley Ann. It was to prove I didn't need them, just like they didn't seem to need me."

She walked up behind him and wrapped her arms around his waist as she leaned her cheek against his muscular back. "Oh baby!" She was silent for a minute. "Did it work?"

"No." His voice was only a whisper of sound. "Damn it. As much as I tried to tell myself I didn't need them, didn't want them. I did. I do."

He wrapped his arms around her. It was time to be honest with her about what was coming. "My father and Cayden came to see me at *The Prankster* yesterday morning, Keeley. Riordan, King of our people, has called a meeting of the Council of Lords for the end of this month."

"About you?" she whispered softly.

"Yes." He stroked her hair. "My mother wants them to reconsider their decision. I'll have to go. It might take several days." He raked a hand through his long hair. "There's always a lot of ceremony that goes with it."

Keeley looked into his eyes and saw what he didn't want to say, so she gave voice to it instead. "And I can't be there."

He lowered his head until his chin rested on the top of hers. "I'm sorry, baby. Until I'm accepted back in, only I may appear."

"And afterwards?"

His arms tightened. "We'll be together, Keeley. No matter what. We'll be together. I'll never let you go."

She hugged him tightly, but in her mind, she remembered back to the first time they went sailing together and he told her the legend of the Silkie. How humans and Silkies couldn't be together forever because the human couldn't live in the sea and the Silkie could never truly be happy on land. If only there were some magic to make it happen.

Could there be some hope for them since she was part Faerie? Keeley wrapped her arms around Ciaran and burrowed against him. How could he have become so vital to her?

"I have to go into the city tomorrow on business." His deep voice rumbled. "Would you like to come with me or stay here?"

She smiled at him. "I'll stay here. Maybe I can convince your cook to prepare a very special dinner for you. I hear she's a real wizard in the kitchen."

"And the most amazing witch in bed." He laughed, shaking off the melancholy mood that overtook him when he looked out the window and saw the *Skerry* anchored in the bay.

She arched a brow at him. "You enjoyed the last bit of magic so much, I think we'll have to experiment with it more often."

His dark brows rose into the shorter strands of hair hanging over his forehead. "You'll kill me, but I'm a willing sacrifice."

Keeley laughed. "I'm a Faerie. I have my ways of keeping you alive."

"Right now I'm starving. Am I allowed in the kitchen?"

"Of course."

"Good because I was hoping I could find a quick snack in the pantry."

"Did you have something in mind? Sweet or salty?"

"Both."

"Mmm."

****

He brought her to two amazing and noisy climaxes before he finally buried himself inside her. She was backed against one of the pantry shelves, her legs wrapped around him as he pounded into her so furiously she was afraid they would knock everything onto the floor. She would never get enough of the feel of him sliding in and out of her slick core.

"I think it fair to tell you," he panted. "Jonathan might not be too happy with us."

"Why's that?" Keeley grunted.

"He likes to watch."

"He *what*?" Keeley gasped and laughed.

"He likes to watch," Ciaran mumbled. "Surely you realized that."

She reached behind his head and pulled the string on the light switch to turn it on. A blush stained Ciaran's cheekbones. "You *know* and you let him?"

Ciaran shrugged. "It makes him happy. He

doesn't want to take part, just observe."

"And I thought you were just trying to piss me off."

"Well there was that, but I caught him early on in his employment peeping. He doesn't want to do more than that. He's got a full social life of his own, but he seems to enjoy the show, so I let him. The Silkie have never really suffered many hang-ups about public sex. Lately, though, he's hit a dry spell."

Keeley was quiet for a moment, taking in the idea. She recalled how both Jonathan and the maid often came back to the kitchen with play by play on what was going on. She thought it was simply an unavoidable circumstance.

"I've shocked you, haven't I?" Ciaran's gaze searched her face.

She let her head fall back. "Not as much as you might think."

It was Ciaran's turn to look wide-eyed. He was quiet for a while as he stroked her cheek and her shoulders. Finally, he shook his head. "I can't believe you're not blowing a gasket, much less that you look faintly interested." He paused. "Would you...?"

She grinned and shook her head. "Maybe, eventually, but right now I want it to be just the two of us."

Ciaran smiled. "Then by all means, let us finish." His face tightened with passion and he slammed himself in and out of her, growling as his climax tightened his nuts and he once again spent himself inside her.

****

"No! No! Don't make me. I don't wanna. I don't wanna!"

Ciaran's eyes snapped open when he heard Keeley's screams and felt her thrashing next to him. He glanced at the clock. Almost three. They'd only been sleeping a couple of hours.

"Keeley, love," he said gently. "You're having a nightmare. Wake up."

It took her some time. He switched on the bedside lamp, watching her in its muted glow.

"It's not real, love."

She closed her eyes and rubbed her hands over her face, then pulled her knees up until she could rest her chin on top of them. After a couple of deep breaths, she opened her eyes. "I'm sorry."

"You wanna talk about it?"

She shrugged. "It's an old dream. I thought they were gone, but ever since that damn card came in the mail after Granddad's death, I've been seeing him again in my nightmares."

"Frank?" He should have tracked the bastard down and killed him. Instead, he'd decided to let it drop, let it stay in Keeley's past where it belonged. Ciaran brushed the hair off her face. "What can I do to help?"

She took hold of his hand and held it against her cheek. "You already have. You've made me whole, Ciaran. You helped me realize just how much power I'd let him continue to have over me. But not anymore. You've replaced those awful memories with new ones. You've shown me in just a couple of days what it means to be loved in every sense of the word."

"Come here," he growled softly. "So why the nightmares?"

She shrugged. "I guess part of me is still worried I'll open the door one day to find him standing there."

He shifted and hauled her between his legs so she could lay against his chest while he wrapped his arms around her. "Forget Frank Wells, Keeley. He's part of your past. Even if he did show up, you're strong enough to handle him. You're not a kid anymore, and he has no place in our future."

Whatever we have left to us. Ciaran tried to banish the thought, but he couldn't. The mere possibility the Silkie Lords might return his pelt kindled his longing for the sea. He kissed Keeley's delicate nape where he had marked her. If they did, where would that leave his little Faerie? He wouldn't think about it now. This was their time to be together, and he would give her everything he was. He would pour it into her, because he feared what would happen if he was offered his pelt.

So many forgot. After being human for so long, they simply forgot to return if they were ever given back their pelts, ever allowed once again into the sea. Staying in seal form was seductive. It was a carefree existence with no worries other than hunting, and the food was plentiful.

His arms tightened around her.

"Ciaran?" she looked over her shoulder at him. "Are you all right?"

He nodded. "Yeah." He bent his head and let his lips trace across her cheek. "I was thinking of a way to help you get to sleep."

"And what would that be?"

"I never really finished that massage last night."

She laughed. "You didn't? It sure left me boneless."

He grinned into her silky hair. "Oh no. You see I only got one side done. I still need to massage your front."

He watched in absolute fascination as both of her nipples instantly hardened in front of his eyes. "I can see you like that idea," he chuckled then groaned as she rubbed her bottom against his already half-hard cock.

"Only if I get to do my own massage afterward."

"It feels to me like it's already started."

Keeley turned over on her stomach on top of his recumbent form. Her green eyes held his as she smiled and slowly slid down, pressing intermittent kisses to his hard belly and the arrow of hair leading down to his cock. "I get to go first then." She squeezed her small breasts together so they enveloped his shaft and rubbed. After licking his stomach and blowing on the places her tongue touched, she looked up at him. "What do you think so far?"

He smiled at her. "I think you know a lot about massage so I should simply observe and learn."

Keeley laughed. "Smart man. Feel free to comment on any of my techniques."

She lowered her head and slipped him between her lips and into her mouth. Ciaran threw back his head and moaned. His hands fisted in her hair as she continued to take him deeper. While she caressed his hip with one hand, her other cupped his testicles and gently rolled them in her palm.

Ciaran's breathing grew heavy and hoarse. "Oh sweetheart! I can't take much of this!"

Slowly she released him and smiled. Ciaran yanked her up his body and devoured her mouth. He felt wild and knew his orgasm was close. Lifting her, he put her thighs on his shoulders. "Grab the headboard," he ordered and buried his face between her legs. He drew in her musky essence before he began laving her with the flat of his tongue. He teased her with his teeth and sucked the small nub at her core into his mouth. She was as sweet as ambrosia, and he ached to fill her. As he continued to suckle her, Keeley's cries echoed in the big bedchamber.

"Let it go and come for me," he urged and buried his face once more between her thighs. His tongue stabbed into her entrance. Her body began to shake. Ciaran kept his hands up supporting her back as she arched toward him.

He felt nearly overwhelmed with the need to

stamp her as his. Almost roughly he pushed her down on the bed, yanked her legs apart and grabbed hold of his aching cock. Sliding the swollen head along her slit, he found what he was looking for and shoved forward, smiling at her moan of pleasure.

Every thought left his brain but the need to spill himself into her tight, welcoming wetness. His. Forever, she was his. When she screamed again with the force of another climax, he ground his hips into her in a circular motion, grabbed her butt cheeks in his big hands and pummeled into her. It was not only an act of love, but one of desperation.

As he hunched over her, his hips jerking to push out the last of what he had to give, he gasped, "I love you so damn much."

****

He was already gone when she woke. He'd left her a note weighted down with a crystal figure of a seal. It was simple and to the point: *Think of me until tonight. C*

Keeley smiled lazily and stretched. The bed felt huge without him in it. Was it possible to become so attuned to someone in such a short time? To be fair, she had to admit she'd always been aware of him. Even disliking him, there was always an unwilling element of desire in her. She now realized it had made her even more critical of everything about him. When had it started to change? The night he fired her? Or the night he danced with her? She shook her head. It hardly mattered now. It was what it was. She agreed to move in with him.

For all his tender gestures, when it came to the way he made love, gentleness never entered into it. He was rough, demanding, and thorough. Keeley loved it, just as she loved the way he responded to her so eagerly. All she had to do was look at him and it was enough. It was incredibly empowering and also incredibly humbling a man as dominant as

Ciaran would be willing to do whatever she asked of him.

Keeley crossed the plush carpet to the cool, tiled splendor of the master bath. The room was nearly as large as the living room in her cottage. As she showered, she decided she would take Ciaran's day in the city as an opportunity to begin packing her things. She could not yet face packing her grandfather's belongings. It was simply too soon.

Jonathan was in the kitchen enjoying a cup of coffee and the paper when she came in. Keeley smiled at the butler and waved him back into his seat when he would have risen.

"Would you like me to fix you anything?" he inquired stiffly.

Keeley grinned. "No. I believe I can handle that." She poured herself a cup of coffee and put a couple of slices of bread in to toast. After buttering them and adding some jam, she placed them on a plate and brought her breakfast over to the table. She sensed Jonathan's discomfort and finally cleared her throat. When he lowered his paper, she reached over to gently touch the back of his hand.

"I hope you will welcome me here. I've always enjoyed your company. Just because Ciaran and I are lovers, it doesn't mean anything needs to change." She looked at him levelly. "I want things to be just as they always have been. Okay?"

"Yes. Thank you, Miss Keeley." There was a faint blush on his cheekbones and she smiled, feeling like he really did understand what she'd been trying to say. She might not be quite at the point where she wanted an audience, but if it happened by accident, and it certainly could as often as Ciaran reached for her, she didn't want Jonathan to feel awkward.

With a contented sigh, she went back to munching her toast and drinking her coffee. When she was through, she stood and dusted off her shorts. "I'm going over to Granddad's house to pack more of my things. There are some other errands I need to run as well, so I'll be gone until this afternoon."

Jonathan looked up. "Do you need any help, Miss?"

"No. I'll take Ciaran's SUV and put everything in myself."

Less than an hour later she was in her bedroom at Granddad's house packing her clothing when she heard a knock on the door. Keeley ran lightly down the stairs. Through the window she saw Stephie standing on the front porch. Keeley ripped open the front door and gave her friend an enthusiastic hug and a kiss.

Stephie stepped back with a raised brow. "I take it the bikini worked?"

Keeley laughed and pulled her inside the house. "Oh better than even I could have predicted."

With her hands on her hips, Stephie glared. "So young lady, would you care to explain where you've been for the past two days?"

Keeley twirled around. "Having every part of my body touched and licked by the most gorgeous man." The thought of it made her skin heat until she thought she'd have to fan herself.

Stephie flopped down into a chair. "Damn. I pick up guys and all they want to do is fondle my breasts, but you find someone who licks you *all* over?"

Keeley nodded her confirmation. "Every inch. But Stephie, if you would let guys take you out more than once or twice they might get beyond your tits. You have to admit most men would find them fascinating. I've always thought you'd be the perfect centerfold, and you wouldn't even need silicone or airbrushing."

Stephie blushed. "That's nice you think that, but it's not all it's cracked up to be. You've got bumps that let you go braless while I've had to harness myself in since I was ten. Do you know what it's like to have every boy in the fifth grade never look higher than your chest? And do you remember that horrible time on the beach when Taylor Barton's friend stole my bikini top?"

God! How could she have forgotten? That's where she remembered Taylor from even though it had been his friend...what was his name? Geoff. Geoff Sanderson.

Keeley looked at her friend, for once really noticing how painful it must be. "You could always have breast reduction surgery, Steph, but at the very least, you should stick with someone long enough to let him see more than your breasts and your blonde hair."

Stephie grimaced. "In theory, I know. But I don't exactly see guys lining up for the job."

Keeley tilted her head. "Maybe you just refuse to look."

Stephie made a face. "Enough about me. Where have you been?"

"We spent the first night on his sailboat. Last night we were at his house. He's asked me to move in with him."

Stephie frowned. "You're not going to, right? That's awfully sudden."

Keeley looked back toward the stairs. "Actually, I was upstairs packing some of my things. Ciaran had to go into the city today, so it seemed like a good opportunity."

"Keeley..." Concern colored Stephie's voice as she drew out her friend's name. "Don't you think all of this is moving just a little too fast?"

She spread her hands as she looked at Stephie. "I trust him. I love him. Stephie, he's already asked me to marry him. I'm the one who is being cautious." She could see she had clearly shocked her friend.

Ciaran's reputation was well-known and well-deserved. He'd made no bones about the women he escorted. But when it came right down to it, she didn't care. She believed him when he said he loved her, and she knew deep inside her those were not words he took lightly or said casually. "I'm moving in with him."

Ever practical, Stephie knew when she was beat. She shrugged her shoulders. "I'll help you pack."

"That's why I love you, Stephie." Keeley grinned.

"I know."

"I'm finding you a guy. Next thing on my list."

Stephie snorted. "You take care of you."

****

Ciaran crossed his legs and steepled his hands in front of him. He hated wearing a suit, but sometimes it was necessary. He found it particularly useful when dealing with his attorneys. Pompous asses. Why was it many human men seemed to think a few gray hairs at the temples magically enhanced their brain capacity? And everyone under the age of thirty was still thinking only with their dick? Granted, his dick had done a lot of thinking for him, but certainly not all of it.

"I believe you heard me correctly, Jim," Ciaran said smoothly, knowing it would irritate the older man he used his first name so casually. "I want a new will drawn up that leaves everything to Keeley McNamara. I want it done, signed, notarized—whatever the hell has to be done to it to make it fucking official—before the end of this month, and yes I do realize that's only a week away. I want a bank account set up in her name." He slid a folded piece of paper across the desk. "Transfer this amount of money into it."

"Mr. Clifton..." The attorney was shaking his head as he looked at the figure on the paper.

184

Ciaran continued to stare at him unblinkingly.

"As you wish, sir."

Every line of the man's posture radiated his disapproval, but Ciaran didn't give a shit. He must make sure if anything happened to him as a result of the council's decision Keeley would be taken care of. He stood and handed Jim Belmont a sealed envelope. "Should anything happen to me, give this to Miss McNamara as soon as possible."

Belmont again shook his head. "You act as if you're expecting something to happen."

Ciaran smiled faintly. "Maybe I'm simply hoping preparation will be my insurance against it. Good afternoon."

He left the chrome and glass offices, rode the elevator downstairs and emerged from the relative quiet of the interior into the noise of the streets. Horns honking, sirens blaring in the distance, people shouting and for just a moment, he swayed, his senses assaulted. How quickly he had become used to the quiet of the island. Even now he longed to be back with Keeley, standing on the point overlooking the bay at sunset or sailing *The Prankster* back to the cove. He would hold her against him, listen to the quiet rhythm of her heart and the slap of the water against the hull and he would feel whole.

"Hey buddy! You mind stepping out of the doorway?"

Ciaran barely looked at the guy glaring at him impatiently before he strode toward the parking garage and found the Porsche. Keeley. He would go back to her, make love to her until she screamed with pleasure. His cock stirred. Easy boy. Just a few more hours.

****

Keeley moved her things into the room that was supposed to be hers in the master suite. Mary helped her unpack. As Keeley looked at her meager wardrobe inside the huge walk-in closet, she laughed. "Wow! Can anyone actually own enough clothes to fill one of these?"

Mary giggled. "Check this out." She opened the door of Ciaran's closet and flicked the light switch. "Judge for yourself, Miss."

Keeley's eyes widened at the suits, slacks, jeans, dress shirts, casual shirts, sweaters, and ties. Pair after pair of shoes were neatly lined up on one end. Most of the time she'd seen him he certainly didn't have shoes on, and often barely any clothes. She giggled. "Well. I guess that answers that question. Perhaps I need to order a different colored cook's jacket for every night of the week. I could team it with some brightly colored Crocs and be just like Mario."

Mary giggled again. "I don't think Mr. Clifton would be nearly as fascinated if you were just like Mario."

There was a knock at the door and then Jonathan entered. "There is a woman to see you downstairs, Miss Keeley. She says she is Mr. Clifton's mother."

Keeley reeled. Catriona Clifton had come to Ciaran's house? To see her? She looked down at her grubby cutoffs and cropped T-shirt.

"Tell her I'll be right down, Jonathan. Offer her something to eat and drink."

"As you wish."

Keeley stared at Mary. "Help! I can't go down to see her looking like this. I'm filthy."

"Hop in the shower. I'll find something for you to wear."

Keeley peeled her clothes off where she stood while Mary turned on the shower and adjusted it. "There you go. I'll find you a sundress and some panties in your things."

"Thank you."

Less than ten minutes later, Keeley entered the sunroom where Jonathan had seated Catriona Clifton.

"Good afternoon, Mrs. Clifton. I'm afraid you've missed Ciaran. He went into the city today."

Catriona smiled, her deep green eyes alight with humor. "I actually came to see you. I believe my son has told you about the coming meeting of the Council of Silkie Lords."

Keeley nodded. "How do you know? Ciaran told me you don't have contact with each other."

Catriona smiled. "The bond between a mother and her children is nearly as close as between a woman and her mate. I think you understand when I say I am sometimes able to see things, sense things?"

Keeley blushed, thinking of the times that had happened between Ciaran and her. Catriona laughed, a merry sound that made Keeley blush even more.

"Ah, I see you do. I lost touch with him for a while; he became expert at cutting himself off from me, from us, until he began to fall in love with you. Make no mistake, he is totally and completely infatuated. It is that way with true mates. Carrick and I share that, so do Cayder and Annabel. I am happy Ciaran has found what could make a difference to him. It's the reason I asked the Council to take another look at their decision and see how my son has changed. I believe there's a very good chance when the Lords meet next week, they will allow Ciaran to take back his pelt, allow him to return to the sea. Right now you know only his human half. Do you really have any concept of who you love? Ciaran is so much more than just a man."

Keeley's hands clenched in her lap. Where was this headed? For some reason, the conversation filled her with dread. She had seen the expression on his face when he looked out at the sea. "He's told me, but no I guess I don't really know. Only that we are in some way linked by blood."

The older woman smiled in understanding. "Yes. It's true, the Silkie and the Faerie folk do go back to the same origins. But there are differences too. Faeries may still be more adept when it comes to casting actual spells, but the Silkie have their own powerful magic. So far, you've seen only the reflection of that. You have a couple of hours. Come with me to the *Skerry*. Meet Carrick and Cayden. Let us show you what we are."

Keeley hesitated. Would she be betraying Ciaran or was this simply a way to understand him and what he faced? This wasn't the time to over think it. "All right."

A young, good-looking teenager waited at the launch. Dressed in shorts, the rest of him was bare with the exception of a leather anklet. She noticed something similar on Catriona Clifton. The youth helped Keeley on board and then bowed his head to Catriona as he offered his hand. "My lady."

Keeley wondered if all the crew looked like him. In her mind she automatically compared him to Ciaran, but there was simply no contest. While the boy was beautiful, Ciaran radiated power and sex. He would tower over this teen. Just looking at Ciaran was enough to make her sex swell and ache. Hell, just thinking about him was doing it. She shifted on the seat and watched as the boy brought them expertly along the stern of the *Skerry*. Two more youths waited to tie the launch and help them on board. Again, Catriona was addressed as my lady and treated with deference.

"Come, Keeley. It's just Carrick and Cayden. Annabel has gone to the house at Barton Point to spend the day with her brother, Taylor. I believe you know them already?"

"Yes. I remember them from summers when I was a teenager."

Catriona nodded. "I recall seeing you some with your grandfather. I wish I had known earlier of your Faerie blood." She paused. "I have told my husband and my son to mind their manners, but they have all the arrogance of the Silkie Lords so they can be a little intimidating until you come to know them better."

Intimidating? Keeley wasn't about to back down to any man, especially these two. No matter what Ciaran had done four years ago, he was different now. She saw what he didn't want her to see, the homesickness and the hurt. These men had the power to help change that, but she would not kiss their asses to make it happen. By the time they reached the deck where the two men lounged by the pool, Keeley prepared herself for a fight. They both stood when the two women approached. She recalled them from the morning at her house and then again along the waterfront, but today was different. Then she had been only vaguely aware of them.

Like Ciaran, they were tall and well formed with dark hair and dark eyes. There was a striking resemblance between Cayden and Ciaran, but the older brother was leaner with features just a bit sharper. Keeley's glance shifted to Carrick and a shock of recognition went through her. This was what Ciaran would look like when he got older. There was just the merest hint of silver at Carrick Clifton's temples. A few laugh lines crinkled the corners of his eyes, but physically he was in magnificent shape.

As Carrick stepped forward at Catriona's introduction, his dark eyes assessed her in one broad sweep. She raised her chin and met his gaze without flinching.

"You're just a tiny thing, hardly bigger than a

girl," Carrick mocked. "Does Ciaran need to dominate everything so much he chooses a child as his mate?"

Okay, so much for nice. Keeley's temper snapped and her nostrils flared. "No one dominates me!" She flicked her finger at him and he tumbled backward into the pool with a resounding splash. Keeley spun around and glared at Cayden. "You wanna say something too?" When Cayden merely raised his brows, Keeley glared at him and then at Carrick who leaped back out of the pool, his black eyes snapping. A brisk wind began to whip around the four people gathered on the deck. Carrick raised his hand and calmed it, but just as soon as he did, Keeley whipped it up again. They glared at each other.

"Stop it!" Catriona ordered quietly. "Carrick! She is a guest, here at my invitation!"

The words might have been aimed at Carrick, but Keeley felt their bite as well. She blinked, felt the anger drain out of her and slowly unclenched her hands. The face she turned to Ciaran's mother was flushed with shame. "I'm sorry, Mrs. Clifton. You invited me to your home, and I'm being rude." She faced Carrick, sighed deeply, and held out her hand. "I owe you an apology as well. Truce?"

Carrick stared at her hand for a moment, laughed and then bent over to press a kiss to the back of it. Keeley snatched her hand away and shoved it in the pocket of her dress. She eyed him warily. "Why did you do that?"

"You're a mean little thing, aren't you?" he eyed her with a gleam in his dark eyes.

She stuck her chin out at him. "If I have to be."

"I like that in a woman. Cat was...is a real spitfire too. Now Bell, she's a sweet thing, but don't let her fool you; that girl is tough. She's had to be."

"Carrick," Catriona said gently. "I don't think we need to give Keeley a history of the entire family, but I did want her to be able to see what we are...what Ciaran is."

Cayden stepped forward and took Keeley's hand. "I'm sure you don't really remember me or my father, but we came with Momma to help the day your Granddad died. I'm sorry for your loss."

Keeley smiled at him. His temperament seemed much quieter than Ciaran, but both men bore the same tenacious set to their jaws. "Thank you. I'm afraid I don't really remember much from that day."

"If you will allow me, I thought I could perhaps explain things and let my parents demonstrate."

Keeley cast an uncertain look over her shoulder at Catriona, but the woman simply smiled reassuringly. She avoided Carrick's gaze and turned back to Cayden. "All right."

She followed them to the stern, barely keeping her mouth from dropping open as Carrick and Catriona calmly disrobed. The two youths standing nearby took their clothing with a bow and backed away. Keeley's eyes widened. If she thought Carrick Clifton was impressive before, nude he was breathtaking, as was his wife. Both still boasted physiques that would put most thirty year olds to shame. Before she could really make the adjustment to such casual nudity, they dove over the edge.

She hurried forward, gasping as Carrick metamorphosed before her eyes. All it took was a touch to the leather anklet he wore and human became a sleek, powerful bull seal. By the time Keeley was able to tear her eyes from Ciaran's father, Catriona had already shifted. Small and infinitely more delicate than her husband, they were both still a picture of grace. As Keeley watched, she recognized with a shock the sensuality that surrounded them. It was so thick it was nearly a tangible thing. As Catriona swam, Carrick darted and twisted around her until she paused and poked her head out of the water. Carrick's form swam under and around her, and air bubbles rose all around Catriona.

Ciaran had done that to her! She looked at Cayden. "What...what is he doing?"

Cayden grinned and looked back out at his parents. "It's a mating ritual. Amazing after all these years he still courts her." Seeing Keeley's expression, his tone lowered. "Ah, I see you recognize this. Ciaran has done it to you even in human form? I did the same to Bell, both as a seal and as a human."

Carrick and Catriona disappeared beneath the surface of the water. When they didn't immediately resurface, Keeley frowned.

"Where did they go?"

Cayden chuckled. "I suspect they'll find a deserted spot of beach, take advantage of the opportunity and then return. While we're waiting, can I answer any questions for you? Since you don't seem particularly shocked, I'm guessing Ciaran has explained most of this to you."

Keeley nodded, but worry still furrowed her brow as she looked out at the bay. "He also said when he first told me about it, a Silkie could never truly be happy as a human. I see now. I see the freedom it gives you."

Cayden touched her hand where it clenched on the railing of the *Skerry*. "There's freedom in finding your true mate too. When you find the one person who accepts you as you are, to whom you feel attuned. That's a very powerful draw, Keeley."

She turned her head back to the sea. Yes, she and Ciaran were incredible together, but if she could never share this part of his life with him, would they lose what they had? She pushed the thought away, wanting to know something else instead, something just as important.

"If your Council allows him to return, will," she hesitated, "Will you?"

Cayden stiffened, and she looked up into dark eyes incredibly like Ciaran's. "Will you forgive him? Will you be able to accept him back with you as a brother? Will you love him?"

Emotions raced over Cayden's face, along with uncertainty, and stiffness.

"I don't know." Cayden shook his head. "So much happened. He nearly killed my mate, Keeley, nearly killed our father. You don't understand."

Keeley glared at him. "I understand he's not the same person he was; he needs his family. I understand if you and your father can't forgive him, then it doesn't matter what your Council decides. He needs *you* as much as he needs to return to the sea."

Cayden's laughter was tinged with cynicism. "Forgive me if I find that hard to believe."

Keeley's eyes narrowed. With a bitter twist to her mouth she spun toward the launch tethered to the stern. "Take me back. There's no need to stay here any longer. I've seen enough. You would let him return to the ocean, but not to his family. And I tell you he longs for one just as much as the other."

Cayden grabbed her arm. "You won't interfere. It would break my mother's heart."

She shook him off. "I won't interfere. It would break *Ciaran's* heart. The rest of you can go to hell."

Chapter Thirteen

Ciaran noticed something wrong as soon as he returned. When he entered through the kitchen door, Keeley stood at the counter beating something with a metal mallet and mumbling to herself. She didn't even seem aware he was there. As he watched, he could tell the moment she did. Her nostrils flared briefly and she closed her eyes for just a second. Then, after putting the mallet down, she gazed at him with eyes wide and dark, like a still, deep cove along a rocky northern coast.

He set his jacket over the back of a chair. "Keeley?" His voice was quiet, questioning and comforting at the same time. She barreled into him, grasping his dress shirt, to pull herself up so she could kiss him. His arms wrapped around her bottom and lifted her to him. "What's wrong, baby?"

She shook her head into the hollow of his neck and then tilted her face back. "Kiss me. Just please kiss me. I've missed you."

Ciaran pulled her in tight against him, instantly aroused. She rubbed against him and moaned. "You want some now?"

"Yes, now."

His breathing hitched. "In the pantry?"

Her eyes blazed at him and she licked her lips. "Here."

He set her bottom on the kitchen table and slid his hands along her thighs under her dress. When he found she was without panties, he smiled and slid a finger along her already moist sex. "Have you been thinking about this?"

"All day." Her fingers were busy unbuckling his belt and unbuttoning and unzipping his fly. She smoothed her hand over the length of him, still straining his boxers, and then yanked his pants and his shorts down. Her hand stroked him, her fingers running over the swollen head of his cock until he groaned.

Just the thought of her already so hot made him ache. He pushed her thighs apart and pulled her hips forward on the table until he could step up and guide his shaft into her warm, wet channel. With a final, sharp thrust, he fully seated himself inside her.

"Is that what you wanted, baby? Is that what you've been waiting for?"

She whimpered, biting her lower lip as she stared down to where they were joined. Her eyes blazed when she looked back at him. "Yes. Hurry, Ciaran."

He grasped her buttocks and thrust in a frenzy. The kitchen filled with the sound of their loving, mingled moans and the sound of his body moving against hers. It was fast and furious, a coming together with no gentleness, no tenderness, just a basic need to possess. As her climax made her arch and clutch her body around his, Ciaran cried out hoarsely and slammed back into her, his hips bucking into her as he climaxed.

They stayed just like that for a moment, their hearts pounding and their breathing rasping. When their eyes met they simply stared at each other. Ciaran smiled first and Keeley followed suit. She brushed her fingers along his beard-shadowed cheek.

"Welcome home," she whispered.

Ciaran cupped her face in his hands and kissed her slowly. "Anytime, love. Really. Anytime."

A sound in the doorway startled them. Ciaran looked to the side and saw Jonathan standing there, his eyes only slightly wider than his smile. “Pour me a bourbon, will you Jonathan? I’ll let Keeley get back to work on dinner.”

The door closed after the butler.

“How long was he there?” Keeley asked, blushing slightly.

Ciaran laughed as he withdrew and tucked himself back into his pants. “Not long enough. I guess he’ll just have to be content.”

Keeley giggled. “Yeah. Dinner will be ready in about a half hour. It’s such a nice evening; would you like to eat by the pool?”

Ciaran’s brow arched. “I’d love to.”

He was relieved to see he had lightened her mood, but he was determined to find out what caused it. He retreated to his study to put copies of the papers Belmont had drawn up in his safe and turned when he heard the door. Jonathan appeared with his bourbon.

As Ciaran took the glass from him, he asked casually. “Did we have any visitors today?”

Jonathan paused at the doorway. “Yes. Your mother, sir. She came to visit Miss Keeley. Then the two of them went out for a while.”

Ciaran smiled at him absently as he sipped his bourbon. “Thanks. Let me know when dinner is ready. I’m afraid if I stay around the kitchen I will distract Keeley too much.”

Jonathan’s thin lips curved in a small smile right before the door shut behind him.

Ciaran’s eyes narrowed thoughtfully as he stared out the window. So his mother stopped by. He wondered why. While he toyed with the glass, he stared toward the pool. He needed to find out about that visit because he was sure some element of it was what upset Keeley, and he simply would not tolerate having her upset. It was too soon after her grandfather’s death. He tossed back the rest of the bourbon and stalked upstairs to change clothes.

After exchanging the business suit for lightweight shorts and a shirt, Ciaran crossed to the terrace doors and pulled them open. In the distance he saw the *Skerry* lit against the backdrop of the darkening sky. He frowned.

****

Something had changed between when he arrived home and now. Something that darkened his mood. Keeley watched as he ate. Sometimes she had flashes into what he was thinking, but not now. As he scowled over the chicken roll she had prepared, she couldn't stand it any longer.

"Is something wrong?"

He looked up, his brow clearing. "No. The meal is delicious, Keeley."

She stroked the back of his wrist. "I'm not talking about the meal. You've been in a strange mood ever since you came back downstairs."

He set his knife and fork aside, took a sip from the chilled white wine in his goblet and slowly leaned back in his chair, letting the glass dangle from his left hand. "Tell me about your guest today."

Keeley blushed.

Ciaran suddenly leaned forward and grabbed her wrist, stroking it as he frowned. "Were you going to tell me? Or just keep it locked inside? I won't let them upset you. What did my mother say to make you unhappy? What did she do?"

Keeley swallowed. His intensity was intimidating. "It wasn't Catriona. It wasn't your mother. You mustn't think that."

"Then why were you trying to beat the chicken to death? You looked so angry and haunted. What did she want? Where did you go?"

Keeley's eyes widened. "Who told you we went anywhere?"

"Jonathan. Oh, he wasn't trying to tattle in any

way. I simply asked if you'd had any visitors, and he told me my mother came by then the two of you went out. He simply assumed it was to shop. Where did you go?"

"To the *Skerry*," Keeley whispered.

"Damn it!" Ciaran jumped up from the table and strode over to the edge of the pool, his fists clenched at his sides. She stared at his stiff back worriedly. Anger radiated from him and left her frightened for him. He was so close to getting back the other half of his life she wanted nothing to get in the way, even if it meant an end for the two of them.

He turned around and his dark eyes blazed. "It was them. My father and brother! It had to be. What happened?"

Keeley fiddled with her silverware, straightening the utensils on her plate. "I think your mother really came by to see if I loved you, if I was good enough for you."

"Like hell. It's not her decision."

Keeley sighed. This was not how she wanted this to go. Damn. Why had she let him see how upset she was? "She meant well, Ciaran. I'm sure of it. She misses you terribly."

He tried to mask it, but she saw the momentary lifting of the darkness in his eyes, and knew without a doubt she was right. Ciaran needed his family, but she wasn't at all sure everyone would welcome him back.

"She invited me out to the *Skerry* so I could see what you were, see the shift and what you looked like in your seal form." Keeley stopped and bit her lower lip as she fiddled with the stem of her wine glass. "I'm afraid things didn't go too well. I butted heads with your father and pushed him into the pool."

Ciaran's gaze jerked back to her. "You did what?"

"I pushed your father into the pool...using magic." When she looked at Ciaran, she frowned in remembered anger. "He criticized you, claimed you were still trying to dominate everything around you by picking a mate who was just a child. So I told him nobody dominated me and shoved him back into the pool."

Ciaran's lip twitched, but he remained silent.

"Then I asked Cayden if he wanted to say anything."

"Did he?"

Keeley saw a definite twinkle in Ciaran's eyes. "No."

He walked back over and took her hand, urging her up from the table. Grabbing the wine bottle and their glasses, he led her over to a lounge, pulling her down to curl up on his lap. "So then what happened?"

"Carrick and I threw some hot air around until your mother intervened. I apologized to her and offered your father a truce. He called me a mean little thing, but said he liked that in a woman."

She stopped, not really wanting to get into her conversation with Cayden.

"There's more, though. Something upset you." He stroked a hand over her hair and along the sensitive skin of her neck.

She leaned her head against his chest. "Catriona and Carrick demonstrated the shift, and Cayden stayed with me to explain it. I-I realized there will be a big part of your life I won't be able to share Ciaran. And—and I worried those you could share it with might not be able to forgive and forget no matter what your Council decides. So I asked Cayden that very thing."

He stroked her hair again. "And you didn't like the answer you got."

"No." She buried her fingers in his silky hair and

held on to him for dear life. How could she let him go if they would not welcome him?

"They don't matter," he assured her in a voice designed to soothe. "It's you I will come back to."

Would he? Keeley kissed him with a desperate passion. She had seen how free Carrick and Catriona appeared after their transformation. How could anyone possibly remember a human, even one with Faerie blood, with all that open water to explore?

"What's the matter, love?" he whispered.

Keeley shook her head. She didn't want to voice her fear, afraid it might show a lack of trust. She turned so she straddled his lap and kissed him hungrily. Her lips teased his, nibbling at his bottom lip, tugging it gently and then licking where she'd nibbled. His mouth opened beneath hers and Keeley plundered. Ciaran groaned at her aggressiveness.

"That's it, Keeley Ann," he murmured. "Whatever you want to do."

Desire tightened her belly and she rubbed sinuously against his thigh. Her fingers slipped beneath his shirt, tweaking the tips of his nipples until he moaned. She urged him to a sitting position and stripped his shirt off over his head before she pushed him back once again against the lounge.

She rubbed his chest and lowered her mouth to flick her tongue over the small pebble of flesh. His hands were busy unzipping the back of her sundress. It sagged open and he slipped his fingers beneath the straps to gently tug them off her shoulders. He smiled as her delicate pink-tipped breasts were bared to him.

Keeley felt his cock jump as his hands cupped her breasts. "I love how delicate you are. Just enough to fill my mouth. I sat in the meeting today with my attorney and thought about these, about cradling them in my hands and squeezing and got the biggest hard on. I want to suck on them. Would you like that?"

Keeley yanked her dress around her waist. "Please. I want to feel your lips everywhere."

She leaned forward, using her hand to guide one of her breasts into his hungry mouth. While he suckled, he slid a hand along her thigh, under the skirt of her dress until it was bunched around her waist. His hand slid around to the cheek of her ass and he kneaded the round flesh.

As he licked her breast, he looked at her with a smile. "He's watching. Are you okay or shall I wave him away?"

Keeley rested her forehead on his shoulder. "Jonathan?"

Ciaran gently bit her nipple. "Yeah."

She shivered. The thought was tempting and somewhat forbidden, but she needed this to be between the two of them. She shook her head against Ciaran's broad chest. "I'm not ready, not yet."

She felt rather than saw him motion with his hand. When his arms came back around her, Keeley knew Jonathan was gone. She slid her hand between them to undo his shorts. Her eyebrows arched when she realized he had gone commando. "Making things easier?" she teased.

"I would never make it difficult for a woman to wrap her fingers around my cock."

She pulled her dress completely off. Naked, she straddled his gaping pants and eased her hand up and down the swollen length of him. Ciaran grinned and put his hands behind his head.

"Come on, Keeley Ann, have your wicked way with me."

Wetness flooded her core. She burned for him with a desperation she couldn't even begin to examine. While she stroked Ciaran with one hand, she slid the fingers of her other hand down to touch herself. He couldn't take his eyes off what she was doing, and Keeley smiled slowly, deliciously, suddenly feeling very powerful. Just looking into his dark eyes was enough to tell her he could never get enough of her just as she would never get enough of him.

"Yes!" Ciaran moaned. He grabbed her hand and pulled her fingers toward his own mouth, slowly tonguing off the sweet clear juices. "Let's go inside."

****

She took off into the house, stark naked. Ciaran followed, laughter bursting forth without restraint as he pursued her. He couldn't believe how happy she made him, how she continued to surprise him each and every time they were together. Before Keeley he would have been the first to say he would never be satisfied with just one lover. He had epitomized the Silkie myth, involved in a few threesomes, even some involving men, and had never encountered anything he did not like when it came to sex. In that, he was no different than many of his kind.

But now? Only Keeley would do. It was only her he thought about, only her who could satisfy the craving inside him.

She adjusted the shower and then laughed as she pulled him inside. They took turns soaping each other. As she lathered his back, his cock went rock hard again.

"Spread your legs. Let me wash your butt."

Ciaran did what he was told, his breath catching in his throat as she ran her fingers down over the cheeks of his ass teasingly. He let his forehead fall forward until it rested against the shower wall. His heart thudded heavily in his chest as her hands continued to move over his soap-slickened body. Unable to resist, he wrapped his cock in his fist and began to stroke himself.

She slapped his butt. "Save that. That's mine." At her softly purred words, his cock jumped.

"Then take me, Keeley. Do what you want."

He felt like his mind was in a fog where the only thing that mattered was finding some relief for the throbbing ache tying him in knots. She led him into the bedroom and told him to lie on his back. Ciaran smiled wickedly at her and Keeley grinned back at him.

"Do you have any massage oil?" she asked.

He arched a brow. "In the nightstand."

He felt vulnerable lying there with his cock so hard it laid flat against his stomach. Ciaran heard the drawer open and shut, then a moment later, she was kissing the soles of his feet. Her fingers stroked and rubbed from his feet along his calves and on to his thighs. He moaned as he watched her slowly work her way up his body.

For an instant, her lips and her fingers hovered around his swollen cock and then she moved on, a teasing smile on her lips and a twinkle in her eyes.

"Mmm. You missed a spot, baby," he murmured.

Her fingers brushed his nipples in a feathery caress that made him inhale sharply.

"Don't worry," she laughed softly. "I plan on giving that spot a lot of attention. Roll over."

After pressing her lips against the nape of his neck, she used her hands and lips to glide down the length of his back. Ciaran quivered, feeling even more vulnerable as she brushed her hands over his ass. When her lips and tongue teased the sensitive area at the small of his back, he moaned.

"Oh, Keeley. Sweet, sweet girl. Please let me touch you."

"No," she murmured as she leaned near his ear. "This time is for you."

The heavy throb in his cock increased and his

testicles tightened, but she was nowhere near ready to put him out of his misery. Lips and hands teased along the backs of his legs, lingering at the sensitive area behind his knee. Ciaran's fingers curled into the sheets.

"Please," he groaned.

"Turn over," she whispered. "Bend your legs and spread them apart."

"Keeley…" he began, but she stopped him.

"Your turn, Ciaran. You've given me so much, now I want to give back."

She crawled between his bent legs and gently cupped his testicles in one small hand. Ciaran chuffed. "Oh sweet love…"

When her mouth closed over him, he nearly leaped off the bed. She pushed him back with her free hand and continued to work the length of his shaft with her lips and tongue. She added a hand and set up a rhythm that had his pelvis pumping.

"Baby, you're going to make me come."

She swirled her tongue around the head of his cock and looked up at him with eyes gone dark and seductive. "That's the idea."

Someone cried out. Was that his voice? She took him deep into her throat and his body overrode whatever rational thought remained. He convulsed with pleasure and was overwhelmed with how much he loved his little Faerie witch.

It was only as his body relaxed, he realized Keeley's fingers clenched his shins for support. He opened his eyes to see her in the midst of her own orgasm. He pulled her across his lap and stroked her with fingers that trembled. When she arched back, he bent his head and slipped her nipple in his mouth.

And then she fainted.

The muscles in his arms bunched as he pulled her off of him and stretched her limp form on top of him. He relaxed his legs, only now beginning to realize how close his muscles were to cramping.

"Oh sweetheart," he whispered against her hair over and over again. He nestled her against him, stroking her back, waiting for her to rouse. He was in awe. Never had a woman passed out in his arms. Tears blurred his vision and he tried to blink them away, but they slipped out of the corners of his eyes. She stirred against him, but then made a noise like a contented purr and burrowed against him. God he loved her!

He was afraid to tell her how terrified he was of the upcoming meeting of the Silkie Lords. Afraid she would insist on going with him. He had to do this alone, but he was scared what would happen if they gave his pelt back to him.

Ciaran remembered what occurred when his father banished him before. Oh he hadn't called it that, simply said he was sending him south to spend time with their cousins, but Ciaran had known it was to get him away from Cayden and Bell. Ciaran spent the time almost exclusively as a seal, hunting and mating often and indiscriminately. Then he let temptation rule him. Would that happen again because he had been human for so long?

He wouldn't let it. If taking back his pelt meant losing Keeley, there was no choice. He would stay a human. As he voiced the thought to himself, he felt again the pull of the sea and shoved it away, but as he rested his cheek against Keeley's head his eyes were wide in the dark room and sleep was far away.

Chapter Fourteen

Keeley awoke just after dawn. Her hand patted lazily next to her, but Ciaran was no longer under the covers. The spot where he'd lain was still warm so he couldn't have been up long. She stretched like a contented kitten. He stood out on the terrace, silhouetted against the morning sky, his arms resting on the railing. He had one leg slightly bent and she could just see his arrogant profile while he stared out at the bay. God he was beautiful, from his broad muscular shoulders down to his tight rounded ass.

She smiled to herself. Who was she? She barely recognized this wanton woman as the same Keeley Ann McNamara who shunned dates or even the touch of a man. There was something about Ciaran, though. And now she could scarcely believe she watched him for two years without reaching this point sooner. Thank God for a messed up dessert!

He caught her gaze on him and smiled softly as he came toward her. Eyes glued to his nude body, all Keeley could do was swallow as her heart began to beat heavily and her sex pulsed in time with it.

"Hey, love," he purred in her ear. The bed shifted as he climbed back in with her. "Is there some special reason you have such a big smile on your face?"

"I was just admiring your butt...and the rest of you."

He chuckled. "And thinking about last night?"

"Of course."

He stroked her cheek. "Come swimming with

me. Right now, in the bay, just like we are."

Keeley's eyes widened. "People will see us."

"It's early yet. Just a few fishermen, and they'll be far enough away. Come on, Keeley."

They both laughed like kids with a secret as they raced out the door and down the path from the point to the beach below. Keeley hit the water first, quickly followed by Ciaran. She splashed him and then squealed as he grabbed her and tossed her in the air. She twisted sinuously so she came back down into a dive, cutting shallowly into the water with Ciaran once again following. She ducked underwater, quickly twisting back underneath him so she was following him. When he stopped to tread water, Keeley swam below him and softly blew bubbles around him as she circled him and surfaced.

He quit laughing. Their eyes met and she saw a hungry, almost wild look on his face before he gathered her into his arms and kissed her. It was long and slow as if they had all the time in the world. Keeley wrapped herself around him, leaving his legs free to tread water while the kiss heated up. Passion was submerged for the moment in a kiss that bore a different intensity. Hands stroked each other's cheeks, tracing jaw lines, eyebrows and the edge of mouths. Their foreheads rested against each other and they simply breathed, inhaling the other's scent.

Keeley looked into his dark, velvety eyes and saw shadows, a shimmer of tears that could have been a trick of the morning light.

"Hey, this ain't no nude beach!" someone yelled from a passing fishing boat.

It broke the spell.

They both looked at each other and laughed again.

"Climb on my back. I'll give you a ride."

She arched a brow at him. "Seriously? Won't I be

too big?"

He tweaked her nose. "No. You're just a mean little thing. I'm sure I can handle you."

As he swam, Keeley laid her cheek between his shoulders, savoring the feel of the smoothly moving muscles. At the end of the point, two seals watched the lovers until Ciaran carried Keeley back up the path while she laughingly told him to put her down she could walk just fine thank you very much.

The morning set the tone for the rest of the week. By unspoken agreement, neither talked about the arrival of the Silkie Lords he expected at the end of the week, but Ciaran was obviously reluctant to let Keeley out of his sight. When she went to her house to begin sorting through things, he came along and helped her pack. He rented jet skis one afternoon and they raced around the cove near his house until they collapsed laughing on the beach. As soon as Ciaran realized no one was in sight, he yanked her bikini off, jerked his shorts down and plunged into her fast and furiously. When they rolled apart, they laughed even harder to see one of Ciaran's blueblood neighbors watching them with an obvious hard-on tenting his khakis.

"You seem to like having an audience," Ciaran teased her.

She swatted at him. "You're the one who picked this spot, not me."

His face sobered and he stroked her cheek. "You make me forget everything else."

The evening before Ciaran expected to be summoned away, they made love again by the pool, but they were so attuned to each other they never noticed Jonathan watching.

"I don't want to stop," Ciaran whispered as he took her for the third time. "But I do want to move it upstairs."

He picked her up in his arms. Keeley didn't

make a single protest, simply resting her cheek against his shoulder so she could watch him. She touched his face and he stopped at the base of the stairs.

"What, sweetheart?" he crooned.

"I love you, Ciaran, so much." She closed her eyes and took the hand she'd touched to his cheek and made a fist over her heart as if she could hold onto the feel of his skin beneath her fingers.

He growled and practically flew up the stairs. As soon as he got her on the bed, he started at her toes and proceeded to lick her entire body. When he reached her core, he took his time, laving her with the flat of his tongue before sliding back to tease the sensitive skin where hip met thigh. "What position would you prefer, Keeley?"

She touched his cheek again and their eyes met for what seemed like an eternity.

"All of them," he said softly answering his own question. He spent the entire night making love to her and having her love him. They would nap a bit and then wake to once again arouse each other, their cries echoing through the house as they came together over and over. The last time, he made love to her from behind, taking the nape of her neck in his teeth and marking her with his passion. His. Just before dawn, Ciaran pulled her close and tucked the covers around them both. "Sleep darling Keeley. Sleep."

He waved his hand over her face, calling on what small amount of magic remained to him and watched in satisfaction as her eyes drifted shut. He waited a moment and then slowly closed his own eyes.

"Don't let me forget," he whispered into the darkness.

She was still sleeping when Cayden appeared on the terrace. He walked cautiously into the room. As soon as Ciaran saw him, he tucked the covers around Keeley, but his brother wasn't looking at her. He glanced around the room before looking back at Ciaran.

"You've done well for yourself."

Ciaran stood, unselfconsciously naked, and stalked toward the door to the sitting room, leaving Cayden to follow. He waited for his brother and then shut the door quietly.

"I assume I am being summoned."

Cayden lifted one brow coolly and glanced about him. "I have no other reason to be here."

Ciaran swallowed the bitter retort that rose to his lips. "I'd like to say goodbye to Keeley."

Cayden nodded. "I'll wait here for you."

His brother moved away to stand by the French doors that led to the terrace from the sitting room. After turning on his heel, Ciaran slipped back into the bedroom. Keeley was curled on her side, one hand half reaching out into the space where he lay just a few minutes before. Her brow was furrowed as if even in her sleep she already wondered where he was. Her eyes suddenly opened and she stared at him. For one unguarded moment, he saw pain and grief in their beautiful depths.

"You're going." It was a statement, not a question. She already knew. He saw the knowledge in her eyes.

"Cayden's here. I've been summoned."

He was at her side as soon as she sat up, pulling her into his arms, holding her as close as he could get. Words poured out of him then, all the things he needed to tell her but kept putting off.

"I love you so much." He reached into the nightstand and pulled out a small box. "Please, wear this until I can come back; then I want us to get married." He slipped an intricately woven band encrusted with emeralds onto her finger.

"Ciaran," she said softly. "I don't need a ring to know you love me."

He stroked her cheek. "It's so everyone else will know. I want them to know you're mine."

Keeley pressed her lips to his. "Heart and soul."

He continued touching her face, staring at her intently, trying to memorize every feature. When he spoke again, it was quickly. "I've made arrangements for you, for the household. If...if I'm not back in a week, you must call my attorney. All the paperwork is in the top right hand drawer in my study. He knows what to do. I've set up accounts for you and given you power of attorney to handle my affairs until my return."

Keeley's face paled. "How long will you be gone?"

He wanted to lie. He wanted to tell her it would be a couple of weeks at the most. "I don't know. God help me! I don't know. I've been in human form for four years. If the Council returns my pelt...sometimes Silkies go a little crazy. They transform. They forget."

Tears. She cried so rarely it undid him.

"Don't love. Don't cry." He held her, stroking her back. When she pulled back from him, he watched as she took the necklace from around her neck and slipped it around his. "Keeley. Don't. Your father gave this to you."

"And I'm giving it to you." Her chin jutted stubbornly, but the effect was ruined when her lip trembled. "Wear it always. Then if I see a seal with it on, I'll know it's you."

The last few words were muffled by tears. He wanted to tell her he wouldn't leave, but he couldn't. He could feel the pull of the sea, the pull of the Silkie, and it was tearing him apart. She must have seen that in his face. Keeley slid from his lap and slipped a robe on.

"Who came to get you?" she asked softly.

"My brother, Cayden."

"I'll say hello while you get dressed."

****

Cayden watched her come into the room, a slender almost boyish looking woman with eyes that burned a bright emerald green. He inclined his head stiffly, still remembering their last encounter. "Miss McNamara."

She waved her hand dismissively, her stance braced like a boxer preparing to fight. Her little chin jutted at him pugnaciously. In any other situation but the present one, he might have laughed. It was like watching a terrier square off with a rottweiler, but beneath her feisty exterior, he saw the sheen of tears in her eyes and the paleness of her skin.

"Ciaran will be here in just a moment, so I want you to keep your mouth shut and let me speak my piece."

Cayden simply arched a brow at her inquiringly.

"If you...and your father...can't forgive him, please promise me you won't hurt him, that you will let your mother be with him, if that's what she wants. I know you don't believe me, and I have no way to make you, but he needs you, Cayden. He does. He's not the same man he was."

She bit her lip. Cayden felt the fear and grief pour from her. He wasn't so hardened against his brother that her emotions failed to touch him. He took a step toward her, but she backed away, her eyes wide and wary.

"I beg you. Don't shut him out."

She turned away just as the door opened. Ciaran's eyes shifted curiously from Cayden's shuttered expression to Keeley's distraught one. His eyes snapped as he looked back at Cayden. "What did you say to her? What did you do?" Ciaran's voice was a low, angry snarl.

"Not a thing."

Keeley put her hands against Ciaran's chest. "It's true. I'm just overwrought."

Cayden watched in fascination at the change in his brother's expression as he gazed down at Keeley. His whole face softened and lightened, as if just being near her obliterated the darkness in him. Maybe what his mother tried to tell them was true. Cayden glowered, crossing his arms over his chest as he waited.

Ciaran's arms went around Keeley and he hugged her to him. His eyes closed and he rested his cheek against her hair. When he started to pull back, Keeley uttered what sounded like a soft cry. Cayden couldn't bear the emotions coming from them. Jesus! It made him ache just watching them.

"I'll come back, Keeley. I won't leave you."

"Go. Do what you need to. Just know I'll be waiting. I love you. No matter what."

"Ciaran," Cayden said. "We need to leave."

He hated to do that to them, but they needed to get back to the *Skerry*. Ciaran twined his fingers through hers and brought their joined hands to his face, simply holding them against his cheek. It was then Cayden saw the ring she wore on her finger and the necklace circling Ciaran's neck. Cayden's fingers went to the gold locket he still wore, a gift from Bell.

Keeley stepped back from Ciaran. With one last stroke along her cheek, he faced his older brother. "Let's go!"

****

She managed to hold it together until she was sure they were out of earshot. Then she simply sank to the floor, crying as if her heart would break. He was gone. In her heart she knew he wouldn't be back soon. She had seen the freedom they had as seals, and she had seen the longing in his face for the sea. It was as potent a mistress as any woman ever could be, and Keeley wasn't sure there really was a way for him to balance the two.

Right now, though, all she could do was feel the pain of him leaving. She cried silently, her hands fisted against the carpeting and her body shaking. She cried until she had nothing left, until weariness and a nearly sleepless night caught up with her, and then she fell asleep.

Jonathan found her there. When calling her name didn't rouse her, he simply picked her up in his arms and tucked her back into bed. She was little bigger than a child, and right now he was sure she was as brokenhearted as one.

He covered her then went to the drapes at the terrace doors. Before shutting them to close out the light, he watched the *Skerry* sailing slowly out of the bay, just as Mr. Clifton had often done over the past two years. At first it had been with a curse on his lips, but lately, a haunted look lingered on his boss's face. There was a lot Jonathan didn't know about his employer, but like any good butler, he would deal with whatever came his way. Right now, it appeared Keeley McNamara had been left to his care for heaven only knew how long.

****

Ciaran's mother welcomed him with open arms. His father was much more reserved. Cayden simply treated him as a duty to be performed. Ciaran knew he was being standoffish, but he just couldn't relax. He felt like a guest on what was once his home. Even as his mother welcomed him on board, his eyes moved distractedly back to the white house on the point. Keeley. He already missed her.

"I've put you in your old room. Your ceremonial clothing is there as well. Riordan has requested a formal dinner tonight for the gathering and wishes you to attend even if you have not yet been recognized. I think that's a promising sign, though, and your father agrees."

Ciaran's eyes darted to Carrick for a moment before he was distracted by the sound of childish laughter and running feet. To his right a black-haired, blue-eyed little girl barreled down the deck.

"Daddy! Daddy!"

She laughed as Cayden bent to swing her into his arms. Love shone from them both.

"I'm sorry," Bell said breathlessly as she reached them. The swell of her latest pregnancy was just beginning to show. "She's getting so fast! I tried to keep her back but she just had to see you, Cay."

The little girl hugged Cayden around the neck and then stared with avid curiosity at Ciaran. "You look like Daddy 'n Papa. Who are you?"

Pain and longing seared through him, nearly making him gasp. She was beautiful. In his mind he saw a little girl with black hair and green eyes. He smiled gently.

"I'm your uncle. Ciaran."

She held out her arms to him. Ciaran's gaze darted from his niece to his brother and then to Annabel. When she nodded, he swallowed thickly and stepped forward to take her from Cayden. His brother glared at him, but Ciaran didn't see it. His eyes were glued on his niece.

"Hi," he muttered, feeling like a fool as he flushed. His niece noticed nothing wrong and quickly wrapped her sun-bronzed arms around his neck and gave him a bone-crunching hug. Ciaran grinned. "Don't kill your Uncle Ciaran, sweetheart."

"Leah," Cayden said stiffly. "Her name's Leah."

Ciaran touched her curly hair with his fingers. "Leah, a beautiful name."

"I'm going to have a brother. Mima says so." He didn't know what to say, so he just smiled at her. "Will you be his uncle too?"

Ciaran nodded, his eyes locked on hers. She grinned at him and gave him a big smacking kiss on the cheek. "I like you."

"I like you too, little Leah." When she wriggled in his hold, he squatted and set her down. Swallowing nervously, he stood and faced Annabel. He jammed his hands in the pockets of his slacks. "Bell," he greeted her softly, afraid she might recoil from him since the last time he'd seen her was during his hearing before the Council for attempting to kill her and his father.

Her dark blue eyes examined him fearlessly. Ciaran refused to look away, instead standing still under her examination.

"You've changed," she said.

He snorted and looked away, toward his house. "I wasn't given much choice."

"Whatever happened you brought on yourself." Cayden put his arm protectively around Annabel's shoulders.

"I wasn't casting blame," Ciaran shot back, "just stating a fact."

"Enough," Carrick interjected coolly. "The Council will decide what will be done."

Ciaran bowed his head in acknowledgement. "As you wish, Father." He turned back to Bell. "You're right, Bell. I have changed. No matter what the Council of Lords decides, I would at least beg your forgiveness. If you can't give me that, then accept my apology. I-I now understand what you and Cayden mean to each other. I didn't then."

She leaned closer to Cayden, her eyes wary. Finally, she nodded. Ciaran felt like part of the load he carried for the past four years had lifted. He nodded in acknowledgement. "Thank you."

He turned back to his mother who had remained silent so far, standing in the background. Fatigue pulled at him, but even more than that, he simply wanted to be left alone. "I'd like to go to my cabin, if you don't mind. I didn't sleep much last night."

"Of course, son." Catriona took his arm and tucked hers through it. "Rory is here along with Faeran and Brayden, but we are still awaiting the arrival of the Pacific contingent."

He listened to her with half an ear as she continued to talk as if this were no more than a social gathering instead of a council to decide his future. Being back on board the *Skerry* was having an impact on him he hadn't anticipated, but should have. His pelt was somewhere on board ship and its pull preyed on him. The longing to be back in the ocean grew, twisting in his gut and filling his thoughts.

Keeley. His free hand touched the necklace she had given him and he felt an instant, warm connection to her. Some of the tension left him.

****

Catriona Clifton paced the spacious cabin she shared with her husband. "Everyone will be here by this evening, won't they?"

Carrick sat back in one of the large, overstuffed chairs arranged in the sitting area of the cabin. "I have heard from Dylan, and he assured me they will. Why does it matter so much?"

Catriona stopped, tugging distractedly at the long braid that hung over her shoulder. Carrick's eyes widened. He had not seen her do that in years. The last time was when Annabel was so terribly injured in the sailing accident, and Cat had already known the girl was paralyzed even when no one else had. He stood and came over to his wife. As he slid his hands over her shoulders and down her arms, he bent his mouth to her ear. "What's wrong, Cat? You seem anxious."

She struggled with something inside herself, something she was reluctant to talk about. "He's changed, Carrick."

"Of course, and from what I can see, you're

right. It is for the better."

She shook her head. "No. It's more than that. He's slipping away from us. I'm not sure he even is one of us anymore. I get the feeling given half a chance he would flee the ship and go back to Keeley McNamara without a second thought."

Carrick raised his head. "I thought you liked the girl."

"I do, but not at the expense of losing my son! Not at the expense of him turning his back on who and what he is!"

He pulled Cat into his arms. For the first time in four years, he saw fear in her eyes for one of her children, and this time it was for the son who had always been such a source of heartache and hatred.

"You think he would deny the Silkie in him for this girl?" Carrick's tone was skeptical, but he could never dismiss Catriona's fears. She was correct more often than not.

Catriona closed her eyes for just a moment. "He is far more attached to her than to us right now. Unless you wish to lose him permanently, the hearing must take place sooner rather than later. He's being pulled in both directions. If he turns his back on his pelt now, the Council will banish him for good. You know it! And you must believe me, he is merely a breath away from doing just that. He may lose her for a while when he takes his pelt back, but if their love is as strong as I believe it is, he'll find his way back eventually."

Carrick stroked her cheeks and then pulled her close to rest his forehead against hers. "This is tearing you apart, isn't it? Because either way, he'll know pain. The girl will too. And we can do little for her."

Catriona shook her head. "Don't underestimate her. She's stronger than you think."

Chapter Fifteen

Ciaran stared at himself in the mirror in his cabin. This was a man he no longer knew. Garbed in the traditional *feileadh* that left his legs and chest bare, he pinned on the family brooch to hold his sash in place at his shoulder. It looked a lot like a kilt and plaid, and he supposed there must be some common heritage there somewhere.

I wish Keeley was here. She would tease me and laugh and make me feel light. Instead all he felt was the weight of his future pressing down upon him, smothering him. As was the custom, his feet were bare. He touched the necklace he wore and felt somewhat reassured. It seemed to him the scent and warmth of her skin still clung to it. "Don't let me forget her," he whispered again at his reflection.

A knock at his cabin door interrupted his musings. He tucked the necklace below his sash and went to the door. His mother and father were on the other side, both dressed traditionally, Carrick in his own *feileadh* and his mother in a draped, diaphanous gown that simultaneously revealed and concealed. All the women would be garbed in such a manner, their bodies on display to be admired by the men. And the men always far outnumbered the women. It was one of the reasons males so often sought human company. He had even heard of Silkie men so desperate for a mate they looked among the seals, but those matings never came to a happy ending.

He bowed over his mother's hand. "You are looking beautiful, Momma, as beautiful as I remember you." He bowed to his father. "My Lord."

The stiffness was still there. Ciaran knew that, as yet, his father was not willing to unbend. Perhaps he never would. Ciaran's mouth twisted. Four years ago, and even longer, if he were completely honest, he was filled with hate for everything and everybody. But his feelings coalesced and focused on Carrick, Cayden, and most of all Annabel. Some of it was jealousy that Cayden found his mate when he was still quite young. He was just ten when Annabel called to him the first time. She'd been known as Poppy then. Seven years later, the childhood friendship became a whole lot more, and yet not enough. Cayden hadn't fulfilled his duty in the eyes of the Silkie Lords, and Annabel's sailing accident seemed to ensure it would never happen.

Cayden was the one banished then. Ciaran basked in being the center of attention for both his father and his mother. He had done everything to curry favor in his father's eyes, but it was all spurred by jealousy, and when Cayden came back, instantly accepted back into the fold, Ciaran had gone over the edge. First he nearly killed his brother, then he kidnapped Annabel with the intention of killing her and his father. It seemed so ludicrous to him now. The whining, puling tantrums of a boy.

The last four years taught him much.

"We will go in together, Ciaran," Carrick said formally. "The Council has arrived. I would like them to see a united front."

Ciaran couldn't help himself. "What of Cayden? Is he not required to complete this show of unity?"

"He and Bell will meet us at the ballroom door."

Ciaran nodded. "My pardon, sir."

As they prepared to walk into the ballroom, Ciaran touched the necklace one more time. Was it his imagination, or had a flash of warmth shot from it and through him? The wide double doors were thrown open by two young men. Light and laughter spilled out from the room onto the darkened deck. Cayden and Annabel led the way in, followed by Ciaran. His mother and father brought up the rear. Every eye was on him. This was a critical moment for him and his family. Ciaran didn't care about himself. The only one who mattered to him right now was his mother. Behind her bright exterior, he sensed a brittleness she tried hard to mask.

While no one would officially recognize him, he would be watched. Ciaran stayed near his mother. Rory kept his own counsel with the dukes, Faeran and Dylan, at his side. Several maids who accompanied their parents giggled and danced near Faeran, spinning to the music so their gowns floated around them and showed more than enough of a rounded breast, a shapely thigh or a shadowed cleft. Dylan's own lady, tall, olive-skinned and voluptuous stood near her husband, her curves barely concealed beneath a creamy white gown. Dylan's eyes shifted to her often, already hot with passion. While he had no eyes for the other maids dancing so enticingly, it was obvious the Duke of the Pacific would take his lady off to a private corner very soon.

Ciaran had forgotten the rampant sexuality. It was at the core of what the Silkie were. His eyes drifted to his brother. Cayden had never been a part of that. Maybe it was because he always knew Annabel was for him, but he was much more fastidious in his sexual encounters. Ciaran couldn't say the same for himself. In the past, he would have thought nothing of luring one of the maids to the side of the room and coupling with her right there. Public sex was not a taboo, at least as long as one didn't engage in it in the middle of the room, but certainly taking a maid, or a man, to the side to pleasure and be pleasured was not as outré as in

221

human society.

But it held no interest for him. All he could think of was Keeley. She would put every woman to shame if she were here. As dainty as a Faerie, as lissome as a Silkie, as bewitching as any mermaid. He pictured her dressed in one of the diaphanous gowns, but quickly stopped that train of thought when his cock became semi-hard. He turned away from the maids dancing and found a tall, well-formed male crew member boldly eyeing his partial hard-on. No. That wouldn't do either.

Somehow he knew the evening would be interminable when all he wanted was respite until he must go before the Council. Ciaran stood on one side of the ballroom and simply observed the society that had shunned him the last four years. Already, the young Silkie women tried to attract his attention. He turned away and discovered Faeran, Duke of the Atlantic Ocean, appeared to be equally put off by their attentions. In the past, Ciaran had wondered if Faeran preferred men to women, but never saw any sign it was so. He was simply an oddity, one of their kind who never replaced the mate and child he'd lost years ago, though he must already be near forty. It was unusual.

As if he somehow knew Ciaran's thoughts, Faeran made his way to that side of the room. His eyes were coolly assessing as he examined Ciaran from head to toe. "I notice you avoid the maids now. Of one thing I could always be sure from the time you hit puberty on, if there was something fuckable within your reach, you would find a way to be inside it. Male, female, you didn't much care as long as you got pleasure from it."

Ciaran crossed his arms over his chest, his jaw tensing. He refused to rise to the baiting. Where was Faeran going with this?

"Ask me, Ciaran," he hissed quietly, "don't just

wonder. You wonder if I want you instead of a maid. I don't. You wonder why I don't take one of the tidbits being so juicily offered. I have my reasons, infant, perhaps not so different from yours."

"You can read my thoughts." It pissed him off. He had enough going on and thought he had blocked them off. He didn't need anyone inside his head, not when he was so torn.

Faeran laughed. "I am far more powerful than even Catriona. Tell me about your not-so-human mate."

Keeley. Faeran knew about her already. His heart ached, and he touched the necklace. "She has a loving soul, as beautiful as she herself is. Just a tiny thing, but feisty enough to stand up to anyone." He smiled. "She threatened me once with a meat cleaver when she got angry." His smile disappeared. "She cried when I left. She never cries."

Faeran nodded. "You tell me what she's like on the inside, not what she looks like."

"Is that a problem?"

The Duke smiled. "Not at all. Tell me about her powers."

"We hear each other and see each other sometimes."

"What do you hear now?"

Ciaran scowled. "Nothing. I think she's blocked herself from me on purpose. She can move things, and when we...make love, she has shared what she feels with me."

Faeran smiled. "A fine thing in a mate, I would think."

Ciaran nodded. His eyes surveyed the room, but absently. His thoughts were back on Keeley. What was she doing? Was she all right? She had tried to so hard that morning to send him away with no regrets. His hand went again to her necklace.

"You are worried you will forget her if we choose

to return your pelt."

Ciaran faced Faeran. They were cousins, though the older Silkie was far more powerful as the son of King Riordan, and Duke of the Atlantic in his own right. "Can you stop that from happening?" He couldn't quite keep the desperation out of his voice.

Faeran shook his head slowly. "Some things none of us can control. That is between you and God."

Ciaran's scowl deepened as he stared out at the brightly bedecked Silkies. Most of the men wore their pelts draped from their *feileadh* while many of the women chose to keep them on as an anklet. He stood out as the only one who did not have a pelt. Any of the Silkie in here could change at will, but they changed so often they did not forget who they were, where they were. But Ciaran knew it would be different for him. He shuddered.

When he felt a hand on his shoulder, he turned, meeting the midnight blue eyes of his cousin. "Brayden and I took you away four years ago. I can go with you again if the Council decides to return your pelt. While I can't make you remember, I can help remind you there is another side of you."

Gratitude flowed through him. Ciaran looked again at Faeran. There was a sadness underlying, one he knew the duke would not reveal.

"I would be grateful, but I believe we get ahead of ourselves. First I must convince the council to return my pelt."

Faeran tilted his head at Ciaran. "No, first you must convince yourself you really want it back."

****

Keeley sat in the dark next to the pool. She had told Jonathan and Mary she wished to be left alone. She refused to think of Ciaran, afraid if she did she would somehow broadcast her longing to him. He must be able to focus. God how she wished there were someone of her own kind to whom she could talk. Her father and Granddad spoke of the Faeries as if there were a great many of them, but Keeley had never seen them. Idly she brushed her hand back and forth, creating waves in the surface of the pool.

What good was her magic now when it couldn't help her hang on to the man she loved? What good had it ever been to her?

She stripped off her clothes and dove naked into the water. She must stay away from the ocean. Somehow she knew if she went into the water, he would know. Ciaran must have the chance to rediscover who and what he was, even if it meant she would lose him. She could not ask him to be any other than what he truly was. She could not ask him to be any less than he was born to be, and that would happen if he did not take up the Silkie in him.

She hauled herself from the pool, grabbed a towel and ran inside the house. Staying next to the pool was reminding her too much of him and how they made love there. But as she went through the house, she realized there were few places that did not remind her of Ciaran's touch or taste. They had played together nearly everywhere except her bedroom. She had never slept there, had hardly been inside it. Maybe there she would find sleep.

Herbs would help. She knew how to brew a tea that would help with that. Several minutes later, she headed upstairs with her mug, headed to the room she now thought of as a refuge. The one spot where she would not be constantly assaulted by thoughts of Ciaran and her together.

How long would he be gone? Right now even one night seemed like forever.

****

Ciaran got little rest that night. He sat next to the window in his cabin, staring off in the direction of his house on the point. Was she sleeping? Was she curled in the big bed they had shared? He liked to watch her sleep. Most of the time she curled on her side, one hand resting next to her head and her lips just slightly parted. He recalled their loving from the night before, the way she had become the aggressor.

It was too much. Images taunted him of Keeley, dressed as one of the Silkie noblewomen. He imagined a diaphanous green gown that did little to conceal the pink, pebbled tips of her breasts, her lean, toned body with her tight, round butt. Everyone would be able to see the nest of dark curls that concealed her hot core. And it would be wet, so wet because she would know everyone was watching her. As much as she shied at the idea of Jonathan watching them together, it nevertheless excited her. Ciaran threw back his head on a hoarse groan and his heart pounded in his chest. He wanted her, needed her.

He couldn't forget this. Surely, he couldn't forget a woman who made him hard just imagining her.

He dressed carefully the next morning, his hand once more clasped around the Celtic knot on the necklace Keeley had given to him. *I love you, Keeley. As I will try not to forget you, please don't forget me.*

Carrick and Cayden arrived at the door. Catriona and Annabel were right behind them. When Ciaran saw the two women, he raised his brows curiously.

"They are here," Carrick clarified gravely, "because it is the two of them who requested this hearing."

Two of them? Ciaran's glance went beyond Cayden to Bell. She asked? He swallowed and bowed to both of them. "No matter the outcome, I thank you both. It means a lot to me." He looked at Bell. "You especially, Annabel."

She nodded stiffly.

He wanted to say he was unaffected by what was going on, but marching back into the same room from four years earlier, sitting in the same spot with two big Silkie guards next to him, did jangle his nerves. He stood as Riordan entered flanked by Faeran and Dylan, and bowed to them, as did everyone else. Once everyone was seated, Ciaran watched nervously as Riordan gazed around the tables.

"We are here today to reconsider the punishment of Ciaran Clifton. Four years ago, we took away his pelt and set him adrift to survive or perish on his own. At that time, I said we would reconsider his case if he could show us he had changed for the better, that he had learned the importance of helping others, of not being contemptuous of everything human."

Rory looked at everyone assembled. "Who has asked for this council?"

Catriona stood. "As his mother, I do."

Rory acknowledged her with an inclination of his head. "A mother's plea can never be dismissed, but it must be tempered by the bias of your love for your son."

Annabel stood. "I too called for this council, as your great-granddaughter and as one of Ciaran Clifton's victims."

Ciaran's eyes swiveled to Annabel. Great-granddaughter? But she was human, surely. He had always dismissed the last name. It was a human as well as a Silkie surname. He glanced surreptitiously at everyone else. No one seemed at all surprised by her revelation. The knowledge slammed into him on two different levels.

He had very nearly killed the great-granddaughter of their king. He might indeed be lucky if the reminder didn't make them decide to kill him outright this time. But the greater concern was secretly he had held out hope if Annabel, a human, could become a Silkie, then Keeley could too. They could find a way to be together. Now, knowing Annabel had royal Silkie blood running through her veins crushed the future he had begun to envision.

"Stand up, Ciaran Clifton," Rory ordered. "Give an accounting of yourself. Tell us how you have changed."

He got to his feet and glanced around the table. "After I was set adrift, I made my way to shore. I was able to secure work crewing on yachts for wealthy businessmen from the city. I discovered by keeping my ears open, I could pick up useful information. And then there were the women." He stopped, but knew he needed to be honest. "They were bored and lonely and more than willing to talk to someone who made them feel good about themselves."

Dylan frowned. "You used them sexually to get information to help you?"

Ciaran jammed his hands in the pockets of his slacks. "Yes."

There was a disapproving rumble around the table. While the Silkie certainly enjoyed sex, it was for the pleasure itself, not for any gain to be had from encounters with humans or others.

"What did you do with the information you got?" one of the Pacific lords inquired.

"I took money I earned and sank all of it into investments based on that information. In two years, I amassed a fortune."

"So then you no longer used these women?" Faeran asked.

Ciaran swallowed. "No. I continued to use them to satisfy myself sexually." This was not going well. Or was it? If he was human he could stay with Keeley. He closed his eyes. The thought was as alluring as the sea calling to him. Ciaran stared around at them. Could he lose the Silkie in him forever and be happy with Keeley?

Taking a deep breath, Ciaran continued, "Look, my lords, I spent most of the past four years fucking every human female I could, married, single, old, young, fat or skinny. If I thought I could get something out of it to help me I did. I made a fortune screwing those women and I spent every damned dime of it on me and what I wanted. I tried with everything in me to flaunt my success in front of my father and family. I have to tell you honestly, I have no idea why you would even consider returning my pelt."

Ciaran dropped into his chair, leaned back, and simply stared down at the surface of the table. Maybe now they would let him go, let him go back to Keeley. He could make it as a human. He had for the last four years, hadn't he?

"I watched him, with no thought to his own safety, run into the ocean to save a young woman who was drowning." Ciaran looked up in surprise to see Annabel Barton standing straight and defiant. She looked at him challengingly. "The Ciaran I knew would never have done that."

Catriona stood. "I saw him deny his own sexual desires when he realized this same young woman was frightened of the feelings growing between them. Since then I have seen how he has come to love this woman. Even now, he paints himself in the worst of lights, hoping to save her the grief of his disappearance."

His mother fixed him with a reproachful look.

Carrick spoke from his seat with the lords. "I saw him comfort her in her grief and watched in the days following as he stayed by her side after her grandfather's death. These were not the actions of a selfish man."

Faeran straightened from where he negligently

leaned on the arm of his chair next to his father. "I spoke with him last night and know that even now he struggles with the pain he will cause this young woman if his pelt is returned and he disappears from her life. He has taken steps legally and financially to see she, and the people who work for him, are protected until he returns or fails to return. Hardly the actions of a man who loves himself more than others."

"I saw the way they touched when he said goodbye," Cayden said quietly. "The man I saw was not the Ciaran I once knew. His depth was infinite as is the love he bears for Keeley McNamara. He is as changed as night from day. As his brother, I ask that you let him return to us."

Ciaran was overcome. He sat stiffly, staring down at the table, not daring to look at anyone until Riordan commanded everyone's attention.

"I would like everyone but the Council to leave while we consider our decision."

Ciaran couldn't wait to get out. He ignored the sound of his name being called and strode quickly toward the bow of the *Skerry*. Once there, he grasped the railing with knuckles gone white from the force of his grip. How could they defend him? How could the very people he had wronged now stand in his defense? Tears burned his eyes and his throat was tight and achy.

"Ciaran."

Cayden stood behind him.

"Brother." Cayden's voice compelled him.

He sobbed then. All of the loneliness of the past four years came together and nearly knocked his legs out from under him. Cayden put his arms around him.

"I'm so sorry, Cayden," Ciaran rasped. "I was so jealous of you it blinded me. Now I see and understand. Please forgive me. No matter what they decide, if you could just please forgive me."

Cayden clenched his fists in Ciaran's hair and forced him to look at him. "I forgive you."

Their eyes locked. "I love you."

Cayden smiled. "Love you too." He shook him slightly. "Somehow, you've managed to make my wife one of your most ardent champions."

"Ever since I saw Keeley McNamara move a garbage can so you nearly fell on your butt."

Both men found Annabel standing just a few feet away. Ciaran was at her side in two strides, taking her hand and pressing it to his lips. "Bell. Thank you."

"Don't thank me yet. They haven't reached a decision."

****

Keeley couldn't sit in the big house on the point. Ciaran had told her the Council of Lords would hold their hearing quickly. When dawn broke, she was up and showering. Dressed in old cut-offs and a T-shirt, she stopped in the kitchen only long enough to pour herself a cup of coffee and toast a piece of bread. When Jonathan walked in, she gave him an absent smile.

"I'm taking the SUV so I can work on packing my Granddad's things."

"I could assist you if you wish, Miss Keeley."

"No. That's all right, Jonathan. I-I wish to be on my own."

It was a relief to escape the house, escape the reminders of Ciaran. His stamp and his aroma were everywhere. She called a realtor to list Granddad's house as a rental unit. She didn't want to sell it at the moment, but saw no reason for it to sit empty when it could bring in a tidy income as a summer rental. Once the rest of the boxes of items had been stored in the back of the SUV, Keeley phoned the realtor and made arrangements for her to stop by later that afternoon. One last look around the house told her it was neat and tidy. There was everything on hand a renter would need. Keeley splashed some water on her face and decided to walk down to the marina. Her footsteps took her to the *Prankster*.

"Keeley McNamara?"

She spun around to see a tall man with honey colored hair and midnight blue eyes. She cast around desperately in her memory, but her distraught emotions left her hanging. Her smile was cool and wary. She might be willing to put her trust in Ciaran, but that didn't mean she would let her guard down around every male she met.

He stuck out his hand and she took it as a reflex. "Taylor Barton. Used to be Taylor Stokes. I'm Annabel Clifton's half-brother."

"Of course. I remember you now." She took her hand back and shoved both of them in her pockets. Her smile was now nearly gone. "What can I do for you?"

He smiled again. "Well, for starters, you could let me take you to lunch."

She was already shaking her head even before he finished. "I-I have some errands I need to run."

Taylor tilted his head at her, his deep blue eyes regarding her with a knowing look. Keeley dropped her gaze and saw the anklet he wore.

"You're one of them."

His eyes narrowed slightly. "One of them? You make that sound like an accusation, like it's something bad, but I'm no different than Ciaran."

Keeley glared at him. "Shouldn't you be with them?"

Taylor shook his head. "No, by being the long lost great-grandson, I've managed so far to get most of the benefits without the responsibilities men like Carrick and my uncles bear."

"What do you mean?"

He chuckled. "Let me take you to lunch and I'll explain."

Keeley took a deep breath. She had to admit to a certain amount of curiosity concerning Ciaran's family and anything having to do with Silkies. And she still had a lot of questions. She bit her lip and eyed him a little nervously.

Taylor put a hand over his heart and smiled at her. "I promise I will neither bite nor molest you. I also have a pretty good shoulder to cry on. It's about the only Silkie thing I seem to be adept at. I guess I spent too much time as a somewhat nerdy human to have become the sex machines most of my relatives and in-laws seem to be. It's a little unmanning."

Once she finished simply staring at him aghast, Keeley laughed. "Are you for real?"

"Oh definitely. Don't you see nice guy written all over me? I'm everybody's boy next door." He offered his arm and she found herself taking it.

"Aren't you an attorney or something?" she asked as they walked back up the dock.

He smiled down at her. "Both actually. I handle most of the legal affairs for the Cliftons, and occasionally take on the odd errand or two. I disarm with my boyish charm and then go in for the kill like the legal barracuda I am. Besides, if you look at my less than stellar record as a Silkie, about the only thing I seem to be good at is putting other people together."

Keeley's green eyes narrowed. "Let me guess, is one of your errands being told to stay behind and watch out for Ciaran's human?"

The faint flush that stained his cheekbones told her everything, but amazingly she wasn't angry. In some ways, she found it comforting his family cared enough about Ciaran to make sure she was okay.

Taylor eyed her cautiously. "You're not mad? Cayden and Carrick said you had a pretty wicked temper and I should work really hard not to piss you off, but then I don't seem to inspire raging fits of any kind of emotion." He sighed dramatically. "So am I in danger of being hexed or cursed or anything?"

Now she did laugh. "Oh, I'm sure I could never accomplish anything so dramatic. I'm more the move things out of your way type if I like you, and move things in your way if I don't."

Taylor grinned. "Poppy—I mean Bell—mentioned she'd seen you make Ciaran trip over a garbage can. Pissed you off, huh?"

She laughed. "Yeah."

They walked in silence for a few minutes as he led her toward one of the many outdoor food joints and cafés along the waterfront.

"You were with Annabel and her daughter that day at the waterfront. I thought I recognized you. Didn't you used to hang out with that other guy—Geoff?"

Taylor nodded. "Geoff Sanderson. He's a good friend. Just came back to start a law practice here."

A furrow appeared between his brows. "Is that a problem?"

Taylor shook his head. "Geoff's just not real happy right now. He hated the practice he'd joined in Boston, and then his fiancée, the boss's daughter, dumped him. I've been trying to cheer him up."

Keeley thought of Stephie, but hesitated. After all, Geoff was the guy who'd stolen her bikini when they were teenagers. Granted it was just a prank, but Stephie had been humiliated.

Taylor guided her through the crowded tables to one overlooking the marina. "Did you really push Carrick into his own pool?" Taylor asked as he pulled a chair out for her.

Keeley grimaced. "Yes. I'm afraid I didn't make a very good first impression."

Taylor patted her hand. "Don't be too sure.

Carrick talked of nothing else and laughed the entire time. He can be kind of grim, so I think you definitely made a favorable impression. Same with Cay. He admired your loyalty. Said Ciaran was lucky to have you."

Now it was Keeley who felt her cheeks flooding with a blush. "I can't take too long for lunch. I'm meeting my realtor at two."

"Are you selling your grandfather's house then?"

"No. I've decided to rent it. Granddad had it for so long, I can't bring myself to sell, but it seems silly to let it sit empty when it could bring in a respectable income."

Taylor flopped back in his chair. "Ah, a woman after my own heart. Practical. And I hear you cook. But as always with my luck, someone else found you first."

His harmless, light flirting brought a smile to her face. Keeley realized with a shock he was exactly as he portrayed himself, a nice guy. By the end of lunch, she had invited him to the house for dinner and he was seating her in his little convertible to drop her back by her granddad's Cape Cod style home. When she climbed out, Keeley turned to him with a laugh. "Thanks for finding me, Taylor Barton. Everyone is right. You are a nice guy, and I'm glad Ciaran's family appointed you my watchdog."

"Seal. That would be a watchseal. I'll come to the house at seven, then, all right?"

"Yeah."

Keeley spent the next hour with the realtor going through the paperwork necessary to allow the realty company to conduct the lease arrangements. They did a quick inventory of the house and she let Keeley know she should have the listing on the internet in a few days. Satisfied it would all work out, Keeley shook hands with the woman and locked the house after she'd left.

As she climbed into the SUV she glanced over at the wooden box holding the ashes of her father and grandfather. "I haven't forgotten my promise, Pawpaw. There are just a few other things that need to be settled first."

She stopped by the market, picked up fresh salmon and vegetables for grilling. She would keep it simple and grill everything out by the pool. Taylor seemed like a nice enough guy, just like he'd said.

****

Carrick came out to get them. His expression betrayed nothing and made Ciaran want to rail at him. Didn't he realize this was his fucking life hanging in the balance? The decision they made would forever alter his future. A trickle of sweat slid down his back as he stood waiting for Rory to return. When he did, everyone bowed and waited until he seated himself. Ciaran sank back into the chair, his glance darting to his mother's pale face. In her hands he saw she held his pelt. The question now was would it be returned to him, or handed over to Rory?

The Silkie king looked down the long table at Ciaran. Dark eyes met dark eyes. "Ciaran Clifton, we have considered your situation and the changes you've made over the last four years. More important to us are the changes observed in you over the last few months. It is our belief you have shifted the focus of your existence so you are no longer the most important being in it. You have shown selflessness with regard to the woman Keeley McNamara, but we're also aware of kindnesses, perhaps more subtle but still there, you have shown toward the people who work for you. You have become more thoughtful and patient, and we believe you deserve the chance to show you can successfully meld the Silkie with the humanity in you."

He closed his eyes for a moment and let out a

236

ragged breath. He heard his mother laugh, the expressions of relief and congratulations from the rest of his family, yet even as his eyes turned toward his pelt, he was reaching for the necklace he wore. Keeley.

Don't let me forget.

The lure of his pelt was as sharp and gnawing as an addict's for his fix. It was part of him, part of who he was. No matter how long it had been, part of him always knew it had been missing. His mother stood before him, turning him and then bending to brush her hands over his ankle. Ciaran looked down and saw the leather circlet resting once more against the bones and tendons of his ankle.

"I know you are anxious to get back to the sea, son, but we would like you to dine with everyone this evening, then we will give you an official sendoff. Humor them, Ciaran. They have done you a great favor, done all of us a great favor."

He saw the tears in her eyes, blinked away the moisture from his own and had to swallow thickly before he answered, "Yes, Momma."

Chapter Sixteen

Taylor ate what she fixed as if he were a starving man getting his first meal in weeks. When he at last sat back, rubbing his stomach and smiling sleepily, all Keeley could do was laugh.

"If you always eat like that, no wonder they asked you to stay behind!"

Taylor smiled ruefully. "I didn't used to, well not quite as much, but there's just something about my metabolism since I first transformed. I can't seem to get enough to eat."

"Do you eat in seal form?"

Taylor nodded. "Hunt and eat."

Keeley toyed with the stem of her wine glass. "You mentioned something earlier today about being a long lost grandson. Whose great-grandson?"

"Rory the Silkie king. His son Taurent was my grandmother Mary Taylor's lover. They had my father, Phillip. When Taurent finally told my father about his heritage, Phillip rejected it and his father. Taurent left to return to his people…"

"What do you mean, he left?"

"I guess the longing for the sea became too much. It's the nature of the Silkie. They spend nearly as much time in seal form as they do human form, and when a Silkie has gone a long time in human form," he shrugged, "their bodies seek balance."

Keeley was floored. Ciaran had been human for four years. Did that mean when he changed he would spend four years as a seal? Her eyes widened. Four years? "I'm sorry, I interrupted your story."

Her voice was a little breathless.

"Yes, well, Taurent left to return to King Riordan, but he was killed in a hurricane during his return so Rory and my uncles, Faeran, Dylan and Brayden, never knew about Poppy and me. Since all the lordly spots have been filled, I can simply go along being plain old Taylor Barton."

Keeley smiled. "You're okay with that?"

"Absolutely. Don't get me wrong. I'm proud of my heritage, but I've spent most of my life as a human and that's still where most of my identity is focused. My friends are human and I'm simply more comfortable in the human world. Now, as a concession, I live in the home on Barton Point when Bell and Cayden aren't there and I take care of details for Carrick and some of the others as well. Many Silkie aren't comfortable socializing in the human world, particularly if it takes them any distance from the ocean."

Keeley sipped her wine and set it down, her fingers trembling slightly. "Ciaran has spent the last four years in human form, Taylor. If...if he gets his pelt back and transforms, how long will he stay in that form? How long will it take him to find balance?"

He was silent for enough time Keeley looked at him. "Taylor? How long?"

"It could be two years."

Suddenly Keeley understood why Ciaran made so many arrangements for her to be able to access his money and his investments. Why he stressed she was to go to his attorney once he was gone for more than a few days. Even as this was all turning over in her mind, a shock suddenly coursed through her body almost as if lightning struck her. It was the necklace.

She felt the transformation and she cried out both from the shock and the realization Ciaran might be lost to her for years. Keeley gasped, stumbling to her feet she ran down the path in the gloom of the summer twilight toward the point.

"Ciaran!" She ignored Taylor running after her, but skidded to a stop at the end of the point just as Taylor grabbed hold of her and pulled her away from the edge. "Stop it! Let me go. Oh God. I can't lose him, please."

Taylor pulled her into his arms. She heard the frantic beating of his heart, felt the tight band of his arms around her and she suddenly slumped against him.

"He's gone. He's gone. He swore he would never leave me, but he's gone."

"Shh! Keeley. He'll come back. Catriona's told me what she's seen. He'll come back. Give him time."

She heard the words, knew they should give her some comfort, but the ache inside was so great.

****

The ceremonial dinner took forever. Ciaran felt the weight of his pelt around his ankle; the call of the open ocean lured him. Yet part of him resisted, wanted to throw off the anklet that bound him as much as it freed him to pursue his other self. He could transform, and in so doing, he risked everything he had with Keeley.

As the dinner ended, the pressure built for him to make the change. Carrick and Cayden approached; the sight of them made Ciaran's stomach lurch. It was time. It could be put off no longer. His fist tightened around the necklace.

"Son, you must do this." Carrick's voice was quiet. "Cayden and I will go into the water with you. This first time you should transform there."

Ciaran's mouth twisted. "So I am back to being just a child again, in need of assistance should I have trouble."

"You know half-transformations can be painful."

"I am aware." Ciaran's jaw hardened. "I apologize. There are things..."

Cayden put his hand on his shoulder. "Annabel asked her brother Taylor to watch out for her, Ciaran, especially tonight. She's not alone."

Ciaran wasn't sure if that was a comfort or not. Another man was with her? He set jealous feelings aside. She needed someone with her to help her understand, to help her through however long it might be. Still.

"I can't lose her, Cayden," Ciaran growled. "Promise you will watch over her if I don't come back. I swore to her I wouldn't desert her, that I wouldn't leave her...and I am doing exactly that. Please...swear."

Carrick touched his other shoulder. "You'll be back. Your love for her is too strong. For now, you must concentrate on changing."

Cayden met his gaze evenly. "I swear to you."

Ciaran nodded. Everyone crowded the deck. He felt as if he were on display as he stripped off his clothing. Carrick and Cayden did so as well. A collective sigh went up from the women and some of the men as well. There was no doubt the Clifton males were truly a sight to behold with their broad shoulders, narrow waists and flat stomachs. All of it blended into high, tight butts and long muscular thighs, and there was at least one additional area most of the younger girls found equally fascinating. They sighed with envy of the women who were allowed to play with such gorgeous specimens.

Carrick and Cayden dove in first, treading water as they waited for Ciaran.

Catriona stepped forward. "Your necklace, Ciaran. Surely you wish to remove it."

In the light from the boat, Ciaran saw the glint of gold around Cayden's neck. "No. I'll keep it on. Maybe it will remind me."

"Son..."

He turned to his mother, feeling again the need to just leave. He could steal the launch..."I must have something. Please!"

Catriona bowed her head and backed away.

Ciaran dove in and surfaced between his father and brother. "I'm ready. Let's do this."

"Say the words, Ciaran. Say them and believe them."

His jaw was tight and his mind on Keeley. He grabbed the necklace again and nearly swam back to the *Skerry*. If he took the launch, he could be back with her in under an hour.

"Ciaran! Say them."

He began in their ancient tongue, "On land I am but man, on the sea a Silkie be. As I will it so will it be."

He felt the change and railed against it.

"Quit fighting it!" Carrick snapped. "Say the words again and quit fighting it before you injure yourself."

Ciaran repeated the words over and over and this time as he touched the pelt on his ankle, he felt the shifting and turning from man to seal.

"Keeley!" her name was wrenched from his throat as human vocal chords became those of a seal. And then his worries were gone. He heard the sounds of the ocean and felt the caress of the water against his sleek hide. With a joyous bark, he leaped and twisted, diving down and spinning through the water. Carrick and Cayden changed with him, shooting off to follow, knowing for now at least they would not be able to send him their thoughts. He was a seal, sentient only in the sense of wanting to swim and hunt, to eat and play. The carefree existence was a powerful mistress few could deny, and after four years confined in his human form, Ciaran was finally free.

He swam until he was exhausted, pulling out on a rocky bit of deserted beach to sleep the rest of the night. Humanity was simply a whisper so far on the edge of his animal consciousness that it was no more than a memory. He was a bull seal, powerful and in his prime. Carrick and Cayden watched for a moment and then left him alone so they could bring news back to those aboard the *Skerry*.

****

Keeley stood on the point as she did each morning and evening and looked for him. Human or seal, she didn't care if she could only get a sight of him. A week had passed. Taylor would be there in an hour to take her into the city to see Ciaran's attorney. She was already dressed in a suit with a skirt that ended at mid-thigh. She carried her high heels hooked on two of her fingers as she stared out to sea. Did he remember? Her stomach turned over again. She had eaten and slept little in the past week.

While she knew in her mind she had to go on, it was so damn hard. Stephie stopped by, but since Keeley could hardly explain Ciaran was swimming around somewhere in the Atlantic as a seal, the only thing her friend saw was Ciaran deserted her. Taylor stopped by almost every evening and walked with her to the point where they sat while she stared out to sea. She sometimes wondered if he was only there to prevent her from going into the sea, but in the end it didn't matter. To him at least, she could talk and let out all her fears.

Taylor kept telling her to trust, but that had never come easy for Keeley. As childish as she knew it to be, deep down inside she always felt her father deserted her. He made the choice to save someone, even knowing what it would mean. Then Frank Wells betrayed her trust. The man who should have been looking out for her, protecting her, instead violated and abused her. And finally, the ultimate betrayal of trust was her own mother who chose to believe Frank rather than her. No, trust wasn't something that came easily to Keeley, but she had learned to survive.

"I thought I might find you out here," Taylor said quietly from behind her. "Are you ready?"

Keeley turned and her eyes widened. This was a Taylor she barely recognized. She had seen him only in shorts, T-shirts and sandals. Now before her stood a tall, golden haired man impeccably groomed and attired in a suit obviously custom-tailored.

"You look different."

"So do you. Do you think Ciaran would mind if we borrow the Porsche? It will be a lot more comfortable than my convertible."

Keeley's mouth twisted. "No. He wants me to take over responsibility for everything. I guess that means the car too."

Taylor offered his arm. "Come on. I know a wonderful place where we can get lunch in the city after we've dealt with Jim Belmont. Did I tell you I almost went to work for his firm? I'm sure there will be a few hard feelings since Belmont is a golfing buddy of my mother's husband."

"Stokes? Wasn't that the name you grew up with?"

"Yes, but after learning the truth and who my relatives were, I decided I felt a lot more like a Barton than a Stokes. I had already filled out all of the paperwork to begin working for Belmont's firm when I discovered the truth. It kind of shifted my priorities, and I backed out of the job."

Keeley stopped on the path as they neared the house. "Taylor, if you're not comfortable with this…"

He grinned at her. "Keeley, I love confrontations. It's why I became an attorney. I only look like an angel. There is nothing—well almost nothing—that excites me more than to twist an argument to prove a point."

Two hours later, they were seated in the waiting area outside Jim Belmont's office. The man was deliberately keeping them waiting and it irritated Keeley. Taylor, she noted with an equal amount of irritation, was remarkably unruffled.

"Sit, Keeley." Taylor said patiently. "It's a game. You have to play it. Never let them see you sweat. It's what he wants."

"I'm not sweating," she hissed. "I'm pissed. There's a difference. I'm also hungry."

"Well that's a switch," Taylor drawled. "You've lost weight in the past week. Ciaran's a lot bigger than me. I don't want him to beat me up when he gets back if you're not in the peak of health."

She glared at him for a moment and then laughed.

"That's better, Keeley girl."

Her eyes widened, startled at hearing the same pet name her granddad had used. What surprised her even more was the instant ache of longing she felt. She flushed and glanced away. Surely she couldn't feel lust for this man. But she knew what it was. Ciaran had stirred her sexual appetites and then satiated them so regularly she'd become used to it. Now doing without him was making her frustration mount.

"Mr. Belmont will see you now." The secretary's cool voice interrupted Keeley's heated thoughts. Good thing. It would never do to be thinking about sex with her fiancé's cousin, brother-in-law, whatever the hell he was.

Taylor kept his hand comfortingly at the small of her back as he guided her inside Jim Belmont's office. The older man stood, his eyes narrowing in recognition on Taylor.

"Good morning, Miss McNamara. Stokes...or is

it Barton now?"

"Barton, Jim, but you can call me Taylor. Like Ciaran, I prefer to keep things more informal."

"Cavalier might be more accurate," Belmont muttered.

"Now, now, Jim," Taylor said, "We're here to deal with Ciaran's instructions concerning Miss McNamara, not your feelings about my change in career pursuits." Although there was humor in his voice, Keeley heard the steel underlying it, and realized Taylor Barton was not simply the easygoing young man he appeared to be. Underneath was a very focused, determined man. His casual attitude was there simply to throw people off guard. "I believe you have some paperwork for Miss McNamara to sign, and some communication for her from Ciaran."

"I believe Ciaran wished me to handle Miss McNamara." Belmont's tone was condescending. "Not some inexperienced attorney. There is a lot of money involved here, not something you're likely comfortable with."

Now Taylor laughed. Keeley didn't like Belmont's tone and was close to telling him just that, but there was such a wicked gleam in Taylor's eye she decided she could hold her tongue a while longer to see what came of it.

"I suspect you're right. Being chief legal counsel for Clifton Shipping would limit my exposure to assets beyond a few billion dollars. However, when it comes to Miss McNamara, I believe, Jim, you're going to find no one, but no one *handles* Keeley McNamara."

For the first time since she entered the room, Keeley felt Jim Belmont finally take a good look at her. Seeing her petite frame and spiky hair, she knew he was about ready to dismiss her as nothing more than Ciaran Clifton's latest bubble-headed trophy. Then the older man's eyes met hers. Keeley stared him down until he swallowed somewhat nervously.

"My apologies, Miss McNamara. Let me get Mr. Clifton's file."

Keeley read and signed the paperwork put in front of her. Finally, Belmont handed her a sealed envelope. "Mr. Clifton wanted you to read this once it became necessary for you to take over his affairs. If you'd like, I'll leave you two alone while you do so."

Keeley held the envelope in her hand as if it were a living thing. "I would appreciate that."

When the door shut behind him, she continued to stare at the envelope.

"Would you like me to leave?"

"No. I'll just take this over to the chair near the window."

Her hands trembled as she opened the seal on the envelope.

My Beautiful Keeley,

If you're reading this, then it means at least a week has already passed since we parted. I am no doubt swimming and hunting somewhere. I have avoided telling you just how long it could be before I come back mainly out of my own fear you would leave me. I couldn't do what I had to do if I knew you wouldn't be waiting. But now I am gone, I won't hold you to me. When I have no idea how long I might be gone, I simply refuse to bind you to any promises, but I will keep mine to you. What is mine is yours. Use it, care for it and care for yourself.

I might not be able to come back to you for years, love. I pray it won't be so. With every breath I take as I write this, I ache for you already. I know this doesn't make much sense, but finding you, loving you, gives me the strength to go, because I know there is something to come back to. You are my humanity. You are the very best of me.

If you see a seal swimming in the bay, think of me. Maybe you can pull me back. I want it to be so.

I will love you forever. C

Tears slipped down her cheeks. Trust. She trusted his love, trusted the strength of their love. He would be back. He wouldn't leave her forever. No matter how long it took, he would remember and he'd be able to make the change.

"Keeley," Taylor's voice was just a whisper behind her. "Are you all right?"

His hand rested gently on her shoulder. Keeley touched her cheek to his hand. "I am all right, Taylor. I think I've finally been able to do what you kept urging me to. Trust."

She turned around and hugged him. His arms circled her loosely. "We've done what we need to do here. Why don't we grab some lunch and head back? Do you like to sail? I have a boat."

Keeley laughed. "I love to sail, and I'm starving. Lunch first, then take me out on the water. I think I'll feel closer to him that way, and I need that right now."

She wasn't sure what she expected, a five star restaurant or something the up and coming crowd frequented, but instead they ended up at a noisy Greek eatery run by an older man and his wife. The food was prepared and served family style with as much love as expertise. When Taylor mentioned Keeley was a chef, the woman blushed and stammered to make excuses about her cooking.

Keeley put her hand on the woman's arm. "This is delicious. I could never make souvlaki such as this. And your pastries? So many people struggle with the filo because they're impatient. It's obvious you took the time to make this right. I've never had better."

The woman beamed, chattering to her husband in Greek as she headed back to the kitchen. Taylor's dark blue eyes were frankly admiring as he looked across the table at Keeley.

"That was very kind of you, Keeley."

Keeley waved her hand dismissively as she picked up the small cup of thick, sweet coffee served with dessert. "It wasn't kind. It was the truth. Half of being able to cook successfully is loving what you do. She does and it shows."

Taylor watched her as she finished until finally she looked at him. "What?"

"I see why Ciaran loves you."

She looked away again. "Don't, Taylor. You must know I'm vulnerable right now. Don't make it worse. You're an attractive man..."

"Shh. Relax. I would never do anything to upset you or Ciaran. Like I told you before. He's bigger than me...whether it's as a man or as a seal. I've always found fear to be a great deterrent to hasty actions."

Keeley's tension disappeared and she giggled. "You make Ciaran sound like a bully."

Taylor's brows pulled together. "He was. But that's changed. Still, I have a healthy respect for someone as powerful as he is. He might not have the same amount of magic Cayden possesses, but what he does have combined with his physical prowess would make him a formidable foe. I have no intention of trespassing where I haven't been invited."

Keeley tilted her head. "You make it sound like an invitation isn't out of the question."

Taylor laughed. "Honey, if you spend much time around the Silkie, you'll realize they have a very different outlook on sex."

She let that slide for the time being and allowed him to escort her back out to the Porsche. She drifted to sleep on the drive back, exhausted from disturbed nights and the tension she had felt about this day.

****

Taylor glanced over at her. Like him, she shed her suit jacket for the trip home, but where he wore a dress shirt and tie, only a thin silk shell covered her. From the rounded curves of her small breasts to the pebbled hardness of her nipples, it was obvious she wore nothing beneath it. His glanced drifted down to the expanse of slender, bare thigh. Did she wear anything under her skirt? His cock swelled, tenting his slacks with its aching hardness. Hell. He was near coming just thinking about her, and that wasn't at all Taylor's normal taste. He preferred his women on more Junoesque lines. Keeley was more like an elf. Truth be told, he hadn't had a steady lover for four years, and barely any sex at all. He and Geoff Sanderson indulged themselves now and then in the past with the same woman, but since his return, Geoff had been withdrawn to the point where Taylor worried about him.

Taylor's jaw tightened. He felt like he'd become the watchdog not only for the Silkie, but for his own human friends.

He glanced at Keeley again, hating at least some of the deception he was putting her through. Yes, he'd been instructed to watch out for her, but Catriona had also pulled him aside with other instructions, and it was those he intended to carry out now.

Why did he always end up with the tough jobs? The tough jobs with no payoff. Taylor drove straight to the Yacht Club marina. He had Jonathan throw a bag in the trunk of the Porsche with Keeley's bathing suit and a spare set of casual clothes.

After parking the car, he took a moment to simply stare at her. Something about her pulled him. For the first time, he wanted to do more than just get her in the sack. He wanted to know her inside and out. Be her friend, her protector...her lover. And that was the problem. She wasn't free for him to claim, and he wasn't sure if the Silkie's relaxed attitude about sex extended this far.

Gently, he shook her awake. "We're here."

She stirred with a little mewl of protest. "Home? Is Ciaran back? I dreamed of him. You were there too. He laughed at me about that."

"About what, honey?"

"The thought of making love with an audience."

Taylor shifted uncomfortably as his prick jerked inside his pants. "How very like a Silkie you must be, Keeley. No, we're at the marina. Jonathan packed a bag with your bikini and a change of clothes. We can head on out. *Sweet Life* is a little bigger than *The Prankster*, so I might need some help. Can you crew?"

She nodded. "Granddad taught me."

Taylor grinned. "Great! Let's go then."

****

He showed her down to the main cabin and left her there to change while he used the galley. The cabin was all very masculine in décor with its wood trim and primary colors.

After stripping off her clothes, she rummaged in the duffle bag and found her bikini. She wished Jonathan had packed her racing suit, but this would have to do. After tying the top and the bottoms, Keeley slipped her feet into her deck shoes, and opened the door to go topside.

Taylor bumped into her as she came out and she instantly put her hands up to balance herself. She sucked in a breath feeling the hard muscle beneath the crisp, golden hair on his chest. Her eyes were drawn down his body. She couldn't help it. As they paused on the distinct bulge in his shorts, she blushed.

"Sorry. I didn't mean to run into you," she

gasped, not daring to meet his eyes.

"Quite all right," Taylor responded, a touch of humor in his voice. "Let's get under way."

He had her steer while he cast off. Once he'd maneuvered into the bay, they worked together to adjust sail. Keeley felt his eyes on her body, and caught herself several times looking at the play of muscles beneath his golden skin. When she once again glanced at his crotch, she heard him chuckle.

"I don't mind you looking," he said when she flushed and turned away. "It's flattering really. I can't really do much to hide the fact I find you very attractive, so I hope it doesn't bother you too much."

Keeley felt such an ache for Ciaran, and Taylor's response only reminded her of what she missed. That just made things worse, thinking of her last night with Ciaran, and she was afraid she might have to go back down to the cabin for a few minutes to relieve the throbbing of her own desire.

"I'm fine," she responded a little breathlessly.

She saw his gaze drop to her hard nipples.

"You can sunbathe topless if you'd like. I can't get in much worse shape than I already am."

Keeley's eyes widened and then she giggled. "That's an interesting way to look at it."

Taylor grinned. "I'm practical. Maybe looking at them instead of imagining them will anesthetize me."

Keeley gaped at him and then just laughed. "Do you think the same thing would work for me?"

Taylor smiled slowly. "Do you need it to? What a wicked girl you are. We could try it and see."

They sailed toward a cove Keeley knew all too well. As she stripped off her top and dropped it onto the deck, she looked back at Taylor. His eyes were glued to her small breasts. She saw what she'd imagined was a hard-on was just a mere shadow compared to what now tautened the front of his shorts.

Feeling the ache of desire, she murmured, "I don't think this is having the desired effect."

"It's certainly affecting my desire."

Keeley laughed. "Yes but it seems to be increasing rather than decreasing."

Taylor bowed. "Thank you for noticing. Maybe a swim will help."

Keeley looked back at the cove. "Why is it such a beautiful cove always seems to be deserted? I never see anyone else here."

Taylor laughed. "Magic."

Keeley's eyes opened. "Magic? I thought that was my purview."

"Oh the Silkie have their own abilities, and Catriona is blessed with more since she was originally one of your kind. You would be the same."

Keeley chose to ignore that for now, more curious about the cove. "So what you're telling me is humans don't see this?"

"Not unless we choose to bring them. They see a swamp. Cayden took care of that."

"So whatever we do here can't be seen by uninvited human eyes."

"That's correct."

Keeley stood and dropped her swimsuit bottoms. "Then I'm skinny-dipping." The truth of the matter was she was so damn horny, she was afraid she would orgasm just standing there unless she could get in the water and cool off. God how she longed for Ciaran! He would laugh at her and then touch her in all the right places.

Taylor looked at her with an odd smile. "Why don't you go on in while I drop anchor. I'll join you in a couple of minutes."

Keeley dove in and quickly circled to the port bow, away from where Taylor had been working. She ached. Oh God, she thought as tears ran down her cheeks, she wanted Ciaran so badly, wanted to feel him touching her, loving her. She hesitated for a moment and then cupped her hand over herself. She was so near to coming it took a moment to realize her own breathing wasn't the only breathing she heard. Throwing back her head, she looked up to see Taylor standing just a few feet away, his eyes glued on her movements. He had removed his shorts and stood leaning against the gunwale.

She started to duck away in embarrassment, but there was something so understanding in his blue eyes all she could do was stare. Her eyes dropped to his erection.

"That's it," he whispered as he watched her and stroked himself. "Get your scent in the water for Ciaran. Touch yourself, Keeley. Let him know where you are. It's why we're here."

Her eyes widened as she took in his meaning. Could that bring him to her? She glanced around her as if just the thought might make it fact, but the waters were bare. Her fingers slipped inside her tight passage.

"That's the way. Call him to you."

Ciaran. If there were any way he could come to her...She moaned softly as her climax neared, her eyes were glued to the movements of Taylor's hand over his hard phallus. In her mind, it wasn't Taylor; it was Ciaran she saw. In just a few seconds more, he stiffened and came. It triggered her orgasm and she cried out. She went still, too weak to tread water, and began to sink. Then something brushed her bottom, pushing her upward. Air bubbles rose around her, thousands and thousands of them tickling her skin and teasing her legs and butt and belly.

Keeley gasped, looking around her frantically until she saw a seal's head pop up a few feet away. She watched, not even daring to hope, and then as it swam toward her, she saw the glint of silver around its neck. Ciaran. He surfaced a little closer, still watching her curiously with big dark eyes.

It was him. Keeley laughed. It was him! He had the necklace on. Joy raced through her.

"Ciaran!" Her voice broke, and she bit down on her lower lip to stop it from trembling.

He swam to her then, nuzzling her, circling her, blowing bubbles around her and at her. She couldn't believe it, couldn't believe how happy she felt, how her heart lightened. She looked up at Taylor who still stood at the gunwale watching.

"Did you know?" She asked.

He smiled. "Let's just say we hoped."

"We?"

"Catriona suggested it."

Keeley blushed bright red. "She suggested you get me out here and do this?"

It was Taylor's turn to blush. "Yes, although I'm not sure the degree of my own reaction was in the plan. Ciaran is very lucky," he continued quietly. "You're so beautiful when you climax."

Ciaran bumped her gently with his big, sleek body.

"Why doesn't he change?" Worry clouded her tone.

"He probably can't yet, but I think it's a testament to the strength of his love that he's here. What you have must be very strong."

She stroked the sleek head lying against her shoulder. "Can he understand us?"

"Most likely. If he was aware enough to come to you, then most likely he also understands."

Tears came to her eyes. Ciaran remained still, his head slightly tilted and then made a couple of soft, grunting noises before diving underneath her where he again circled her, blowing bubbles. He surfaced in front of her and hovered there, his head turned over his shoulder.

Taylor laughed. "He wants to give you a ride. Cayden and Bell used to do this. Hold around his neck or at the top of his front flippers."

Keeley swam to him and did that, surprised by the feeling of coming home as her body slid along his wet fur. Her breath hitched on a sob and she laid her head next to his. He grunted again softly and slowly swam off with her riding on his back. It reminded her of the time in the bay when he'd let her ride on his back while he swam. Keeley stretched out on him, reaching for him with her mind, but she couldn't breach the differences between them. He brought her into shallow water, nudged her onto the beach then disappeared.

"Don't go!" She started to panic, but then realized he had simply moved nearer *Sweet Life*.

A few minutes later, she saw Ciaran and Taylor both swimming as seals, rolling and playing together. She watched, fascinated at the rough and tumble interaction between the two. It was beautiful, graceful and wild. As they came toward shore, Taylor transformed, but Ciaran continued onto the beach as a seal. Keeley's glance went from his dark liquid eyes to Taylor who shook his head. She knew she'd been unable to mask her disappointment.

"He doesn't have enough strength to change." Taylor murmured, then stopped awkwardly, a blush staining his tan cheeks. Ciaran growled. Taylor sighed. "He wants me to pleasure you for him."

Keeley's eyes widened as she looked from Ciaran to Taylor. "He wants you to have *sex* with me?"

Chapter Seventeen

She recoiled from it, partly because, just for an instant, she found Taylor attractive, but mostly because it was Ciaran she needed, Ciaran she wanted.

"No!" Taylor shook his head. "No, not mate with you. He wants me to arouse you, to give you pleasure." He stopped for a minute to gather his thoughts. "I told you earlier, the Silkie have very different ideas about sexual pleasure. Public sex is okay and threesomes are not at all uncommon."

Keeley looked from Taylor to Ciaran's whiskered face and back again. She liked Taylor, but it wasn't him she longed for with everything inside her.

"He wants to mate with me while he's like this?"

Ciaran growled and Taylor blanched. "No. No, of course not. Damn, I wish you could talk right now Ciaran, buddy, because I have so lost my gift for gab, and I'm fuckin' this up pretty badly."

Ciaran grunted, rolling over in the water to clap his flippers together. It lightened the tension surrounded them all. Keeley giggled. Taylor flopped down next to her. "Oh hell, let me just give it to you straight. He would really like to change and make love with you, but he doesn't think he can. In the meantime, it would give him pleasure if it would give you pleasure for me to...to play with you. You know, kiss you and uh...give you an orgasm...if that suits you."

Keeley's glance darted to Ciaran. "And he would watch, so maybe it would help him turn and we could at least make love?"

Taylor sighed with obvious relief. "Yes. Exactly."

Ciaran scooted far enough out of the water to lick the bottom of her foot. Heat shot through her. He grunted and nudged her toes.

"O...kay. But in the water so he can be part of it," Keeley whispered. Taylor took her hand and led her back into the water until they stood waist deep. He turned her so her back was to him and slid his arms around her. Slowly, he kissed the side of her neck, the shell of her ear, then tilted her face just enough to finally brush her mouth with his lips. He felt different than Ciaran. While she didn't feel the overwhelming passion she did with him, knowing Ciaran watched, that he wanted this helped her response. And with him behind her, she could almost imagine it was Ciaran. Taylor nibbled at her neck, his hands stroking ribs and down across her belly, pulling her close against his swelling cock.

"Touch my breasts," she murmured, covering his hands with her own. That was always one of Ciaran's favorite things to do. Maybe it would help now. He brushed against their legs under the water and bubbles floated around them. "Yes," she moaned. "Watch us and change. Please, Ciaran. I need to feel you inside me again."

She arched against Taylor, her moans increasing as he slid one hand over her belly and covered her sex. She parted her legs for his seeking fingers, crying out as he caressed her slick core. Ciaran swam around them stopping to bump them gently, then slipping below the water to blow more bubbles around them.

"Let me take you to the edge of the water," Taylor groaned. "I want to taste you. Inhaling your sweet fragrance is incredible. God Ciaran, I owe you for this."

The big bull seal lay next to them snuffling softly as he watched Taylor kiss his way down

Keeley's body, suckling at her breasts, nipping at her stomach and then gently parting her thighs with his hands. He stopped for a moment and just stared at the pink, pouting lips of her sex visible through the wet curls.

"She's so swollen," Taylor whispered. "I can just imagine what she would feel like wrapped around my cock."

A low growl came from next to them. Keeley giggled, her slumberous eyes turning to Ciaran. Taylor's tongue suddenly licked along the length of her, its broad, flat surface laving her. Her eyes closed and she fisted her hands in his wet golden curls. He became more aggressive, pleasuring her with his tongue and his fingers. Keeley moaned as wetness flooded her. Her eyes were on Ciaran. Suddenly he blurred, and changed, his body lengthening and streamlining. Fur disappeared to be replaced with golden skin and a light coating of body hair.

****

God, it hurt! Every fiber of muscle and bone protested being forced to change so soon, but Ciaran was desperate.

"Keeley!" He needed to be inside her, and he knew he had little time. She cried hearing the sound of his voice. Now he shut his eyes with a different pain. Never would he have done this to her, and now when he most wanted to take his time and be tender, he had to take her quickly.

As he uncoiled, stretching his legs and the length of his arms, Taylor broke off what he was doing and rolled out of the way. Now. Ciaran had to do it now. He covered her body with his and thrust into her. Their moans filled the air as he pumped in and out, frantic to bring them both to completion. As they coupled on the sand, their heads turned toward Taylor, who watched them with hot, blue eyes.

Ciaran stared down at Keeley, wanting to memorize every expression on her face. It had taken almost all the strength he possessed to change. Now he needed to hurry because he couldn't maintain his human form for long. Too many years denying his Silkie existence. He had to make up for that, but just this once he could give her part of himself. She called to him with her tears as much as her scent. This much he could do for her. He thrust deeply inside of her, filling her just as he saw Taylor climax. He hadn't wanted him to touch her, but there was no other way, and for that he owed him.

Ciaran kissed Keeley frantically as she spasmed around him.

"I love you, Keeley Ann. Love you. I have to go. Can't stay. Can come to you as a seal."

The change came over him now whether he wanted it or not. He simply could not maintain his human form. Ciaran cried out as his body reverted and rolled away from her so he wouldn't crush her. *Keeley*. It was his last thought. He had to get away for a while. Being near her was too much. It demanded more of his control and his emotions than he could stand.

With a lurch and a powerful lunge he pushed beneath the surface of the water, once more locking his humanity behind a wall so he could survive in the dangerous world beneath the wave.

****

Barely a ripple remained where he had been.

"Ciaran," she whispered. "Come back." But the water remained still. No shadow sped beneath the surface. She rolled onto her side and curled into a ball.

Taylor watched from a few feet away, stunned at the powerful emotions swirling around them. He had thought Cayden and Annabel were closer than any two beings could be. Until now.

260

Ciaran Clifton and Keeley McNamara weren't two people. They were two halves to a whole, neither totally complete without the other. He swallowed and closed his eyes, feeling their pain deep inside and finally understanding this was his version of Silkie magic. A curse more like it, the ability to be empathic.

Taylor rose to his feet and closed the distance to where Keeley lay curled in the wet sand. When he picked up her slender body, she curled against him, burying her face in his chest.

"How do I stand it?" she breathed.

He stared down at her sadly and swallowed around the lump in his own throat. "You share your pain, Keeley. That's why I'm here."

While she silently shook with sobs, Taylor carried her back out to his boat. Once he brought her on board, he gently dried her naked body, laid her in the berth in the main cabin and tucked her in.

Inhaling deeply, he forced himself to concentrate while he brushed a hand across her eyes. This type of magic was still difficult for him.

"Sleep, Keeley girl. Sleep."

****

A month. One month had passed since that unforgettable afternoon in the cove. Keeley sat on the beach watching the fishermen head out for the evening. Summer was nearing an end. Already many of the temps had left. Her hair had grown longer, whipping about her face as a brisk breeze blew.

"You're mighty pensive." Stephie plopped down next to her. "Heard anything from Ciaran?"

Keeley stared out to sea. "No. Not for a month."

"Mighty long business trip." Keeley dug in the sand with her bare toes as Stephie continued. "Of course, you don't seem to lack for company. I've seen you around town with Taylor Barton and Geoff Sanderson. Neither of them is anything to turn your

261

nose up at."

Keeley turned her head where it rested on her knee and smiled wanly at her friend. "They're friends, Stephie, like us. Besides, Ciaran and his family have asked them to keep an eye on me."

Stephie laughed. "I wish someone would ask two hunks like that to keep an eye on me."

Keeley tilted her head and slowly smiled. "I could use some female company. Are you off tonight?"

"Yeah. Next weekend will be a bitch, so Stan's trying to give us some time off now. Why?"

"Come over for dinner. Bring your bathing suit. We'll stuff our faces and flop around the pool. I could use the company of my very best friend."

Stephie smiled. "Sounds good to me. Will you give me the grand tour of the playboy mansion?"

Keeley stared back out at the water. "Yeah, and then I think maybe it might be time for you to learn a little more about Ciaran." *And me.* She was tired of hiding everything from her best friend.

"Cool. I gotta go right now. I promised my mom I'd help her this afternoon. She's cleaning a few more summerhouses and getting them ready for the off season."

"Okay. See you around six?"

"Sure thing."

Keeley watched Steph head up the strip of beach to the walkway. Her eyes narrowed on her friend as she reached into her pocket and retrieved her cell phone. She punched Taylor's name and hit call.

"Keeley," he answered on the second ring. "Everything okay?"

She smiled to herself. "Want to come over for dinner? And bring Geoff."

There was a pause on the other end. "We can do that. Are you sure you're all right?"

She heard the concern in his pleasant baritone.

"Yes. Geoff knows about you, right?"

"Yes. I told you that. He actually called to me."

Keeley laughed. "Tell me, Taylor, how are you doing in sexually satisfying him?"

There was a snort on the other end of the line. "I haven't quite figured that one out yet. I'm not quite as open as some of the Silkie when it comes to sexual partners. Men just aren't on the menu."

Keeley smiled. "I might have a solution for you. Come to Ciaran's house, say about seven? And don't ask questions. I think you'll see."

"Okay."

After saying goodbye, she shoved the phone back in her pocket and stared out to sea. Maybe it was time to try and do her own good deed.

****

He watched her from far enough away that she couldn't see him. She was changing, and he wasn't there with her. Ciaran growled, struggling with the urge to go to her, to try to change. In the last week, he had at least become aware again, and he was grateful for that, grateful he did remember. Now he felt trapped. He knew with no doubt the more he attempted to go to her, to change into human form so soon, the longer he would sentence himself to remain in the sea.

She needs me.

Ciaran stared at her bent head, the sorrow he saw in her eyes and the shadows that lay heavily beneath them. All was not right.

****

By the time Steph arrived that evening, Keeley had the steaks in the fridge waiting to go on the grill. Now all she had to do was wait for Taylor and Geoff. In the hour she'd given herself between Steph coming over and the two men getting there, Keeley plied her friend from a rather potent pitcher of frozen margaritas.

And she felt absolutely no guilt. Taylor told her how down in the dumps Geoff was, and she already knew Steph had watched both men off and on since they were teenagers.

As they sat out by the pool, Steph commented. "I'm surprised you don't have Taylor and Geoff here. They seem to be pretty regular guests."

"They've been good friends since Ciaran left."

Steph twisted her head sideways on the lounger where she reclined. "You have all the luck, Keeley. For someone who always gave men such a cold shoulder, suddenly you have three hunks panting after you."

Keeley smiled. In the background behind the music she had playing, she heard the crunch of tires on the drive, a noise Stephie apparently didn't hear.

"It's Ciaran I love, Stephie. Taylor and Geoff are friends, nothing more."

"We should all be so lucky to have two such devoted friends." Keeley's eyes suddenly sparkled with laughter, but she remained silent while her friend continued, "I can think of a lot of things I wouldn't mind doing with those two."

"Is that a promise?" Taylor asked, flopping next to Stephie. He grinned mischievously at Keeley and then directed his gaze back to Stephie. Geoff still stood near the gate to the pool, his dark gaze drinking in Stephie Brooks, from her golden hair all the way to her pink painted toenails.

Keeley tried to wipe the smile from her face as Stephie faced her, her cheeks bright red with embarrassment.

"Keeley McNamara! How could you not say something and just let me go on like that?"

Taylor took Stephie's hand. "Stephanie Brooks, right? I remember you from summers here when I was a teenager. I spent a lot of time fantasizing about you."

Stephie snatched her hand away. "It's the boobs, right? Nobody can get past them." She jumped to her feet. "See you around, Keeley."

Keeley started to protest, but it was Geoff who suddenly stepped forward. "Please. Don't go." He glanced a little nervously from Keeley and Taylor back to Steph. Keeley wished she could see her friend's expression better, but she could see the sincerity in Geoff's face. "I was hoping to see you. I've stopped by Stan's a couple of times, but it always seems to be when you're off."

Keeley jumped up. "Come on, Steph. I'm sorry. I should have told you. I just thought we could all have a nice evening. You know, share some food and drink, swim, talk. Besides, I really want you to understand this part of my life and what's going on right now. I know it seems strange to you."

Stephie shifted her golden gaze from Geoff Sanderson back to her friend. "You're right about that, Keeley. It does seem strange; I feel like you've been shutting me out."

Taylor came up at that point and rested his hands on Keeley's shoulders. "You want her to know, Keeley?" he asked quietly.

Keeley looked at Taylor's familiar features. "Yes. She's my best friend."

Geoff touched Steph's shoulder. "Please stay, if for no other reason than to give me a chance to apologize once again for stealing your bikini top all those years ago."

Stephie flushed, but Keeley could see her curiosity was aroused. Stephie kept stealing glances at Geoff Sanderson, exactly what Keeley wanted. Taking hold of Stephie's hands, she tugged her friend back to the side of the pool where they'd been sitting.

Taylor poured drinks, raising his brows slightly when Keeley said she'd stick with the Perrier. Geoff sat in the chair nearest Stephie and Keeley smiled. Two people who were a better fit for each other she'd never seen. Geoff had never been as stuck up as some of the rich kids who spent their summers on the sound, never looked down on Stephie or Keeley because they lived on the sound year round.

"Taylor?" Keeley sat up. "Would you come to the kitchen with me and help me carry everything out? I'll cook out here while you all talk."

****

"Okay, Keeley," Taylor said as soon as they reached the kitchen. "What are you up to?"

She turned from the refrigerator with the platter of steaks in her hand. "Haven't you ever noticed the way those two have looked at each other over the years?"

Taylor shook his head. "Honestly? I was spending too much time staring myself."

Keeley snorted. "Staring at her boobs, right?"

"Actually, it was her shapely ass I fantasized about. Me and Geoff. We'd sit around in the dark at the Yacht Club and jerk off imagining ourselves both doing her at the same time. But Geoff had it a lot worse than me."

"Well, here's your chance," Keeley told him. "Do your Silkie matchmaker thing or whatever it is you do. I mean, won't you be off the hook if he's sexually satisfied even if you're not the satisfier?"

Taylor shrugged. "I guess." He glanced out the window to see Geoff smiling at something Stephie was saying. "They do seem to be hitting it off. But boy, I have to admit to some envy. If I fix the two of them up, I'm still not getting any sex. What kind of a Silkie am I?"

He turned when he felt Keeley's delicate touch on his arm. "The kindest one I know?"

He smiled into her upturned face. "Why couldn't I have been the one to get to you first?"

Keeley surprised him then by hugging him tightly. "You know I love Ciaran, but if it weren't for him I think I could've fallen for you pretty hard, Taylor Barton."

He closed his eyes as his hand stroked over her dark curls. Still holding her loosely in his arms, he commented quietly, "You look a little washed out, honey. Other than not seeing any sign of Ciaran, is everything okay?"

She shrugged.

"Come on, you can tell me," he coaxed. "I notice you're not drinking any of the margaritas."

She slipped from his arms. "I don't want to be drunk while I cook."

He watched her. She was lying. The faint flush on her cheekbones gave her away. "Keeley..."

Her fingers clenched against the counter. "I think I'm pregnant."

"Oh honey."

She waved her hand. "Don't. I don't want to go to pieces here, okay? I'm only a couple of weeks late, but I did a pregnancy test and it came up positive."

"I can call Carrick and Cayden or get in touch with Faeran to see if they can find Ciaran."

She shook her head and bit her lower lip. "No. I don't want anyone to know just yet. I don't want Ciaran to worry about this right now. I want him to do what he has to do so when he does come back he can really and truly come back." She swallowed and brushed a shaky hand across her eyes. "I don't need a few minutes with him, Taylor. I need him."

God what a mess. Taylor went around the counter and pulled her into his arms again. "Okay. Whatever you want. I'm here to help, you know that."

"I'm okay, really. I could just use some company this evening. If...if you don't mind, I'd really like you to stay. I sleep better with you and Geoff here.

You're like my own personal teddy bears."

Taylor rubbed her shoulders. They had spent more than one night with her cuddled between them until she fell asleep. Taylor usually tucked her in bed. "You know I'll do whatever you need." His glance strayed to the pool where Geoff now sat at the end of the lounger Stephie occupied. "Now Geoff might desert you. It looks to me like things are going well poolside."

Keeley looked out and uttered a quiet laugh. "I so hoped that would work."

"I think it has." Taylor picked up the tray that held the platter of steaks along with marinated vegetable kabobs and a loaf of freshly baked bread. "Now how much do you want Steph to know?"

Keeley looked at him. "I want to show her what I am. What I can do. And I'd like you to show her what you are, so she can understand what's going on with Ciaran."

Taylor nodded. "Okay."

****

While Keeley cooked, she was relieved to see Stephie relaxed enough she was now smiling and laughing between Taylor and Geoff's attentions. Keeley had forgotten just how attractive Geoff Sanderson was. With his dark wavy hair and warm brown eyes, Keeley was sure he turned a lot of women's heads, but he didn't seem to notice, in the same way Stephie always seemed to be unaware of her own attractiveness. It was more than just physical good looks; they were both caring, intelligent people. What made it even better in Keeley's mind was Geoff was tall enough and big enough he could make Stephie feel dainty for once in her life.

Taylor stayed near them both, refilling glasses and generally doing everything he could to keep them both relaxed.

As they all sat to eat, Keeley smiled when Geoff pulled out a chair to seat Stephie. During dinner he leaned toward her, buttering her bread and then laughingly feeding it to her.

Keeley caught Taylor's eye and winked. Taylor smiled back.

"Keeley," Stephie said, "you said this afternoon there was something you wanted to tell me about Ciaran. I'm guessing Geoff and Taylor both know already?"

Keeley nodded. "I'm going to ask you to suspend belief here for the next little bit." She glanced at Taylor who nodded. "Steph, your dad's a fisherman. Has he ever talked about some of the sea legends?"

"You mean like mermaids and stuff?"

Keeley nodded. "Yes, but one legend in particular. Have you ever heard of the Silkie?"

Stephie grinned. "The creatures who turn from seals into people so they can seduce humans?"

Keeley nodded. "That's the general idea."

"But not completely accurate," Taylor said. "We're the aquatic version of Faeries."

Stephie raised her eyebrows and laughed. "We? Taylor, are you trying to tell me you are a Silkie?"

When he nodded, she hurriedly glanced at Keeley. "It's true, Stephie. So is Ciaran. That's why he's not here right now. He's somewhere in the ocean."

Stephie's golden eyes narrowed angrily. "Keeley, if this is your idea of a joke, I don't think it's funny."

"It's not a joke," Geoff said in his quiet way. "I nearly passed out when I found out about Taylor."

Stephie started to get up. "I don't believe you."

Taylor stood as well. "I'll show you. Will that convince you?"

"You're going to turn into a seal?" When Taylor nodded, she glanced at Keeley and Geoff, her eyes widening as she read the confirmation in their faces.

Crossing her arms across her chest, she said, "Okay. Prove it."

Keeley tensed as Taylor calmly stripped down. As he dove into the pool, he touched the leather anklet and morphed right there in front of them. Stephie stumbled back; Geoff was right there to catch her.

"Oh my God. Holy shit! Keeley are you one of them too?" Stephie's eyes were wide and frightened as she stared at Keeley.

"No." Keeley shook her head. "I'm no Silkie, but Ciaran is. So is the rest of his family."

Stephie pulled away from Geoff. "And you?"

Geoff held up both hands, palms out. "Human. Just plain, all American human male."

"Well, thank God for that." They smiled at each other.

Taylor morphed back into human form and stood in the shallow end of the pool. He raised one brow at Keeley, who shrugged. Honestly, she wasn't quite sure how Stephie was taking this. She supposed it was a good sign her friend hadn't stormed off.

Stephie moved closer to Geoff and turned back to Keeley curiously. "So if Taylor can switch back and forth, why can't Ciaran?"

As Taylor climbed out of the pool, dried off, and dressed, Keeley explained what happened with Ciaran, and why they were now not sure when he would be coming back.

Stephie's eyes widened. "It could be a couple of *years*?"

Keeley nodded and felt her mouth tremble.

"Oh sweetie." Stephie hugged Keeley to her. "There's more you haven't told me, though, isn't there?"

Keeley sighed. Stephie knew her so well. She was her first and really only friend after she arrived to live permanently with her grandfather. "Yes. It's about me."

Stephie leaned back and looked down at her. "Does it have anything to do with the way you can move things?"

It was Keeley's turn to be surprised. She gaped at Stephie. "You know?"

Stephie laughed. "We've been friends nearly half our lives. The first time I saw it, I thought I imagined it. Then I started to look for it. I never said anything because you didn't. You were always so private about your personal life and your past, I didn't want to lose you as a friend. You were my only friend too, so I let it go."

Keeley sagged in relief. "Well, then I guess it will be a little anti-climactic to tell you my family is descended from the Faerie folk."

"So does that make you cousins with all the Silkie we've apparently been surrounded by over the years?"

Taylor laughed. "If we are, it's so distant it hardly counts. Are you really okay with this, Steph?"

Stephie looked from Taylor to Keeley and then at Geoff. She smiled. "Yeah. I guess I am. You're my best friend. Nothing can change that. And I've seen Taylor with my own eyes. So yeah, I guess I am okay with it."

Keeley suddenly felt overwhelmed with emotion. Maybe it was finding out she carried Ciaran's child, she wasn't sure, but suddenly she humiliated herself by bursting into tears.

When Steph started to go to her, Taylor waved her away and picked Keeley up. He sat in a chair and simply held her.

She wiped her eyes after a couple of minutes and sniffed. "I'm so sorry. It's just starting to get to me you know? I miss him, and right now I really need him."

Stephie sat next to Geoff on a cushioned loveseat. "I don't know much about what you can do Keeley, but can't you call Ciaran somehow?"

****

Taylor looked down into Keeley's pale face. It worked the one time, but after a month of no sightings of Ciaran, it was doubtful he was even in the area. Keeley shook her head.

"We've communicated thoughts a couple of times, but not over any great distance."

Keeley shivered, and Taylor sat up straighter. "It's getting a little chilly out here. Why don't we go inside? We'll get all this stuff cleared away, then you can give Stephie the grand tour."

Taylor was worried about Keeley. He would honor her request not to tell anyone of her pregnancy right now, but he really felt like she was keeping too much locked inside, and holding herself together by the finest of threads.

They ended up in the sitting room of the master suite. With its overstuffed loveseats and the large-screened TV over the fireplace, it was the perfect retreat. Taylor watched the easy way Geoff sat next to Stephie. In just a few minutes, he had her nestled next to him, her head resting against his shoulder.

Taylor felt a stab of envy. In the past, he and Geoff occasionally shared a woman, but he had the feeling that wouldn't be the case this time around. His arm tightened around Keeley. He had other concerns now, not only to take care of Keeley, but also the baby she carried.

"You tired, honey?" he asked quietly.

"A bit." Keeley looked at Geoff and Stephie. "Make yourselves at home. Taylor?"

Stephie's glance darted between Keeley and him. "What?"

Taylor put his arm around Keeley's shoulders. "She has trouble sleeping since Ciaran left. All I do is sleep with her, Stephie." It certainly wasn't all he could have done or would have been willing to do, but it was what Keeley wanted, and it seemed like that was to be his role with her.

As he followed Keeley into her room, he glanced over his shoulder. Geoff had already shifted positions so he was half facing Stephie. Both were already oblivious to everything else. Taylor smiled. At least that was developing nicely.

He stayed with Keeley until he was positive she was asleep, then as quietly as he could, he slipped from the bed and put his clothes back on.

When he returned to the sitting room, the lights were off. He wondered if Geoff had taken Stephie home until he stepped into the hall. From the other side, he heard the unmistakable sounds of lovemaking coming from the guest room at the far end. Taylor smiled again. Keeley had a whole lot better instincts, it seemed, than he did when it came to their two best friends.

Now it was time to do something for her. Taylor frowned for just a moment. She said she didn't want anyone to know, but this was a trust he felt compelled to break. He needed advice, and the only people he felt he could go to were Carrick and Catriona. If he sacrificed her friendship, then he would do it for the best of motives...concern for her.

They were still sitting on the deck of the *Skerry* when he came on board. After throwing on clothes supplied by one of the crew, Taylor headed up top.

"Taylor!" Catriona greeted him with a smile and a hug. "It's always nice to see you outside of business. What brings you here?"

He clasped arms with Carrick and then took the seat the older male gestured to. "How is Ciaran's feisty little Faerie doing?"

Taylor sighed in relief. Trust Carrick to get right to the heart of what brought him on board this late.

"Actually, that's why I'm here."

"Is she all right?" Catriona's green eyes glowed with concern.

Taylor sighed. "I'm violating a confidence here, but I need your advice."

Carrick leaned back in his chair. "You know we'll help anyway we can, Taylor. You're like a son to us."

"She told me this evening she's pregnant."

Catriona's hand went to her mouth in surprise. "She's sure?"

"She did one of those home pregnancy tests. I asked her if she wanted me to find Ciaran, but she said no."

"What?" Carrick and Catriona both spoke at once, their brows furrowing.

"But a babe is always a reason to celebrate among the Silkie. Why would she not want him found and told?" Catriona murmured.

"That's what worries me. She needs him, but she said she needs him for more than just a few minutes. She's afraid if he's found now and tries to come back, it will be for only a few minutes or hours and then he'll have to change."

Catriona nodded. "She's worried if he's found now it will ultimately delay him being able to come back to her for good."

"Exactly. But I feel like someone needs to know and keep tabs on his whereabouts," Taylor paused. "You know, in case there is some sort of problem."

Catriona's brows arched. "Is she ill?"

Taylor shook his head. "No. But she misses him. She has trouble sleeping, and she's tired."

Catriona sighed. "I'll call Faeran. He's the strongest telepath among us. If anyone can locate Ciaran, he can."

Taylor stood. "Thank you. I'll return to Keeley." He paused, hoping they couldn't see the flush on his cheeks. "She sleeps better when I stay with her."

Carrick's eyes narrowed. "Ciaran is okay with this?"

"He suggested it. I'm her friend, Carrick, nothing more."

"But that's not by your choice."

Taylor sighed. "No, but that's the way it is." Carrick and Catriona both knew him too well.

Once back at Ciaran's house, he stood near the window in Keeley's room and simply stared at her slight form curled in the bed. Taylor closed his eyes and clenched his fists.

Soon, Ciaran. You need to come back soon because I'm not sure how much longer I can remain only a friend.

There were times when he wished he were simply human.

Chapter Eighteen

Ciaran sniffed the air as he hauled out onto a rocky beach along the Maine coast. The seasons were changing. Along with cooler water temperatures, there was a bite to the breeze. He tried several times to reach out with his mind for Keeley, but his telepathy simply wasn't that strong. The temptation to try to change back into human form hung before him like a piece of candy just beyond the reach of a kid. Each time he came on land, heard and smelled the signs of humanity, the need to try, to see if he could change on his own nearly overwhelmed common sense.

His parents always considered him stubborn, and it was stubbornness that now kept him firmly away from his house along the bay. When he came back to Keeley, it would be for good. He couldn't bear another visit where he barely had time to hold her, much less tell her of his feelings. If only he had some way of knowing how she was.

She's lonely is how she is, infant.

Ciaran's head swung around as Faeran morphed in the shallows and stepped ashore, dragging his pelt around his hips. God, if Faeran had taken the time to find him, something must be wrong. Ciaran's throat and chest tightened with worry.

"Settle down. There's nothing physically wrong with your little Faerie, but she pines for you. I think it's time you gave up the I'll-go-back-for-good-or-not-at-all attitude. She needs you. So get to it. Let's see you change."

She needed him. Ciaran dug deep inside him.

The thought of her unhappy was more than he could bear. If seeing him, even for a short time would make her smile, how could he deny her? He forced himself to concentrate; being in human form was no longer the norm it once was and change did not come easily. It rippled over him with pain, not the smooth and easy skill it was when he could simply morph in mid-air. Now it was a struggle, a painful, agonizing struggle.

It was infinitely easier to stay below the waves. Life there was without conscious thought, without worry. Hunting and sleeping, existing only for today.

"Ciaran!" Faeran's harsh reminder brought him back. "She sits on the point every morning and evening looking for even a glimpse of you."

Ciaran's voice erupted in a bellow of pain as limbs lengthened and stretched to unaccustomed length. On his hands and knees on the coarse sand, his head hung, hair falling in wet ropes around his face. In one hand he clutched his pelt, completely unable to manage the magic that would have turned it back into the anklet most of them wore.

"Faeran. Is she well?" his voice was hoarse and gravelly with disuse as he slowly rolled to his knees and wrapped the soft warmth of his sealskin around his bare hips.

The Duke of the Atlantic crouched next to him and touched his shoulder. "You will work with me. Every day until you have enough strength to go to her. She is feisty, your little Faerie, but not nearly as self-sufficient as she would have everyone believe.

Fear stabbed through Ciaran's chest and he looked away to the west. "They are looking after her? Tell me that much!"

"Yes, but you must build up your strength and return, even if you can't stay for long."

Ciaran's body rebelled against the time in human form, once again shifting without his consent. He groaned in pain, but couldn't stop it. After so much time walking only as a human, nature demanded balance no matter how much he might fight it.

Ciaran hated the pity in his eyes. "I will stay with you, work with you, and help you."

That was what worried Ciaran most of all. Faeran's sacrifice told him as his words would not something was not right with Keeley. She needed him. He deliberately stayed away after realizing he couldn't be near her and not want to change back into human form. Instead he went north, seeking refuge among the clans off Nova Scotia.

****

Keeley stared at the results of the latest pregnancy test. Positive. They had all been positive. She thought to begin with the first test might have been a fluke, but it wasn't. There were other signs as well. Her breasts ached, she craved sushi, something she'd always detested, and she already had the beginnings of a small baby bump. Not surprising she supposed, as small as she was.

Two months. Two months since she'd seen Ciaran. Throwing on sweats, she ran barefoot to the point and stared down at the bay. But as always, the water was empty of any seal. Her shoulders slumped.

Labor Day weekend was over. The last of the summer residents were headed back to the city, back to school, back to work. And still no sign of Ciaran. He'd said he'd come to her as a seal, but though she looked for him every morning and every night, he wasn't there.

Catriona and Carrick invited her out to the *Skerry*, but the thought of getting on a rolling deck of a ship made her nauseous so she'd declined and avoided them. She hadn't told them, but she could hear the knowledge in Catriona's voice. Keeley sighed. At this point it didn't much matter whether she heard it from Taylor or simply picked up on Keeley's thoughts. It wasn't something she could keep secret any longer.

As she stood staring down, her hand went to her belly. She needed Ciaran. The brave front she'd tried to maintain crumbled. There was no use denying it, especially to herself. She craved the feeling of him holding her in his arms, and right now she didn't care if it was only for a few seconds. If she could just feel him, hear the rhythm of his heart, and the rumble of his voice!

The wind ruffled her curls. Her hair had grown out from the spiky look she'd worn for so long, it hung in short blue-black coils. Pregnancy only tightened them more. Keeley lifted her face to the dawn. The breeze blowing in from the northwest was cool and she could smell the tang of autumn in the air.

"Come back, Ciaran," she whispered into the breeze. She stood, outlined against the sky and raised her hands to it. She seldom attempted to use her magic for anything other than to move objects. It was only when she was with Ciaran she sensed the mental connection between them. Could she use that? Could she consciously call him to her?

She stared at the empty water and felt tears slowly slide down her face before they were caught and swept away by the wind. Lifting her hands, she tilted her head back and whispered, "Help me wind to bring this change, give my voice a wider range. Let my whispers in his heart make sound, let what is lost to me now be found."

She thought she heard it echo on the wind, but it could have been her imagination. Keeley turned away from the sea and trudged back along the path to the house. She needed something to get her mind off of her troubles.

It was early afternoon when her cell phone rang. She snatched it up, hoping it might be Ciaran.

"Keeley here."

"Oh! I'm so glad I caught you." It was her realtor. "Listen. I have someone interested in looking to rent the house off-season. They want to come by tomorrow first thing and I can't get by to make sure it's shipshape. Could you possibly swing by to make sure last weekend's tenants didn't leave a disaster?"

Keeley smiled. "Sure thing. I'll do that now." She tucked the phone back in the front pocket of her lightweight sweatshirt and slipped on her sneakers.

"Hey! Jonathan!"

He poked his head in from the living room.

"I'm going down to Granddad's house to check on it. Liz says she's got someone coming by to look at it for a long term rental, so I'm just going to tidy up a bit."

The butler wiped his hands. "I can do that for you."

"Oh no. You and Mary have enough to do around here, especially with as much time as Taylor, Geoff, and Stehpie have been spending here. I'll do it."

She grabbed the keys to the SUV, threw in a bucket of cleaning supplies and drove to the small house. The whole town looked a bit forlorn now the temps were gone. Several businesses put up closed signs so they could take some time off for their own vacations. A gust of wind blew and Keeley looked at the sky. Sure looked like a storm might be headed their way. Would Ciaran be all right in bad weather? She'd never really thought about it. Where did seals go to ride out a storm?

She unlocked the door and walked in. The living room looked neat enough. She went through the bedrooms and stripped the sheets, grabbed the towels from the bathroom and the kitchen and started a load of laundry. While it was cycling, she returned to the bathroom and cleaned that and then the kitchen. After sweeping and running the vacuum, Keeley curled on the couch to wait for the dryer to finish. She'd just fix the beds, put the fresh towels out and then give Liz a call.

She was in the process of switching the sheets and towels from the washer to the dryer when she heard the front door. Pausing for a moment, she tilted her head to listen.

"Liz?"

When she got no answer, Keeley returned to her task.

She smelled him first. It was an aroma she would never forget, one burned into her memory like a brand onto a calf. Cheap lime aftershave and mint mouthwash.

"Did you miss your daddy, baby girl?"

For a moment her throat closed with nausea and her mind went totally and completely numb. It was just long enough for Frank Wells to hit her along the side of the head. Keeley couldn't even get a scream out before her world faded.

****

"I can do it, damn it. How many times do I need to show you?" Ciaran panted with his latest effort and impatiently swept his hair back off his face.

Faeran crossed his arms across his broad chest. It was just after dawn; they stood along a rocky deserted beach at the far end of the Atlantic coast side of Long Island. Ciaran was practicing changing back and forth from human to seal as he dove into the surf and then changed back to walk out on land.

Faeran arched a brow. "Just making sure, *infant*, before I let you go back to your family and that pretty green-eyed Faerie of yours."

Ciaran stopped and spun around, his eyes narrowed. "How would you know what she looks like?"

Faeran tapped his head. "You send an almost unceasing stream of fairly erotic images. Even I can't tune everything out."

"Shit! Don't look. Keeley wouldn't like it. She doesn't know you."

The brows went even higher. "It would make a difference if she did?"

Ciaran grinned. "It might if she liked you."

"Hmm. Invite me for a visit once you've settled back in."

"I can go?"

Faeran nodded. "Yes. You're back to normal as long as you remember to spend about half your days in the ocean for a while."

"Yes, your grace."

"And Ciaran? I'm serious about the visit. You're not under the same restrictions as your father and brother. You *can* mate with a non-Silkie, especially a member of the Faerie folk."

Ciaran's eyes lighted with relief and laughter. "You'll be our first guest and I'll let you give the bride away."

Faeran laughed. "Be careful I don't keep her."

"Not a chance, cousin."

Ciaran dove back into the sea, changing to a seal as he hit the water. It had taken days of hard work to reach this point. The effort left him lying exhausted on the beach at night, with Faeran watching over him. The swim back would take hours, but that was okay. He was going back to Keeley and nothing could be better. Now he would be able to do more than just think about her. His arms ached with the need to fold her close to him, to rest his cheek against her hair.

As he raced through the water, gliding along the bottom, he cocked his head and then shot to the surface. He shook his head and looked around. For just a moment, he could have sworn he heard her call. He touched his necklace, surprised it felt warm in spite of the cold water. Diving once more he swam with a single focus in mind, returning to the bay and Keeley.

There were plenty of willing females, but Ciaran turned them down. There was only one female he wanted. Keeley. He thought of her midnight hair, her porcelain skin, and her vivid green eyes and swam that much harder. Faeran had dropped hints Keeley had something important to share with him.

Ciaran leaped in and out of the surface of the water. He was going home. Home to Keeley. He hunted as he traveled, but in a playful way, not with the single mindedness with which he'd approached it over the last two months. In order to keep his thoughts off Keeley, he hunted alone, only occasionally with others. It was the middle of the afternoon before he left the sound and entered the bay. He swam toward his house on the point. Keeley. She was a song in the water that flowed around him as he sped homeward.

****

She felt his eyes on her as awareness returned. It was one of the things that stood out from the years she'd lived with her mother and him, the fact he watched her constantly. A sick, greasy feeling pooled in her belly, bringing with it all of the insecurities of her girlhood. She wouldn't look at him. She couldn't let him have that power. Right now she was more concerned to find he'd tied her up. Her head was jerked sideways by the roots of her hair. Keeley's eyes snapped open at the pain.

"I see you're awake now, baby girl. I always did like it better when you were aware enough to struggle."

Keeley glared at him. "You don't scare me anymore, Frank. I'm not a child you can intimidate, so why don't you just get the hell out of here, you sick pervert!"

Wells snarled at her and slapped her across the mouth. "You watch your smart mouth, you little bitch! I've come for your mama's share of your grandfather's money. I know the old coot squirreled stuff away. So where is it?"

Keeley tasted blood and knew he'd split her lip. She also felt some puffiness around her eye, but without being able to touch it or look in a mirror, she couldn't be sure. What she was sure of was it was no longer fear she felt for Frank Wells. He was the nightmare of her childhood, but not anymore. He might have caught her by surprise, but that element was gone. She was no longer a weak, frightened little girl.

More important, he'd grossly underestimated what magic she was now capable of, especially when threatened. There was absolutely no way she would allow his filth to harm her, and the baby she carried.

Keeley laughed. "There is no money. Granddad's medical bills ate through his savings and everything I could earn as well. You're on a fool's errand."

He slapped her again. This time blood spurted from her nose as her head swung sideways. Even as pain ricocheted through her, so did fury.

She faced him again. "I'm not a little girl any longer, Frank. You're making a big mistake."

"Try that on someone who believes it. You can't do shit. I've got your hands tied."

Her mouth twisted, she stared at him levelly and chanted, "Stop this one who breached my door, knock his ass upon the floor."

Frank yelped as he flew backward, landing flat on his back near the fireplace. Before he could begin to recover, Keeley stared at her bound hands. "From these bindings set me free, as I will so will it be."

The rope fell from her and she stood.

"Jesus!" Frank Well's eyes widened, and then a

sly look spread across his face. "Come on, baby girl! It's just a joke. Just relax. Didn't I always show you a good time?"

Keeley paused to simply stare for a second before she laughed. "You are so up shit creek, you don't even know it." She flicked her wrist at him and he was suddenly hanging upside down. "It's payback time, Daddy dearest."

****

Ciaran shot through the water, hope and joy flowing through him. When he saw her he would hold her, just hold her. He wanted to feel her against him, skin to skin. He was nearly to the point by his home when he felt as if something slammed into him. In his mind, he suddenly felt Keeley's fear as a living, tangible thing. And then it was gone. His heart pounded as he changed. Without considering it was broad daylight, he dashed out of the water and ran nude up the path to the top of the point and down to the house, his pelt once again around his ankle as most of his kind wore it.

"Mr. Ciaran!" Jonathan nearly fainted with shock as the back door slammed open and Ciaran stood there breathing hard, his eyes wild and his body soaked and naked.

"Where is she?"

Jonathan recovered from his momentary loss of butlerly decorum and handed Ciaran a towel. "Miss Keeley went down to her granddad's house to clean it up some so the realtor could show it tomorrow."

"Something's wrong. Don't ask me how I know. I just do." Ciaran hastily dried himself off. "Get me pants and the keys to the Porsche. Hurry!"

He gasped as a wave of pain washed over him. And then he no longer felt her emotions through the haze of rage and anger clouding his. Dammit! He would kill whoever it was causing her this fear and pain. Jonathan returned and Ciaran jerked on the

285

jeans, barely pausing to zip them before he snatched the keys and raced out of the house.

The Porsche's engine growled to life. Tires squealed as he backed out of the garage and then he was roaring down the driveway. He screeched to a stop in front of the Cape Cod in just a couple of minutes. His narrowed gaze took in his SUV and another car that appeared to be a rental. After leaping from the black sports car, Ciaran pounded up the path and into the house, his concern exploding when he found the door ajar.

He resisted the urge to go crashing inside, instead, pushing the front door open cautiously and peering around the empty living room. Ropes lay on the floor behind a hard chair. He searched for Keeley. A cold born of fear for her trickled down his spine.

From the kitchen he heard the sounds of things crashing and breaking, along with the sound of a man's voice swearing. "Leave off, you witch! Enough!"

An inarticulate voice muttered in a language that didn't sound like English.

"Aargh!"

Ciaran burst into the room and stopped dead. In the middle of the kitchen, a middle aged, greasy looking guy hung upside down in midair, his pants around his ankles. Several butcher knives flashed around his bare penis and testicles. Keeley stood just a few feet away with her back to Ciaran. Her hands were upraised as she continued to mutter, but now he could understand her.

As a rolling pin smashed into the man's nose and blood spurted, Keeley growled. "That's for smacking me upside the head, you worthless piece of shriveled testicle." She bent down almost to eye level with her captive. "Shall I make your penis turn black and your nuts dry up and fall off? Hmm. That might be a good idea so you can't hurt any other little girls. And there have been others, haven't there, Frank? I was just the first. Admit it!"

"Yes! Yes! There have!"

"How many, Frank?" Ciaran watched her hold a cell phone out toward the frightened man. "How many, *Daddy*?"

"Five. My nieces and two neighbor girls."

"Just five?" The knives flashed again near his ball sac.

Ciaran thought the man was going to piss himself, but now realizing just who it was, he leaned against the doorway and watched. She was magnificent. Keeley held one hand toward the man, keeping him suspended while she put the phone in her other hand to her ear. "Did you get all of that, Mother? You didn't believe me, now your nieces and your neighbors' have been his victims as well. You either agree to turn him over to the police once you bail him out here, or I swear I'll cut his dick off and let him bleed to death all over the floor while I laugh."

As much as he might agree it was a fair punishment for her stepfather, the last thing Ciaran needed was to have his fiancée jailed for murder.

"Keeley." Ciaran's voice was quiet, soothing.

The phone fell from her suddenly nerveless hands at the same time Frank Wells dropped to the floor, her spell broken. She turned slowly to him and Ciaran's heart clenched. Her nose was bloody, one eye was swelling shut and her lip was split. The tiny spark of sympathy he had felt for Frank Wells disappeared, and he very nearly picked the man up so he could kill him barehanded.

"Ciaran." It came out on a sob before she rushed on, "I've missed you so much. I called to you, but I didn't really have any hope you could actually come to me. And I..." She stopped, swallowed, then stumbled forward and collapsed into his arms.

"Shh," he soothed while he held her as close as he could. With her limp body held next to him in one arm, he pulled his cell phone out and called the police. He glared at Wells with an icy rage and took deep breaths to prevent himself from picking up one of the knives and gutting the man.

His gaze went to Keeley again. My God! Her face looked bad enough. What else had he done to her?

As Wells stirred, Ciaran snarled. "Move, asshole, and I'll gut you like a fish!"

Rather than take his eyes off her, he called Taylor on his cell phone. "Get everyone over here to the McNamara house. The police are on their way. Keeley's hurt."

"Jesus!" Taylor swore. "Is the baby all right?"

Ciaran's heart went cold, and his eyes stared down at the sweatshirt Keeley wore. "Baby?"

"Ah shit! We've been trying to find you, to get the word to you."

Pregnant. He thought about the way Faeran had suddenly shown up, saying Ciaran needed to practice morphing to see if he was ready yet to go home. Faeran kept pushing him with torturous persistence to the point where Ciaran had begun to get irritated. Now he understood.

He stared down at her bruised and bloody face. She was so pale and still. Ciaran lifted eyes to Frank Wells that glowed black with rage. "What else did you do to her, you son of a bitch?"

"Nothing! I swear!" Wells voice squealed in a high-pitched whine and cracked.

Ciaran heard a siren, the squeal of tires, and the sound of feet approaching both the back and front doors. "Police! Mr. Clifton? You in there?"

"Yeah! Come in and get this piece of shit before I kill him!"

"Calm down, Ciaran," the chief ordered quietly

from just behind him. "We'll take care of him. You need an ambulance?"

Ciaran stroked her hair away from her face. It had gotten long and curly, he noted inconsequentially. Beautiful. "Yeah," he whispered. "Let's take her to the clinic and get her looked at."

The chief's hand touched his shoulder. "We'll take care of him. Take her in the other room until we can get them over here." He spoke into his handheld radio, but Ciaran paid him little attention. His focus shifted entirely to Keeley.

He carried her carefully out of the kitchen and back into the living room. He knew he should lay her down, but he couldn't bring himself to let go. Instead, he sat on the couch and cradled her against him. Surreptitiously, he felt along her ribcage, and then closed his eyes as he ran his hand under the elastic waist of her sweatpants. His heart stopped. There it was, just the slightest of swells. He buried his face against her hair, inhaling her familiar scent, losing himself in touching her again, and still he continued to rock them both.

"Ciaran?" his mother called his name softly. Tears clouded his dark eyes when he looked at her.

"He beat her. She's having a baby, and he beat her up, Momma."

His mother's eyes darkened with fury and fear. She touched her hands to Keeley's head and to his where it lay over her belly. Slowly, she smiled. "The baby's fine, son. The ambulance is arriving. Will you go with them?"

He nodded. Although he knew he would have to turn her loose, he had no intention of letting her out of his sight again. Carrick stood just behind Catriona, his jaw hard and his face grim as he watched the paramedics preparing Keeley for transport. She came to as they moved her from Ciaran's arms to the stretcher.

She cried out in protest. "Ciaran!"

"He's coming with you, Keeley," the older man told her with the familiarity of long acquaintance. Like most people in the area, he'd known her since she first started visiting Andy McNamara, had seen her grow up. "He'll be right with you, sweetheart."

Her eyes searched for him, the panic only disappearing from her expression as she saw him hovering just a few feet away. As soon as they lifted the stretcher onto its wheels, he came back to her side, holding her hand. As they rushed down the sidewalk he saw Taylor hurry toward them. Behind him was Stephie Brooks with a taller, darker haired man holding her hand.

"Is she all right?" Taylor's voice was tight with worry. Ciaran saw the same concern reflected on Stephie's and the other man's faces.

"She will be."

"What about..."

Ciaran grinned. "Momma says the baby will be fine too."

Taylor and the other man grinned and clapped each other on the back. Stephie stepped forward and touched his arm. He looked down to see tears in her eyes.

"She'll be fine, Stephie," he reassured her and on impulse gave her a friendly hug. "She just looks a little worse for wear."

"I should have been here."

Ciaran smiled at her. "Trust me, Keeley had the situation well in hand. I want to get her checked out, but we'll be home by this evening. You can come by to check on her."

Stephie smiled in relief. "Thanks."

Ciaran turned his attention back to Keeley, who watched him quietly through the eye not swollen shut. He squeezed her hand gently and felt an answering squeeze back. Neither one of them paid much attention to the attendant who sat on the opposite bench once the doors were shut. As the ambulance moved off, Ciaran leaned down so his face was just inches from hers.

"I love you, Keeley Ann McNamara. Will you marry me?"

"Yes," she whispered. "Oh God! I love you so much."

"Shh!" He laid a finger over his lips because her lower lip was swollen and cut. "Let's get you checked out and cleaned up baby, then I'll get you home and spend all night telling you how much I love you."

Her eyes clouded with tears for a moment. "You don't have to go away again, do you?"

"No." When she closed her eyes, tears trickled from beneath her thick, sooty lashes. He could explain it in detail later. For now, she needed the reassurance he would stay with her, and he would. "Never again, baby. I promise. Faeran, the Duke of the Atlantic, has even agreed to give you away."

Keeley's green eyes searched his face. "Just so long as he only gives me to you. Only to you, Ciaran. I've missed you so much."

He touched her face with gentle fingers. "You're the air I breathe and the heart that beats inside me. I'm sorry I didn't take care of Frank Wells a long time ago. I'm sorry I wasn't here for you."

She touched his hand. "Don't be hard on yourself. Maybe it was better this way. Now I know what happened to me...what he did to me. It's in my past. I conquered it...and him.

Ciaran touched his lips to her fingers. "I cannot imagine a life without you."

291

Epilogue

"It was so kind of Faeran to take care of my father's and Granddad's ashes," Keeley said softly. "It was Granddad's final wish they be returned to the home of their forefathers."

"He was glad to do it," Ciaran commented as he eyed his wife appreciatively. In fact, ever since Faeran set eyes on Keeley, he bent over backward to smooth the way for them, letting her know that once she gave birth, they could discuss whether she wished to become one of them, a process he assured her would be eased by the kinship that already existed between Faerie and Silkie. He had been impressed when Ciaran shared his discovery of her capture of her stepfather, nodding his head and saying Carrick was obviously correct in calling her a mean little thing, but he would add she was a courageous, mean little thing. Ciaran smiled in remembrance. Faeran didn't hand out praise unearned. He was a hard man. His attention came back to the present when his bride squealed.

Keeley's eyes widened as she looked in the mirror at the dress Annabel and Catriona had handed her.

"Ciaran! You can see right through this thing!"

"Uh huh. It's a great view too, baby."

"I can't wear this!"

He came across the room, his feileadh leaving most of his chest bare except where his pelt was pinned with an ornate brooch to his shoulder. Around his neck glinted the silver of the Celtic knot necklace he never took off. When he stepped in close behind her, she felt his cock beneath his kilt. It pressed hard against her bottom. "And if you don't have this same effect on every single man in that room, I'll be surprised." He chuckled. "We already know at least one other man who would do anything to make you happy."

"That was just while you were gone, and really Ciaran, Taylor was far more concerned about what you would do if he stepped even an inch out of line."

He kissed the side of her neck and trailed his lips down to her shoulder where he lightly nibbled. When her nipples instantly hardened into pointed little pebbles, he laughed again and rubbed his hand over her rounded belly.

"I find myself very interested right now in bringing you pleasure. Perhaps we should get that out of the way unless you're feeling up to a little public display of affection."

Keeley's hand reached back to rub his cock. "I think now would be a good idea. I don't think I'm quite ready for you Silkies and your enthusiasm for open sex."

"I thought you quite enjoyed some of the displays at our wedding."

She giggled. "Oh, don't get me wrong. Watching is one thing, doing is another."

"Perhaps we should start with a smaller audience."

Even as he spoke he lifted her. He sat in her vanity chair and then set her down to straddle his lap as they faced each other.

"His Grace won't be upset, will he, that we're late for the party in his home?"

Ciaran brushed the diaphanous material out of the way so he could slip his fingers between the wet folds of her sex. As his thumb circled her clit, she threw her head back on a moan.

"No, in fact, I believe he expects it. You are so

incredibly sensitive to any stimulation since you got pregnant. How do you even walk without coming?"

Keeley panted as his fingers slipped in and out of her. "It's not easy. And I think about it constantly." Her hands were busy caressing him.

"I want to bury myself in you. Are you ready?"

"I thought you'd never ask."

****

On deck, Carrick scowled. "I fear I must apologize, your grace. It is difficult to get Ciaran and Keeley anywhere on time."

Faeran closed his eyes for a moment with an odd smile on his firm lips. "They're newlyweds. Don't rush them, Carrick."

"I don't know what they're thinking."

Faeran's smile widened. "I do."

About the Author

From the moment Rhett walked out on Scarlett, Laura's been hooked on romance. Deciding truth really is stranger than fiction, though, she chose a career path in journalism. Laura now teaches English and has returned to her first love—writing fiction.

She lives with her husband and son in central North Carolina along with a menagerie of animals that includes three rowdy Jack Russells and a gentle white mare named Tweed. When she's not reading or writing, Laura enjoys riding, photography, and baking the best darned carrot cake you've ever tasted.

Visit Laura at
www.laurabrowningbooks.com

To chat with Laura and other Wild Rose Press authors of erotic romance, join us at www.group.yahoo.com/group/thewilderroses.

Also Available

The Silkie's Call

by

Laura Browning

Book 1 of the Sea Lovers Series

For seven years, Cayden Clifton's had to stay away from the woman he can't forget. But now his banishment is over and he's returning to claim Annabel Barton, if she'll accept him for what he is...a Silkie.

Annabel has returned to Long Island Sound to close up her father's home. The place holds nothing but bitter memories of a summer that changed her life forever. She lost the boy she loved and the use of her legs. The last person she wants or expects to see is Cayden. He walked away from her when he found out she was paralyzed, so what could he want with her now?

Chapter One

"You don't have to finish this right now, Poppy," Taylor said as he watched her cover her eyes with her hands. "I could take you back over to our place."

Taylor still persisted in calling her by her childhood nickname of Poppy. But now, at the age of twenty-one, she was known to everyone else as Annabel Barton. Placing her hands back down on her father's desk, she stroked the leather surface of the blotter with loving fingertips. Sadness, regret...what was it she truly felt when she thought of her father? Along with those emotions, there were good memories as well.

She smiled as she looked up at her cousin Taylor. With parents like George and Helen, who would have thought he would turn out to be such a good friend? It was too bad they were cousins. Not only was he fun, generous, and her best friend, he was damn fine looking! With his blond-streaked hair and sapphire eyes, they were often mistaken for brother and sister, something that constantly angered Helen Stokes. Annabel sometimes felt that resemblance was part of the reason her aunt disliked her so much.

"I do need to do this, Taylor. At least make a start on it. It's been a month since Daddy's funeral."

"Yes, and you've already gone through the apartment in New York, cleaned it out, and put it on the market. You're driving yourself too damn hard. Why don't you take a break and enjoy a few weeks up here to just relax. It's been years since you've been here."

She looked out the window. Yes, seven to be exact, and she hadn't wanted to come back now. She had few fond memories of the bay and the sound. Seven years ago, she'd come here as a normal, healthy, if somewhat lonely, fourteen-year-old and left as a physical wreck. At least she had never had to worry about anyone trying to push her onto the field hockey team, she thought cynically. Nor had she been obliged to make her debut at the debutante ball. No, she'd never danced with her father nor needed Taylor to serve as her escort.

Instead, she spent seven years learning to move out of a wheelchair to the point where she could manage with crutches for at least part of the day. She was focused and determined. Everyone commented on how mature she was, how well she handled her personal tragedy. And she never let them see her private pain, never told anyone of the dreams that haunted her, of the voice she heard over and over. *No matter what anyone tells you over the next few years, believe me. I love you.*

But she had quit believing. Oh, not for the first year, or even the second or third, but by the time she left for college she quit believing she ever meant any more to Cayden Clifton than a chance to play around with a naïve little virgin. At least until she chickened out. And she began to believe what her father and Aunt Helen told her. That he deliberately turned his back on her when he heard she would never walk again.

Being here in this house was a reminder of that last summer. It made her uneasy. She had moved on. The accident had forced her to. And she didn't want to be here now. But she did need to sort through her father's belongings. Then she would put this house on the market too. She planned to finish her degree in finance this year, and then she would go after a Master's. This was just a temporary and unpleasant interlude. An obligation she must fulfill.

"I had your boat sailed up here for you. It's docking now."

Annabel's head snapped up and she glared at her cousin. "Taylor! You had no right. I don't want to stay here."

"You need a fucking break!" His lean face reflected the stubbornness coursing through her veins.

"But not here!" She clenched her hand into a fist when she saw it tremble. There were too many memories of sneaking out to meet Cayden, of swimming in the dark water, the way the moonlight shone in his dark eyes. And his kisses. Even as young as they were, the longing was there. Longing from which they both shied away, too naïve and hesitant to do anything about it.

Taylor sat in the chair across from her, crossing his legs and staring at her with an intensity that made her shift in her seat. "Don't practice your legal eagle crap on me. I won't stay here." He had just finished law school and would soon join a practice in the city.

"Why is that, Poppy? What the fuck happened that last summer you were here? Was it something with that guy Cayden Clifton?"

"Don't talk about him." she snapped.

Taylor watched her, his eyes never wavering from hers. "He used to ask about you."

"You've seen him?" A shaft of longing hit her right in the heart, and she hated herself for it. Hated herself for caring when Cayden so obviously didn't.

"Not for several years. He had a big fight with his family. I got the feeling he was out on his own. He worked around here for a summer. Hiring out as crew at the yacht club and then he disappeared. His parents have been back, but he wasn't with them. Just the other brother, the younger one."

"I really don't want to talk about this," Annabel said coolly but firmly, shutting the door on any further conversation about Cayden.

Taylor studied her for a moment. "Come out with me. Take the wheel and I'll crew, Captain."

His grin disarmed her. She was never able to resist it.

Her father had installed a ramp all the way from the house to the dock years ago, perhaps hoping she would come back during the summers, but she put her foot down and created such a scene when he suggested it that he finally just gave up. Remorse ate at her now when it was too late. He'd made such an effort, and she'd rejected it. She squeezed her eyes shut. More than rejected, she had positively thrown a tantrum. Sometimes she hated herself as much as she hated her condition.

While she had healed her relationship with her father on many levels, she'd kept some parts shut off from him in the same way that he'd shut her out. She'd never been able to touch or heal some of his deepest grief. And that was what had finally overwhelmed him once she'd left for college. When she'd come home for holidays and breaks, she'd seen that he was deteriorating, but she'd been helpless to do anything about it. She hadn't understood it. The grief had been about more than her mother, but he'd never talked about it.

Then came the call right after she finished her finals, the call that he had been found dead inside the New York apartment, an empty bottle of sleeping pills by his side. *You have your wish now, Daddy. You can finally be with Momma.* It was what he always wanted. She had known it ever since she was seven. Somehow, she had never been enough to hold him. Even his career as a writer had never been enough.

From the moment her mother died of cancer, her

father had been little more than the walking dead. He would have willingly turned her over to Aunt Helen until Annabel's accident changed that. In fact, he had planned to, but the accident forced him to go on for a few more years. She had no doubt that had she not been paralyzed that summer when she capsized the *Silkie*, he would have ended his life years earlier.

She walked carefully down the ramp now, balancing on the crutches that hooked around her forearms. Taylor strode on ahead, getting the *Revenge* ready to go. He hopped back onto the dock when she reached the side of the boat and lifted her in. While Annabel would have rejected such help from most people, she accepted it from Taylor. He was more family to her than anyone, and she loved him like a brother.

"Ready?" he grinned as he untied the lines fore and aft and jumped in.

She smiled back at him. "Yes, but you're not. Lifejacket, Taylor. You know my rule."

It had saved her seven years ago. It was perhaps the one smart choice she'd made that day when she was fourteen, deciding to put on the lifejacket. If she hadn't, she would have drowned. The boom had cracked her skull before it damaged her spine, leaving her not only semi-conscious in rough seas, but partially paralyzed from the waist down. Without the lifejacket, she would have been helpless to stay afloat.

She remembered very little from that day, only what her father had told her. That Carrick and Cayden Clifton found her and pulled her out. She'd heard the story of how the Coast Guard took her by cruiser to the station and then airlifted her to a trauma center.

Annabel jerked herself back to the present. Taylor dutifully donned a lifejacket and was busy unfurling the sails, so she started the small motor on the boat and came about to head out into the bay.

"Hey, Poppy! Did you wear your suit under your clothes?"

"Yes. Why?"

"Let's go to that cove you used to visit and go for a swim."

She blanched. "Not there, Taylor."

He stared at her. "You can't let him haunt the rest of your life, you know."

"Who?" she asked innocently.

"Clifton. Make some new memories, Poppy."

So in the end, she set off in that direction. It didn't take long to reach the cove. The *Revenge* was faster than the *Silkie* had ever been. They dropped anchor in the middle of the cove and Taylor set the ladder on the stern so that she'd be able to get back in. After stripping down to his trunks, he dove over the side. Annabel took her time, keeping her gaze carefully away from the small beach where she and Cayden first kissed each other.

Using her arms to keep her balance, she sat on the edge of the *Revenge* and swung her legs around. To a casual observer, she looked perfectly normal. She now had enough control that she was able to maintain muscle tone in her legs, and when she was in the water, could even swim using a dolphin style kick that relied heavily on the muscles in her abdomen and back to create momentum. That at least was something that hadn't been taken away from her. She had always loved the water, and even her accident hadn't changed that.

It felt wonderful to swim in salt water again. It had been a while. At school, she regularly exercised in the pool, not only using aqua therapy to work her body, but swimming laps to make her stronger. The salt water was so buoyant she could spend more time swimming and less time trying to stay afloat.

303

She sighed blissfully and floated on her back, staring up at the gulls wheeling and turning overhead.

****

Cayden sensed her as soon as she hit the water. The shock to his system almost made him forget to hold his breath as he shot through the water. Breaking away from the school of fish he pursued, he turned out of the sound to search the bay. He followed her scent and her sound as carefully as any predator in the sea. And as a bull seal at full maturity, that's exactly what he was, a predator. Seven years. Or not quite seven years, so he couldn't go to her, not until the seventh day of the seventh month, but he could look. He would look because he could do nothing else.

If he could just see her again. Did she remember what he'd told her? Was that why she was here? He didn't dare hope for that much.

It had been a long seven years, he thought bitterly, separated not only from her, but from his family as well. He closed his eyes as he remembered what happened after Bell's accident. They had taken her away while he watched, his father holding his arms in a vise-like grip to prevent him from following. He'd tried to see her, but Carrick forbade it. Then when he managed to sneak into the hospital in the city, a place he never wished to see again, Phillip Barton physically barred the door and then had him removed by armed security guards. He'd tried again the next day, and this time he'd been arrested. Carrick and Catriona had come to get him.

But it wasn't just human law he had violated. His father soon broke the news that they must travel to the islands off Scotland, the ancestral home of the Silkie, to appear before the Council of Lords.

"But why, Dad?" Cayden had asked.

Carrick sighed. "You answered the call of a female and didn't fulfill your responsibility to mate with her. The Council doesn't understand human beliefs about age and sex. In their eyes, you've flaunted our traditions, and because you are my son, they will make an example of you."

And they had. What had made it even worse was that Carrick had to sit in judgment on his own son. The outcome was a foregone conclusion. He was banished for seven years to live on his own. His mother cried, his brother, Ciaran looked coldly victorious, and his father slipped a piece of paper into his hand even as he embraced him one last time. Cayden was escorted from the hall and turned out into the night. Shunned by his own kind, he sought shelter with humans while he figured out what to do.

His father had given him a letter with instructions about where he could access a bank account set up for him. "Use this as an opportunity to grow, my son," his note had said. "I have supplied you with enough funds to provide for you, if you are thrifty. Learn all you can. On the seventh day, of the seventh month, in seven years, we will find you again."

So Cayden had returned to the sound and the town on the bay. He'd found a job cleaning and fixing boats during the off months and crewing during the summer. He'd finished high school and then gone to college, completing a degree in Marine Management. It hadn't been easy. His father had left funds for him to survive, not to pay for an education, so Cayden had spent the seven years working hard and fitting in classes around whatever jobs he'd been able to find.

And he'd tried to forget Annabel Lee Barton. Poppy to nearly everyone in her family, but to him she had always been Bell. His beautiful Bell. He hadn't found anyone else, and he'd never forgotten her. For seven years, he'd lived in the hope that he would find her again.

Now she was within reach. If she called to him again, he would go to her. He had to. As a Silkie, it was his nature to please the human who sent for him, and Annabel Barton was the only female who had ever called to him. The only female he had ever wanted.

He hovered at the entrance to the cove, his dark eyes examining the small sloop anchored there. *Revenge.* From there his gaze scanned the cove, coming to rest on two heads bobbing close together in the water. Her laughter traveled across the surface to him, at once arousing yearning, jealousy, and anger. Damn her! How could she sound so carefree when he had spent seven years agonizing over her, longing for her?

He ducked under the water and swam closer, hovering in the depths below them, scenting and listening. He saw the long, slender length of her legs and the way they blended so smoothly into her rounded ass, her flat belly and the slight protuberance of her sex. The cold water had tightened her nipples until they poked, pebble hard, against the thin material of her suit. His Silkie instincts roared to life. Cayden wanted to take her in his mouth, suckle her breasts and bury his erection in the soft folds between her legs.

He started to move on the human male and then realized two things. His seven years had not yet ended, and the man with her was Taylor Stokes. Some of his jealousy evaporated as he realized she was with her cousin.

"I told you, Taylor," she protested. "I don't want to go to the yacht club. It was bad enough before. It would be torture now."

"No one will pay any attention."

Her laughter had a hard edge to it. "Please! Just leave it alone. All I want to do is go through everything at the house and get it sold. After that, I never want to see this hellhole again."

She swam away from her cousin then, her stroke just as strong and graceful as it had always been. Cayden watched her with a longing so great he was afraid to stay any longer. Turning swiftly, he torpedoed his way out of the cove and into the waters of the bay. He had to stay away from her. There were just two weeks remaining, but even then, she had to call him.

And now he feared she wouldn't. She'd said as much. She wanted to get away from here. While he remembered their summer with longing, she apparently had no such similar feelings. Hope disappeared to be replaced by anger and bitterness.

****

Annabel pulled herself back up the ladder. It was a slow process, and not particularly graceful, but it was a damn sight better than it had been. At least now she could rest her weight on her legs even if she still did most of the actual lifting with her upper body. Taylor wasn't far behind her, levering himself back into the *Revenge* without using the ladder.

"Come on, Poppy! Let me take you out to dinner, even if it's just so I don't have to eat your cooking."

She turned her face away unhappily. Taylor was so good to her, and she did always have a good time with him.

"Taylor, it's just...I'll have to use the chair."

He knelt next to her. "Poppy, the only one it bothers is you. Yes, people might look at first, but you make them forget when you let yourself forget. Come on. Put on something pretty and let me take you out."

She brushed the hair off his dear, dear face. "You don't know how often over the years I've wished you were my big brother. You have always been there for me, Taylor. Out of everyone in our family, including my dad, it's always been you."

He tweaked her cheek. "Somebody has to look out for you, Popper."

To purchase *The Silkie's Call* and other erotic titles, visit www.thewilderroses.com.

www.ingramcontent.com/pod-product-compliance
Lightning Source LLC
Chambersburg PA
CBHW070550260626
47161CB00002B/556